The Racing Line

Also by Kelly Frost

The Kings Head

The Racing Line

KELLY FROST

Definition: In motorsport, the racing line is the optimal path around the race track

atlantic · *fiction*

Published in hardback in Great Britain in 2026 by Atlantic Books,
an imprint of Atlantic Books Ltd.

1 2 3 4 5 6 7 8 9

A CIP catalogue record for this book is available from the British Library.

Hardback ISBN: 9781805465836
E-book ISBN: 9781805465843

Printed and bound by CPI Group (UK) Ltd, Croydon CR0 4YY

Atlantic Books
An imprint of Atlantic Books Ltd
Ormond House
26–27 Boswell Street
London
WC1N 3JZ

www.atlantic-books.co.uk

Product safety EU representative: Authorised Rep Compliance Ltd., Ground Floor, 71 Lower Baggot Street, Dublin, D02 P593, Ireland. www.arccompliance.com

FSC
www.fsc.org
MIX
Paper | Supporting responsible forestry
FSC® C013604

‘The only helmet a woman should use is the one
at the hairdressers.’

(Race director of the 1958 French Grand Prix to
Maria Teresa De Filippis, after forbidding her from racing)

Prologue: *What's My Line?*

April 1968

The first thing she heard when she emerged from behind the curtain was whistling.

Not just any whistling, but the kind of noise men make from their cars to women on the street. Wolf whistling. There was no chance of hiding from it as she stepped onto the stage. The television studio's cardboard walls and gummy matt-black floor fenced her in, the spotlights trapping her in their glare. Rows of audience members looked at her expectantly, hands poised to clap, gagging for a laugh, as the theme tune played itself out in the background: *overseer, undertaker, pest destroyer, boilermaker. It's… BBC's* What's My Line? And then the host:

'We've got some *very* interesting occupations to trouble you with on tonight's episode of *What's My Line?*' he said, fast and slick. 'You all know the rules. Our panel have got to guess the occupations of our guests before they reach ten 'no's. And without further ado, let's meet our first contestant. Come on, don't be scared.' He beckoned her over. She finally let go of the curtain.

The whistling resumed as she edged towards him in the high heels the producers had told her to wear. They had chosen her outfit as well – a shrimp-coloured satin skirt so tight that her thighs strained at the fabric, and a blazer collared with pink feathers that tickled her nose and itched her neck. Her blonde hair had been wound around foam blocks and hairsprayed stiff until it resembled a wig. Glamour was *essential*, the stylist had told her.

The host shook her hand and instructed her to write her name on the blackboard.

She did: *Winifred Vaux* in neat cursive.

He read it out to the audience incorrectly, pronouncing her surname like *Vox*.

'It's *Vaux*,' she said. 'The x is silent. It sounds like *bow*, like what you use to play the violin.'

'And is it Miss or Mrs Vaux?' He leaned in, like he was speaking to a child.

'It's Ms.'

'What, the letters between the *m* and *s* weren't good enough for you?' The audience laughed, but she remained unsmiling. 'Oh, alright.' His lip twitched. She was bucking the script already, ignoring the cue cards flashing behind his head.

'Now, *Ms*' – he exaggerated it – '*Vaux*' – and exaggerated that too – 'may I present the panel.'

She turned towards the right side of the stage and saw two male faces, two female ones – four stiff sets of hair. Then, the host took her arm and led her towards the desk on the left side, directing her into the seat next to him.

'We'll let the audience in the theatre and at home know exactly what your line is. If you want to play it the hard way like our panel, then close your eyes for a moment.'

Her line flashed up on the screen: AUTOMOBILE RACE DRIVER.

The cue card – APPLAUSE – lifted up, but the response was slow. A few claps, then some more. A rush at last. She smirked. It was a hesitance she knew well.

'Alright, we can tell you that Ms Vaux deals in a service, and we'll begin the general questioning with Dennis.'

Dennis looked up at her through his thick-paned glasses. He took a deep breath.

'Ms Vaux, have you anything to do with show business, and if not, why not?'

Urgent laughs filled the studio.

'No.'

'That's one *no* down and nine to go. Alison?' The host clipped along.

Alison arranged her petite upper body to face her.

'Well, Dennis asked that question, because you are a very attractive lady, but the reason for all the laughter must be because you do something quite unlike what it *looks* like you do. Is that possible?'

'Yes.'

'So day to day, on the job that you have, you wouldn't look like you do tonight.'

'I try not to,' she replied with a smile. The audience's laugh changed colour.

Her eyes pleaded with Alison to *go on. Get me out of this satin.*

'Do you do something that requires dexterity?'

'Yes.'

'Perhaps with heavy machinery?'

'Yes.'

'Is it some kind of automobile?'

'Yes.'

'Do you drive a car that is different from a regular car?'

'Yes.'

'Does it go very fast?'

'Sometimes.'

Alison shifted in her seat, suddenly uncomfortable. Was someone holding up a cue card behind her? Had someone – Dennis, perhaps – pinched her under the table? Why had she stopped, when she knew? Alison sank under the weight of her hair, reeling herself back in as if she had overstepped.

'Is it larger than the average car?' she finally asked, quieter this time.

'No.'

Alison looked at her in apology, then brushed her hair to the side and stared down into her lap. She had been so close.

*

It lasted for an agonizing twenty minutes. During which time the panel had tiptoed around what they all knew until the host threw up his hands and announced they were out of questions. He had then turned to her and said *it seems that the panel could not guess your line, why don't you tell them what it is?* When she did, their mock surprise bored her – and the host proceeded to ask whether she found television or racing more terrifying.

After they let her free, she rushed through back corridors to her dressing room while shooing away men with clipboards. She pushed aside the make-up brushes and tissue boxes, searching for the telephone. Dialled.

'They talked in the present tense,' she shouted at the man on the other end, breathless. But this man – her publicist, manager, something inbetween – was used to the lack of hello.

'So what?'

'You didn't tell them I was a *former* racing car driver?'

'You're on a long hiatus, no?'

'Rich, I quit. It's finished.'

'Freddy, that's what you say, but I think—'

'You know why I quit.'

The line went silent.

'Tell me how it went otherwise,' he said.

'It was terrible, they had no idea who I was.'

'My dear, I believe that's the point. The trick is not to take offence.'

'But they played it out like I was some joke. And one

of the producers mentioned something about an *obituary*. Care to explain?'

'That's how they found you,' he said, after some hesitation.

'But I'm not dead.'

'Evidently. They were after some Countess who raced with you once, wanted to get her onto the show but she was… you know, dead. Your name was mentioned alongside hers.'

She bit her lip and tried not to catch her eye in the mirror.

'I never should have agreed to this – it was a bad idea.'

'I could have told you that.'

'Then why didn't you?'

'Tell you what to do? Fred, I value my life far too much to do that.'

'Maybe I don't want the next thing written about me to be an obituary.' She paused. 'Just tell me there's a difference.' To his silence: 'Tell me there's a difference between vanity and not wanting to sink into obscurity.'

'Whoever said you had to *sink* into it? I'd say it's been a rather pleasant walk into the sunset.'

Something occurred to her, then. 'Why did you set this up in the first place, Rich? I'm not even your client.'

A long pause.

'You'll always be my client, Fred. You know that. I promised you that.'

Freddy put down the phone and waited for the final trembles of embarrassment to burn off. She heard her forty-two-year-old body uncranking, cooling, like something mechanical. It was an old habit she had revived over the past few months, this listening to her body. Calculating the speed with which her mind sent neurons to her feet when she walked, trying to catch a lag in the system, feeling each individual muscle expand and contract. When the cars shunted her against their cockpit walls, she could predict the colour of the bruise from the force. The insistent noise of her being had always stood out from the haze of drills and exhaust cracks. But such sensitivity had faded over time, like most other things.

Until her hand had smoothed over that faint lump in her breast, a little less than a month ago.

She had been in the shower when she felt the strange bauble just in the side of her left breast – untender, untended. She felt it over and over again, how it bobbed and escaped the pressure of her fingers, had almost named it by the time she emerged from the shower. And she spent ten more minutes scrabbling with her breast, examining it in the mirror and trying to spot the little nudge in her skin.

It must have been from the crash in Monaco, she had thought, remembering the chicane that chucked her around like ice in a cocktail shaker, and how the debris had hit her breast awkwardly. *Or was it at Monza?* The Italian racetrack where she ran around the back of her car to chase the boys to the pit lane and slammed into the rear wing, then spent more than three weeks pretending she was not in pain. *It could even have been Spa*, the Belgian track where a thirty-one-mile-per-hour wind was always battering the side of her car at precisely the wrong angle. She had replayed the beats of her life, asking whether she might have avoided this fate if she had hit some of them differently. She tore through her career at the bathroom sink.

Now, sat in front of the dressing room mirror, she took off the feathered pink blazer and twisted her torso, noticing the small protrusion even through the blouse. She cursed Rich for no particular reason. The lump was why she was here backstage at a television studio. Her hair had still been wet from that fateful shower when she answered his call about *What's My Line?*

She had barely listened to him as he explained the premise and, after blindly agreeing to the show, she had run through the options again: perhaps it was scar tissue, perhaps it was a gland gone awry, or a cyst or an ulcer. Women get those sorts of thing. But then there were the questionnaires at the doctor's office that she had filled in: Do you have a history of breast cancer in your family?

Yes, she would always tick, thinking nothing of it. She called the doctor. The doctor called for a scan. The scan led to a mammogram. The mammogram to a biopsy. The biopsy to that frown on the doctor's forehead that spelled what she already knew. *Yes*, she ticked again.

How long? she asked – but all she remembered from the doctor's appointment was the word *aggressive*. The only place she had brought aggression was the track, shoving herself onto the apex of the racing line before her opponent could. But this was something she could not overtake or outpace. It had the jump on her. Its aggression had trumped hers.

Six weeks? Eight weeks? It was only a matter of time. And time was matter now – it was thick, quantifiable, something to wade through, heavy with dread and doubt.

She closed her eyes and listened to her body again, the cumulative bumps and bruises on her arms. In the dressing room, sat so still, she itched for the ever-breathtaking speed of the car. The host's question came back into her mind then: *do you find television or racing more terrifying?* One thing was for certain: neither was as terrifying as the prospect of all that speed, all those bruises, being for nothing. She understood that the universe did not owe her anything, and she had never driven simply for the trophies or the fame. But she had dared to think that her efforts to scorch a path in the sport would make some small mark on the world and its way of thinking. Respect, at least, if not recognition. Opening her eyes, she caught herself in the mirror.

She reached for the phone and dialled it again. This time, she called a different number. The instant the line connected, she asked:

'What's your driver line-up for Le Mans looking like this year?'

1. Victory Race

May 1945

It began at the end. As Freddy sat tracing the rim of a champagne-filled coupe, she thought she was probably the only person in the club, in London, and probably in all of England, who wasn't thrilled that the war was over. She was struggling to admit this to herself, as the chandelier swung above her, and a shirtless boy from it, and two girls danced with their two boys and trod right over her toes without even noticing. In the grand scheme of things, she reasoned, there was nothing to complain about. Nothing at all. Future historians would scoff at questions about the mixed mood after the news came that it was over. Her dread, her hesitance would be swept under a carpet of *utterly wonderful.* And it was, wasn't it?

There was nothing to complain about. Other than that she wouldn't be able to drive from now on.

She would be able to *drive*, she tutted to herself. Of course she would. But not for her occupation, not for her country, and not – certainly not – fast.

Gingerly, she touched the breast pocket of her uniform, feeling for the four corners of the letter poking at the fabric. Not that she needed to read it again; she already had it memorized.

Miss Winifred Vaux has been promoted to the rank of Junior Commander in the Auxiliary Territorial Service. This will replace her previous rank of second subaltern, and she is to report to the Aldershot Training Facility on 11th May to captain her division and receive additional training. She is to be congratulated on this achievement.

Please see the enclosed medal and insignia, which can be attached to the regular ATS uniform. No new uniform will be supplied.

It was dated 4 May 1945 – only last week, but it could have been from another time. A promotion for a service that would be disbanded and wound down. She could burn her uniform, unpin her hair, ditch the hat. An auxiliary to nothing. She had half a mind to throw it away altogether, but then there was that other half that told her to keep the letter pressed against her chest, just so she knew it was there.

Without it, someone could convince her the previous seven months had been a hallucination. That all those night circuits in ambulances and recovery vehicles around the East End had been a recurring dream; that the uniform she wore was a costume; that she had never learned how to drive four different types of military vehicle through pitch-dark at seventy miles per hour; that she had never touched the engine or greased the tyres of a moderated military Humber. She almost wished it had been a dream. If she had never had the chance to drive like that, she would never have the chance to miss it.

The pleasure of it came from the awfulness. There was an odd liberation in being given licence to become a regulated nuisance on the bomb-torn streets, hand-brake turning and skidding around junk playgrounds. When wailing women were loaded into the back of her truck, she knew, with guilty giddiness, that they had called her because she was the best driver on the force – the one who could get them to the hospital quicker than anyone else. They were the most terrible circumstances in which to feel so gratified – but did the blood on her backseat invalidate her skill? Was she not allowed some shaded glee for finding a shortcut to what she was born for, using these men and their machines for her own gain? She had driven for country with the rebellious, childish notion that she was outsmarting them at their own game, undercutting their grand plan. They hated putting their delicate young women behind the wheel and she had lapped it up – their hate, and the speed.

After so much acceleration, for so many nights, being stationary had never seemed so still. She was desperate to move, but her brothers had said *wait there, we've got a surprise for you* and disappeared across the dance floor. She had stood up to follow them but John, the eldest, guided her back down into the chair. *I'm serious, don't move.* He ordered her a drink and left. It had been nearly ten minutes now and she wondered if this was one of their pranks.

She scanned the sprawling dance floor, searching for them. The once-pristine chandelier that loomed over the dancers had tarnished, displaying rusted edges and two missing bulbs, and the white curtains hung by the stage were repurposed bedsheets. The floor pinched and squeaked when people danced on it, polished to excess. The drink she had left on the table was so sweet it became sour, and then the sour gave way to a further edge of sweetness. Endings kept fluttering into new beginnings, and beginnings into ends. Glasses and spoons clinked without pause. The band knocked out tune after tune. Loud shouts of joy from all directions. Men threw their dance partners in violent glee.

Soldiers in various layers, styles, versions of uniform veered near Freddy's table, but all took wide berths when she scowled at them. While she could be considered enticing, she had a habit of making herself look the opposite. Standoffish was her aim. She was gamine – petite, but not curvy. Her hips and thighs, still clad in uniform under the table, were straight, narrow, boyish, and she wore her blonde hair short, so that only a few flicked ends would peek out from under her cap. She heard an American soldier walk past her and remark that *some of these English broads ain't broad where they oughta be.*

Good, she thought. With any luck, she could get through tonight without touching the hand of a man that wasn't one of her brothers. She had no intention of nearing any of these soldiers, nor letting one near her – not after what had happened to Carrie Dalton, the girl she had met over a pair of engines at training camp. The only one in the service she could stomach. Freddy had never fitted in with other girls growing up, their friendship threatening to distract her from her ambition to be the best – or at least half as good as the boys. *Other women are a threat* was the mantra she often chanted to herself without realizing. Had someone else instilled this idea in her head, or did she generate it herself?

But things were different with Carrie. She cared as little for friendship as Freddy did, and their relationship was more one of comfortably sharing silence and occasionally telling each other how to gearshift that bit more efficiently or find the better line around the corner. Never giving away *all* the secrets, of course, because they were both keen to remain one step ahead of the other, but Carrie was someone to learn from, to stick close to – she was from a farming family and had grown up with her hands deep inside the guts of tractors. There was no worry either of Carrie getting involved with one of the men, like the other girls always dreamed of. She seemed to show no interest in them – and when she did talk to someone she liked, red-haired Carrie's face flushed so violently that it was difficult to tell where her hairline began, and she started spluttering and giggling in a way that drove off her fellow conversationalist. Even Freddy was more experienced with boys, and that was saying something.

On the night the company went down to the pub after completing their initial training, Freddy knew they were in trouble when Carrie whispered to her that *a man keeps looking at me* and there was no chance of distinguishing Carrie's hairline. *What man?* Freddy had asked. The man who crossed the room and put his hand on Carrie's waist, and then his arm around it. He never even told Carrie his name. She never asked, but never said *no* to anything he asked, too in awe of his attention.

A month later, it was *discovered* – in the words of the commander – that *Miss Dalton has got herself pregnant*, as though no one else had played a part. Freddy knew the rulebook by heart, and she knew what it meant: according to paragraph eleven, auxiliaries who became pregnant were to be discharged with immediate effect and their conduct throughout their period of service investigated.

If the choice was to be a prude or pregnant, then she would choose prude in a heartbeat.

It was easy to spot Eric picking his way through the tables, as one of the only men not in uniform. Instead, he wore a blue pinstripe suit, a neatly folded white handkerchief in the breast pocket, and expensive horn-rimmed glasses. While he was almost as short as Freddy, he left quite the wake, bumping into chairs and dancing couples. He knocked a woman right out of her partner's hands, and John – appearing behind – had to rescue him to escape a fight. John, then, with his monstrous, uniformed shoulders and broad hands pushed his younger brother, like a wheelbarrow, towards her table. Freddy always hoped that her brothers acted like this merely for her amusement, but she could never be sure.

'What's this surpr—?' Freddy began.

John placed a finger on her lips and nodded behind them. She threw off his hand and looked around him.

'He just dropped off his coat.'

'Who?'

Eric and John slapped at each other, clearly in cahoots.

Freddy narrowed her eyes and searched the crowd. Two men shoving each other in the middle of the dance floor drew her gaze. The taller man, who shoved the hardest and swore at the other, straightened himself, brushed back his hair, and turned to look at her. She knew that face instantly.

'Vernon?'

'You're blushing,' John whispered into her ear.

'No, I'm not.'

She was. And there was no way to unblush her cheeks, not with him stood in front of her, grinning down, tall enough to block out the light from the chandelier. She rose to meet him.

'This can't be little Winnie...?' Vernon laughed, a deep rich sound, looking at her brothers in turn. The gleam of his white teeth was sharp, and she felt throttled in the bright blue of his eyes. He was tanned, noticeably; when his face relaxed, there were small white marks in the creases around his eyes. Days of foreign sun were baked into him and his lightly bronzed hair.

'She goes by *Freddy* now,' Eric said.

'I've always gone by Freddy,' she jumped in. 'But you never listened to me when I told you.'

'I'm sorry,' Vernon said, playing offended, his ruse so good it made her uncomfortable. No man should be this fantastically at ease with people, she thought. 'No, it can't be. *This* is Winnie Vaux, the ten-year-old who came to her brother's rugby matches and tried to join in?' He stood back, crossed his arms, shook his head as though admiring newly acquired artwork. 'I've never seen someone more beautiful. I thought the ATS was supposed to make all you girls look horrid and independent and with no need for us anymore? That when we came back you would be a pack of sexless beasts, mawing at each other?'

Even John looked to the ground with that one, and her father had washed his mouth out with soap more than a few times. Freddy looked around to see if anyone had heard – *prude, prude*, she kept telling herself.

'Who said I ever needed you?'

'Fred, no need to be rude! Verne arrived back in town yesterday, just in time,' John said.

'Where from?' she asked.

'Classified.' Verne tapped a finger on the side of his nose. 'Nothing to worry your pretty little head about.'

She wanted to swat him – that's what she would have done to her brothers, but she held back. Here he was: the only one who could threaten that strict code she had set for herself ever since Carrie. How could she be a prude with a man like Vernon smiling down at her? She was angry at her cheeks for blushing, angry at her heart for beating. *Stop it*, she said to herself, as she often did when she was around him.

Granted, that was not often. He had been to boarding school with her brothers, and she had probably spent less than a few hours with him in her entire life. But she had dwelled on him for entire summers. The thought of them being together was so unrealistic, she lived on it – he could have anyone, so why would he have her? She became so infatuated with him that she would feel guilty for not thinking about Vernon every second of every day – correcting herself halfway through doing something important to remind herself that Vernon was what should be on her mind. Schoolgirl stuff that had lasted longer than she liked to admit.

When war broke out and the boys had been away at Oxford together, she had heard distant tales about Verne and his prowess in the Air Force, strapped fearlessly into

Spitfires. Sometimes he had shot down ten Germans, sometimes fourteen. The numbers varied. But there were always some Germans shot down and it was always him who did the shooting.

She barely knew him at all, in truth. She wouldn't be able to tell you whether he was the type of man to crush a spider with his bare hands or cup it gently in his palms and take it to the window. His eyes certainly gave nothing away – and his smile even less. Absence, she supposed, made the heart grow fonder and she was captivated by the possibility of knowing him, of becoming *his*. She suspected he was a man who thought in the conditional mood and she considered herself a woman who did the same thing. Both unable to kick their obsessions with potential. But she hesitated to look too closely at the cut of his jaw and the attractive way his uniform fell on his shoulders. It might draw her in. If he was a brute, she preferred it kept a mystery. There were too many brutes these days and she didn't intend to fall for one – or anyone, she reminded herself.

'Where are all your girlfriends, Winnie? I thought your service was like the Wrens. Are you all plaiting each other's hair and gossiping about the lads in uniform?'

'It's *Freddy*.'

'What did you even *do* anyway?'

'She was driving the maimed around, weren't you, Fred?' Eric came to her rescue. 'We were all very proud… after, of course, the initial shock.'

'I don't think Father spoke to her for several months.'

'That being said…' John began. 'He doesn't really speak much anymore, just sort of grunts.'

'I don't think he could handle a second disappointment,' Eric mumbled to himself, pushing up his glasses. Freddy nudged him in camaraderie.

Eric's mind worked in ways his body didn't. He had spent half his childhood as an invalid, and now his bones were weak, he got out of breath walking upstairs, and his eyesight was poor. Poached midway through his mathematics degree, he had spent the war at Bletchley Park behind a desk, producing results that their father struggled to see. Unlike John, the brother who had created muscles and scars and anecdotes for enough campfires to light up the country.

'No, but I'd like to know. Your ATS isn't a *real* wing of the army, is it?' Vernon continued. 'It's ceremonial. I heard that you don't have to salute other officers and that you can't fire the guns you're trained to use. Like the Home Guard, blowing whistles when Granddad forgets to turn off his bedside lamp.'

'*Ceremonial?*' Freddy repeated.

'Oh no.'

'Here we go.' From the brothers. She had a tendency – when she began – not to stop.

'There's nothing ceremonial about dying.' She crossed her arms. 'Believe me. Someone who trained with us got transferred to an anti-aircraft battery in Plymouth. Until then, I didn't think there was anything funny about shrapnel, Vernon. But I discovered that there is. Do you know what it is?' He shook his head, amused. 'The funny thing about shrapnel is that it hits the men on the batteries but it hits the women too. Apparently, she ran back to snap off the searchlight, but the bombs were already falling. I heard she—'

'That's quite enough of that,' John placed his hand on her shoulder. She shrugged it off, her heart rollicking in her ribcage. 'It's a party, we're celebrating things going back to normal, back to how they were, alright? We're here to have fun.'

Freddy's mouth was pinched tight – probably in a way that was unattractive. *Good*, she thought again. Vernon was inspecting her. She inspected him back.

'Seeing as your ladies-in-arms are nowhere to be found, then it's only fair you have a dance with me.' He held out his hand.

'There is nothing I want less than to dance with you.'

'That's not very nice. Did they train all those manners out of you in your service?'

The fact that he continued to call it *your* service grated her.

'Dancing was *strictly* forbidden, so I'm afraid I am out of practice.'

'Then we shall have to put that right.'

'No, Verne.'

'Come on, don't be difficult, Fred.' John nudged her. 'It's fun.'

'For who? Me? Or Verne?'

'Look, how about a bet? A dare. And if I win, I can dance with you,' Verne took off his jacket and draped it on the back of a chair. Freddy grinned.

'Alright. Anything?'

'You pick,' Verne said.

The two brothers urged him not to – but he waved them off.

'Did you drive here?' she asked.

'Yes, I picked up my car—'

'And John, is your car—'

'Yes, it's outside.'

'Then, a race. I bet I can drive faster than you.'

Verne spluttered a laugh, but he could see that she was serious.

'Well, go on, then. John, give the lady your keys.'

The lengths she had to go to in order to prove she was *not* flirting with this man.

2. Lessons

It wasn't the first time she was glad her father had taught her to drive. Not of his own free will, as the story went. Rather, when she was five (or eight or ten, depending on her father's mood that particular day of telling), she had clambered into the driver's seat of his car and pressed the horn. When he asked her to *get down from there*, her response was to press the horn harder. She wouldn't move until he agreed to drive with her around the estate, her small hands pattering on the leather wheel of his Austin Seven – the Baby Austin, as she came to call it.

It was the kindest thing she had seen him do. Closely followed by letting her drive around the grounds behind their farmhouse all alone, then on the country lanes with him, then – and only very occasionally – on the country lanes alone. Not to be forgotten was when he showed her how to fix up the engine of the Baby Austin, then gifted it to her on her sixteenth birthday. If she ever tried to thank him, he refused and – in denial or sudden amnesia – claimed that he had never done those things at all.

He was the owner of a no-longer-modestly-sized car manufacturer, so had *plenty of old models lying around*. That was his defence. He had to shop around, try out all the designs on the market to make his company's the best. Besides, he was a motoring enthusiast, so who could blame him for wanting to hear those old engines roar, no matter who was behind the wheel. *A respectable man does not teach his only daughter to drive*, she had heard him say at dinners she was not invited to. *Respectability is a waste of time*, she had also heard – at dinners she was.

Another of his kindnesses was taking her away from the nuns. Sister Sophia had sent Freddy into the corridor so many times, she figured that she spent more time outside the classroom than in it. And what for? Grease on her clothes, dirt under her fingernails, a loud voice. Her father and mother were called in and asked *if it was perhaps not sensible for Winifred to move to another educational establishment*. Freddy pleaded. She was old enough; she could ditch educational establishments for good. Her mother protested, but her father agreed, which meant she was to finish her final years of schooling at home with a private tutor. *Greek, Latin, the works*, he said. *And engineering, and maths*, Freddy added. He had never said no.

It didn't take long to realize why her mother had been so irritated by her removal from school. With her father's business situated on the other side of Surrey, he spent his days out of the house – and her mother spent them bringing other men into it. She made no attempt to hide it, and continued as though Freddy wasn't there. When the latest suitor would drive up to the house, and Freddy was in the garage tinkering with an engine, polishing the Baby Austin, she would meet her mother's eyes over the bonnet. She never forgot their blue. Never asking for forgiveness – but rather for understanding. A compromise. *Just let me have this*, she seemed to say.

Freddy could never bring herself to say *no*. Something in those eyes held her back, and often she stood under the window, listening to her mother argue with these nameless suitors. She was brash with them, snappy. Horrid, almost. Anger bursting out of every pore of her thin, sharply pointed body.

Rarely did the same man visit twice. Freddy tried not to see them at all – that was the beauty of her Baby Austin. Whenever the talking stopped and something else began, she cranked the engine and positioned herself in the driver's seat. She accelerated through the long tunnel of trees lining the drive, imagining herself crossing the wide and open plains of distant countries. On rainy days, she drove fast circuits of the nearby empty fields, trying not to let her wheels slip on the wet grass. It was best when she went fast enough that she could feel her heart dislodge and rattle around inside her ribcage.

And then there were the times when driving had saved not only her, but others as well. She was thirteen and hanging bunting to the outside of the house with her mother for some patriotic reason, Freddy supporting the ladder as her mother did the attaching. Back-beating sun scorched the drive. The little union jacks smacked and flapped in the breeze. She was in the midst of a bargain; help her mother with the decorations and then be released for the afternoon to her own devices (the Austin, which winked at her from the garage).

'You really should go to the village and meet some girlfriends, Winifred.'

Without fail, her mother's sentences contained *should* and were punctuated by drags from the Goldflake cigarette hanging on her bottom lip.

'I don't have any *girlfriends*.' Freddy didn't even like the word.

'You should make some, then.'

'But girls are dull and *you* don't have any girlfriends, you don't see anyone apart from—' but she had stopped at her mother's look.

'That's because, at my age, girlfriends are good for one thing – gossip.' She ploughed onwards, 'But when I was your age, I would have loved to be where you are, to have the upbringing you've had.'

'When you were my age, you *were* where I am.'

The two couldn't speak without descending into nonsensicality.

'All I'm saying is that if I were young and with so many opportunities at my fingertips, I would take them. I would wear nicer clothes, because I could afford to,' she looked down at Freddy's grease-smeared pinafore, 'I would meet girls and boys, I would socialize, I would focus on my studies, I would do it all differently.'

'But—'

'Oh, shut up,' she snapped. Freddy could see her red-rimmed eyes. Her spiked nails fiddled with the bunting, and the two continued in silence. The sun burned down on them, and although she begged her mother to stop, to come inside, she continued. Her blonde hair had turned brown with sweat, and her housedress was soaked through. Freddy wanted to leave her, but someone had to support the ladder.

Perhaps she was distracted, or the sun seared off the top layer of her concentration, but the next thing she heard was a *thud* on her right – not clean, but flailing, as though several parts of the object had hit the ground at different moments. She turned and saw a lifeless puppet, stuffed limbs spread at wrong angles. But it was not a puppet. It was her mother.

Freddy stared at her for several seconds, stiff with confusion. She called for her in a wavering voice, but there was no answer – and then she started to move. Keeping the panic at bay, she ran into the house, picked up the phone and called for an ambulance.

'There's not one in that area at this moment,' said the voice on the telephone. 'We'll dispatch an ambulance shortly. There's a high demand because of the heat.'

'Shortly?' Freddy shouted into the receiver. 'How shortly?'

'Within the hour.'

The nearest hospital was only twenty minutes away.

'What if I… what if I drive?'

'How old are you, miss?'

'I can drive, I can.'

'Is there no one else at home who could drive you both?'

She slammed the phone back into the wall.

By the time she returned to the drive: blood. Spilling from her mother's head. Freddy leaned down and heard short, resilient breaths. She placed her fingers to the neck and retracted them as soon as she found a pulse. She had never found her mother's living so blatantly repulsive. The thought of dragging her to the Austin rose and floundered.

Instead, she left her mother there, whispering apologies, and ran across the drive to the garage. She placed her hand on the Austin's door handle. The keys! She sprinted back inside. On her father's desk. Ignition, gear. She manoeuvred it next to her mother's body. Opened the back door. Panic gave way to focus. One long limb at a time, she folded her mother into the back of the car. Her mother's eyes fluttered as she did so.

'I can get you there, I can get you there,' Freddy chanted. She sped forwards and through the gates, up the steep hill, along the familiar country lanes, onto the more unfamiliar Surrey roads that she was forbidden from driving on.

Perhaps her mother had suffered a heart attack. Perhaps it was the heat. Perhaps she simply fell. *Perhaps you should focus on driving*, her mind replied. She did. She drove through two crossroads. Horns blared, shouts flew, but Freddy dropped them all. That thrill in her heart – she scolded it, but it remained. She could drive faster than death. The grim reaper in a race car wouldn't have a chance.

As her tyres screeched on the entranceway of the hospital, she threw open the back door. She yelled for help and it came. And the nurses marvelled at the steaming hunk of metal that had kept her mother in this life. A gurney wheeled up to the back door, and she helped to lever her onto it. She followed them inside and, despite everything else, she grinned when she saw it – when she saw her mother alive. And when she was told that a few minutes more and her heart would have given out. An ambulance would have been too late.

Later, when she went to see her mother propped up in the bed, there was a scowl on her face. She attributed it to the pain until—

'You should be ashamed of yourself. Driving like that, a hooligan. It's not becoming.'

'Don't you want to thank me? I saved your life.'

'You shouldn't be so conceited, Winifred. The doctors saved my life.'

She held her mother's hand, nevertheless. Over the bedsheets.

Freddy believed she could drive faster than death until her mother's heart gave out a year later. She had spent that year in curtained rooms. *Headaches when I move, heartburn when I breathe* – a constant refrain. Flies landed on her mother as though she was already dead. No more men came to visit. When she called for Freddy – which was rare – it was only to lob statements of disappointment. Sometimes these morphed into pieces of advice that someone might say to themselves in the mirror. *Smile for them, dance with them, play by the rules of the game.* But, as much as Freddy continued to believe, she could do nothing to outpace the slow lulling of her mother's heart.

When she was gone, Freddy mourned strangely. Mourned what they never had, and what could now never be. The friendship that might have blossomed between them when Freddy was finally old enough to understand her. All those answers to questions about womanhood and relationships that she would never be able to ask. At the funeral, she cried the least of anyone – she had been mourning her mother's absence her whole life.

Afterwards, she sat on a bench with her father. He watched John and Eric weeping at the grave like good sons. There was a lit cigarette in his hand, but he wasn't smoking it.

'I knew.' He was staring at the ground.

'About what?' Freddy picked at her hem.

He looked askance at her.

'I knew about the others. All of them.'

The final knocks of soil were falling on the coffin. There was nothing to say in response.

'Did she tell you how we met?'

'On a golf course.'

'But did she tell you what she was doing on the golf course?'

'Spectating, I suppose. You were the one playing in the tournament.'

'She was playing, too. In fact, she could have won.'

'I never saw her play.'

'No, I bet you didn't. She couldn't bear anyone knowing she had tried and failed. She would rather not be known at all. She…' He sighed. *I've done it now*, she could see him thinking. 'There was one day left in the tournament, and she was due to win. Victory was almost certain. But that evening, when we were in the clubhouse and discussing the day, we were told that she had been disqualified, and that it was in fact a men's tournament. No stipulation about it before, but the decision had been made. I went to comfort her and she latched on to me. She never let go. I don't know how she was told, too harshly maybe, but she stopped playing. She was a fantastic golfer. She could hit a drive over three hundred yards.'

He shook his head. 'But after that came this terrible *anger* that just swallowed her up. There's no excuse for it, but it's a reason for her hate, I suppose. Her only fun was degrading me, making me feel like a fool. It was only right that I let her.'

There were too many words to say and none to get out, so she watched the blackbirds fight. Her mind turned to the day she drove her mother to the hospital.

'She never liked that I drove.'

'I think she wanted to keep you from discovering a passion for it. Save you from the blunting.'

'The blunting?'

'That's what she called it. The not-quite-making-it. She said it blunted her. And she was blunted and angry for too long afterwards.'

Freddy had never been sadder nor prouder to be compared to her mother.

'She spent longer on this earth because of you, though. Never forget that. It was lucky then that I taught you to drive.' He slapped his hands on his thighs and stood up. That was certainly enough sincerity for one day.

Freddy pressed the accelerator pedal once, twice, three times.

'Please bring it back in one piece,' John said, leaning in through the passenger window and shoving the old newspapers and cigarette packets on the seat into the glove box. He walked around the front of the car to Freddy's window, reached across her and placed her hand on the gearstick. 'Now this…'

'I know what it is. I can drive anything.' Freddy swatted his hand away. These were the sorts of phrases that she had once dreamed of saying, and that she *had* said when she flew to the recruitment office: *I can drive anything. Ambulances, emergency vehicles, you name it*, she told the man behind the desk just over a year ago. His eyes licked her all over. *Age?* he asked. She said *eighteen*, and he knew it was seventeen, but he didn't care, because she had popped the top button of her blouse and neglected to wear her slip that day. She was desperate for a rematch with death. Who cared what it took.

Eric leaned in the other window.

'Go easy on Verne, Fred. He's not slept in a week.'

'Neither have I,' she said.

Vernon jabbed his horn several times. He had collected his car from around the corner and parked it in one of the two left lanes on Seven Sisters Road. John's car, with Freddy inside, was in the other. Distant traffic lights rolled through their greens, ambers and reds – as they had continued to do throughout the Blitz – but the roads were free from traffic. Free from any cars at all, it seemed. Everyone who was still awake was on foot, either inside the clubs, singing on street corners or splashing around half-naked in city-centre fountains. No one would think of chasing Freddy and Vernon down for traffic offences or speeding, not on a night like tonight. Most people were off duty anyway (except for the fire service, who were having their busiest night of the war attending to bonfires all across London).

Somewhere irrelevant, a bell tolled midnight – but the night was nowhere near over. Howls rang from within the club, people thronging in the entrance lit with spangly yellow pinlights. No hint of sunrise yet either, and the dew that had turned the road into a long black slick of grease was nowhere near morning dew. After months of blackout, the authorities had switched the streetlights back on, flooding the city with light, but someone was clearly still looking for the switch that controlled this borough and most of the lamps remained off. Freddy leaned into the night's sensation that everything was tipping. That smell of possibility – or perhaps it was just the smell of exhaust fumes as she revved the engine again.

'You don't need to do that!' John snapped. 'It's already warm. It's a warm night.'

'I know it's warm! I'm doing it for two reasons,' she shouted over the noise. 'One, I'm making sure the carburettor doesn't choke on all that fuel. And two, because it shows Verne I mean business.' Eric laughed somewhere in the background.

'Be careful, please. The engine has been playing up.'

'I can take a look at it for you, when—'

'Just… be careful. Of *yourself*.' Eric patted her forearm.

'Yes, of course, of yourself.' John coughed. Then leaned in further, whispering: 'Go on, beat him. It will do him some good.'

He withdrew from the window to reveal Vernon, who shouted:

'If there's this much talking involved in racing cars, then it's no wonder you girls are starting to get involved.'

Oh, she wanted to knead his face into the ground. That anger – she revved. She could outdrive death, she had outdriven death many times, and she could outdrive Verne.

'All this for a dance, eh?' Freddy shouted between the cars, over the engines. 'You must have been pretty desperate out there in the service.'

John stood between them and recited the rules.

'When I lower my arms, *drive.* The first to the Beaumont theatre *and back* wins. You know the Beaumont?' Nods from both. 'It's half ruin, but the sign and green brick is still there. Capiche?'

John lifted his arms. Freddy bounced the accelerator pedal, the car in gear, brake still clenched tight. As his arms fell—

—she released it and pressed full on the accelerator.

And pushed it almost to the floor, but little power answered her foot and she began to drop back. Something was wrong, the carburettor choking on all that air, or else some piston misfiring and barring her from the higher speeds. She pictured the sleek body of the car, its nerves and organs and vessels all connected in one machine, and listened closely to identify the source of the grinding whine. The gearbox, it had to be. She skipped between gears, searching for the unharmed one, and found it – third, the highest. Her foot touched the floor again and the speed boosted. The rear of Verne's car was not only in her sights, but she was all over it.

Climbing up beside him, she relished his glare. She passed him. Drunk men and women hooted from the pavements, cheering her on. Their faces wide with victory.

She preferred to take turns without her foot on the brake. Her hand yanked on the parking brake and the car skidded around – so quick that Verne was still driving in the opposite direction. She faced him head on, and quickly passed him. The car ate the road. A long snake of black tarmac gliding down its throat.

As she accelerated, she outdrove her rival, she outdrove her mother's obscurity. Shops and restaurants and train stations – all closed – blurred and melted away. Instead, the plains opened on either side; she was in her Baby Austin again, trundling down to the hospital in second gear.

Eric waved in the distance. There was no one in the back of her car now. She was doing this for herself. She had never felt so free, pushing the edge of acceptable. Finding the place beyond, where it made no sense to fear. At high speed, a clarity came over her. She couldn't see herself doing anything other than driving. If she couldn't drive ambulances, then she would drive for sport. She would drive to win.

Her mind was so caught up in plotting her own story, she didn't even hear the engine choke. With spluttering, the car spat to an undignified and smoking halt. She smacked on the dashboard, once, twice, three times. The finish line, where her brothers stood, was twenty metres ahead.

As Verne drove past, he looked back in the rear-view mirror – not even over his shoulder.

3. Honeymoon

Spring 1947

Freddy denied that she let Verne win all the way to the dance floor, then to the bedroom, then to the altar. Even into the bridal suite afterwards. Never once did she give in – and never once did he believe her. Tangled in sheets, almost restrained by them, her arms caught in cotton, Freddy told him again.

'I swear it. The engine went kaput. I would never lose on purpose, not even for a dance with you. Are we going to argue this for our whole marriage?'

'It can be our secret.' He kissed her on the cheek, one of those hard ones that threatened not to end. 'But just tell me, tell me that you wanted to dance with me. From the ring on your finger, it wouldn't be difficult to believe.'

'I *didn't*.'

'Then why not say anything to John and Eric? Both of them ridiculed you for the entire night. But you danced with me for *three* dances. The deal was only for one. I will never understand you,' he said, in that way he said it – not affectionately, but with irritation, his brow crunched.

Freddy had no answer. That night, nearly two years ago now, had rattled in her mind ever since. She sometimes wondered what would have happened if she had won the race on Seven Sisters Road – whether she would have danced with him regardless. Whether she would have won and walked off into the night alone, somewhat empty other than the rush of the race bouncing around inside her. Whether she would have avoided this marriage, which felt like it was bookending her youth.

'What are you thinking about?' A question he asked regularly. With a prodding insistence, not curiosity – like a child too desperate to know why the sky is blue.

She wouldn't tell him that she was thinking about the resident pit of dread in her stomach. She could point to it, lodged somewhere between the folds of her gut, lifting and falling with her diaphragm. And she wouldn't tell him the real reason why she had twice rearranged the date of the wedding. The first time, it was due to a clash of dates. Eric was finally graduating and she demanded – despite her brother's insistence to the contrary – that the entire family *had* to be there. But by the time the wedding was called off, the church that Verne had picked was booked up for the next five months. So, it would have to wait until the winter, and it would be a ceremony among dead leaves.

The second time, there had been a disaster with the wedding dress. It was ruined. *Ruined* was a generous way to put it – she had gone through her father's liquor cabinet, spilling half of it on the dress, and then walked around neighbouring fields barefoot until the early hours of the morning. *I refuse to get married in any dress other than that one.* She played the difficult bride, and it worked. *Anything for my darling*, Verne said, and a month was required for the repair of the dress, a prolonged amount of time that had nothing to do with the pound notes that Freddy slipped the dressmaker under the till.

There was no chance she would tell him about what had happened at the door of the church either. In the photos, there was a wet patch on the lap of her skirt from where she sat and cried into the dress for ten minutes. The bridesmaids muttered at the entrance, none sure how to approach. One of them said: *What's the problem? I'll marry him if she won't. She's crazy.*

It was her father who found her curled in the grasses outside the church. He hadn't entirely approved of the engagement, so he wore a tight smile when he placed a hand on her shoulder. No words exchanged between them and she could sense he was torn. Let his barely adult daughter marry her crush or suffer the town gossip if he allowed her to leave him at the altar. He looked at her deeply and she nodded. With that, she stood, brushed down her skirt and went into the church to say her vows.

When she had first sprung on her father that she was getting engaged to Vernon Dawson-Hayes at tea one afternoon, his first question was:

'Who are his parents?' He seemed shocked by his own question – a traditionalist despite himself.

'You know, *Dawson-Hayes*,' she said. She saw her father nod, catching the whiff of nobility. Lord Dawson's oldest son. Lord Hayes' only daughter. Both too in love with their links to the past to relinquish a letter of their names. Behind that whiff of nobility came the full reek of empire. A family of dashing sons raised to conquer overseas, gathering manly handfuls of land, stretches of property, in England and further afar. Awash with old money, their manor house was lined with portraits of men in military uniforms, thick strokes of oil paint texturing the moustaches that launched a thousand ships. Other than living off their extensive acres of land that stretched across half of Wales, their business was dogs. Verne's parents spent their leisurely lives breeding champion pointers, training race-winning greyhounds and trading English setters.

'If he won't follow in his parents' footsteps and take over the breeding or greyhound business, then I suppose he'll manage the land,' Freddy explained to her father. Even though he took every opportunity to label his parents' canine passions *frightfully dull*, Verne had never expressed an interest in pursuing anything else. For now, he trailed his father around races and kennels in between visits to his various social clubs and the estates of fellow members of his graduating class. But he had studied Rural Economy at Oxford.

'Does that mean he's simple?'

'No, actually. He's very smart.'

'Smart? At what?'

'People.'

'People?'

'Will you stop repeating everything I say.'

'But everything you're saying is so ridiculous, I can't help it. You're talking about *marriage*, Winifred.'

'When I say smart, I mean he's very attentive and insightful. He can see what's going on with you.'

'A *sensitive* man?'

'Don't say sensitive like it's a dirty word.'

'Is it not?'

'No. Besides, he's not sensitive. He's... perceptive. I like that.'

Freddy also liked how he made her feel like no one else ever had. She simply could not stop smiling, even when she was miles away from him. *How did people do this?* she wondered – just go about their lives, completely besotted. She had no girlfriends to ask this question, but the magazines told her that it must be love. She remembered what she cared about when she was with him and the answer was always, frustratingly, him. He had faults, his little quips and asides, but she deserved them, she told herself. She was a nuisance and he was a dream. And he was patient enough to love her whims and her standoffishness, and he didn't even need to say it. She should be lucky, she supposed, that he had chosen her, when she had spent all those summers agonizing over the fact that he was too good for her.

After countless nights at dances and movies and restaurants, none particularly more special than another, he had leaned down and whispered into her ear that he wanted to marry her. *To make you mine*, was his exact phrasing. He'd already bought the ring, he added. She had crumpled her weight onto his chest as they continued swaying on the dance floor, thinking that she had finally found it – a third option between prude or pregnant that allowed her to be neither and both: married. It was a huge relief to get it over and done with. The marrying of someone was a tale she had been sold as long as she could remember. And now she had done it, and with someone that she could trust with her blushes. Someone who knew how to handle her. A mighty sense of achievement fell on her the evening he proposed. She had set herself free from something that could have taken quite a few years to sort out, and now all was clear ahead.

'Anyway, he's going to ask for your consent and you're going to say yes,' Freddy told her father.

'Isn't the groom meant to do this part?'

'Yes, but I know you don't like surprises.'

'I don't mind surprises, especially if there's cake involved, but what I don't like are men who are not good enough for my daughter.'

'When he asks, you'll say yes.'

No response.

'Please?'

'If you're asking for my legal consent, then yes. But blessing? You won't get that. I don't want this on my hands if it goes south. My marriage was unhappy enough, and I don't intend to get involved in another.'

'Charming. But I think ours will end fine.'

'Well, hopefully it won't *end* at all.'

'That's not what I meant.'

'But what are you going to do about your driving and all that?' He waved a madeleine around in his hand.

'That's…' she paused. 'What are you talking about? Is this why you're being funny about Verne?'

'After the war ended, you came bounding in here saying that you were going to race cars. You're still planning on pushing on with that, I suppose. What does *he* think about all of it?'

It was the first time this topic had surfaced in months, since things had become serious between her and Verne. Last time it came up, she had dismissed her proclamation as a *moment of madness* and her father had scolded her, saying: *Don't call it madness.*

'Well, we haven't exactly discussed it.'

'You should probably do that.'

'Yes, thank you.'

'You know, just in case he doesn't like the idea of Mrs Dawson-Hayes in a helmet. Mrs Dawson-Hayes in a race paddock surrounded by men of all ilk. Europeans, Italians…'

'Italians are Europeans.'

'If you say so.'

She squinted at him. 'The matter at hand.'

'Go on with it, then. It's not my business.'

'That's an approval?'

'It's not *not* one.'

'For goodness' sake,' she sighed and stood up to leave. Stomped across the lawn. 'I'll be telling Verne that you were over the moon about it.'

In her bridal bed, she turned to her new husband.

'I'm thinking about nothing.' She smiled. 'I'm happy.'

'Yes?'

'Yes.'

But he wouldn't take that as an answer several weeks after returning from their honeymoon.

'You're moony,' he said one afternoon, leaning over the arm of the sofa while she lay on it.

'Is that a nice way of saying moody?' He had a way with euphemism.

'What are you thinking? And don't say nothing. I'd hate to believe my wife was dumb.' She put on a stiff smile. 'You're happy, yes?' He clenched and unclenched her hands in his.

'Of course. The honeymoon was… perfect.'

Perfect was one word for it. The entire week in northern France she had barely known what it felt like to walk into a room without him beside her, to walk unheld by his hand, to move unsupervised in bed. When Verne let her drive his new Rolls-Royce, a wedding gift from his father, along the coastal roads, he held onto the side and directed her how to change the gears. She let him, meekly.

If she could have chosen somewhere to honeymoon, it would have been further afield. You could practically see the English coast from their hotel room window. And he whisked her through museums and historical sites, assuring her it was all boring and she didn't need to focus on anything but him, as if not wanting to make her too aware of the world that existed outside their marriage. Anything that didn't involve him was deemed an unnecessary distraction.

The only place she stood her ground was, surprisingly to her, the bedroom. It was a place that had never featured in her childish fantasies – and yet she still found herself disappointed. Sex with Verne was a transactional, scheduled affair that she avoided for as long as she could and then always ended early once it started, every movement overshadowed by the fear of what came after. This was one of the only things her mother and her countless affairs had taught Freddy – how to be with a man, but not tied to him forever. *Women can pull out too*, her mother had once mumbled at the tail end of a conversation.

Her aversion to getting pregnant was no secret between her and Verne. In fact, she had mentioned it to him very early in their relationship – on that first night. After she lost the race on Victory Day, after she danced with him, and continued to dance, they wandered all the way to Oxford Street with the taste of alcohol still in their mouths, stopping only to kiss against lampposts. A grey sun tried to rise, and it was like the sky was hungover. Stragglers sprawled on benches. Trails of confetti and bunting laced across concrete, and silence: no motors, no planes, no marches. She had sat on a bench with his arm around her and said: *I feel like I should tell you that I'm not sure I want children.* He responded: *Let's not ruin the moment.* She said: *But I think it's important.* He closed his eyes and leaned his head so far back it almost fell between his shoulder blades. *We'll see. We can talk about this another time.*

He kept pretending to forget this conversation each night of their honeymoon, at some times more playfully than others. But she knew from his long, deliberate pauses that he remembered. Still she had to repeat her reasons to him: she was young, only twenty, and they had so much of their lives ahead of them; she wanted to spend some time as husband and wife before adding more humans into the mix; she was worried about the toll it would take on her body, her narrow hips that grandparents and great-aunts had ominously labelled as *not child-bearing.* Always with a distracted look, Verne would nod as she recited these reasons and insist that he understood, but then repeat that same refrain. *We'll see.*

The phrase circled through her mind once more as she lay on the sofa, his hands twirling strands of her hair. He had just arrived home from the club, still smelling of the outside. It was rare for him to return while it was still daylight. It probably meant that he wanted them to rehearse their tiring performance in the bedroom once more.

Here: the inevitable outcome. What came after the aisle and altar and bridal suite. The excitement wearing off. *Mrs Dawson-Hayes*, the name she had once scribbled at the front of her notebooks, sounded clunky now it was printed on letters and documents and bills. She wandered the house, the kitchen, with the odd sense of being already dead – beyond life. There were times when she wondered how she could claw her way back. Times like this one now on the sofa.

'I want to know what's the matter, tell me,' he urged.

'Well...'

'I think it's a little too early for an affair, don't you think? Who was it, some chap in France?' He had given her the floor to speak and he was still on it. He realized and held up his hands. 'Sorry, darling. Go ahead.'

'The dressmaker.'

'What dressmaker?'

*

The one who owned the wedding dress shop, to whom she had slipped pound notes under the till. She had been older, stockier, with black-green eyes and dark wiry hair bushed around her face. Sharp flicks of eyeliner bought from shops that Freddy had never walked into. She had seen her nip quick sips from a hip flask and she called her *pal*, *darl* and *sweets*. When she measured Freddy around the bust, she was brusque, pinched her with nimble, practical fingers and gave her more advice in her appointment than her mother had ever thought to give in her lifetime, common-sense stuff that sounded like gospel coming from her – *wear nude-coloured underwear so you won't see it through the skirt*. Then, without Freddy's assent, she had fetched it and put it on the bill. Either she was a remarkable saleswoman or cared a great deal.

Freddy had exchanged no more than the pleasantries, shallow talk, until the day she came to pick up her dress. She sped the Baby Austin into the small lay-by outside the shop.

The dressmaker was watching Freddy before the bell dinged above her.

She moved to the counter.

'I need to pick up—'

'I know what you need to pick up, darl,' she said, but didn't move. She leaned on the counter, arms crossed, looking at Freddy.

'Is something wrong?'

'That your car?' She pointed out the window. Freddy turned.

'Yes.'

She squinted.

'You wouldn't happen to be that girl who drove her mother to the hospital and saved her life? I recognize you from the newspaper.'

'That was years ago.'

Freddy remembered with shame the journalist coming to the house the week after the incident. *Pose with the car, young lady*. The headline still made her cringe: *Little Miss Avoids Near Miss for Mother with Driving Skills*. And then scattered throughout, phrases like *she may look as cute as a button, but she's a devil behind the wheel... with no concern for her hair, she drove her father's car... she managed not to crash it into the hospital when she arrived*.

'What are you doing next week?' the woman asked.

'I'm...' She looked at the wedding dress hanging on the rack. The woman followed her gaze and, seeing it, laughed.

'Of course. And then it's off for a honeymoon, I suppose.'

'Yes.'

The woman sighed and retrieved Freddy's dress from the rack. She didn't let go of it, though, and the two held it between them over the counter.

'Take care.'

She let go, eventually. Freddy walked to the door. She paused, her hand on the handle.

'If I wasn't getting married, what would you want me to do?'

'If you weren't, not that it matters now… You seem to know your way around a car. I drive rallies most weekends. I need a partner.'

'I can *drive*, but I don't think that qualifies me for a rally.'

'You'd be surprised. Besides, you would navigate. I would drive.'

'Are *you*… married?'

'It's an arrangement I have with my husband. He drives also. In the other direction.'

Freddy opened the door and stood on the step. She could only half-look at the dressmaker as she left.

'Thank you, that's very kind. But no, I don't… I don't think so.'

'Alright,' she heard, as she walked towards the car. 'I'm here when you're ready.'

'I've been thinking of taking her up on her offer.'

'Hold on.' Verne was now lying with his head in her lap as she sat on the sofa looking out at the garden. 'There's a dressmaker who drives rallies.'

'Yes. Well, I don't know if she's the dressmaker. She seems like she owns the business.'

'What's her name?'

'I don't know.'

'Did you imagine this woman, sweet Win?'

'No, of course not.'

'Does this mean that all those times you've said *I'm happy, it's nothing*,' he mimicked her, 'that you've been lying?'

'Not at all.' She stroked his hair. 'But you're away a lot, Verne. And I'm left alone in this house. This could be a pastime for me. You know I'm a good driver, after that night…'

'All I remember about that night is you losing.'

'Yes, well you would.'

The muscles in his neck tensed and she stroked slower.

'Is this woman married?'

'Yes.'

'And her husband lets her drive around the country, with hundreds of other men?'

'They have an arrangement.'

'I don't like the sound of that. Not at all. For all we know this is some whore who uses the cover of rallies to sleep with any man she wants.' If she had said these words, he might not have spoken to her for hours. *In shock*, he had once muttered, when she dared to say 'bugger', *that you would use filthy language like that.*

'I very much doubt that.' She searched desperately for solutions, wondering if she would have to disobey him. This thought unnerved her. Not because she had intended to be an obedient wife, but because obedience – the idea of being or not being obedient – had never crossed her mind. 'It could be a trial. If it doesn't work, if it goes horribly wrong, then I'll know it's not for me.'

He remained silent.

'You're away next weekend, Verne. If there's a race, we can both be back for Sunday night.'

He leaned up and grabbed onto her chin – so that he could kiss it.

Verne would never say no, he was too wedded to the idea of the devoted husband to do that, but he wouldn't mind if she chickened out. She could hear him waiting for her to change her mind. She rubbed her hands on the velvet and sighed as the breeze picked through the room.

'If you must.' He snapped the strap of her bra. 'You could do with a trip to the dressmaker – you need some new underwear.'

She liked to think she would have gone without his approval, but she could never be certain.

The dressmaker – whose name was Vanessa – was where she had left her. When the bell rang as she opened the door, Freddy had the sense of returning from an overlong detour.

'How was the honeymoon?' Vanessa asked. No formalities. Freddy copied the frankness.

'Oh, you know… delightful. But I'm glad to be back.'

'Are you ready?'

'For what?'

'Our race. Tomorrow. Meet me here at six a.m.' It sounded like she was going to say *or else*, Freddy thought. Caught off guard by her firmness, she found herself nodding, returning Vanessa's grin.

Considering the speed with which Vanessa entered, and then exited, her life, sometimes Freddy wondered if she had imagined her after all.

4. *Daily Express Rally*

November 1947

Freddy had forgotten the part about navigating. The following morning, when Vanessa thrust her the road map, a list of reference points, an instruction booklet, a separate map for the mountainous areas and then a further map for the coast roads, she realized that she could barely steer herself through her own life, let alone steer someone else through theirs. Vanessa caught the look on her face, maps splayed over her lap, and tutted:

'There's a briefing before the race starts. No need to worry.'

'I'm not.'

'Your face says otherwise.' She had been in the car with Vanessa for not even ten minutes and already the dressmaker was exposing her. 'Read this,' Vanessa leaned behind her to grab another stack of papers from the backseat and handed them to Freddy. She had never felt slow until she was next to Vanessa. 'A friend of mine who works in the press for these sorts of things leaked it to me. It's the pre-write for the race. Go on, read.'

'This Rally is being organized by the M.C.C. for the Daily Express. *At last we have a real "man's rally" again.'* Eyes poised to roll, Freddy looked up for Vanessa's response, but she gave none. *'The 1,000 miles have to be covered at a 26⅔ m.p.h. average, with the exception of 24 m.p.h. average for the communal stage from Chester to the finish at Torquay. This will take quite a bit of doing, especially if fog is encountered, as these speeds are inclusive of all stops.'*

'The starting places will be Plymouth (Car No. 1 leaves here at 11 a.m., Nov. 8th), Norwich, Harrogate, Cardiff, Glasgow, Leamington Spa, London and Manchester. The first car is due at Torquay on Nov. 10th at 7.30 a.m. Cars will be examined for condition at the finish and there will be a Concours d'Elegance on Nov. 11th.'

Freddy stopped reading. She had agreed with Vernon to be home by the evening of the 10th at the latest, which was when he returned from the races. She would have to miss the Concours d'Elegance, the line-up of the winners' cars.

Right there, she snagged it: the first time she had considered that she could win. The first time she imagined herself shaking the hand of some official while he handed her a trophy. Dreams, buried deep inside her like bulbs, had begun to sprout and bloom – and Vanessa's smile was helping.

She looked at her watch, which read just after six o'clock.

'Aren't we cutting it a bit fine? If the race starts at eleven, then what time is the briefing?'

'I've done this before, we're alright for time. It's less than three hours to Plymouth from here.'

'But what about the car, when we get there? Will we have time to test it?'

Vanessa's laugh was so rich that Freddy felt honoured to have given her the opportunity to let it out.

'Test? Whatever do you mean, darling?'

'Well, the car. The one we'll be racing in.'

'What do you think we're driving?'

'We're racing in *this* car?' Freddy said.

'It's not so bad, is it? I know it's factory made, but it's a Sunbeam-Talbot, it's got style, it's got speed, what more could a woman want?'

'A woman could want… a proper rally car.'

'This *is* a rally car.'

'I suppose it'll do,' Freddy sighed. When Vanessa first ushered her inside, she had glanced at the backseat for signs of children, crumbs or toys or little shoes, because it looked like a family car. She found none. The model was new to the market, but it was bulky and not exactly suited to a high-speed cross-country rally. Perhaps it was all Vanessa could get her hands on – but Freddy suspected there was something deliberate about this choice of car. She crossed her arms.

'I don't know how you're going to hold the maps with those arms crossed.'

'Do you mind me asking something?'

Vanessa – she could already tell – had a problem with assenting to things, so she ploughed into her question anyway.

'How old are you?'

'Forty-one.' Then, to Freddy's look of surprise: 'What, did you think that would be a tough question? It's not something to be ashamed of, merely a number and nothing more. A rather nice number. The glorious age beyond the possibility of children.'

Freddy did small sums in her head and realized that Vanessa was just about old enough to be her mother. Perhaps that explained the maternal sway this woman had over her.

'I'm long past believing that I could do this for a career,' Vanessa continued. 'But it's the best use of the life I've ended up with, don't you agree?'

Freddy was also beginning to have a problem with assenting; she was starting to flick her hair like Vanessa, laugh richly, deeply. She felt both more and never less like herself.

'We should step on it, then.'

'That's the spirit.'

'I still don't understand how we'll get there in time.'

'With an expert navigator, who can find me the short-cuts. Come on, let's practise.'

Freddy opened up the maps – and through the rustles, she heard the only snap of cynicism that had slipped from Vanessa's mouth since they entered the car: 'You should get used to this. We have to win a race, against time, against circumstances, against the day, just to reach the start line.'

Not for the first time that morning, Freddy was unsure who was navigating. Whether she was guiding Vanessa – or Vanessa was guiding her.

They had missed the start – or had they? Had the first car already gone? What were all these vehicles doing? Surely they had missed it, because why were the cars already on the start line, warming their engines under the *DAILY EXPRESS RALLY 1947* banner at five minutes to ten? If they hadn't missed it, then why had the briefing *wrapped up*?

'What do you mean *wrapped up*?' Vanessa argued with the race steward. It was the third time she had asked the question; the first two times, he had continued to mark down numbers on a clipboard as he walked along the start line. She chased him, stuck to him like his own elbow. Freddy trailed her. 'When is the briefing?'

He sighed, turned to her. His face was too small for his glasses – or was it that the glasses were too big for his face? The nerves turned her mind into a basket of questions. She found herself hiding behind Vanessa and her bushel of black hair.

'The briefing *was* at nine a.m. The race start is at ten a.m.'

'But the race start is at eleven!' Vanessa waved the paper at him. He smirked. He was the master of time and paper, and who was she to play him, let alone beat him, at his own game?

'Is there a bathroom?' Freddy begged. The long drive to Plymouth hadn't been kind to her bladder.

'A women's bathroom?' the man repeated. 'No, I'm afraid not.'

'Then what do you expect me to do? Go in that field?'

'That's what the other women do.'

'The other women?'

'The two I've seen today.'

'You saw them—'

'I'm sorry, but the timings are all wrong,' Vanessa interrupted.

'Your timings are the ones that are wrong. Miss, I believe you have been given false information.' His sentences irritated Freddy. They were too long, too full of letters.

'It's *Mrs*,' Vanessa replied.

'*Mrs*. Is your husband here? Perhaps he's on the start line already. Have you come to spectate, because you still have…' he looked at his watch, 'five minutes until the gun.'

'*We* are racing. My husband is at home. I entered a Sunbeam-Talbot, number 23.' His frown grew like fungus on his face. He looked at his clipboard, his glasses slipping down his nose. Freddy wondered why he had never changed them for a smaller pair.

He ticked a box and handed a small sheaf of paper to Vanessa.

'Number 23. Please proceed to the start line.'

'Thank you,' Vanessa snatched the paper from him and turned. Without her partner as a buffer, Freddy curled her fist; fury boiled inside her. She opened her mouth—

—and Vanessa tugged at her arm, dragging her away, before she could say a word.

'Don't get angry.'

'But he's…'

'Don't. If this riles you up, then you won't last the weekend. You've not seen the worst yet. Besides,' she continued, her fingers firm around Freddy's wrist. 'He's not the one you want to be angry at.'

'Who, then?'

'The bastard who gave me the wrong time. He knew it was wrong. The *son-of-a-bitch*!' she swore. Breathed. Continued in a measured voice: 'After what I did for him.'

'What did you do?'

Vanessa looked at her.

'Oh, sweetheart. Use your imagination.'

Freddy's face flared.

'You mean…'

'Yes, I do mean that.'

Freddy shook her wrist free. Disgust washed over her. Similar to the disgust she felt when it was announced that

Carrie had *got herself pregnant*. She was a wife. A good wife. An obedient wife. She was nothing like this woman. If Verne really knew who Vanessa was and the ideas she was putting in Freddy's head.

'You think I'm dirty? A good girl like you, you don't realize what needs to be done.'

'That doesn't… that doesn't *need* to be done.'

'In an ideal world, no. But we don't live in an ideal world. We have to make do with our practical one.'

'I don't believe that.'

'Then you might be the best of us.'

After striding past the other cars, they reached their platinum Sunbeam at the end of the line. Somewhere on their drive here, Vanessa had finally admitted that this car's strength was *resilience* and *reliability*, what the racier cars lacked, but Freddy was still unsure as she heard the more ostentatious cars around them roaring and flaring their engines. That said, the Sunbeam was what they had, and they clambered inside – Vanessa in the driver's seat, Freddy in the passenger seat.

'Look,' Vanessa said, as the door shut with a neat *clock*. 'You can think I'm a whore all you want. It's an agreement I have with my husband. You wouldn't understand. It's my business what I do and who I do it with.'

Freddy nodded, unconvinced.

'Put your helmet on. The little prick had a little prick, so I should have guessed. What I've learned, anyway,' she was testing the gears, warming the engine, 'is that if someone's trying to sabotage you, they think you're a threat. Take it as a compliment.'

'A compliment, but…'

'But what?' They were beginning to know each other's silences. The gun went, shocking them. The first car drove. Then the second. Freddy could see them peeling off ahead. Vanessa put on her helmet. The banner fluttered.

'But we missed the briefing. Isn't that important information? What don't we know?'

'I've listened to them before, and it's not essential. Weather warnings, speed limits, aid stations, mile checkpoints. The usual.'

'Those sound important.'

Freddy leaned forwards to survey the weather: a surprisingly warm November morning had yanked the dew from the ground to make thick fog. Magpies chattered and crows cawed. It looked more like a cemetery than a start line.

'The weather looks… variable. Should we be worried?'

'Not if you're a good driver. And you're a good driver.'

'Aren't *you* the driver?'

'Yes.' Vanessa smiled. 'Of course. I'm driving. I don't know what I mean.' She shifted into gear and bounced on the clutch.

The car next to them rolled down its window and fingers tapped on their door.

Vanessa rolled down hers.

'Bob, how are you?'

'Vanessa, a pleasure. The same car, I see. Hopefully you can make it to the end this year without putting it into the fence,' he said.

Bob's face was wrinkling badly under his tartan flat cap. He was smoking a cigarette and had opened the window to throw the stub into the mud.

'Who's that with you?'

'This is Freddy Vaux.' Freddy wanted to correct her – *it's Dawson-Hayes* – but she lost the moment.

'Another protégée?' Bob raised his eyebrows. 'Sometimes I think you only have these girls around so you can corrupt them with your ways. Which of the drivers are you taking home this time, Vanessa?'

'Best of luck, Bob.' She rolled up the window. Freddy marvelled at her ability not to rise to it.

'Who was that? What did he mean?'

'Focus.' Vanessa looked forwards. Not to the side, not to Bob's car, and certainly not back.

But one final question appealed to Freddy before it was their turn to shoot off into the fog.

'Vanessa, why did you ask me to be your navigator?'

She looked across at her, but it was too late. They were about to start. Vanessa's grin was huge. She released the clutch.

Two hours later, she asked Vanessa the same question – probably because Freddy had navigated them into a field, where perplexed farmers were staring at them.

'Why did you ask me to be your navigator? I'm hopeless.'

Vanessa held the map, turning it this way, that way, flipping it over. Fog curled around them. A cow moo-ed not too far off. When they were driving, the mist had been so thick, it had covered the road signs, and she had thrown confidences Vanessa's way she didn't really believe. Freddy looked at her watch and wondered if she could catch a train back home; what a story this would make for Verne.

'You've been holding it the wrong *bloody* way up. You *bloody* moron. Did you go to school?'

'I did, for a while.'

'And who taught you? Martians?'

'Nuns.'

'Bloody *nuns*,' Vanessa threw her hands in the air. 'Do they not plan their route to Jesus or whatever?'

'No, I don't…'

'Wait here.'

Vanessa walked off to speak with the farmers. Freddy leaned against the car, watching her communicate with them; hand gestures pointing to the left, laughs. When she returned, stomping across the rows of new seed, she threw the keys at Freddy, who caught them against her chest.

'I hope you drive better than you navigate.' She walked around to the passenger door. When Freddy didn't move: 'Get in the car! Now! I hope the nuns taught you what a race is.'

'Yes, they did. Among other things.'

Things like: the inevitability of damnation; the sacred covenant to populate the earth; that a husband, should you be lucky enough to get one, is the bishop of the home; that wives should know their place, and that place is behind the sink or the stove; that men should not be overshadowed; that women should stay beautiful, their bodies temples for men to explore; and that *Winifred Vaux, you should not stick your nose where it does not belong.*

The driver's door remained open, the seat gaping at her like a newborn. *To hell with the nuns*, Freddy thought, and closed it behind her.

'The gear shift is clunky,' Vanessa said. 'Take it easy.'

Before she could finish the word *easy*, the Sunbeam was back on the road.

As the checkpoints passed by the windows, it became clear that Vanessa was a much better teacher than she was a driver. Freddy hadn't mentioned it, but Vanessa's spiky turns had been making her feel queasy. Her wheel control was too harsh. With a brutally clear thought, Freddy realized that it was no wonder Vanessa had never won. All that rage and disagreement that Freddy had thought Vanessa was able to tamp down inside her – when she rolled up the window in Bob's face, when she walked away from the man with the clipboard – actually flowed out through her driving, to jerky consequences. She might as well have been muttering the words *Bob* and *bastard* under her breath as she yanked the gears up and down. There was too much of the past in her every movement.

'The next left,' Vanessa pointed. 'Then you want to take the stretch at high speed, to keep our average up. Third should do it for the corner. Don't be scared and drop down to two.' Freddy followed her command.

'Faster. You can do better than that.'

Freddy pushed it. Vanessa smiled.

'That's it.'

They sliced through the fog. Before long, they were on the rear of another car in the race. It was one of the first they had seen after dropping off the back. Freddy pushed down on the accelerator.

'That's it,' Vanessa whispered. 'Now…'

Freddy pulled out wide, in harmony with Vanessa's commentary. She drove parallel to their competitor.

'Make sure to look. It's always good to remember their faces.'

Later on, Freddy would decide that was the best piece of advice that Vanessa had given her. The faces of those men stayed with her. The little black Os where their mouths should be.

When she pulled back in, ahead of the car, Vanessa was giving her that deep, rich laugh.

'Oh, I bet you're glad that you came to my shop for your wedding dress. Look at that smile.' Freddy touched it; there it was, teeth and all. And there was a burst inside her too, somewhere under her ribcage, a bonfire. 'There's two turns up here. I'll direct.'

That felt like a good moment to ask the question for the third time.

'Vanessa, why did you ask me to be your navigator?' With dread, she continued. 'Did you just want someone to cover for you when you sneak off with men at the finish line?'

Vanessa laughed again.

'Good lord, what have I done to you? Half a day in a car with me and it's like you've been reading pulp fiction your entire life.'

As well as assenting, Vanessa had a problem with answering.

'Then what? Bob said that you do this often, that I'm just the latest one you've brought with you to navigate. How many have there been?'

'You wouldn't understand.' Vanessa shook her head.

'We've got another seventeen hours in this car. Try me.'

'Straight ahead.'

Freddy passed over the junction, without looking in either direction. She knew Vanessa would tell her if someone was approaching.

'Call it my duty,' Vanessa sighed, so quiet that Freddy could barely hear. Then, her voice growing louder: 'It's long past the days when I could drive and win, but I've learned a hell of a lot from my years of trying. It seems useless to keep all that to myself now, doesn't it? These aren't secrets. Or they shouldn't be. There comes a time when a woman racer's responsibility might not be to race anymore, but to teach others how to do it instead. I think I could die, knowing that one more girl like you has driven because of me, that I… *live on* in the way they shift the gears or overtake an old bastard.'

'Like that,' Freddy said, as she took out another competitor on the road.

'Pull out later. Stay in his slipstream longer.'

She nodded.

'What do you mean a girl like me?'

'Someone who has got the ill-advised idea stuck in her head that she wants to race cars.'

Freddy grinned.

'Then what happened to all the others?'

'What always happens.' She pointed to the ring on Freddy's finger. 'What's already happened to you, which is why I think…' She paused. Freddy felt Vanessa inspecting her. 'I think there's something different about you.'

Freddy thought of Carrie. 'You mean that I've got my head screwed on right… and not stuck on meaningless things like knitting patterns and *muscles*.'

Vanessa was quiet, then she sighed. 'There's nothing wrong with knitting patterns, Freddy. And certainly nothing wrong with muscles. I used to think like that too, but beating down other women to make your own path doesn't mean you'll get there any quicker. It just means you'll end up alone and exposed.

'You'd realize there's no need for all that nastiness, if only you saw how *good* you are.' To Freddy's look: 'I'm not blowing sunshine up your arse, Fred, but you're *good*. Really good.'

Freddy opened her mouth to reply, then shut it again.

'All I'm saying is that these young women deserved a chance, and there was no one else to give it to them. At least I let them try. Let them see what they're missing out on.'

A silence settled over the car. Wind gushed past the windows, but the interior was calm. It was the purest space Freddy had known, free of complication and distress. Her hands fell on the wheel, smoothing the varnished wood. A sweet melancholy emanated from Vanessa. She was an unhappy woman with so few ways to turn that into happiness; a woman who knew she was a teacher and not a doer; stubborn, bitter, but determined.

'Thank you,' Freddy whispered.

'For what?'

Freddy shrugged. 'For asking me.'

She wanted to thank her for more than that: for allowing a future to open up in the road ahead of them, a future in which she drove with Vanessa as a pair, and the two talked torque for hours, and the fog bowed to them, and they went to Monte Carlo and East Africa and Ireland for their rallies. Since the wedding, she had known she wanted more – and Vanessa had shown her that *this* was what she wanted. And another thing she wanted to thank her for: she had barely thought about Verne since the race began.

Freddy couldn't be sure, considering how dark it was, but it seemed there was a dead man on the side of the road. It was dawn on the second day and her hands were beginning to cramp, her eyes aching to shut, her mouth dry, the car hot and stuffy, but after blinking once, twice, she was certain: he was dead.

She swatted Vanessa, who was dozing in the passenger seat.

'Look, there.'

Freddy pointed and slowed to a roll. Half-awake, Vanessa reached out with her cold, sharp hand and pressed Freddy's thigh down onto the accelerator pedal.

'What are you doing?' Freddy shouted.

'Don't stop.'

Freddy grabbed her hand and threw it away, lifting her foot from the pedal.

'Would he stop for you?' Vanessa spat.

'That makes no difference.'

'Kindness doesn't win races. And this is a *race*, Fred, not a tea party where everyone needs a fair share of the cucumber sandwiches. You'll have to learn,' Vanessa sighed as the car came to a stop. 'Don't get out of this car.'

'*Get in the car, get out, turn left, turn right,*' Freddy mimicked her voice. 'Who do you think you are?'

'Your navigator. I suggest you listen to me. I know more than you.'

'Not about this.' She pressed down on the brake and opened the door. Vanessa tutted as she tried to grab the back of her jacket. But Freddy slipped out. At dawn, the road was sweaty with dew.

A pillar of smoke rose from a mangled car in the ditch near the body. Adorned with a Daily Express Rally competition banner like the one on Vanessa's Sunbeam, the wrecked vehicle was custom-built, sleek and fashionable; the last time Freddy had seen one was on a movie screen and Jean Kent had been driving it. Now the black hull was crumpled like the rucks of a satin dress, all but one wheel fallen off, the windshield broken. And out of it, a man had been thrown. There was a trail of his blood from the driver's seat. The helmet was cracked – his head on the floor.

'Sir? Excuse me?'

'Fred, get *back* in this car,' Vanessa hissed from behind.

'I'm not going to leave a man for dead.'

'Too good to be good,' Vanessa shouted. 'That's what you are.'

'Sir!' Freddy urged again, only inches from the body.

He twitched.

'Sir?'

He turned and grabbed her wrist.

'I lost… concentration,' he forced the word out.

'He's alive!' Freddy shouted to Vanessa in the car. She turned back to him. 'Don't speak. I'll get help.'

'My navigator…' the man whispered.

'Yes? Is he in the car? Does he need help?'

'No. He went for help. Ages ago.' The man sat upright without difficulty. He cradled his arm. 'I've broken my arm, miss, but I think I should be fine.'

'But you were lying down?'

'I was tired. I'm part of a rally, see. Driving for twenty-four hours will kill any man.'

'I'm part of the rally too.'

He frowned, then began to chuckle. 'I needed a good laugh.'

Freddy stepped backwards. 'You're fine?'

He couldn't reply for laughing. 'Oh, I'm just fine. I'm *tip-top*, lovely.' He leaned back to open his lungs for more breath – so that he could carry on laughing.

Freddy walked back to the car.

'Is he alright?' Vanessa asked.

'He's fine.'

'Can we keep moving?'

Freddy's mind was absent; she shifted the car into gear. Her mouth couldn't find words.

'He's… fine.'

A car was approaching in the rear window. She recognized the make and number – Bob. He rolled the window down and stuck out his head.

'Madams.' He doffed his cap, which he was wearing instead of a helmet. He was of the generation – Vanessa had explained – that didn't believe in safety; good drivers live and bad drivers die, there were no two ways about it. 'Aren't…' He grinned before finishing his sentence. 'Aren't you sitting in the wrong seats?'

They both froze.

'It's a quick change, so that Vanessa can get some rest,' Freddy said.

Bob snapped up the window and drove off. She heard his hoots long after the car had disappeared.

'As if we needed to give them another reason to disqualify us.'

'Disqualify us?'

'That's *why* you don't stop,' Vanessa huffed.

'But he could have been hurt.'

'Sure.' Vanessa shook her head. 'Just drive. You won't make that mistake again.'

Vanessa was right; she wouldn't.

Freddy would never know what information had been circulated at the safety briefing. Perhaps the race directors had given instructions about slowing at junctions in the fog or double-guessing the map because the farmers spring up stone walls like crops. Perhaps it had been a waste of time. The point is, she would never know.

But she would wonder about that safety briefing for years to come – after Vanessa told her on the second night to *cross the road, go straight ahead* and Freddy drove straight into a wall. There was no ahead.

First, her mind registered the crash. A gasping twist of metal and machine. And second, Vanessa. Slumped over the dashboard, her blood dribbling down the speed dial.

The pain in Freddy's own body took a few seconds to seep in, and then once she felt it – *there it was* – she pushed it off again.

'Vanessa,' she whispered. The body in the navigator seat was still. The car – still. Hissing, the bonnet crumpled, the shield and headlights smashed. 'Vanessa, please. You've got to tell me where to go. You've got to tell me what to do.' As with her mother, it wasn't fear that crossed her mind. Those tears streaming down her face – they weren't tears, not at all, just blood from the cut – but what cut, where? It was Vanessa she needed to worry about.

She had no car to outdrive death with anymore; but Freddy flipped open the glove box and found a torch, a scarf, and a handkerchief. That would do.

'Stick with me,' she shouted. Owls hooted in the woods to their left. Horses roamed the open plains to their right. She scanned the horizon for chimneys, lights: nothing. The next checkpoint was two miles away, according to the blood-stained map on Vanessa's lap.

'Vanessa, hold on.'

She touched Vanessa's black mane, withdrew her hand, touched it again, and this time carefully lifted the head back to the headrest. It was heavy, and Freddy heard crunches in bone and skull and glass all at the same time. Freddy clicked the torch and shone it onto the dashboard, working its beam around to Vanessa's face—

—she gasped. A shard of windshield had cut into Vanessa's forehead, underneath the rim of the helmet and sliced a big flap of skin, which folded down over her eyes like limp ham.

Her hands acting for her, her mind catching up, Freddy touched two fingers to Vanessa's neck and felt resilient pumps of blood. She had checked pulses hundreds of times during the war. *Stay with me*, she thought, then held up the wet flap of skin and slapped the handkerchief hard onto the gash, blood oozing out. She wound the scarf tight around Vanessa's head, wadding it in the gaps of the helmet. She knew better than to take the helmet off. Vanessa made no sound throughout the brisk operation.

A car was approaching. She saw its headlights first, and then, twisting in her seat, saw the rest of the car, and the two helmeted heads inside it. She screamed: *help!*

'Please, someone get some help!'

She rocked side to side in the car – with her door smashed against the wall there was no chance of opening it. Perhaps a rolling, steaming, hissing Sunbeam might attract them.

'Wait!' she shouted at the car. Her eyes locked with theirs, but the car sped up at exactly that moment. She would never know who those two men were, her mind spinning too much to see the number plate, but she would have… what would she have done, reported them? She could almost hear Vanessa laughing about the *fat lot of good* that would do.

'I'll get help,' Freddy mumbled, watching the fog pool around their steaming wreck. This woman would not die. She kicked in the final hanging shards of the windscreen and lugged herself out the car, cutting her hands on the sharp edges. She made no sound, no yelps or grunts; no one was around to hear her.

She had to leave her shoes wedged under the dashboard – a fact she felt particularly keenly when her feet hit the wet, slippery surface of the country lane.

But she had the torch. She clicked it, took one final look at Vanessa and hobbled down the lane towards the checkpoint.

The three men sat under the gazebo, minding their own business. None of them noticed Freddy as she appeared from the fog, dragging her feet like broken hooves, her blonde hair darkened with mist and blood.

'Excuse me.' She tried to wave, but her arm was too weak. 'Over here.'

They continued talking, not seeing her.

One of the men finally turned towards the noise. He took a beat, then said with mild irritation: 'What is it, dear?'

'My navigator, she's hurt. Please, I need help. She's a few miles that way.'

And as much as he tried to hide it, she heard the second one mumble into his flask of tea: *women drivers.*

'Well, at least there's one less of them now, isn't there?' Freddy yelled.

'What happened?' The first stood. A tall man with watery eyes, a Barbour jacket, flat cap, and wrinkled, blue-veined hands.

'A crash. The wall came out of nowhere. And the fog, it was so thick.'

'Did you not listen to the briefing, my dear?'

'No. I did not.'

'It has some vital information.'

'So I've heard.'

She had cried all her tears out on the way here and now there was only rage left.

'Roger said he'd kill us if we knocked on his door before eight,' the third mused to the others from his seat.

'I suggest you call on Roger anyway, considering there is a woman missing half her face a couple miles down that road.'

'Right. Yes.' The first fidgeted. Then remembering something.

'Ah, what's your number. So that we can inform race authorities.'

'Why does that matter?' Freddy cooled herself again, hearing Vanessa's commands.

'It's procedure.'

'Number twenty-three.'

'Twenty-three,' the second spoke, looking up and down a clipboard. He paused, smacking his pen at the paper. 'I should suppose it's lucky that you've crashed out. Stops you from a waste of effort.'

'What do you mean?' Freddy asked.

'You've been disqualified anyway. Unauthorized swapping of positions. Another driver reported it when he passed through here last night.'

Freddy dug her nails into the palm of her hand.

'That's convenient, isn't it?' She tried Vanessa's sarcasm, and it felt better than expected.

'If you want to look at it that way.' The first rubbed his hands together.

It took Freddy to slump against the wall for them to move with any urgency. How long she might have stood there arguing the worth of a woman's life, if she had remained upright.

They had helped her out of the bed so she could call her husband from the hospital.

'How many?' Verne's voice crackled down the line on the matron's telephone. She leaned all her weight on the wall of the busy corridor, only just remaining upright through the haze of painkillers.

'Seven.' She was talking about the stitches at her hairline, the ones that the doctor had threaded into her skin moments ago. Vanessa was in the operating room. She had been in there for hours.

'Darling... what did I tell you? Perhaps this isn't...' He stopped himself, waiting for her to complete the sentence. When it became clear she wasn't going to, he continued: 'Are they looking after you?'

'Funnily enough that's a priority in most hospitals,' she said. 'The car is a write-off, Verne.'

'That's alright, it wasn't ours anyway, was it? It was that woman's.'

'She's in surgery, if you were wondering.'

He took a moment to reply. 'Sorry?'

'Verne, are you busy?'

'I am, but it's alright. I'm glad you're fine.'

'Well, not really, I'm—'

'I'm not sure if I can make it to pick you up.'

'Could you try?'

'Darling, we're about to leave for the races in Cardiff. Father wants to catch sight of a new hound in action... he's quite marvellous. But you don't want to hear about all that.'

'Well, could you—'

'I'll sort it,' he snapped. Then in the background: *Dash, stop that. Stop. Put it down.* 'I'll sort it, Win. Someone will be there to pick you up. Hold on tight.'

He hung up. Her mind whirred; she wanted to vomit. Unforgiving light from the electric bulbs studding the ceiling made her squint, and the nurses walking over the linoleum in squeaky shoes were too loud. Her ears were sensitive, like she had been underwater for some time.

As she was preparing to shuffle back to the ward, the phone rang. She picked it up.

'Oh, thank goodness you're still there,' Verne said.

'Yes, a high-speed crash has the remarkable effect of slowing you down quite considerably.'

'Right. I just needed to check… where are you again?'

'I'm in Royal Devon and Exeter Hospital. Ward Three. Bed Two. The nurse is called Jemima.'

'Right. Thank you.' The line clipped.

When she returned to the bed, she dozed, woozy from the head wound. Life slipped around her. She fell in and out of consciousness and dreams, unable to tell which was which. At times, she still drove while Vanessa offered directions on her left. At others, she lay in a bed and waited for Verne to collect her, Vanessa several walls away with needles in her head. How close the two worlds were together, only a thin membrane of sleep to separate them.

When she woke, it was late afternoon. The bitty end of day. Sick of being stationary in the bed, Freddy padded down the corridor, towards the line of doors that they had wheeled Vanessa into, her head hanging off the back of the stretcher, that black hair flirting with the floor.

There was a line of wooden benches against the wall outside, and she slumped down on one and waited.

After some time, two doctors emerged from the room, snapping their rubber gloves off and shoving them into the bin. Neither noticed her.

'A waste of good thread, if you ask me.'

'In a car race? A shame that a woman like that had to tear herself to pieces behind the wheel.'

'A damn shame. God rest her soul.'

They strolled down the corridor, as if they had walked out of a bar.

So there had been no final words between them. There had been so much left to say, so many rallies left to drive. It seemed too unfair to curtail that, and Freddy crossed her arms like a toddler. *I don't know how you're going to hold those maps with your arms crossed*, Vanessa quipped in her head, and she had a feeling that the voice was there to stay. The numbness gave way then, and Freddy creased over on the bench, letting her tears out all over her knees. Who did she think she was? Why did she think *she* could race cars? Had she killed a woman last night?

After the crying was done, she must have dozed again, because when she opened her eyes there was someone unfolding her arms.

Her father. His mouth set and flat.

'She's dead. I couldn't save her.'

'She wasn't yours to save. By the sounds of it, she was far gone. Come.' He tugged her from the chair, and the tears began to fall again; because she remembered her father dragging her from another hospital, her mother in the ward. *It was lucky that I taught you how to drive.* Now, she believed she might have been luckier, and Vanessa too, had she never sat behind the wheel and never known what it felt like – how good it felt.

'We need to sort paperwork and…' Freddy protested.

'The woman's husband is in reception. I think it's best we make our exit now.'

He led her down the hallway.

'Speaking of husbands, where is mine?'

'He's… tied up. He called and I offered.'

She nodded – the itching disgust she had anticipated never came. She was glad Verne would never see her like this.

When she exited the hospital doors, she saw the Baby Austin waiting for her outside.

'You brought her,' she breathed. Freddy walked around to the passenger seat.

'Where are you going?' he asked.

'I'm getting in the car.'

'Wrong door.'

'You can't be serious.'

'Deadly.' The word *dead* struck her. It turned out that, as well as an obedient wife, she was an obedient daughter. She opened the driver's door and sat. Turned the keys in the ignition. Shifted into gear. She shuddered.

But she drove. At first, her back was rigid, the muscles in her forearms tense; she heaved for the first mile, sighed for the second, and by the third she was breathing normally. When her eyelids began to droop, her father said her name gently and righted the steering wheel to keep them within the white lines.

Whenever she thought of Vanessa, or her mother,

or the race, the windshield, the junction, and her chest started to shudder, her father said:

'Try not to think about it. Just drive.'

Just drive.

She drove all the way back to the house. At the time, she hated her father for making her drive through the pain. But she became grateful for it.

If he had never forced her to drive home, she might never have driven again.

Halfway through her bacon and eggs the following morning, it became clear that Verne had decided to pretend that nothing had happened. To treat her weekend as one spent at home among the flowers and rose-coloured cushions that his aunt had picked out for them from the season's catalogue. His only acknowledgement of the whole ordeal was the quick kiss on her bandaged cheek as he walked up to her at the hob, collected a plateful of breakfast and sat down with the newspaper.

She had facilitated it, in a way. Before he got back in the early hours of the morning, she struck up a hashed bonfire in the garden and burned her bloody clothes; she hid the helmet at the bottom of the cupboard; she soaked in a bath and scrubbed every pore until not a trace of the race – or Vanessa – was left. She wanted to scour it from her mind too, but there was no chance of that happening. Vanessa's words, her dangling skin, her hair over the edge of the stretcher – the memories dug in their heels. They were staying put.

When he said nothing at breakfast, but slapped the paper against his thigh, licked his fingers, turned the page, she realized he had taken a bait she had laid without thinking. He was behaving so normally that perhaps it *had* all been a dream – or a nightmare. And she had the chance to leave it as one. Here, on the breakfast table, next to the butter oozing in the sun, Verne's knife scraping on his toast, was the opportunity to dismiss it. To end everything there. Call it what it was: a moment of madness. Verne had started to mention more often that he wanted a son. Could she give him one, put her resolve aside? She had no idea that surrender would be this easy.

Without looking up from his page, Verne slid over the Motoring supplement to Freddy. Out of kindness, out of what, she never knew. She dragged it towards her corner of the table and had to read the headline several times: *ANOTHER FINE M.C.C. DAILY EXPRESS RALLY.* Underneath the headline, she found remarks on the weather – *Although the fog never let up, it was a glorious race* – and a list of the results, short biographies of the men who had stood on the podium, a brief interview with the winner. To end the article, a short paragraph: *Four disqualifications. Eleven did not finish.*

Freddy turned over the page, but a report on the latest championship race began. Where was the rest of the article? Where was the mention of Vanessa and herself?

Not even between the lines, but completely outside of them.

She couldn't leave it like that. What about Vanessa's legacy, all her talk of sharing secrets? What of all those rallies she had never driven? There had been so much left to say, and no record of Vanessa's voice anywhere.

Freddy flipped to the obituary pages. V… V…

'Win, do calm down. Do you need to go back to bed?'

'No.'

The phone rang in the hallway. Freddy stood and mumbled *I'll get it*, glad to move from the table.

'Hello?' she answered, picking it up.

'Is that Freddy Vaux?'

'It's… Mrs Dawson-Hayes. Who's this?'

'I'm calling about a woman named Vanessa.'

'Yes?'

'You see… I believe you killed my wife.'

5. The Puck

Of all things, he invited her to tea. He passed his address over the telephone and said *so I'll see you Wednesday at four?* and Freddy supposed you couldn't say no to a man who had just lost his wife, so she said *yes.* When she put down the receiver, she was unsure whether she had been invited so he could hear her apologize, to make her acquaintance or to strike off her head. There was a deep blue thrill in the pit of her stomach.

'Who was it?' Verne asked, not looking up from his newspaper when she returned to the kitchen and began to clear away the breakfast things.

'No one. A friend.' She wasn't planning to lie to him when she re-entered the room.

He looked over his paper, those blue eyes darting into her. She saw his hand tighten around the side of the page, almost ripping it.

'So, which one is it? No one, or a friend?' It wasn't the first time he had spoken to her with that clenched voice.

'A friend. Sally-Anne.'

'I don't know her.'

Of course he wouldn't; she didn't exist.

'She lives in East Tessley.'

'I've never heard of that?'

Again – because it didn't exist.

'It's one of the villages over the river.'

He nodded, not really listening.

'And what did she want?'

'She's invited me to tea. On Wednesday.'

Folding the newspaper, he tore himself from the chair and left the room. She heard his footsteps weaken, before strengthening again and he stood in the threshold, his arms pressed against the doorframe.

'Is she married? This Sally-Anne? She's not one of those rally drivers like that… Valerie.'

'Vanessa.'

'Of course.'

'And no. Sally-Anne is married. We talk interior design and embroidery over cups of Assam, is that acceptable?'

He gave a stiff nod.

'I'm glad to see you're getting out. I'd hate for you to be lonely while I'm away. The Greyhound Derby is coming up soon, so I can't help it. Father needs me.'

'I know.'

Vernon edged towards her and smothered her cheek with kisses, not unlike a dog. She leaned into it. As he kissed her, she imagined where Sally-Anne had been born and what the names of her children were and how many bedrooms their house had and who her husband was and what he did for work and on and on and on.

She found him exactly where he said he would be. Buried deep in the not-so-wilds of Berkshire, and buried deep within his estate, buried deep within the bonnet of his car.

He emerged from the garage, and stretched out a spotless hand, chalky white.

'Will Truston. I know who you are.' He spoke without pauses – as if he feared someone would interrupt him. Brisk, clipped sentences of posh schoolboy English, unbroken by grief. He was small and slim, with a toasting of cotton-blonde hair, milky-blue eyes and cheeks that bloomed red even in November sun. While his delicate skin gave him the pallor of a porcelain doll, his grip was harsh and his baby face was rucked with the slight creases of someone nearing forty.

'I want to express my sincerest condolences,' Freddy said.

'Yes… Vanessa.' He looked down at the gravel for one, two seconds. Then, with great effort, he waved a casual hand to dismiss the matter. And looked back up at her with a pained smile. He carried on in a sombre tone. 'Not your fault at all. I've raced in rallies and I know how these things happen. It was a tragedy, but Vanessa always wanted to die behind the dashboard of her Sunbeam. I know she would have been happy to go like that.' His mind seemed to wander far from the drive, before he reeled it back in and said: 'That's not why I invited you here.'

'Oh.' He was leading her into the garage, and she was following him. 'Do you mind me asking… if that's not why you asked me here, then why did you?'

Will planted them in front of a hull – what might one day be a car, but was at present several twines of metal with an engine in the back:

'Why is the engine behind the driver?' Freddy burst out, before she could stop herself.

'It helps with the weight balance.'

'But—'

'She's a work in progress. Give her the benefit of the doubt.' He flicked his eyes the length of Freddy's body. 'She's not got a name yet, but she'll be a fantastic rally car, and she needs a small, nimble driver. Someone who might have raced in a rally before, but not so many that they're too used to the usual models and couldn't adapt to this one.'

'Are you saying…?'

'Oh, I'm not saying anything, not before tea.' He swivelled on his heel and started walking fast. As if the thoughts might catch up with him if he stood still for even one moment.

As she followed him down the gravel to the manor house, grey stone and turrets, his voice chipper, she realized he hadn't looked her in the eye once; that his right hand was twitching; that he had brushed off Vanessa's name with such subtle violence. She had never seen a man in a deeper state of mourning; he simply hid it remarkably. She wondered what else he was hiding, and if he had a talent for it.

'The parents left the house. The parents left the cars. The parents also left me in my final year of boarding school when they got on a ship to America and found their way to the bottom of the ocean floor,' he said, nonchalantly.

'I'm sorry.'

'For what? I was eighteen. I barely knew them anyway, after they carted me off at twelve.' He wafted the explanations at her while moving around the tea things. 'Besides, at that point, I had already started to make a name for myself as a driver. I won my first rally at seventeen.' He smiled, remembering. 'It's addictive, that sudden fame. But it takes its toll, in other ways. Connections… are not my forte.'

He whisked her through the grand old house, most of the rooms shuttered and dusty. There were no maids or staff or gardeners that she could see. With curiosity, she followed the mannered man who made no use of his manners. She marvelled at the skill in his hands, the quick flips of the teapot lid. He smothered the loneliness in his voice with tinkling and tapping and the whistle from the kettle.

'I hope you like cheese soufflé. It's about the only thing I can make.'

'My husband can't make *anything*.' She hadn't planned on bringing Verne into the conversation, but now she had summoned him into the room. Most people might have then taken the opportunity to ask *what does your husband do?* or *what line of work is he in?* but Will continued on about the soufflé.

'Is one allowed to call it a speciality if it's the only thing I can make?' He spoke to himself, and beckoned her towards the parlour. Their heels clicked the tiles, echoing around the empty house. Embellished columns, chandeliers with candles, it was all a little much. But the parlour had next to no traces of two things: racing and women. The staples of a racer's life.

'You still race?'

'Sporadically, and without results these days. I devote most of my time now to making the cars rather than driving them. Which is… expensive.' He put the tea down on the table and began to pour. 'Yes, I'm afraid those days are gone, but I may have won the Monte several times in my day. Not long after the first war.'

'The Monte?'

He looked at her, stunned.

'My dear, you really don't know anything, do you?' She braced herself. Expecting condescension, expecting laughter. Instead: 'Well, that's just marvellous. I'm *so* pleased I found you.'

'You still haven't told me what you asked me here for...'

He gestured her to take a seat on one of the sofas. He sat on the other, upright, his long-fingered hands pressed in prayer between his slim legs.

'I think you're very talented,' he said. 'I've heard reports from some of the folks in that rally. I know you swapped seats with Vanessa, and she never swapped seats, not with anyone. She was stubborn as a brick.' He held his breath. 'She must have thought you were talented, so I do too.'

'Excuse me, but... I killed your wife.'

'Yes, but before that, I heard you were quite remarkable on the road.'

She wasn't sure if he had heard.

'But I *killed* your wife. You said so.'

'I know I said that on the telephone, but I wasn't myself then. For obvious reasons. That said, I suspect you wouldn't have come here unless you thought it was to grovel and apologize. You seem like someone who wants to apologize for their mere presence in the world. Someone who wants to find reasons to give it all up.'

It was an unusual feeling to Freddy, that someone could read her this well. She searched for a response but came up short. He continued, 'No, it was the car, the road, the conditions, the force, the impact... that's what killed her. Not you.' The truth felt like a hot spotlight.

'The race authority said they're thinking of banning me from future races.'

'A good friend of mine is the co-president. I can sort that out. We'll have to.'

'Why?'

'That car in the garage needs a driver. It needs a woman to drive it.'

She shot up, the napkin in her lap falling onto the floor.

'Goodness, what is it?' he said.

'I know what you want. You're a car manufacturer. You want to sell cars. A pretty woman adorning your cars will help, won't it? Some good press. Well, I'm not interested. I'm not going to sprawl on the bonnet.'

'My dear, who said anything about getting on the bonnet? I should hope you were inside the car. There would be no use for you *on* the car. No,' he stood and took her hands in his. 'I want you to *drive* it. I want you to compete in it. I want to sign you to Truston Motors.'

'What do you mean *sign me?*'

'I want you under contract.'

'Why on earth would you want that?'

'Because Vanessa would.'

Within the hour she was in Will's spare pair of overalls and inside the bonnet of the car.

'Do you mean this?' She held an oil cap out the side.

Will – who was inside the car – stuck his head out.

'Hold it for a second. Wait. I'll give you the signal.'

He gave the signal.

Things were much the same the following day, when Freddy returned and was once again out of her dress and into the overalls, crouching near a wheel rim and muttering about *bolts* with Will.

'Too big?'

'*Far* too big.'

'Change them?'

'Hand me the wrench,' he said.

She did.

After a week, there was real progress. The car was looking like less of a hull; it had side panels and wheels and seats and four circular headlights under plexiglass covers fitted flush to the nose. And suspension of double wishbones at the front and live rear axle. It tipped the scales at just over six hundred kilograms. A dainty little thing.

'She needs a name,' Will said.

'The sprite?'

'Too ethereal.' Freddy shook her head. The two were sat on crates drinking tea. The December chill meant they couldn't sit still for too long – in fingerless gloves, their fingertips were blue when not black with grease.

'Ariel?' Freddy suggested.

'If we're doing Shakespeare, then we had better go with Puck.'

'Puck. Light, small...'

'Underestimated...'

'Tough to spot...'

'Harder to catch.'

'She's perfect.' Freddy slurped the dregs of her tea before switching up the gramophone and swatting Will on the shoulder.

Two weeks later, Will blurted out:

'You'll need a partner, you know.'

'That will be you, won't it?'

'It should be an all-women's car, so that we can compete in the all-women category.'

Freddy stuck her head out of the interior. She was testing the gearbox capability, the wheels up on a sandbox; she was driving at eighty miles per hour, but she was going nowhere. Will leaned on the window.

'Do we have to?'

'If we want a shot at winning the Coupe des Dames, then it needs to be an all-women team.'

'But can't we just enter the normal race?'

'We do enter the normal race. But we won't win it. There are veterans who have been doing this since before the war. We'll be lucky to finish. But the Coupe des Dames is awarded to the first female team that finishes. It's a huge honour. There's a cash prize. And a big trophy.'

Freddy sighed and clunked the car out of gear.

'Do you have someone in mind?'

'Yes,' Will smiled. 'My cousin, Louisa.'

'What's she like?'

'She's sweet.'

'And can she drive?'

'No, not at all. Wouldn't know a steering wheel from a Catherine wheel. The driving is all down to you.'

Freddy grinned and hoped Will wouldn't see it – but she knew he could; rear mirrors worked that way.

'Look, she's getting married in the spring and she came to me and said she had to do something dramatic and glamorous in her life before *she was chained to a sink*.' He began acting the scene out, with Louisa's high voice and a deeper voice that she supposed was Will's. 'I said, *You don't have to be chained to a sink*. And she crossed her arms and said, *Willie, wake up and smell the coffee*.' Freddy was unamused, but he continued, 'Anyway, I told her about the rally. She liked the idea. I said that I know a brilliant woman who will be driving. This woman thinks she killed my wife and she goes on about it, but I try and tell her every day that it's not her fault. She's still an incredible driver, even if she thinks she killed someone.'

'Let me guess, that's me.'

'Oh no, there's another woman I'm talking about.'

Suddenly, that familiar sharp pang in her chest. When she knew she had to wipe the grease off her hands and change back into the dress that hung on the back of the bathroom door and drive home.

'I have to get back to my husband.'

'Usually when someone says they *have to* do something, they don't want to do it.'

'I've told you, it's not like that. He's just… busy. He wouldn't understand.'

'Yes.' Will looked down at her, unconvinced. 'Have you tried to speak with him? You'll need to tell him where you're disappearing off to next week.'

Her silence answered his question.

'You won't know until you try, otherwise the secret between you… it will fester.'

Freddy stepped out of the car and slammed the door behind her. 'What do you know about marriage, huh?'

'I never said I did.'

'What about that agreement between you and Vanessa?'

'You don't understand.'

'I think I do.'

'You think she was some tramp? It wasn't like that.'

'Then what was it like?'

'It was *different*.'

'How?'

'She had the licence to do whatever she wanted, and I could do whatever I wanted.'

'So, you could see other women.'

'Something like that.'

She shook her head and began to walk to the house.

'The only thing Verne would hate more than me racing is socializing with people like you.'

'What do you mean people like me?'

She turned and spat the word at him.

'*Modern* people.'

He laughed her all the way out the drive.

Telling Vernon had always been on the cards. The cards that disappeared when she was with Will, or was fiddling with the innards of the Puck. It was only on the drive home, with her hands clenched on the wheel, that the cards were visible once more, spread all over the dashboard, and she was reminded that she would have to tell him. One way or another.

But he never arrived home before seven, so she always had time to make excuses not to: it's not the right moment, he'll be tired, he never likes to have serious conversations after a long day.

Tonight, she was resolute. She had to tell him. But tell him what? That she wanted her own arrangement, like Will and Vanessa's? Something between prude, pregnant or married? A fourth option – to be *modern*, like them. The thought – and that she had even *thought* it – shocked her. She had never wanted to be modern before. All she wanted was to drive, and for him to understand, but that seemed even more fanciful than that mystical fourth option.

Verne, she might say, *I have something to tell you.*

You're pregnant, he might reply.

'What *then*?' she said aloud, practising her responses to the windscreen. 'Verne, I'm driving the Monte Carlo Rally. Verne, I'm racing from Glasgow down to Grenoble.

Verne, I want to win the Coupe des Dames.' She opened the window onto a fresh December evening.

What about John and Eric? she wondered. If she could tell her brothers, she could get them to do the dirty work for her.

But Eric would sooner die than stand up to Verne, the boy that broke his nose twice at school. And she remembered John's complicit laugh last week at a dinner party with all their friends when she returned to the table from the bathroom to hear Verne saying *that's why they don't put women in the driver's seat.* It was like he had never heard anything funnier. The women at the table, a string of bejewelled wives, had tittered at the comment as well.

No, she had to do it.

She would tell him: *Verne, I'm driving the Monte Carlo Rally in two weekends' time.*

Who would want you to drive the Monte Carlo Rally?

She couldn't mention Will, that's for certain. Nor Louisa. Nor Truston Motors. But who then? Sally-Anne Motors? Sally-Anne's husband has a motoring company. She could hear herself saying it.

But what's it called? Verne would ask.

Did all wives have these conversations with themselves?

When she did tell him a week later, Verne took it like medicine: with slow, careful swallows. He tipped his head back to look at the ceiling as she talked to him.

'Next weekend?'

Freddy nodded.

'What if I had plans next weekend? What if I was planning to take you into London?'

'Were you?' Freddy nuzzled against him on the sofa.

'No, but I could have. Is this…' The words like stones in his throat. 'Something you'll keep doing?'

'I don't know.' Every response was a new hold on a cliffside she was scaling. 'But to be asked is a lovely thing. We'll just do this one and see how we go.'

'See how we go,' he repeated. Took a swig from the tumbler of whisky he'd been resting on his thigh. There was a little damp ring on his trousers, and he rubbed at it. Freddy grasped his hand and held it still.

'Thank you, Verne, for being so understanding.'

'Yes, that's it. The understanding husband.'

'It's very kind.'

'Oh, *very* kind.'

He was drunker than she had thought when she started this conversation. But it was more than alcohol filling him. He was a full-to-bursting dam of a man, an ocean of fury crashing on the backs of his eyeballs. He thought he was hiding it well, but she could sense it. She had the *audacity* to make him feel self-disgust for all that anger inside. He was loath to be angry with her.

Freddy could see the version of this scene where he gave in to the anger; and she watched it play out with him; she watched him hate himself for it, for what she had made him do; for his shouting – *Freddy, I don't like you doing this, I don't like you racing, I like you at home.*

Vernon leaned back.

'You never ask me how I'm doing,' he said.

'How are you doing, sweetheart?' She put fingers through his thick hair, but he pushed them away.

'Remember that I was a pilot?'

'Of course. John talks about it all the time. You're their hero, and the number of Germans you shot down was—'

'But here's the thing about that,' he interrupted her. 'Look at me. Do I look like a man that shot down fourteen Germans? Look at me,' he slammed down his drink on the side table and ridged his body towards her. 'Do I look like a hero?'

'Yes, of course, you're…'

He shook his head.

'I didn't even shoot down one. Well, I did, but that was an accident. I crashed into it.'

'But…'

'I wanted to be a man who shot down fourteen German planes, so I had to become the man that lies about shooting down fourteen German planes, and it doesn't feel good, Winifred. And what feels even worse is that now I won't ever have a chance to shoot down fourteen German planes again. I won't even get the chance to shoot down one. I'll always be the man who lied about it. I'll always be a liar, and a man who never shot down anybody. I got close once. I did. I flew right by him and I fired and it… missed.'

She began to reply, but he left no gap.

'So, it doesn't help me, is all I'll say, Win, when you insist on these races. It doesn't help.' She hated to point out that it was only her second race.

'No, I don't think it would.' Her mouth found words, but from his face she had a feeling they weren't the right ones. 'You don't want me to race?'

He frowned.

'That's not what I said.' Those squinted eyes – he was telling her to come to the realization herself. He wouldn't debase himself by telling his wife he forbade her from something. No good wife should drag her husband to those depths.

'You could fly again,' Freddy urged him. 'The Air Force base has a club where you can fly military jets. You could fly display, you could return to the Air Force.'

He looked at her, horrified.

'Good God, no. I would rather live with this feeling than give in to it, not become some dancing monkey.'

Sympathy – there was some for him, but only some.

'Verne, I'm sorry.'

'Don't say you're sorry, that makes me feel like a puppy someone scolded too harshly.'

If she couldn't say that, then what could she say? In defeat, she announced:

'The race starts in Glasgow. I'll get the train.'

'Alright.' He nodded.

'You're so sweet to let me do this.'

'Yes I am.' He liked the sound of that. She pressed into his shoulder and waited for his head to rest on top of hers. When it did, she held tight.

If someone had asked her when she felt more fear, this conversation with Verne or in the car with Vanessa's body, she would have to say this conversation. Fear riding the back of love, the two so close that she couldn't separate them from one another. And the love, she realized now, *was* it love? She had never questioned it before. But what was her love for him anyway, other than her first?

Freddy had a lot of courage, enough to fill quarries, but not nearly enough to tell her husband that she had always known – and almost everyone did – that he had never shot down any Germans.

6. Monte Carlo Rally

January 1948

She arrived late to Glasgow – through her own fault. Leaving it far too late, she had joined the queue for tickets at Euston Station only to realize that the money she thought she had in her purse was no longer there. And when she went to the bank to withdraw a small sum for the fare, the transaction couldn't be authorized without her husband present. She cursed herself – and herself alone – when she missed the first train. And then the second. And by the time she had missed the third, she hated herself for her stupidity. She could have sworn that the money was in her purse the previous evening; she could have sworn that the last time she went to the bank to withdraw funds, she had been able to without Verne. She swore all over the train station until an attendant asked her what was wrong.

He suggested she call her husband and have him ask for the funds to be released. And she went to the phone box, planning to do that, but she paused.

Verne would laugh. Verne would make her feel like a fool. And she didn't want to feel like a fool right now, not when she was about to drive across Europe.

She fished a coin from her pocket and dialled.

'John?'

'The connection said Euston Station,' he said. 'Euston Station? Where's Winnie headed off to from Euston Station?' Rhetorical questions, it seemed, because he continued. There was a mild frenzy in his voice. 'Lovely to hear from my sister. Are you in the city? Why didn't you come into the office for a drink?'

It was a good question – and one she had been asking of herself on the journey from home, when her train passed through the station near John's law firm. With almost too much clarity, she realized she had simply not wanted to see him.

John was always in his office nowadays, a fact she only knew because his new wife wrote Freddy endless letters on the subject. Before Alice was Mrs Vaux, she was a sister of one of John's friends from school; the wedding was the chummiest thing she'd ever seen, men playing at boys, calling each other by their surnames – Dales, Yallop, Robertson, MacDonald – and reciting jokes about hiding Mr Teele's cane behind the door, night-time raids of the pantry, *that time we beat old Jenkins.* Straight from school to the army to the law firm – Freddy sometimes wondered if John had had the time to become John, instead of *Old Vaux, he'll stub your toe.*

John spends all his days at the office, Alice wrote in the weeks after the wedding. She left long paragraph breaks after these bitty sentences in which Freddy guessed she was supposed to read something else. Begging for some sisterliness. Alice implied that they were both going through the same newlywed difficulties and they could *be there for each other.* But what did Alice expect her to do? Drop everything to help out a woman she barely knew? Marriages were not exactly her forte either, and intruding into someone else's seemed like an overestimation of how equipped she was to deal with her own. It was all quite pathetic, if you asked Freddy. Alice should just get on with things, as she did.

'I'm wondering if you could do me a favour,' she continued to John, tentatively.

'Go on then, what is it? Are you out of your favourite shade of lipstick? Is it a dress emergency?' She often wondered why he continued with the childish jokes. Her heart sank when she realized perhaps it was the only way he knew how to communicate with her.

'Would you have a minute to come down to the station? I know it's not far. I need to buy a train ticket and… I don't seem to have any money.'

'What did you do, spend it on magazines?'

'No, I just don't have it. I thought I did, then the bank wouldn't give me any.'

'You lost it?'

'No. I never had it in the first place. I don't have any of my own money, John. As you know.' She was breathless and loosened her grip on the phone.

'Alright, where are you trying to get to?'

'Glasgow.'

'What on earth are…' He trailed off. 'Oh. You're going for your little race, aren't you?'

'It's quite a large race actually, if we're talking about mileage.'

'The Monte Carlo something or other.'

'Rally. How do *you* know?'

There was some silence on the line – not much, but enough for a sibling to sense its significance. John knew he'd been caught out.

'Verne called me this morning,' he sighed. 'He wasn't well, the way you left him. It wasn't very proper what you've done. He had half a mind to chase after you and try to convince you not to do this.'

'But he seemed…'

'He might have *seemed* alright about it, but you've left him in quite a state. I think perhaps you should… reconsider.' This from the boy who had egged her on that May night.

'John. Did Vernon ask you to talk me out of it?' A lull on the line that overstayed its welcome. 'You're on his side.'

'I'm not *not* on his side,' he said after another pause. 'But is it worth it? All this trouble for some driving?'

She slammed down the phone without a reply. Verne had got to John. Of course, he had. She remembered *Old Vaux, he'll stub your toe* with his best man *Dawson-Hayes, who doesn't play* at the wedding, smashing cake into each other's face like it was the first year at boarding school, the guests clapping them on. The word *traitor* slipped into her head. But since when were she and Verne on different sides?

Someone banged on the door of the phone booth and she snapped back: *hold on a bloody minute*. There were two more coins in her pocket.

Eric picked up on the second ring. He drove to the station within the hour, cash in his hand, no questions asked. Either Vernon couldn't get to him, or her husband had never even bothered to call the younger brother. She always hoped it was the first.

She used her final coin to call Will's hotel and tell him she would be late. He was surprisingly calm about it, relieved almost, and sounded as though he had just woken up. He told her to head straight to the hotel, and then said *I'll see you near the start line tomorrow*. She responded *I'll see you*. It was more threatening than she had intended.

But she felt like threatening him when she arrived at the start line the following morning. He had undersold how busy it would be. Crowds crammed the roads outside the Blythswood Square Hotel, hooting for their favourite drivers. Lines of polished black and cream cars tailed around corners. The sky was the heavy purple-blue of bruises. Chunky buildings, black with soot, rose from the ground like weeds. She had never seen anything like it before, with people bumping into her, buses careening around corners, loud and unfamiliar adverts for Clyde Cold Storage and Loch Lomond Scotch Whisky shouting their wares at her from every direction.

Will was nowhere to be found. Her heart pulsed as she followed the line of cars, looking for their Puck, which Will had driven up earlier in the week.

Here was another race, she thought, where she would be running to the start. Where she was behind before she even began. She missed Vanessa. In a moment of frenzy, when she saw a high-backed barnet of black hair, she followed it. But all that was left of Vanessa were the platitudes she had said on that long drive to the race start: *don't get angry*; *it's a race before you get to the start line*; *if someone's trying to sabotage you, that means you're a threat.*

Determination, instead, took root. She began to ask around, bothering the drivers who were readying themselves or talking to the press. Halfway through an interview with a news outlet:

'Excuse me, sir.'

'Oi, what are you doing, ruining my interview?' the reporter bellowed in a deep Scottish accent. She had never felt more southern.

'Have you seen Will Truston?'

'Will who?'

'I'm driving and he has my car, so…'

The man grinned so wide she thought she might fall into his mouth.

'*You're* driving? And with queer old Truston? Good luck.' He turned back to the driver he was questioning, and the interview carried on, as if she had never interrupted it.

She made her way down the line, asking, asking. *Have you seen Will Truston?* The crowds thinned as she neared the back, and there it was: the Puck. Like a friend. She laid her hand on the side and pulled at the door handle, but it was locked. No Will. No Louisa. She wanted to kick it, but realized one does not kick friends. *One does not kick friends. Race to the start line, race to the start line.* Vanessa's voice – in her head, now saying new things Freddy had never even heard before. She turned. The rain had begun to slap hard drops on the pavement next to her and the coal-thick air grew only thicker with the rain. To walk forwards was like trying to prise apart treacle.

She fell into an alley, seeking shelter, and pressed her back against the brick. It was warmer than she thought it would be, muggy. The noise of the crowds faded. And another noise climbed on top.

Moaning. Small lip smacks. Noises like the slaps of cake batter on the side of the bowl. She tried to compare it to things she had heard before, to the things that she and Verne did in their bed, but none fit. Curiosity got the better of her, and she edged towards the sound, which was coming from deeper in the alley.

The rain had settled into a mist. But through it she could see them: three bodies, all men, combined to look like the sculptures at art galleries where muscled Greeks twisted around each other, straining at the marble. It was like all those artefacts and yet also like nothing else she had seen before. How did those bodies get like that? The nuns had never told her about this. And neither had her brothers. Or her father. Her mother had never had the chance. She had no idea what she was looking at.

Two were in dark-blue mechanic suits. One of them had dirty blond hair, the other dirty orange; dirty, both of them, oil-smeared and greased. The one in the middle was older and blonder; he had his mouth on each of them in turn. His white flannel suit had handprints of oil. There was a smudge on his pale cheek, and streaks in his hair from their caresses.

'Will?'

The ginger one tapped the other. She stepped backwards. Her footsteps were very loud now. They followed her, though – and Will's voice:

'Fred. It's not what it looks like,' he said. 'Well, it's exactly what it looks like, but I need to explain, so you don't get any ideas.' He mumbled something to the other two and they disappeared in the other direction. Freddy walked to the alley's opening, where the Puck glinted in the brewing sunshine.

She put her hand on the car door and yanked. Nothing. Then his breath, hammering on her neck. She shuddered.

She had never been so disgusted in her life, and she didn't have the faintest idea why. It was shock, but not as she knew it.

'Unlock the car, Will.'

'Freddy, I should explain.'

'When you said you and Vanessa had an *arrangement*,' Freddy remained with her back to him, 'this is what you meant.'

'Yes, it is.'

'She knew?'

'From the very beginning.'

'I don't even know what you are… what it is they call it.'

'I should explain,' he shook his head.

'No… you shouldn't.'

He narrowed his eyes, cocked his head.

'Are you saying that you *don't* find me hideous?'

Not exactly, she wanted to reply, but her mouth struggled to form words. No one had ever discussed homosexuality with her – which meant that no one had ever told her it was wrong. There was a freedom in coming to her own conclusion about it. And her conclusion, which she realized she had to form quickly, was that Will was her friend, and that was what mattered.

'It's just a surprise. It's the first time I've come across someone… of this ilk.'

'Of this *ilk*?' he whispered, a small smile on his lips.

She swallowed awkwardly in response and reached out to brush the dirt from his shoulders. But she hesitated.

Now that she thought about it – there had been other times when she saw black smudges on his suits. He followed her gaze. Leaned forwards to whisper:

'It's my way of hiding it and not hiding it at the same time.'

She would have asked more questions, but a blonde girl popped up on her left.

'You must be Winifred.'

She was petite and plump, in a mink fur coat, emerald leather gloves, rouge on her cheeks, and a basket tied with a red-and-white checked ribbon.

'You must be Louisa.' Freddy thrust out her hand.

'Willie has told me *all* about you.'

'Did he tell you how I killed his wife?'

Louisa's face drooped like a daffodil after sun.

'Yes, but let's not bring that up.' A girl, it seemed, who warded off misery simply by not talking about it. 'We're going to have such fun. I brought sandwiches and shortbread.' She turned to Will, spitting on her handkerchief and dabbing at the oil and grease smears.

'Oh, Willie, what have you been doing? You're covered in muck!'

'I've been simply *rolling* around in the gutter, Lou,' he laughed. His face was out of joint – his mouth was laughing, but his eyes said to Freddy that *we'll resume our conversation later.*

Two thousand miles between them and the truth.

*

It was hardly a surprise that they didn't win, or come anywhere near to winning – and the road was the toughest she had known, the turns sharp as needles and decked with January ice – but Freddy had never enjoyed any two thousand miles as much in her entire life. She was in the mood for superlatives when the clouds parted for the final descent into Monte Carlo. It was the most beautiful thing she had ever seen; the sky was the truest blue; the mountains sculpted at the most perfect angle. Louisa was also the most annoying girl she had ever known and her foot was the most tired it had ever been, after four days of pressing on the throttle, but that didn't matter at all. It was ridiculous, how happy she was.

When she pulled up at the finish line next to the harbour, the press noticed. One of them even approached her. *Now, the thing about rallies*, she would go on to tell people (as she remembered Vanessa saying when they passed Cardiff), *is that you've never really got an indication of where you've come.* Sometimes you don't even know you've won until you reach the finish line and wonder *where's the party?* So, there was a moment when Freddy stepped out of the car, holding onto the side of the door, because her foot hurt to touch the ground, when she thought, *did we?*

She even said it, 'Did we?'

'No, madam. Countess Gravonne Van Strasbourg Steerum won the Coupe des Dames,' a reporter said with the strongest German accent she had ever heard. He pointed to a tall woman sat daintily on the bonnet of her car, wrapped in a fur and holding a slim cigarette between two long, alabaster fingers. 'You and your partner are the second female drivers to arrive.'

'Second?' Her smile widened. She turned to Louisa.

'Louisa! Hey, Louisa, we're second,' she leaned down and into the window. 'That's not bad!' She turned back to the German. 'That's not bad!' He nodded, under duress.

Freddy walked towards the harbour wall. The race flashed behind her eyes, the moments rolling into one another, with no help from Louisa, who came tottering out of the car, her face an ashy grey. She spent the long drive down from Glasgow to Dover with a shortbread in one hand and a map in the other, mumbling directions around the biscuit in her mouth. Luckily, Freddy had studied the maps on the train, so she could speak Louisa's crumble-language. On the overnight ferry across the Channel, Louisa had decided that she preferred cars to boats and said farewell to the shortbread she'd eaten over the side of it. The two of them watched the waves eat it up, and Freddy spent the night half-asleep, half-turning through lanes. The next day, she drove through northern France, Holland, Belgium. Louisa never shook her sickness, and spent the rest of the trip too nauseous to open her mouth for fear of what might come out of it. She simply pointed her finger left, right, forwards, and Freddy nodded. The two had barely spoken since Calais.

When the Alps reared over the crest, the road narrowed, turned icy. More often, they passed cars with

'Rallye Monte-Carlo' plated on the front, and their bonnets lodged in snowdrifts or signposts; one even turned over on its side, two drivers crawling out. Freddy knew to keep on going, even when Louisa whined at her to stop. The pass was designed to kill a man, Freddy concluded. But not the Puck. It was nimble enough to dive around the corners. Their Puck played tricks with the elements, and she passed three cars that picked their way carefully around the tight bends. She was not here to be careful. She was here to drive fast. She had to outdrive death. It could never catch her, not when she drove that quickly.

Freddy sat on the harbour wall, and then lay on it, the weak winter sun good on her skin. With her eyes closed, she listened to the boats clinking in the heavy wind and cars still piling into the finish. Louisa laid next to her. After several seconds, the other girl whispered:

'I can't wait to get married and never do that again.'

Freddy didn't reply, but an instinct crossed her mind to say, *I can't wait to do that and never be married again.*

For no lack of searching, she didn't find Will until she was four glasses of champagne into her evening. And that was only after she had talked to several reporters and received her medal for second place from the Prince of Monaco. After she had gone with Louisa to purchase an evening dress (with the small cheque of prize money). After she had descended to the ballroom of the Hôtel de Paris and sat at one of the high tables, frowning at the tall Countess and at the glittering Coupe des Dames trophy perched beside her. After she had wondered if she would ever become like Vanessa and help the few other women in the race, because all she felt now was jealousy. After she had accepted flute after flute of champagne. After she saw Will on the other side of the ballroom, with two glasses, looking for someone – and she caught his eye.

Louisa was fetching a fur – *why do the Monégasques like everything so frigid and cold?* she had whined – and Freddy crossed the floor.

'Our train was delayed in all that snow, so kudos to you for driving through it.' He held the glass to her. 'Drink?'

'I've had one. Several, actually.'

She kept her hands around her clutch, awkward in front of her. After a small silence, she continued, 'The car, Will. It's a triumph.'

'There's already a car called the Triumph.'

'You're not listening to me. It's fabulous. It took the corners like a bull by the horns.'

He grinned. 'I know. And I know about second place. And I know that Lou probably didn't help one jot with the drive. Well done, you.' He went to embrace her, but both his hands were full. Eventually, she took one of the glasses.

'We didn't finish.'

'Yes, you did. In second place.'

'No, our talk. Will, we didn't finish it.'

'You want to finish it now? Here?'

'Not here but…' She bit her finger, and nodded her head towards the open doors that led onto the terrace. 'There.' He followed her across the floor.

'You look lovely by the way.'

'Only because I had to,' she muttered. 'I had no idea there was a dress code.'

'Goodness, you take compliments *terribly*.'

On the terrace, she looked down at herself in the moonlight. She could admit that the black dress wasn't too bad. It scooped low at the back, edged with small gems, the straps fine on her shoulders. Louisa had bundled her locks into some knot on the back of her head, exposing her neck. All these nooks of her skin she usually forgot and stuffed away – they weren't for her, they were for Verne. It was only in the bath that she remembered she had a body and that she was inside it.

Will walked to the wall of the terrace and leaned against it. The wind lifted his hair from his forehead, then placed it back down, over and over. A half-moon fell on the sea, the beaches with their staggering drunks, the palm ruffles, the hotel roofs. Black. Silver. Blue. If there was beauty in it, Freddy wanted to find it. She felt her eyes rolling like vicious little marbles in her head, inspecting the night, wondering how she had got here. The space behind her eyes was crammed with anger and rude ambition: the need to be another step up on the podium, a name more well known, for the Puck to go faster.

'You're lying about yourself. You're not who you say you are,' she said eventually. The sea lashed its tongue.

'Neither are you, my dear,' he replied after a deep draw on his cigarette. 'You claim to be a prim English wife with a quaint hobby of driving cars, but we both know that's not the case. Don't lie to yourself.'

'I'm not.'

'Well, you seem to come to personal revelations a lot later than everyone else, so either you're stupid or you're short-sighted or you're lying to yourself, and I don't think you're stupid. Or short-sighted. You wouldn't have made it here if you were.'

'This is *not* about me.'

'Oh, it's not?'

He took another draw on his cigarette.

'Tell me about Vanessa. It seems cruel to marry her and then deny her.'

'Trust me, I wasn't denying her anything. She had everything she wanted, and more. She had every*one* she wanted.'

'But why? She married you and she knew about your… inclination? Was she… did she find herself attracted to…?'

'Women, Fred?' he finished for her. 'These are just words, you would do well to say them. And no, she wasn't.'

'Then why was she with you?'

'Call her a free spirit. Call her what you want. She never had any intention of settling down, of marrying, children.'

'Then why marry you?'

'No need to sound so disgusted. I was quite the bachelor in my day. Which was why my parents couldn't stand the fact that I was never interested in anyone. I think my father suspected something, and he left a ridiculous clause in the will about me not being able to take up the house until I was married. I've never quite known if they actually wanted me to marry, or if they were just so afraid what people might say if I didn't. They were that sort of folk. You know, smiles on faces, even if the house is burning. Held dinner parties during the war.

'The other reason was the racing, of course. It was becoming *excruciating*, every time I wanted to race or I was at the track, women throwing themselves at me, really quite exhausting. I had to put a stop to that and quick. Besides, there were speculations and… none of it was good. Marriage was definitely the answer.

'Vanessa was a friend. I can never remember where we met exactly. She may have walked into the motorcar club and demanded to join, I might have asked her to. We discussed it. Her parents wanted her to marry. She was getting older. We were in the same predicament. It worked out for both of us. She operated like a single woman, did all the races she wanted. And I could operate as a single man and do all that I wanted.'

'Do all… the mechanics.'

'Not every mechanic, but some of them. Usually the blonds,' he added.

He stubbed his cigarette on the wall and took her hands in his.

'It doesn't mean it has to be like that for you and Vernon. That's not the only way to be happy. That was just our unique situation.'

'That's not what I was thinking,' Freddy murmured – even though it was, and Will's eyes were close enough to know it. She could see the fringe of his pupils, the tunnel into his head. *Is that the only way it could work? Separation, for the other to do as they pleased?*

'Didn't you get lonely, in among all those lies?'

'They were the best lies for me.' He took out another cigarette. Freddy knew he didn't want one, he just wanted something to do with his hands, and somewhere to put all that sentimentality that had oozed over the terrace.

'I do… understand, Will.'

He tutted.

'Look at you, all modern.'

'You've got to help me with this, though.'

'Help you?'

'Explain it to me, teach me about you. Tell me how to be a friend to you.'

'It's not my job to teach you how not to hate me. That's something you can learn to do for yourself.'

She could have sworn the moonlight was warm on their backs. The need to apologize passed, carried off by the light breeze. They leaned back on the wall, side by side. Inside the terrace doors, the orchestra swelled, walls of suited backs chattered over string music. It was one of those moments where Freddy remembered that England was not Europe, and that she was not European.

'I don't know,' she began, 'whether to leave my gloves on and stand out because I'll look like an awkward English woman wearing gloves that don't suit her… or whether to throw them over this wall and I'll look like an uncultured English woman who didn't bring gloves… or…'

'Goodness, not *another* option. Your head must be an *exhausting* place.'

'You use the word exhausting a lot.'

'Because I'm very tired, Freddy.'

She continued after a pause.

'Or whether to ditch them and put my racing gloves on because those are the only gloves I care to wear.'

'Or whether to jump this wall and swim in the bay.'

She looked at him, smiling. The terrace was cool, fragrant. The ballroom was warm, sticky, red-orange frescoes crescendoing up the wall, chandeliers nearly on the ground, low with extravagance and tradition. She latched onto Will's hand.

'We've got to head in.'

'And we've got each other to do it with,' he smiled.

'I don't know anyone here.'

'Now *that* is something I can help with.'

And patted her cheek lightly with his free hand. Both of them walked into the ballroom together.

*

Harmony and order were what she expected to find, but instead a sort of chaos had broken out near the bar. The orchestra had stopped playing and lowered their instruments, and the attendees put gloved hands near their mouths – but not so near to smudge their lipstick or ruffle their moustaches.

Will held onto Freddy's arm, a curious smile on his face.

'What is it?' she asked.

'This is overdue, this fight.'

Over the heads of other racers and their partners, Freddy watched two unremarkable men do an unremarkable thing: shove each other. One spoke in Italian and was dressed in a fine suit, a sharp-pointed handkerchief folded in his breast pocket and a thin, little moustache above his lip. The other was still in a race suit. He held his helmet at his side and curls spilled out over his scarred forehead. There was a nick in his cheek, and a nick out of his chin. He was missing half a pinkie finger. If someone had taken him apart, they hadn't put him back together very well. Bits of finger left scattered around somebody's workshop, the chunks of his face somewhere for a cat to munch. This man, Freddy thought, left pieces of himself everywhere.

In a French-tilted boom, he swore at the Italian and pushed him; he fell back into a gash of waiters, trays clattering.

'The piston blew with a touch.' His hands mimicked an explosion. 'The rest of the engine is somewhere on the descent from the mountains. I like to drive cars and that car is one that makes me never want to drive again. This is *not* acceptable, *not* for me. I walked from the hills to this room to tell you this, and I find you drinking *champagne*.' He flicked the glass and it landed with a tinkle.

The Italian raised a fist, and the other laughed. Freddy couldn't help but snicker too; it was like an ant curling its spindly fist at a boot.

'Who's the Frenchman?' Freddy tugged on Will's sleeve.

'He's not French. Jersey. Technically he's British.'

'I don't care. *Who* is he?'

'Yves Le Brocq.'

'Last year's winner?' She had seen the honour rolls dotted around the room. The name YVES LE BROCQ etched in gold next to the years 1946 and 1947.

'That's the one. And he's won a fair few Grands Prix, also with Ferrari. He wins championships… or at least he did.' He shushed her, even though he was the one talking. Freddy looked around; no one was lending a hand, no one was stopping them. They welcomed it like fate, with the certainty that the fight would play out.

'What about the car, huh?' Yves yelled. 'The other Ferrari drivers all made it to the end, did they not? I spoke to the press outside. I told them that Ferrari have given me a bad car. The engine is not right, the chassis is an old one, outdated. Why, for Yves Le Brocq? What have I done? Are you trying to get rid of me?' Freddy was almost impressed by his arrogance.

'You spoke to the *press*?' the Italian asked.

'Enzo Larini, Ferrari team director.' Will filled her in with a whisper. 'Ferrari doesn't like it when you say bad things about their cars in the press. They don't like it at all.'

'You're enjoying this?' Freddy asked him.

'No evening is complete without Yves doing…'

'Without Yves doing what?'

'What he does best. Fight. Lose his lid. Lob his helmet to the ground.' At that moment, Yves did in fact toss the helmet to the marble floor. It cracked and he yelled, *Even the helmet they give me is bad!* He yelled to his audience (the room, somehow, had become his). 'He wears his heart on his sleeve, that's for certain,' Will added.

Yves tugged at his race suit then and Freddy thought he might also take that off, set fire to it to prove that the suit was faulty too. Will's comment rolled through her mind. To wear your heart on your sleeve was spoken of as a bad thing – but it was better than hiding your heart away, right? She was trying out defences for this man and she had no idea why. She only knew that she preferred a man who did his fighting in public; at least she knew that he didn't save it for behind closed doors. He swore and kicked his foot against the table, rippling the glasses.

'You don't *respect* Ferrari and all its honour,' Enzo seethed.

Yves lifted his hand to punch the Italian, but he seemed to realize himself, and he loosened it, dropped it to his side. *The kind of man who would not crush a spider*, Freddy thought. She had known less about her husband when she married him.

He retreated towards the door, the manager of the hotel pursuing him despite Yves' flaps of dismissal.

Enzo lifted a trembling finger. 'I will not see you at the factory next week. I don't want to see you there!'

Yves' back twitched. He tried, with every nerve and plate of spine, not to turn and respond. But who was he kidding? He swivelled.

'What do you think I came here to tell you? Ferrari can go fuck themselves. Yves Le Brocq no longer drives for them.'

Will exhaled, went to clap.

'He never fails to do it. A dramatist. A real artiste.'

Yves stormed out, throwing his racing gloves to the ground one after the other. The room eased back into itself, like water flowing over a rock.

'I've been waiting for him to do that since Ferrari put him in the second shift for Le Mans.'

'He sounds conceited.'

'He is. But he doesn't care.'

'How did he lose his finger?'

'He's missing a finger?' Will asked as he accepted two

more glasses from the waiter. 'I can't say I noticed. I wasn't looking at his hand, or his fingers. If you were wondering whether he was wearing a wedding ring, he's not.'

She hadn't been looking for a wedding ring, Freddy wanted to say, but Will had already begun to push her through the crowd. He was telling her the names of men she only wanted to remember so she knew who she was overtaking.

All the talk of wedding rings reminded Freddy of her own, which she had taken off for the rally and stowed in the breast pocket of her race suit now lying on the floor of her hotel room. No wonder her hand felt off balance, lighter.

As Will led her through the ballroom and introduced her to Reggie and Raymond and Tony – and Louisa joined them once more – and Robert and Rob and Bert, she wondered if the wedding ring was still in the race suit pocket or if it had fallen out onto the carpet or worse, somewhere in the Alps. What would Vernon do if she lost it?

Too overcome with anxiety, she excused herself and stepped out to the lobby. She asked the concierge for the phone booth and he pointed her towards a leather row on the opposite wall. She called her husband.

'Monte Carlo? Who's calling me from Monte bloody Carlo?'

'It's me… Fred… Winifred.'

'I assume you finished the drive then?'

'Yes. I wanted to call and tell you that we made it. And we came second.'

'How brilliant,' he said. She felt foolish for telling him.

A crash sang in the background. A brush of laughs and boyish singing.

'Are you alright? What's that?'

'I have company, darling. It only seemed fair, considering…'

'Considering what?'

'Considering that you *left* me.'

'I hardly think…'

'John has very kindly stepped in to comfort me while you're away,' he slurred, the words falling over one another on their way out of his mouth.

'Make sure John doesn't drive home. He's a terrible driver after a drink, as well as before one.' *She just called you a terrible driver*, Verne shouted to John. 'And don't offer to give him a lift, either.'

'Don't tell me what to do,' he mumbled. 'But also tell me what to do. I want you. I want you here. Not there. Win, when are you going to stop all this?'

Her voice, which seemed so small, hitched in her throat.

'What?'

'Stop this hobby. Come home, sweetheart.'

She was glad he added the *sweetheart*; it was all too brutal before.

'Soon, Verne. I'll be home soon.'

'And you'll stay there?' he moaned through the phone.

'We'll see.'

'I'll see that you do.'

'What does that mean, Verne?'

'Did you get to Glasgow alright in the end?'

'Yes, I did.' She paused. She had never told him about her struggles at Euston. 'Verne, what do you know about it?'

'Your brother told me about it.'

'Which one?'

'The only one I can stand.'

John, of course. Freddy sighed, relieved that he hadn't said Eric's name.

'Sweetheart?'

'Yes,' she said, her voice small.

'I love you.'

'Very much.'

She slammed the receiver. A cold sweat had broken out under her armpits – her heartbeat was faster than it had been on those Alpine corners.

A head popped up from the neighbouring phone booth. The man was even more nicked and scarred up close, like a cratered moon.

'Boyfriend or father?' Yves asked, arms crossed on the divide between the booths.

'Husband, actually.'

'I should have guessed,' he tutted to himself. 'Only the married talk to each other like that.'

'Only the exceptionally rude listen in on other people's conversations.'

He smacked the divider and left the booth, striding towards the lobby doors.

'It's Yves, yes?' She rushed behind him and held out a hand. He shook it, and his grip was the gentlest out of all the men she had met that night. 'I'm Freddy Vaux.'

'Congratulations on second place, Freddy Vaux.'

'What will you do now that you've left Ferrari?'

'I suppose I'll just have to go and start my own motor company.'

'Yes?'

He wore ambition as well as he wore his race suit.

'That call I made,' he pointed to the phone booth. 'I wish you could have heard it. The first of a new beginning. Le Brocq Motors.'

'Good luck.'

'You too, Freddy Vaux.'

7. Rally Season

Spring 1948

Her ambition, the force of it, swept her off her feet. Like she was a bride all over again.

After she arrived home from Monte Carlo and slipped into the bed next to her husband, she knew she wanted to enter more races, and she wanted to win. And when she returned from the next rally, she wanted to be at two more. And when she was done with those two, she wanted to race ten more. She wanted to race the Countess again and she wanted to beat her, and beat the men too.

There came a point – a sharp and distinct one – when she revved at the start of her second Daily Express Rally, six months after she had met Vanessa, and she was further up the start line, on time, with a better car, her hands clenched on the wheel. A point at which she realized that she could never turn back now. The tide had claimed her, and all she could do was surf to keep from drowning.

The hitches knocked her forwards, she told herself. All these setbacks were necessary, right? She considered herself lucky for having all that adversity.

Take the Highland Rally, which saw drivers race around the twists and turns of Ben Nevis and Ben Lawers, circling through mountainous mists before punching into clear sky. She knew the other drivers would be difficult before she even showed up to the paddock. Her reputation preceded her, and she watched it walk out in front and tap them on the shoulders, the men turning towards her and inspecting her up and down. *The woman. Sticking her nose in where it doesn't belong. Ruining our fun.* She had heard it all. By the time she had made the final changes to her car and slammed the bonnet shut and shoved her helmet onto her neat cap of blonde hair, there was a man with a clipboard standing over her. There was always a man with a clipboard.

This particular man inspected the Puck while holding the rims of his glasses. Freddy snuck a glance at Will, who stood far off talking to two mechanics. Their arrangement was that, when the car was race-ready, the time was his to do with as he pleased.

'Miss, we've received some complaints about your car. Some of the other participants have expressed a concern that it's not compliant,' the race inspector said in a strong Scottish accent.

'Excuse me?'

'Some of the other…'

'I don't need you to repeat it.'

She leaned out and looked around his clipboard to see Bob with two other drivers. The previous month, she had managed to overtake him in the final mile of the Brighton–London sprint to win the race. But she had to stand alone on the podium. He would rather collect his second-place trophy from the post office than receive it next to her.

'Did they express a particular concern?'

'The headlights, miss. And the weight of the car. It's too light.'

'Are you going to *weigh* the car? I don't think she'll take that very well.'

'Miss?' He squinted.

'Never mind.'

'May I?' He leaned towards the headlights with a tape measure.

'Take all the time you need. She's compliant, built to specification, built to regulation.' While he tweaked and tapped the Puck, she bored her eyes into Bob until he turned his back on her.

'It seems…' The inspector looked down at the clipboard. 'All in order. I'm sorry about that. Have a good race.' The inspector made to walk off, but Freddy latched onto his arm and held him back.

'But sir, what about all the other cars?'

'I beg your pardon.'

'If mine is getting inspected, then everyone's needs to be, right? It's only fair.'

Under her grip, he writhed; his eye twitched. The clipboard drooped. She had learned how to play this game of regulation from the best: Vanessa.

'Yes, I suppose.'

She pointed behind him – towards Bob.

'Then over there. You may want to check their tyres. I believe the pressures aren't quite right.' Then added, chuckling, 'But what do I know, I'm just a gal? Call it a hunch.'

He nodded and trotted off towards the other cars.

Will approached.

'Everything alright?'

She smiled, watching. It was more than alright, when she saw the inspector hand a red slip of paper to Bob, marked with the word: DISQUALIFICATION. Another driver she had come to know after first racing him in the Monte received the same slip of paper. Will tutted – at her or them, she couldn't tell.

'He'll never share a podium with you now.'

'Good. His breath smells. And he's got a wandering hand.' Freddy opened the door of the Puck and secured her helmet.

Starting up the engine and lifting the brake, she began to drive the car towards the start line, but Bob all but threw himself in front of it. He slapped the red paper onto her window and pointed at it in a strange mime act. She rolled it down.

'Can I help you?'

'You f…' He screwed his mouth tight.

'What? Go on.' She egged him on, willing him to lower himself and call her whatever horrible word was in his head. Cow? Bitch? Bob resisted, looking around for Will and pointing at him. 'You and that *dandy* are…'

'We're what? Race compliance isn't something to be trifled with,' Freddy notified him. 'Lodge another complaint about my car and you'll keep finding ones sent your way.' And she meant it, as she pushed down on the accelerator and he hopped out of her path.

She went on to win – comfortably. As she held the cup, beaming to the cameras, she wasn't too proud to admit that she might not have won so easily if Bob had raced.

The podium grew lonely. But the attention on her only increased. Who was this mysterious woman, always with a different partner, sometimes without, claiming the top spot at the country's biggest rallies? The question expanded to include Europe's biggest rallies too. She heard that her win outright at the inaugural Dutch Tulip Rally caused such anger that it almost made the organizers wish they had never come up with the idea of a four-day race across 1,800 miles. The press was hesitant to involve itself too closely with her and these wins, but the interest wailed around her anyway. The more she was spurned, the more she was spurred on, and the more races she entered, the more races she won, and she won and she won and she won.

She entered race upon race – even two in one day. In the midnight hours next to Verne, she made an intricate plan of how she would complete the Boscombe Hill Climb and then the Salisbury Sprint. Both of them took place within miles and hours of each other. She would have to get a spare car and line it up at the start of the Salisbury Sprint near the river, so that it was waiting for her when she finished the hill climb, and someone would have to give her a lift between the two races – Will, perhaps. Or Eric. He had begun to step in and support her hobby-turning-obsession-turning-career, when he had the time around his maths doctorate. She hoped it was out of brotherly love and pride; she feared it was out of a long-held grudge against Vernon and John, a chance to rub them up the wrong way, in payment for all the broken noses and Chinese burns. Her little career merely the settled debt of a schoolboy dispute.

When the day came and she reached the top of the hill climb, Will was there waiting. She grabbed the trophy from the race officials while running to Will's car, throwing back a quick *thanks, I'm honoured* over her shoulder.

'You're absolutely mad,' Will grinned.

'Faster, faster!' She bashed on the dashboard.

'You're not afraid of it, are you?'

'Of what?' She looked behind her and saw, blissfully, nothing on the road.

'Of going too fast. Of the speed. Any of it. You're not afraid of the other drivers.'

She stilled. Then, with realization in her voice, as if this was the first time she had ever considered *fear*, 'No.'

'You sound disappointed.'

'Well, it would make it easier, wouldn't it? To stop all this, I mean.' She said it as though it was obvious. 'If I was scared witless of a hairpin bend, if I never wanted to go near one…'

'Why ever would you want to *stop all this*?'

She shrugged.

'Sometimes I do think you drive *too* fast,' Will said.

'You go slower, and people catch up with you. *Things* catch up with you. What's the point of a car if it doesn't leave all that behind?'

'But…'

'Drive!' Freddy pressed on his thigh to push the accelerator down, all of Vanessa coming into her hand. They laughed as the countryside disappeared around them.

The drive should have ended after they crossed the Avon River – but it ended when they reached the bridge. Will braked hard and still the car's nose brushed the chain link fence studded with *closed* signs. On the other side, across the rickety bridge, a long line of cars stretched from the start line into the distance. All of them twinkling in the sun, picturesque and distant. The exhausts coughed smoke, but Freddy and Will were too far to smell it.

'Sorry, Fred, it looks like that's the end of the road.'

Her heart dropped in horror.

'No, it… We can go round the long way.'

'We were already short of time, we were barely going to make it as it is.'

She looked at her watch.

'We've got ten minutes. That's enough time.'

'They've probably disqualified you by now.'

'There's time. There's always time.'

Her eyes flew over the scene before her, searching.

'What are you going to do, Fred? This is the only bridge for miles. It's a waste of time.'

'That's what Verne said about this entire day.'

She scrambled out of the car, her heart in her eyes. Below her, the river churned within its banks; more white on the surface than she expected, and a gushing sound trailing up through the reeds and willows.

Will saw where her eyes were trained.

'No.'

With helmet and race suit still on, she began to pick her way down the riverbank. Will stayed at the top.

He yelled, 'Can you even swim?'

She braced herself as the brownish water gushed up to her knees, then her waist, then her chest. English rivers rarely lie; if they don't look inviting, then they probably aren't.

'I swam in the river all the time when I was younger!' she lied. Her brothers never let her anywhere near it.

'You're going to kill yourself one day,' Will shouted,

his hands cupped around his mouth. 'You're pushing it too far.'

'You wouldn't say that to a man!' Freddy returned – well, she tried to return it, but a mouthful of water gulped into her throat as she attempted a messy breaststroke across the river. People on the other side had caught on, and a crowd built to watch this silly girl swim across the river in April. In a helmet. And a heavy race suit.

'Oh, I *have* said that to a man, Fred. I said it to him several times. And he never listened.' Will's voice was getting louder, more strained. It cracked altogether on the last word, and Freddy turned to catch a desperate look on his face.

She turned back, reaching for the riverbank, and hauled herself up. Covered in mud and weeds, dripping. Against all odds, she presented herself to the race officials.

'Car fourteen. Winifred Vaux.' Cheers – mixed with groans. Men who were debating whether to go home, because their chances of a win had been slashed by this wet river creature. Her reputation once again preceding her.

Will remained on the other side, arms crossed. She waved. He shook his head.

The official looked her up and down, then lowered his clipboard.

'I'm afraid you're too late. Drivers have to be registered and on the start line by 11.55 for a noon start. It is… 11.55.'

'It's 11.53,' she protested, pointing at his watch.

'Miss, you're disqualified.'

Her life consisted of sweet-talking men with clipboards.

'Look—'

'Don't even try.'

'I was *going* to be here much earlier, but the bridge was closed.'

'That's very well, but everyone else managed to get here in plenty of time.'

'Even after I crossed that river?' She narrowed her eyes.

The official leaned in and whispered his response – too close to her ear. '*Because* you crossed that river.'

She didn't achieve it that April: two wins in one day. But the following month, she did. And she had sent ahead someone to check the road was open. Podiums were deserting themselves all over the country. The next task she set was three races in one day.

With what money? It was the burning question that she asked herself every time she found a rally in the newspaper and set her heart on it – because it never came from her husband. And it never came from her father. She never asked. They never offered.

Verne never raised the subject of racing. He gave Freddy the impression of a fugitive always blustering forwards with blind hope that their crime would never rear its head, that the police would never darken his door. Their best-kept secret. It was usually an accident, if she ever talked about it. A slip of her tongue. A lapse into forgetfulness. Sometimes, she would find herself short of a train fare, missing pound notes that she thought were there. *A woman's brain*, Verne would tut as he left the house. He never offered to replace the money, to fund the trips, to give her access to the bank account. She never expected him to. The word 'never' made its way into her mind too often.

The money was mostly Will's. And she poured all her winnings straight into funding the next race.

'Will who?' Verne narrowed his eyes, after he asked her how she was funding her trip to Sicily that weekend for the Giro di Sicilia.

'Truston. Of Truston Motors.'

'I think I know a Truston who went to Radley College. He's not your man, is he?' Verne pointed a piece of bacon at her. This was at breakfast, as most of their conversations were now – before he disappeared for his long days seeing to his estates and his hounds and his friends and his long evenings that found their way to long nights. 'Is he married?'

Struck cold by Verne's easy knowledge of Will, and without the heart to tell him again, about Vanessa, about it all, Freddy answered: 'Yes.'

She was quite sure that he would throttle the life out of Will if he suspected she was having an affair with him; but she was even more sure that he would kill him if he knew what Will really was.

'As long as you'll be back Sunday night.'

*

'You'll never be back by Sunday night,' Will muttered to her through the open window as they rolled the Puck to the start line of the Giro.

'Of course I will. Or at least I will have been *supposed* to, but the boat will be cancelled.'

'Will it?'

'Yes.' She leaned into the car and fiddled with the gear shifts. 'And there will be nothing I can do. The next one I'll be able to catch is on Monday morning.'

'I don't feel good about all this lying, Fred.'

'It's not lying. It's… selective telling.'

He gave her a look. 'That sounds like lying to me.'

She put her helmet on and looked at the clock: three minutes until the race. The start line was rowdier than she was used to – in a throng of Italian shouts, Sicilian barons driving unusual models in black and red and green, she and Will and their little silver-purplish Puck stood out like a sore English thumb.

'Tell me about him,' she said, getting into the driver's seat, making her final adjustments.

'Who?' Will handed her the gloves. She began to put them on.

'*Him*. When I was crossing the river to start the next race, back in Salisbury, you were yelling at me about someone you told to slow down. The man.'

'You heard that over the river?' Will looked down.

'Who was he?'

'Peter was a friend.' To her look: '*More* than a friend. I

don't need to tell you this, Fred, but this sport can take someone out of the world at any point. It's hard not to speak in platitudes about how deadly and dangerous it is, even when I know a man, even when I…' he leaned in closer, 'even when I loved a man who was taken by it.

'It's the only thing that makes me want to believe in all that claptrap about fate, the metaphysical. *God*, even. But it's all mechanical. His death was mechanical, the angle at which he hit the wall was mechanical, the way in which his skull was bent out of shape was mechanical.' He paused to sigh. 'When you're at the height of a race, when you're on top of the world, you can be taken out of it like that.' He clicked his fingers. 'It is completely uncontrollable, but if you want to be good, you have no choice but to give yourself over to it, to ease into that lack of control.'

'The only time I have any control is *in* the car,' Freddy mused.

'That's pessimistic.'

'No, it's realistic, Will.' She paused, then returned to the topic of Peter. 'Is that why you only ever mingle with the mechanics? No drivers?'

He nodded.

'No drivers. In fact, it's going against my rules to be friends with a driver. I should really cut you loose.'

She laughed.

'Peter what? What was his surname?' Freddy asked, unsure why she wanted to know so much about this.

'No, I don't think I want to tell you that. It was an affair that we kept between us. I don't much fancy having it dragged out as an anecdote in your memoir.'

A weak smile lazed onto her face.

'I've never done anything in my life deserving of a memoir.'

He grinned at her.

'Not yet.'

Over the tannoy, the race officials announced in Italian that it was one minute until the start.

'I'm short,' Freddy realized, looking out the window at the white lines on the ground that marked the grid positions. 'Give me a shunt.'

'You can't just roll?'

'No, quick!' she yelled as the flag went up – ready to come down. Freddy secured her helmet, while a small nudge from behind levelled her with the car on her right.

'Thank you,' she said to Will in the rear-view mirror as she went speeding off.

He shook his head as she disappeared into the Sicilian hills.

That shunt – a thousand kilometres later – cost her the race.

'*Excusi*? Are you kidding me?' she shouted, while Vanessa in her head shouted at her to stop.

'Signora, several of the drivers have sent complaints that you broke the rules,' an official explained. He spoke to her like she was an imbecile.

'What rule is that? That I don't have a…' She couldn't quite bring herself to say it – not the prude, pregnant, married or modern Freddy – so she pointed at the race official's crotch. His face enflamed.

'Is there a husband I could speak to?'

She released a short, sharp laugh like a baby's hiccup. 'A husband? Just any husband? Any husbands here?' She turned around, threw up her arms. 'I'm sure I can find at least one, if that's what you want.'

'Someone… a mechanic on your team or…'

'You won't even speak to me? Are you *that* offended by me?' A rush of disgust rolled through her stomach. Searching for a friendly face, she felt outnumbered, out of her league. For the first time in her racing career, she longed for another female driver, someone who would understand. Being the only woman at this level had always given her a sense of pride, but now she felt further behind than ever. She couldn't remember the last time she had seen the Countess at any races; the word was that she had fallen pregnant and had to quietly disappear from the track.

'What's going on?' Will's voice punctured through the crowd. And then his crown of blond hair, even blonder after several days in Palermo. She stepped backwards to give him space. 'Will, I'm disqualified. They've disqualified me for a push-start.'

'Don't worry, I'll handle this.'

'But I don't want you to. *I* want to handle it.'

'Please, Fred, it's easier this way. You can't mess with the Italians.'

'It's not the *Mafia*.'

'It's not? We're in Sicily, and they take their driving very seriously here.'

'The rules clearly state that drivers cannot be push-started,' the official read off a clipboard. He mumbled to another official in Italian. The other nodded. Another nodded too.

'I wasn't push-started. I was short of the line,' she interrupted their murmurings. 'The other drivers just want to get rid of me.' They stared at her, then continued to talk to one another.

'Fred, please,' Will was stern with her. 'Let me sort this.'

She stepped back further and turned, unable to watch as he began to speak to them in fluent Italian. In front of her were the dense streets of Palermo, with their shaded alleys and lines of laundry hung between buildings. Shoeless children had scuttled out into the sunshine to examine the cars at the finish line, their mothers emerging from the shade to chase them back into cool apartments. One young mother caught Freddy's eye and looked at her with such intense confusion – *what are you doing there?* – that it unsettled her, made her turn away.

Will suddenly burst out in English: 'You made a girl drive over one thousand kilometres on your shitty Sicilian roads only then to disqualify her!' Other drivers raised their heads and looked.

The Italian officials began to shout back.

'Signor Truston!'

Voices overlapping each other in a tapestry Freddy couldn't pierce.

And then another, speaking in more measured Italian. Freddy whipped her head around: Yves Le Brocq.

'*É pazzo*,' she heard him say. *This is crazy*.

He threw his hands in the air.

'Signor Le Brocq… Signor Truston… la signora è…' And the words trailed off into Italian again. Freddy stopped listening, tired of trying to understand. After several minutes, when the mood seemed to calm, Will left the gathering and walked back to her.

'What did they say? Was that Yves Le Brocq?'

'Yes, he was positively *outraged*, but he was also positively unhelpful. You're not disqualified, but you've got a penalty, which means you're as good as disqualified. You came in seventh.'

'I *won*.'

'Not according to them.'

'But Yves Le Brocq?'

'If you want a knight in shining armour, then look elsewhere. Yves has a finger in seventeen different pies, and seventeen different women. He just likes to get angry so much that sometimes he does it for other people.'

'Did he place?'

'No,' Will smiled. 'He didn't even finish.'

'But seventh…'

'At least we can go to the winners' celebration. The top ten are invited. I'd take it, Fred.' Will looked at her, expectant. 'What?' he asked.

'I could slap you.'

'For saving you from disqualification?'

She clenched her teeth. 'I don't want to be *saved.* I would rather not drive at all than have to be *saved.*'

'Then you won't drive at all.'

'I can't believe you play their game. You don't understand how humiliating it is.'

'We've had these scenes before. I do understand. And I do play their game. I know that's the only way to continue to race. I cope with it so that I can carry on.'

'I can't cope with it!'

'Then you're not made for it, Fred.'

'But it's not fair!' she whined, and smacked the wall, because hearing herself saying those words was enough to make her nauseous. She recoiled, cradling her pulsing hand. The tears wanted to come, but she wouldn't let them.

'It won't be fair, not for a while. But this will make you better than all of them.'

At dinner, she sat at a different table from Will. Distance, she thought, might make it better. But things were only worse when she found herself stranded and lonely at the edge of the ballroom. The light was low. And there were no windows. The room was thick with cigar fog. She felt like she was sat in a man's mouth, elbowing his fillings, held captive by his tongue.

She was seated next to the only other British man on her table, Roderick Cartwright. He had been drinking the wine like water, and then the whisky like wine, slurring his way through introductions and small talk.

'I should talk to you. You're the next big thing, 'pparently.' It sounded like he had worked himself up to admitting this.

'I am?'

'That's what I heard from a gentleman over there. *Winifred Vaux, watch out for her.* Perhaps I should get a photo with you this evening, to say that I sat next to Winifred whatshername when she was a little upstart.'

'If you like,' she smiled politely, entertaining him.

'So, tell me what it's like for a woman to drive.' He put his chin in his hand with a slapping noise.

'I'm sure it's much the same for me as it is for you.'

'Oh, I'm not a driver,' he shook his head. 'I'm *the money.* I sit on the board of Aspen Motors. If you were interested in being one of our drivers, there are people I could speak with.'

He leaned back, hands behind his head, and surveyed her like an unusual museum exhibit. She was already leaning back in her own chair, her legs crossed, the top one in free air. She wore an evening dress of thin, slinky material that half-covered the leg, keeping her from melting in the Sicilian heat. But she saw him looking.

What did he think – that she was wearing it to show off her legs to men like him? Men who sit on boards?

Before the conversation went any further, before she could cover her leg and free herself from his gaze, he snapped forwards and grabbed her ankle. She pulled back, but he held on. Then, while holding on, he rubbed his hand up and down her leg with harsh pressure. She gritted her teeth and he continued to rub, up, down, further up, down, even further up, down. He soon neared the tops of her thighs. She looked around the room to see if anyone else noticed, but everyone was too drunk to mind their own legs let alone hers.

She didn't know what to say. There was no chance of running. There was no chance of kicking him in the face. There was no chance of saying anything. He acted in such a measured manner that if she made a fuss then *she* would be the one accused of indecency. No matter the fits that Yves Le Brocq threw in a room full of people, she was not afforded the same privilege of anger.

After half a minute of this, he leaned back with a satisfied look on his face, and crossed his arms over his stomach.

'I hope you don't mind.' Whenever she thought of something to say, it would get lost somewhere on the way to her mouth. 'I have a psychological condition, you see, about women with hair on their legs. It can cause me terrible stress. But I'm very grateful that you've made the necessary… preparations. It's made my evening far more enjoyable, and I am very thankful to you, my dear.'

He said it as if explaining the tax system. She looked at everyone around the table and almost expected them to nod in agreement. Her violation was the status quo. Perhaps it wasn't that bad – it was only her leg. It wasn't like he had touched anything *important*. But if that was the case, then why had her heart jumped loose in her chest? Her eyes felt like they were bulging. Were they bulging? She reached to touch them, and found the start of tears there.

'Come, let's get that photo.' And he reached towards her and slung his arms around her neck in an over-friendly embrace. 'Where's that photographer got to? This is a very talented young lady and I'd like to have a record that I met her.' He spread a wet kiss generously on her cheek.

No one took him up on his offer. She broke loose.

'I need some air.'

She threaded through the tables. His touch was still on her leg and she shook it, hoping the fingerprints might fall off, but they remained stuck. She would carry them into bed with her tonight and she feared they would writhe on her every night onwards.

As she brushed through the tables, disappointment nestled into her bones. She had seen it coming for a while, but here it was: this is how she would react.

It had only been a matter of time before she found out how she would define herself in these kinds of situations.

As one that speaks out, or one that remains sheepish. It was clear that she wouldn't be someone who protested – not like she did when it came to push-starts and race compliance. She might have guessed this was how she'd be, but it was still disappointing, when she had hoped for more.

She turned around to check Cartwright wasn't following her, but he remained at their table, hands clenched on his stomach. Still looking behind her, she suddenly collided with a man. Another. What did she expect in a room full of them? And he looked just like Cartwright: that big jowly face that shook when he spoke, and wrinkles so deep that the room's shadow crept into them.

Her voice had been lost to the wallpaper, so she stood gaping at him. All her mouth could make were little Os.

The man held both her arms, right at the top near her shoulders, and looked into her eyes.

'Isn't that a coincidence? You're the person I've been looking for.'

'I am?'

'Are you alright, dear?'

'Yes, I was just talking with…' She had forgotten his name and pointed in the direction of the leg-toucher. This new man, who kept hold of her, looked into the background.

'Oh, Rod. In that case, I can understand your haste. He's always been one to over-indulge. I hope he didn't say anything untoward to you?'

'No, he was friendly… that's all.'

'You know what people can be like after a drink… he means well.'

Straining against his vice-like grip, she tried to turn.

'It's Winifred Vaux, is that correct?' He let go then, and offered her a cigarette. She declined. The two stood in the middle of the ballroom, other guests brushing past them occasionally.

'I prefer Freddy.'

'Yes. Yes, of course you do. I knew that.' He pretended to smack his forehead and laughed.

'You know me?'

'Yes, can I get you a drink?' He was already gesturing to a waiter.

She eyed the open doors – and next to them Will, at his table.

'Who are you, exactly?'

'Larry.' Without the surname, it seemed she should know him. She nodded.

'Right, Larry. What can I help you with?' Her tone was hard as flint.

He looked taken aback. 'I suppose I'll get on with it then.'

'Yes. I only have one more night in Sicily and I intend to enjoy it. I can see a friend over there…' She pretended to wave to someone on the other side of the ballroom. 'There is someone who wants a dance with me.' She was being cruel. But she needed to prove she could be cruel too.

'I can imagine. A pretty young thing like you. I wanted to speak with you about an opportunity. I'm the competition manager for Hollis, you see.'

'Hollis,' she could only repeat. The leading automobile manufacturer in England. Another Freddy would have been falling over herself to speak with him. But the Freddy in this ballroom, the Freddy who had just escaped a man who had touched her like he owned her, said: 'What does that matter to me?'

'Well, I have a reputation for sniffing out the best talent in our country, and signing them to Hollis as works drivers.' To her blank look. 'Works drivers test for us, then drive for us. It means being *factory-backed*. Sponsored and signed, they operate under our bank account, with custom-built cars. Salaries, perks. We'd like to discuss an offer with you, if you're interested.'

She was technically a works driver with Truston, she supposed, but the size of the team meant that there was no salary and no huge factory churning out new models every three to six months. To be contracted to a manufacturer like Hollis, to have their financial support, was every racer's dream. She would be stupid to turn it down. But she *was* being stupid.

'So when would I get to race?'

'Well, you have to understand that it would be a while before you drove competitively. It's quite an adjustment from rallying to the open-wheeled formulas. We like to sign all our drivers for at least one year of test work first.

Testing the new models, the cars that we hope to get into Formula Three and even Formula Two.'

'You want me to be a *test* driver?'

'No, Miss Vaux. You're taking all the worst parts of this and twisting it around. This is a huge opportunity.'

'As opposed to a small one.'

'Miss Vaux, please. We're making you a tremendous offer here. You could become a star with Hollis.'

'What's the use of stars?' she almost spat at him. She turned and saw Cartwright making his way towards her. 'Excuse me, Larry. I have to dance. I've spent enough time with old folk this evening.'

'The offer stands, Miss Vaux. I understand it's been a long day, but please, take my card.'

He held out a crisp manila card with his name embossed on it: *LARRY DARKE*. It smelled like after-shave. She took it, waved it in the air, as if to say *thank you*, and shoved it into her clutch.

Cartwright, meanwhile, was still following her. And she pushed on through the room. She turned backwards only briefly to see that Cartwright had caught up to Larry, and now both were pointing at her, discussing her.

She lunged towards Will's table.

'Was that Larry Darke?' he said, their quarrel forgotten. It remained a friendship where the arguments, as real as they were, always faded before too long. 'What did he want?'

'To sign me on as a works driver.'

'And you took him up on it?' He hailed a nearby waiter. 'Champagne!'

'No, no…'

'No, you didn't take him up on it? Or no you don't want champagne?' He gripped her shoulder. She tried to steady her thoughts. 'What's wrong?' She must have looked as panicked as she felt.

'I didn't take him up on it.'

'*Why?*' She wanted to sit still. She wanted to sit down. *Why?* Because she had wanted to escape Cartwright. Because she wanted to race, not test. Because she didn't believe him. Because she didn't understand what he was offering, not when her head was on the other side of the room. But there was another reason too:

'I can't leave Truston Motors. I can't. I'm indebted to you, after all that you've done for me. You gave me my start. You gave me the Puck. I can't race anything other than the Puck.'

'I would never want to hold you back.'

'You're not.'

'I will be, soon. The Puck was fantastic, but it's time to move on. You've outgrown my garage, Fred. You've outgrown yourself. This is not something you can pass up. Look.' He turned her shoulders, and she saw Larry and Cartwright bumbling over themselves to reach her. She couldn't. Her leg still tingled.

'I need some air.'

'Let's speak with Larry, now,' Will grabbed her hand and tried to move her towards him.

'No, I can't. Not right now.'

'And that's Rod Cartwright. He's with Aspen. We should speak to him too.'

'No, I'm so tired. I need air. I need to be alone.'

She pushed her way out of his arms, and out of the ballroom. It was a relief when she finally entered the clear night air.

John – of all people – attended the Royal Automobile Club's International Rally of Great Britain with her. Will had decided he couldn't attend, which she suspected was his way of persuading her to sign with Hollis. Usually, he funded their travel and race fees, when her rally winnings failed to cover the cost.

Three days before the rally in June, she called anyone she could stomach the thought of borrowing money from. Verne had been away all week at the races in France. Eric was in Scotland on his first junior professorship. Her father was, well… he was still her father. Instead: John. She convinced him it would be nice if he came to see his sister rally. *It is your fault after all*, she tried, referring to the bet on Victory Day.

When he agreed and said he'd book a hotel in Northampton the night before, she said: *book two rooms.* And would you have a spare eight pounds? *For what?* An emergency – and by that, she meant the race fee.

Not that she didn't love her brother in that buried, princess-and-the-pea, it's somewhere under the mattresses way, but the thought of spending several hours with him made her palms clam with sweat. Most siblings will have a connection from sharing the same childhood. Only Freddy and John hadn't. When John was young, their father was still starting his business and money was tight; he ran around country farms in bare feet and ate potatoes dug from the neighbouring fields and loved his darling mother until she died when he was nineteen. He went to boarding school at eleven, just when Freddy was beginning to take on memories. She felt as though she was chasing the scent of him around the house. Letters of his achievements – his rugby wins, his exam results, his acceptance into Oxford, his gallantry in the war – were all filtered through the letterbox, which she considered a special object that created a brother once a week. He studied law with professors and she studied sewing with nuns. And now they had grown older, they had grown apart.

It was no wonder, then, that when the two discussed her rallying trackside at Silverstone the evening before the event he didn't understand.

'Why don't you ask Verne to come with you to races?'

'You know why.'

They sat cross-legged in the tall grasses next to the track, dew creeping up their trousers. It was after nine, and he had agreed to meet her here after she had completed her track walk, tracing the worn racing line and the fresh wheel-skids from last month's Grand Prix. With the solstice just past, a waning sun hung above the horizon, a smudge of orange burning between the brown earth and the navy sky.

'Why?' John asked.

She turned to him, wondering if her breath was worth it. She looked at his full-grown body folded like a child's. That sniff of jealousy returned, when she saw his long limbs and remembered how he would lope through fields, her three steps to his one. She had always wanted to race with the boys, compete with them, win against them, and it frustrated her that she never could. And she had felt inadequate for it her entire life, for no reason other than biological coincidence.

But in a car, she could press the pedal as quickly and handle the machine as keenly and turn the corners as smartly. The car cancelled out their differences. In a car, she was a man and he a woman and it didn't make a difference. In a car, she was both of these things and something in between.

'Verne's busy,' she lied. 'I know he can't make the races in between his own competitions, or wherever he is, and that's fine. But I can't stay home alone. It's difficult keeping house when there's no one else in it.'

'I see.' He didn't. 'I'm not sure if I've ever spoken to you about that phone call, when you went to Glasgow,' he began, picking at a strand of grass. 'But Verne doesn't like to talk about… weaknesses… no, that's not right… what he's going through… that's not right either. He doesn't like to talk about what he wants to talk about with you to your face.'

'You're not making sense—'

'Just listen, Win. He was in pieces. He… struggles… no…' John plucked another strand of grass.

'I know that, since the war, it's not quite been the same for Verne.'

'Exactly!' John jumped on it. She had said it for him, seeing as he was so unwilling. 'Yes, and he phoned me in pieces. He phoned me several times to say that it upset him when you weren't there for his return.'

'I try to be, but sometimes the rallies overrun or I'm late or…'

'He still *does* call me in distress, at least once a week. Have you ever thought about what you're doing to him? It's selfish, and it's not fair of you to keep leaving him like that. Everything has to be about you, but have you thought about him, and what he wants?'

'And what does he want?'

'Come on, Fred, what all men want.' He paused. 'A *son.* Children.'

'I've spoken about this with him. And he's not said anything recently…'

'No, because he's not that sort of man. I suppose he expects that you'll change your mind on your own. He doesn't think he has to ask his wife to want children.' He sighed. 'And why should he? Don't all women want to be mothers? Isn't it ingrained in you?'

'Is it? Where?'

'In your…' he pointed at her abdomen. 'You know, your *womb*.'

'Just because we have the gear doesn't mean we have to use it.'

'Are you saying you don't *want* children?'

'John, please. I want to talk to my husband about this, not *you*.'

'He's been waiting for you to talk about it for months, but from the sounds of it, you keep missing each other, heading out the door as the other heads in.'

'Keep your nose out of my marriage. I don't stick mine in yours—'

'How can I, when yours stinks all the way to London? Verne isn't happy and you're… never happy. I've never seen you happy other than behind the wheel of a car.'

'You know that children… that's the end of rallying.'

'Well, of course.'

'Then what about what I want? Doesn't that matter? What if I *don't* want children? What if I want to drive cars for the rest of my life? Why do *his* needs matter more?'

'If you loved Verne—'

'I do love Verne. I'm his wife… but I won't *give up* my life for him. He could come to the rallies, we *could* spend time together.'

'But he can't. He has to be at the competitions. That's his livelihood.'

'And I have to be *here*. I have to be at the rallies. This is *my* livelihood. I don't understand how it's any different.'

'You know it is.'

'Why?' she pleaded. The sun had slipped under the horizon. 'What's the difference? Tell me. I want to hear you say it, John.'

She wanted him to explain Adam and Eve. Go on, talk about Genesis. Make up excuses. Excuse his own bigotry.

He crossed his arms. Dark was settling now and it obscured his face.

'The rallies don't pay much, I'm assuming,' he continued. 'At least if you want a career, then you should have one that brings in a salary.'

'You *can* make a lot of money racing. But that's only in the championships, the Grand Prix, and only with the big manufacturers. I win the non-championship rallies, sometimes the female-only cups and there's not much for those. They're engraved pieces of tin.' She paused. 'But I *was* offered a contract, with Hollis.'

'I've heard of Hollis.' He seemed impressed. She thanked the dark as it hid her giddy grin.

'I turned him down, though, I think.'

'You think?'

'It was a confusing night.'

'Were you drinking?'

'No, there was just a lot going on.'

John paused, regrouping.

'That's disappointing. Verne will be disappointed.'

'What do you mean? Why?'

'He told me not to…'

'Tell me, John. What's this all about.'

'I'm not supposed to tell you… and Father isn't supposed to find out…'

'Find out what, John?'

'I'm surprised he's not told you himself.'

'Told me *what*?'

John looked at her, his eyes hard shells glinting off the final dregs of sunlight.

'Verne is broke. Flat broke.'

8. *Walking*

Autumn 1948

At least when she offered to work, Verne was against that too. This was the thought that kept her going through a long autumn during which he told her not to rally, not to race, not to drive. During which he told her he needed her support through what could be a *rough few months.* During which she waited at home while he went off to salvage their livelihood.

The first thing she had done when she arrived home – without racing at Silverstone – was apologize. For her absence. For her ignorance. She couldn't be sorrier. And she meant it.

'It seemed like everything was fine.'

'I was too ashamed to come out with it,' he told her as they embraced in his study, her tears spilling onto his back.

She made breakfast the next morning – and the next. She offered solutions like another cup of tea.

'I could get a job. I could work as a…'

'As what? You left school, the ATS is ancient history, and your only skill is driving, which costs more than it brings in. John told me that you blew your chance for a contract.' She excused his cruelty, even when there was no excuse for it.

'I could learn to type.'

'I sincerely doubt you could master that skill before the end of the century, my dear. You're fast at driving, but not a great deal else, I'm afraid.' He held her tight and sniffed her hair – and while he rounded the insult with a chuckle, his words had sharp edges. When they pierced her, she remained still to limit their damage.

Every morning, she stood at the sink, counting the number of leaves that had fallen since the previous night, green turning to amber turning to a thin parchment-brown.

'What about the house?' She faced him, bubbles dripping from her hands where she was washing up. 'Can't we sell the house?'

He laughed, licked his finger and turned the newspaper page.

'Dear, we don't *own* the house. We never have. Our parents bought it for us.'

'No, but you said that you…'

'Why are you contesting me on this? I'm quite sure that I know the finances of our living situation better than you do.' She nodded. He put down the paper and beckoned her over. She kneeled next to him, rubbed his thighs. 'Not only does that mean we can't sell it, but there's no money in this old house anyway. It's a lovely spot for newlyweds like us, but who else would want a crumbling cottage southeast of nowhere?'

Other newlyweds might buy it, she wanted to say.

He patted her head as he left for the day, kissed her. Treated her like a sweet child, quaint with her suggestions that dinosaurs were just like us, that the sky could rain wine gums, that there would never be war again.

She was told she didn't understand the situation, the money, any of it; that she had no idea how to manage it or trade it or make it. Vague wafting explanations were thrown her way – bad harvests on Dawson-Hayes land, historic debts being due, the spending habits of his mother catching up with her. She heard of antique sales at the Dawson-Hayes estate. If Vernon's mother was parting with her portraits of all those stocky sons, then money must be tight. Without the rallies, without anything to press her foot against, she believed it – believed *him*. She trusted that he had dragged her away from what she loved for a good reason.

It didn't stop her from those moments where she mulled it over. Moments of *perhaps* and *but what if?* and *there's always a chance*. Doubt.

'I don't understand.' Freddy shook her head. She paused halfway up, back still bent, from picking up apples from the ground with Will. After a silence of several weeks, he had called and invited her to his estate. *There's all these apples on the ground*, he had said over the telephone. *I can't pick them all up on my own. I'll need someone with a good back*.

She had taken two buses and a train, and Will picked her up at the station.

'Why no car?' His first question, when she settled into the passenger seat.

'Verne's using it. He says we can only afford for one of us to be guzzling fuel.'

But it made no sense, she realized, as they drove towards the manor. Verne had taken the train before, so why begin using the car now?

'He's never spoken about a lack of money before.' Freddy rummaged around in the mulch of dead leaves at her feet, picking up another apple. 'He mentioned debts, but debts from what? I don't remember him borrowing money, or talking about borrowing it. What do I know, though? I was too busy with…' She scolded herself for doubting Verne. If he didn't have her support, then whose did he have?

She continued to find apples on the sodden ground and place them in the basket. Picking up the fallen bits of autumn was comforting.

'Inspect them, Fred.' Will grabbed the one she had just thrown in and showed it to her; a maggot squirmed its way through the waxy red skin, the tail flicking out like a whale's.

'Sorry, I was just…'

'It's fine.'

She leaned down again to pick and pick and pick – and talk, and talk, and talk.

'I'm going mad,' she shook her head. 'Sorry.'

'Stop apologizing. You're not mad.' He paused. 'In fact, you might be on the right line.'

'What are you saying?'

She grabbed a few more apples, checking them, then putting them into the basket.

'I'm saying that if you're suspicious, I would trust your instincts.'

'What?'

'Jesus Christ, Freddy, don't be a fool. I'm saying that maybe he *is* lying to you.'

'About the money?'

'Yes. Maybe he isn't telling you the truth. Maybe it all seems a little fishy because it *is* fishy.'

'But why would he lie?'

'I don't know. Maybe it's because you're not driving anymore, because you're at home all the time for him.'

She spurted out a laugh, which fell short on the air.

'You're saying that I'm gullible.'

'I'm saying that Vernon is controlling.'

'Verne isn't controlling.'

'He's not? Do you remember all those times you hitch-hiked and begged and borrowed and stole—'

'I never stole.'

'—to get to races. Do you remember? I was worried sick about you, but you yell at anyone that tries to tell you what to do. Where did the money go, Fred? All those notes that you said disappeared from your purse. Because they didn't vanish by themselves.'

'Take that back.'

She held an apple tight in her hand, so tight she began to feel the juices between her fingers.

'What about driving, Fred?'

'Is this why you brought me here? To try and make me doubt my husband, to meddle in my personal life? I wouldn't expect you to understand what a good marriage looks like.'

'I wasn't going to bring up Vanessa, but now that you have, I might as well say that she would be disappointed in you. To see that you've dropped it so quickly. I brought you here because you're my friend and I want you to remember.'

'Remember what?'

'The rallies, Fred. The offer from Hollis. Is this the end of it? For a girl that wanted to drive, you sure don't do a lot of it anymore.'

'It's only been a few months.'

'But then it will be a few years, and a few years will turn into a decade…'

'Will. Stop.'

She lifted her hand and threw the apple towards him. He ducked.

‘You’re angry. I understand,’ Will held up both his hands to calm her. ‘The truth can be hard to swallow.’

‘This isn’t the truth. You’re trying to trick me and turn me against Verne. You only ever wanted me to sell your cars, and you want me to keep doing it.’

‘That’s not true.’

‘It is,’ she yelled and lobbed another apple at his head.

‘Wake up! Vernon is a jealous man who wants you at home. And he’s winning.’

‘How *dare* you.’ She threw another and this time it clipped the side of his head. This violence felt good – a way to ignore the whirl of *perhaps* and *could he?* that had begun to form words, reason, sense. The panic of truth clambering into her brain. What was she to do with it, all that truth, when it arrived? Where was she to let it take her?

Will shielded his head with a hand, a smudge of apple-mud on his temple. Freddy lifted her hand to throw another, but she left it there. It fell to the ground instead. She gathered up her things.

‘Don’t call me. I don’t want to hear from you,’ she hissed at him, and strode across the orchard, kicking through the fallen apples.

‘How will you get to the station?’ he yelled behind her.

She walked there.

She barely stopped walking over the next few weeks. Endless walks through the countryside. Until her feet questioned the movement. She walked until she was someone else. A tourist. A curious hiker. When she re-approached the house, her body would swerve and she took another loop through the forest, curiosity brushing over her. She was a visitor, she had never seen this house before. *Who could possibly live there? What could be around that corner?* The woman who lived in that house wasn't her.

The woman who sewed in the conservatory wasn't her either. Or the one that read the ladies' magazines that came through the letterbox. Or the one that spent two hours washing and drying and setting her hair and then lay stiff on the pillow at a precise twenty-degree angle when she went to bed in order to keep it neat. None of them were her – but, of course, that then raised the question about who she was, walking past that house.

When friends or neighbours asked them to dinner or tea or a party, Verne turned them down, and she would find out about these invitations only days after they were extended: *and that's why I didn't want to subject you to dinner with the Herons* or *if only you knew how many times Jones down the road was trying to make us take tea with him*. Verne worked hard at isolating them.

Freddy saw her body in the mirror as he would see it – and as he wanted to see it, with a huge swollen belly, a child inside. She had been lying to him, and to herself, whenever she asked Verne to delay this part of their marriage *for now*. Perhaps because she had known that this delaying would get her nowhere in the end. Perhaps because she had already made up her mind about not wanting children. What she wanted was irrelevant. The world, and her husband, would take no notice of how she wanted to live her life, and this was simply another piece of it that would fall exactly how he wanted.

This difference of opinion about children was a problem they should have solved before getting married – but she *had* solved it, hadn't she? She had told Verne clearly enough on Victory Day and many times since, clinging onto those conversations like insurance. *We can talk about this another time.*

Another time was here. The leaves were here, crushed into the mud under her feet. All those women were here, in the conservatory, in the bathroom, in the parlour reading *Woman's Own*. And Verne was here, walking towards her, his arms outstretched.

He decided that they would spend Christmas alone.

'We don't want to get the families involved, do we?' He pulled her closer in the firelight.

That was the way most of his sentences worked now – a statement which turned upwards at the end to give the illusion that it was a question.

She smiled.

'Of course not.'

'Besides, gifts are expensive. If we send a letter and something homemade to them, that will keep from raising eyebrows, won't it?'

She nodded.

'It's a good plan.'

New Year's Eve, however, was an exception, because Eric was returning home. After his time in Scotland, where he had been barely reachable by telephone or letter, he had travelled down to see them for New Year's and then take up a research post in London.

When she told Verne, knowing she had real grounds for a case here, he sighed. Why she had to make a case to see anyone was another question that she had to dismiss almost immediately.

'If I could spend New Year's, just the two of us, like we did at Christmas, then I would.' He pulled her close on a Sunday morning, freshly washed pillows crunching between them. 'I had some special plans for New Year's Eve. A way to ring in 1949 that involved only me and you… and this bed.'

Prude or pregnant – perhaps there *were* only two options, and Freddy would soon fit into the latter. She had somehow remained a prude throughout her entire marriage, never really becoming comfortable with her body or with his. Having sex had remained a rare and relatively loveless routine, and she didn't know whose fault it was. She always approached it with a kind of dread. It wasn't that she hated sex with Verne, but he tried terribly hard, which she suspected was the reason that it didn't feel very good. She would glimpse his face during it, and he would look like a boy concentrating on drawing a perfect circle without a compass. He never seemed to be aware of her displeasure – or at least, never admitted it. And then there was always the anxiety of the following morning, the following days. The relief when her period came.

But on New Year's Eve, she could see herself letting it finally happen, forgetting her mother's tricks. This agency over her body was feeling more and more like rebellion, and she was tired of being a rebel. Racing was a distant dream from another life, none of her concern any longer. There was nothing stopping her from this now. Verne was running out of patience and, it seemed, she was running out of it too. She could see Verne's excitement at what could be, and she knew she would give in. She would give him a child.

But first, she needed a farewell.

'Let's do that New Year's Day. Please, Verne, I want to see Eric.'

'I forget that he's your favourite brother.'

'He's *not* my favourite…'

'You don't speak to John.'

'We have some differences of opinion, that's all.'

'You should make amends with him, considering he's the brother that lives an hour away, and not the one who's off teaching mathematics to highlanders.'

'Please, Verne.'

He leaned his temple on his right fist and inspected her face. Then, he nodded.

'Alright, we'll go.'

She left no inch of his skin uncovered in kisses, forgetting that what he had done was no great act of charity. He was letting her see her family.

There was no reason for her to leave early. No reason, of course, other than she wanted to. Which didn't feel like a decent reason anymore.

As the evening wore on and Verne remained out with one of his friends, she walked to the garage where her husband's Rolls-Royce sat waiting for her. The Baby Austin was back at her father's house.

The Rolls' keys were already in her hand, she realized. And soon she was sat inside it, and she had put the keys into the ignition, and she had driven onto the road. When she was more than halfway there, beetling down the road – well, at that point, it was too late to turn back.

'Verne will meet me here,' she told her father when he opened the door and saw no one beside her. He looked at the empty air like it was a body.

'You and him, you're not… in *trouble* are you?' He whispered *trouble* and looked behind her. How well did he think his neighbours could hear?

'Gosh, no. He said he'd be late. He's with an old friend.'

Unconvinced, he ushered her in. The only thing worse than having a failing marriage was your child having one. She noticed him look down at her stomach to assess its flatness. Whether the scrutiny was one of care or judgement, she couldn't tell. She stared back into his eyes as he stared at her body. Eventually, he gave in and turned away. He had grown quieter since she last saw him.

He beckoned her through to the parlour. Music from the gramophone lilted through the air, the fire crackled. There was nothing more comforting than bookshelves in the same arrangement they had been since she was a child. The same cricket bat in the same corner with the same layers of dust encrusted on its handle. The burgundy carpet with its familiar red-wine stain. Years unreeled themselves in the furniture – especially the sofa, where Eric sat.

'You look smart,' he grinned.

She had chosen the dress from the Monte Carlo Rally. That felt like a lifetime ago, instead of just over a year.

'As do you,' she returned, embracing him. He had grown taller and filled out slightly, but he was still that shy codebreaker from Victory Day, barely out the tunnel of adolescence. Even with his hair styled differently, his new glasses, and the gold band on his fourth finger that looked suspiciously like a wedding ring.

She flicked her eyes to his face, and back to the ring. He saw her do it, then fumbled it off and slipped the thing into his pocket.

'Don't,' he whispered, as their father fussed with something on the other side of the room. 'I was going to tell everyone later… when we were all together.'

'Did Father not notice the ring?'

'Fred, he would barely notice anything was different if I'd showed up tonight with my wife at my side.'

In Eric's letters, he had talked about a new friend in Scotland who was showing him *this beautiful country*. He had never mentioned that this new friend was a woman. Or had Freddy simply never noticed that detail and the meaning behind his comments, too wrapped up in feeling sorry for herself in so many ways? She had been easily deterred from replying to his letters by Verne's argument that it was insensitive to ruin her brother's happiness with discussion of their situation.

'How was Scotland?' She changed the subject. He thanked her silently.

'Dark, dull…' he paused. 'But *beautiful*. The Scots, not so much.'

'*Apart from one*,' she murmured under her breath.

'What was that?' her father asked. He approached with glasses filled with ice and tonic.

'I was telling Freddy about how the Scots are an odd bunch.'

'No surprise there,' he said, reclining into a chair.

'Where's John?' Freddy asked.

'He's at his office still,' her father said. 'I told him it was rude, that his brother was home, but he seemed adamant to finish up something. Apparently, the banks don't close on New Year's Eve anymore.'

Their father burst out of his chair again, in search of the prawn cocktail. The moment he was out of the room, she turned to Eric.

'Who is she then?'

'Stop.'

'Is she Scottish?'

'Stop.'

'Was she at the university?'

'No.'

'Was it in a bar?'

'I'm not telling you.'

'A dance club?'

'No.'

'Please.'

'Why are you so keen to know?'

'Besides being your sister, let me imagine what it's like to be a newlywed again. In love, without a care in the world.'

'You can't remember that? It was only a few years ago that you and Verne—'

'I know, but time flies. Things change. Struggles appear.'

'What struggles?' Eric asked. 'What's going on between you and Verne?'

'Nothing,' she rushed. 'Nothing's going on.'

'Can I trust you to tell me the truth, Fred?'

'Yes.'

Eric narrowed his eyes at her for a moment, then fiddled in his pockets and lit a cigarette.

'I didn't know you smoked.'

'You didn't know I was married five minutes ago.'

Their father rushed back in and set down a bottle of champagne on the table.

'It's too early for champagne,' Eric mumbled.

'It will be midnight in just a few hours.'

'Yes, but in a few hours' time the champagne will be warm if you leave it there.'

He pointed at Eric in agreement and retreated back to the kitchen with the champagne, something cartoonish about his movements. Freddy giggled and her laughing muscles twinged, weak from disuse over the past few months.

'What happened with that race?' Eric asked. He tapped the cigarette on the side of the ashtray.

'What race?' she asked.

'The one where I rushed to Euston Station with a wad of cash in my pocket, like I'd just pulled off a heist.'

'Oh, that race. I didn't win.'

He nodded.

'How is the driving going?'

'I don't do that anymore.' She looked down into her drink. Took a sip. Placed it on the coffee table. 'Verne convinced me it wasn't worth my time. What's the point if you can't win? Anyway, it wasted more money than we had.'

'None of what you just said is correct.'

'What?'

'It's worth your time if you're good at it, which you are. That means there's a point even if you're not winning. And as for the money, Verne has tons of it. His family has tons of it. He can fund it.'

Her hand froze over the drink.

'He never funded it. And he's… we've… not got any money, Eric. We're broke.'

Eric's face remained still.

'What are you talking about, Fred?'

'We're broke. He told me we're broke.'

'How could you be broke when he's been seen winning big in the casinos all over London? When his father bought another holiday home in the Scilly Isles? If this is some ploy to try and mess with me…'

'It's not… You're saying that we're not broke?'

'Not that I last heard.'

'But he told me we were. And I believed him.'

'Of course. Why wouldn't you?' Eric said.

'Why wouldn't I?' she repeated. 'And how would I have known the truth? None of the bank accounts are mine. I see no one. I go nowhere. I have no life that isn't his.'

'Fred.'

'Don't.' Tears bulged in her eyes and she kept herself from blinking, kept herself from spilling them.

Their father re-entered, this time with a bottle of wine. She shot from her seat, offering to pour three glasses. Cheers, cheers, cheers. If fools could smile, she thought, then she was a fool. For an hour, they spoke without speaking. They talked frantically about their lives and Christmas and what spring could bring. When she laughed, it was never deeply. And when Eric looked at her, she looked away.

Someone knocked on the door, and her father left the room to answer it.

'Fred,' Eric whispered. He placed his hand on top of hers.

'I don't know what this means,' she muttered.

'I don't know either. But I know numbers, and I know equations. And I know that the equals sign means both sides of the equation are the same. And when one side is made to be less, then the equation is broken. And that side should probably do something about it.'

'Are you saying I have to leave him?'

'I'm talking about numbers, Fred. I wouldn't want you to think I was giving you any ideas.'

As she feared, it was John at the door.

He waltzed in, shaking off his coat and pouring it over one arm, moaning about the cold, and bent down to give Freddy a casual, one-armed hug. John's form – his body and his personality – was so large that it pushed everyone else's concerns completely out of the room, and their previous conversation evaporated. Their father padded off to get something.

'How's it all going? Where's Verne?'

'He'll join later.'

'How's he doing? I know it's been a rough few months for you two. I offered—'

'Do you not know, or are you lying to me, John?' she snapped.

'About what?'

'Fred,' Eric grabbed at her dress as she stood to face their older brother.

John continued to spread himself around the room, dripping rain onto the carpet.

'Which one is it?' Freddy said. 'Did you just believe him, because he's your friend… or were you lying to me?'

He leaned back and let out a sigh. He shook his head and looked dead into Eric's eyes.

'Well done, Eric. Top job.'

It was enough to answer her question.

She grabbed her coat and stormed out, with a re-awakening sense of power stealing over her. More guests were due to arrive soon. Glasses of champagne were to be clinked. She should have been there, waiting for them.

But she had truths to see to.

Vernon was sat at the table when she arrived home. His head in his hands. She had never seen a better enactment of melancholy. Even after she had skidded the car into the drive, opened the front door and let it bang against the wall – he remained there, still, looking like he hadn't heard a thing.

'Where have you been?' he asked, head down.

'I went ahead.'

'Without me?' He forced out a weak cough, then touched a palm to his chest and began massaging the tight skin over his sternum. 'Something about that cold air has got into my chest. I don't feel too well, so I don't think I'm up for it.'

'Cut it, Verne.'

'What?'

'Stop lying. You're fine.'

His hand dropped from his chest. And when he stood to meet her, she remembered how tall he was. How well built.

'You were fine earlier. You're fine now. Don't lie to me.' She kept the car keys in her hand, wedged between her fingers. The door was open behind her, wind gushing through. 'You weren't planning on letting me go tonight, were you?'

'*Letting* you go?'

'You weren't planning on us going. You were going to return late, then make excuses not to go. You didn't want me seeing Eric. You didn't want me to talk to him, to find out.' She saw the evening splice in two, and the version that he had been planning – where they crawled into bed and made love – crumbled away. And her version of the evening, this one she had forced into happening, overlaid on top of it.

She watched his face calculate his response.

'Find out what?' he tried.

She dropped her handbag to the floor, and her shawl slinked off her shoulders. Rain lashed against the blacked-out windows. Until now, she had done her best not to mind Verne's taunts, his challenges. She almost felt like they were a strange badge of honour, or that she was becoming stronger through her ability to withstand them – or even, sometimes, that this was a competition she could somehow win. But she liked to know when she was in a competition, and what the rules were. There was no excuse for blind manipulation.

'We're not broke, Verne. We never have been. I've lost months to this fantasy that you created to keep me here, but…'

'Would you have spent any time with me, if I hadn't?'

'You admit it?'

'Do you love me, Winifred?'

'Yes, of course,' she said. 'I loved you enough to let you take my life away.'

He shunted his chair back with a deafening screech and stepped towards her. She stepped back.

'Oh, please.' He crossed his arms, shaking his head in disbelief. 'I've done nothing that's not within my rights to do as your husband. My job is to look after you, and I have. I've *protected* you.' He moved closer to her. She stumbled, knocking over a chair. The noise startled her, and, while she looked down at it, he lunged towards her and looped his fingers around her wrist.

Then, he retracted, tutting at his hands. Pointing at them.

'Look… look what you've made of me.' He knocked another chair over. Then another. And took the plate on the table and threw it to the ground; and the brushes in the sink, the draining board, the spatulas. He deconstructed the kitchen one item at a time. She hoped the neighbours could hear it. 'You made me do this, because you were so hesitant about what comes next.'

'And what does come next?' she asked.

'Well, I was hoping for some children, but you tell me, considering you're the one who decides everything. What do you want?'

What did she want? She wanted not to be in this situation. She wanted a world where she could race cars and her husband would understand and she could spend time with him and he would support her and she would support him. She wanted what couldn't be wanted. What she couldn't have. She wanted to make herself miserable, she realized. This was a practical world, not an ideal one.

He wanted her to say she wanted *children*. He wanted her to say *only you, Verne*. He wanted her to forgive him for the lies. She saw the evening play out, like looking at a sheet of music and knowing how the tune will sound from the arrangement of notes on the page. She saw herself falling into him. Putting his wants above hers and remaining wanting.

Instead: Vanessa, in her head. Vanessa in the walls. Vanessa in her ears. Vanessa with the map.

She stepped backwards again.

'Do you know how you've made me feel?'

He shook his head.

'Weak, Verne. You've made me feel like an invalid, like someone who can't even walk down the road without an arm to lean on. I feel worthless.'

'We went through a rough patch, we did. Perhaps it wasn't as bad as I said, but that doesn't mean—'

'Broke. That's what you told me. You're the man who had to lie about shooting down fourteen German planes. You're the man who lies.' She paused. 'Because you're worried that just Vernon wasn't enough to keep his wife at home.'

He pushed down the last chair, and she jumped. Then, a silence.

'I'm going home,' she said.

He pawed at her arm as she marched towards the front door.

'Winifred, I could never…' He held himself back from apologies – because they would admit fault. 'What I did, it wasn't even… I could have been a monster.'

'Who's to say you weren't,' she shot back. 'And for the record, I didn't let you win that race outside the club. I would never let someone win.'

She strode out the door and onto the drive. Big, bruising drops of rain cut into her skin. Her hand on the car door, her other with the keys. A final hesitation. He had followed, feet crunching on the gravel. There was still a chance to salvage this. The night continued to splinter into its lines; there were other routes open. An apology could be on his tongue. She turned towards him and—

He struck her so hard that she thought her head might come off.

Dull, slow, in the moments afterwards, she watched from the ground as he gaped at the offending – shaking – hand. Taking advantage of his distraction, she reached up for the car door handle and pulled herself up. Opened the door, then threw herself into the driver's seat. He snapped out of his horror and reached after her, into the car. More reasoned than afraid, she yanked the door onto his extended arms and heard a bone crack. He moaned, but his mouth trapped the scream tight behind his teeth. He retracted his arms in pain, and she slammed the door, securing herself inside. Begging, he knocked on the window with his good wrist and shouted reassurances – but she couldn't hear him over the engine, which became louder the faster she drove.

It turns out: it didn't matter how long he held off for, or how much effort he'd put into stilling his hand, because when he hit her, it still hurt. And it still hurt an hour later when she pulled into the drive of her father's house, unable to hold onto any thoughts. The rain had calmed, washed itself out. Meanwhile, the house was dark. The lights off. The phone had probably rung back in their house; Verne would have answered it and told them that he wasn't feeling well, not to worry if they didn't show up. She checked her watch: it was nearly one in the morning. She hadn't noticed the new year begin.

Her heart ached to put the key back in the ignition, fire up the motor, drive back. Apologize. Get down on her knees. Beg him for forgiveness and a place in his heart.

Why did this feel like more of a loss than a win? That she had failed. It had been the right thing to do, hadn't it? To confront him, run from him? She wasn't sure she'd even be able to remember her favourite colour anymore – all her likes had become his, her dislikes his. If he saw red, she saw it. His blue was her blue. But now she saw blankness.

She started the engine. Then yanked out the key. Then started it again. Then threw the key out the window and smacked the wheel. She wanted to cry but her tears didn't come. She had forgotten how to tell her body what to do.

She only knew she'd fallen asleep because she woke – to the sight of her father in his dressing gown, rapping on the window. It took her a few moments to realize she was still in her evening gown, parked on the drive. Fresh dawn poured in the windshield. The ivy on the front of the house was wet with morning dew. She went to crank down the window, but once her father saw she was awake he wandered off towards the house. With his back to her, he waved two fingers over his shoulders that said: *come inside.*

Ignoring the ache in her cheek, she staggered out of the car and into the house. Her father was making tea. She knew the noise of the kettle, the scrape it made when it hit the stove.

She pulled out a chair and sat at the kitchen table, not quite sure what she was in for. He was silent, placing tea leaves in two cups, shuffling in his slippers.

'I don't want to know what happened,' he said, facing away. 'I don't want to know, not because I don't care, but because I'm too old to go to war.'

Finally, he turned to her and leaned against the counter. He set his eyes everywhere but her swelling cheek.

'You can stay here, if you need to.'

The first words she'd said since waking up: 'Thank you.'

'Don't mention it.' He moved towards the kettle, which had begun to whistle. Over his shoulder, in a sterner tone, he repeated: 'I'm being serious, Winifred. I don't want people to know what happened between you and your husband. *Don't* mention it. Not to anyone. Not even to your brothers.'

'They're not here?'

'They fell into an argument after Eric told us about his recent nuptials. Nothing *wrong* with the marriage, of course, I've no problem with a Scot being brought into the family and you know I don't like weddings, but who knew young people could be so... *free* with their emotions. But anyway, John said something hurtful and Eric left not too long after you did. Your eldest brother stayed to ring in the new year, but he went off to join Alice at another party. There's something going on with those two as well, but he didn't want to talk about it.'

She nodded, taking in this new information. 'I'm sorry.'

'For whatever are you apologizing?'

He made no effort to be kind – and yet he couldn't help it. He was almost disappointed at how soft he'd gone, she saw, when he shook his head.

He poured water into the cups and mashed down the leaves. The cup of tea, she knew, would be terrible. But it was the gesture, she supposed.

When he clunked the saucers onto the table, she saw the strain on his face and knew: this was where the conversation ended. There would be no more talk of it from now on. To confirm as much, he leaned over the back of the chair and took a letter from the drawer next to the sink.

'I was intending to give this to you last night.'

He placed it in front of her: *MISS WINIFRED VAUX*. There was a London stamp in the corner. She looked up at him for an explanation, but he only sat back and sipped his tea. With still trembling fingers, she opened it and read:

Dear Miss Vaux,

We were delighted to receive your letter accepting my offer of a place on the Hollis team as a works driver. It was a pleasure to meet you at the rally celebrations in Sicily, where I failed to adequately express my admiration for your driving skills. I drove behind you for more than two hours on the cracked mountain roads and discovered you had more than average ability. You seemed the only one alive in all those cars. If you would like to confirm your availability to begin on the team, please respond to this letter with some potential start dates, and a phone number, and we can arrange a day for you to visit the factory and discuss your contract.

Yours sincerely,
Larry Darke
Hollis Group

She looked up from the letter.

'John told me about it, months ago.'

'You responded to Hollis?'

'No. *You* did.' He sipped his tea.

'You went behind my back?'

'Of course that's what you pick up on first.' But the tone wasn't scolding – more that he should have spotted it himself. 'I knew that something must have happened, that you would regret it, because this is your chance. Hollis is one of the largest manufacturers in the country. It would be an honour…'

'But it's to be a works driver, which means a test driver for a year. And I won't have any control over which races I enter, how often I drive, what I'll do. I'll belong to them.'

'For goodness' sake, grow up. Have patience. You have time, so much of it. *This* is what you need to do.' He paused. 'You'll drive for Hollis, or I'll never speak to you again.'

It was the most affectionate threat she'd ever heard.

'I'm so confused.'

'About what?'

'Do you support me or not? You seem to show no signs of it and then you do this.' She waved the letter at him.

He leaned forwards, as if letting her in on a secret.

'To tell you the truth, I'm not quite sure myself. But I have always tried to treat you like one of your brothers, and this is what I would do for them.'

She left the letter splayed open on the table and didn't dare fold it or place it in her pocket. It might disappear if she didn't keep her eyes on it.

Freddy sipped her tea: it tasted even worse than she expected.

9. *Almost*

Summer 1949

Just over six months later, her life was almost perfect – almost exactly as she had imagined it.

Unthinking, she rose with the sun, ate two eggs on two slices of toast, and drove the hour from her father's house at the edge of Surrey to the Hollis manufacturing base in Acton, while dew melted off the windscreen. She discarded her dress in the changing room someone had hastily slapped a sign outside saying *Ladies*, and put on her racing suit. She greeted the mechanics one by one as she walked through the workshops; she thanked the woman who had her tea waiting for her on the little plastic table near the car. When the sun started to shoot rays across the track, she discussed with the engineer – a Dutch man called Nik – what the day's problems were and how she was to drive the car to sort them out. These discussions could last for an hour.

It was usually around lunchtime when she received the first call. The woman who brought her tea rushing out to say *Miss Vaux, your husband is on the line* – a phrase that Freddy had never ceased to find ridiculous. She was Miss Vaux here. Mrs Dawson-Hayes had disappeared. *Tell him I'll call later* was her reply.

Later in the afternoon, when there was discussion to be had about the engine and how to shortcut the carburettor, the call came again – *he sounds stressed, Miss.* She would shoot back: *Say I'm busy.*

There came a point later in the afternoon when Nik and herself had reached a critical edge in their discussion, when she was poised over a nut or bolt and ready to make the vital move, when once again an employee or secretary (because the woman who made her tea had gone home by now) rushed in to tell her that he had called again. *He says he really wants to speak with you.* And because Freddy had been here before, and she knew that he would only continue to pester her, she threw down the wrench or knocked over her tea or stepped out of the car. And she would rush to the phone box.

'Verne, stop calling,' she shoved her voice into the receiver.

'How can I? It's my wife on the other line. *You're* my wife. Why are they calling you Miss Vaux?'

'Leave it, Verne. We need some time apart. I've told you this, I'm not coming home, I'm living with my father for the moment.'

'*I* don't need time apart. I want to be with you.'

At this point, the threats entered the conversation.

'Look, I *know* people. You're only still at Hollis because I haven't intervened yet. I could stop this. I could stop it right now.'

'You breed dogs. Not cars.'

'No, but I *know* people in the competition industry.'

'The competition industry,' she scoffed.

'I could put an end to it with one phone call. I could tell them that you're a whore and a liar and that you don't deserve funding. You're a cheat, and no one wants a cheat on their team. And it would be over. And you'd have to come back to me. You'd have nothing. But I wouldn't do it, not unless you continued with this. This is your last chance.'

Every day was her last chance. And she'd begun to doubt two things: first, whether he knew these so-called 'people in the competition industry', and second, whether he would ever call them if he did. She guessed his threats – if not empty – were at least performative.

After some time, she found the best way to deal with them was simply not to reply. Rather, to hang the phone up and return to the track, put the helmet back on, press her foot down, push the car to its limits, and let the outside world froth away with the engine roar. She only knew the day was over when Nik stood at the side of the track, tapping his watch. She would have continued in the dark, but she knew her body couldn't withstand more than eight hours of driving per day. Not if she wanted to do it all again tomorrow.

As it was, she went home sore and bruised from being thrown around the cockpit. That's what she was building with Nik, a softer cushioned compartment where her shoulders could hit the sides without so much impact; and padding to enable her to reach the pedals. The steering was heavy, so Nik had tried to lighten it for her, but even then, her arms had turned to steel, her skin thick and tough like leather. She drove home slowly, the dull ache in her calf from pushing on a pedal all day.

When she returned to her father's house, there was one final thing to look out for: her husband's car in the drive. Or traces that he had been in the house. Empty mugs on the tables, coats on pegs, wet boot marks. Even the smell of him.

In the early days of their separation, he would be there most nights – his engine idling as he parked near the gates, hand leaning out the window, the cigarette between his fingers dripping little piles of ash onto the tarmac. Freddy had become acquainted with the hidden layby half-a-mile down the road where she would watch and wait, sometimes for hours, for him to drive off and unblock the entrance.

Only once he'd driven all the way up to the house, when she was out. Her father later told her how he'd had no choice but to let Verne in, only for her husband to break down at the kitchen table. Her father described how he couldn't stop looking at Verne's fist, thinking about what it had done to her face. He couldn't believe the audacity – for him to cry like that. In no uncertain terms, he told Verne not to return.

Two weeks of silence later and someone mentioned that he had retreated to a family estate in Wales. He was taking the time to recuperate, as though he was suddenly ill, vulnerable. Rumours spread across the social scene that he was being treated by a doctor for a touch of madness – just a touch, not full-blown. A stylish kind of sickness. He was the one who had been persecuted, and of course the Dawson-Hayes family rallied around their own. The only thing that Verne had ever truly devoted himself to was escaping from the truth, so it made perfect sense to Freddy that he would try to shake it loose dressed in hunting gear among the sheep of Snowdonia. The man he is, what he had done, lost somewhere in all that strong drink and those clear skies. The rumour mill said that there was another woman involved. A ballet dancer who could coil her leg around her neck. *Vernon Dawson-Hayes? Unfaithful?* She could tell that Verne wanted his adultery to shock her, but probably the only one he shocked was himself – that he had become a man who has affairs, as well as a man who lies about shooting down fourteen Germans.

But even this other woman, even his retreat to Wales could be a lie, she reasoned, as she sealed herself between the covers in her childhood bedroom. She was always listening for his footsteps somewhere in the house, watching for his shadow on the carpet. She had never doubted doors but now considered them flimsy as curtains.

And it was that part of day – as night fell and she reached for sleep, abreast of every tick and creak – that she became too aware of the *almost* in *almost perfect.* Her *almost* was her past, her husband, her life.

And then there was the problem of Will.

'I knew this day would come,' he told her on a visit to the Hollis track. It was late summer, when the heat began to harden, and there was a wobbly haze above the ground. No inch of her body was free from sweat; her hair a mess of unpinned curls and flyaways. She couldn't fathom a world in which she looked put-together or even clean anymore, but she didn't care. She was just glad to see her friend. Will continued, 'When you surpassed me and my little cars, went on to greater things. It just feels very soon. *Incredibly* soon.'

'I didn't plan for this to happen. If I'd had it my way, then I'd still be driving with Truston. I would still be rallying around Europe, not stuck driving circles in this hunk of metal.'

Nik protested from the workshop – his ears were superhuman – and Freddy shouted an apology.

'She's no Puck, is she?' He circled the car, inspecting it, his hands in the pockets of his white linen trousers. He'd begun to carry a cane, and wear a straw hat, drawing the looks of the mechanics, the drivers, the engineers. But he looked right back.

'It's completely different, open-wheeled racing.' As she talked, his eyes met hers over the car. 'It's like running naked. There's no drag, there's nothing holding you back but your own body and the weight of the car. For the first time, I can see the wheels and I can put them *exactly* where I want to. It feels like you can always be going faster. I've got more senses than I used to have, in this car. Far more power than in the other rally cars, even the Puck. I'm solely responsible for what happens to this one and where it goes.'

'Which is terrifying?'

She shook her head, biting her lip to stop the grin from spreading too wide.

'No, it's wonderful.'

'Well…' he huffed. 'I'm glad to see that you miss me so much.'

'Oh, I do, Will.' She met him at the back of the car and held onto his hands; she smudged oil onto his fingers, which he looked at in amusement. 'I'll always be so grateful to you. Not only for giving me the opportunity, but for allowing me to… open myself to more opportunities.'

'You won't forget about me, will you?'

'I could never.'

'I would forgive you if you did, you know? Sometimes you have to move on, Fred. I know that it can feel unusual, even wrong, but it's often best to butterfly out of your cocoon, rather than remain where you are.'

It was only after he left that she realized he wasn't only referring to her driving career – but to her *almost* as well.

Larry Darke had never quite forgiven her for their meeting in Sicily. He was a man who took first impressions to heart, she discovered too late, and he couldn't help but mention the *Palermo incident* – as he called it – whenever she closed the door of his office behind her.

'Winifred.'

'Larry.'

'Have you got time for me today?'

'Always.'

'Not like in Palermo.' And then: the urgent chuckle that came afterwards. Like clockwork, she thought.

'No,' she said. He thought it was a joke between them, and she let him think that. He was insufferable, but not unbearable.

The two sat in his office, which was bedecked with the entrails of a failed career. Participation medals, photographs of himself with cars that had never sat on the podium, children from marriages that hadn't worked out. All this memorabilia was behind him. On the desk was a stack of business cards, a telephone, and a Filofax. *He* had moved on from his past, but he still wanted others to be aware of it. He wanted to be both Larry Darke, the guy who raced in the Monte once, and Larry Darke, the competition manager for Hollis.

'I have some news to share with you,' he said.

Her heart lurched. There was the *almost*, a shark fin on the surface of a calm sea. She listened for the phone, for Verne's voice shouting: *I told you. I know people. I could fix it, make them release you from the contract, make the money disappear. I told you I could do it.* It seemed he was in the room. She shifted in her seat, looked behind her at the door.

'It's not bad news,' Larry reassured her.

'Is *not bad* news the same thing as good news?'

'You tell me.'

'What is it, then?' she asked, frustrated.

'It might be time to race.'

'Oh,' was all she could manage.

He choked another laugh out. 'Oh?'

'Sorry, I just… wasn't expecting it.'

'This is what you've been asking for, isn't it? For months? Or shall I give this race entrance to another one of our talented drivers?' Jokes within jokes with jokes. After Freddy had signed with them, she learned that there were two other works drivers who had been with Hollis for years, and both were currently competing in the championship. It was rumoured that one was due to retire soon, meaning a space would open up for another Hollis driver on the track.

'You're not… you want me to progress to races?'

Her *almost* slinked into the background.

'Yes. What would you think about the Madgwick Cup in September?'

'You're not withdrawing the contract, or anything like that. You've not heard from…'

'Heard from who? My first girlfriend? No, she told me she never wanted to speak to me again.'

She would kill him if it made him more serious. Her career was a punchline to him, but it was keeping her alive.

'Unless you want me to withdraw funding,' he mumbled.

'No.' She reached out to him.

He looked at her hand.

'It was a *joke*, darling.' He gave it an awkward, fatherly pat.

'It sounds ideal. But September? The season is basically over by then.'

'Exactly. The car's not ready. But this will give us a chance to burst onto the scene with a little less attention. We can play it off as a trial. Testing the waters, if you will.'

'And there will be no press attention. I don't want any cameras or newspapers begging for quotes on how it feels to be the only woman on the track.' Her status as a curiosity had already made it into the motoring press. While there were a smattering of women entering rallies – because those were slightly more accessible, meaning they could be raced in cars bought from regular dealers – open-wheeled racing was another story. One in which women simply did not feature.

'No,' he crossed his heart and mouthed *hope to die.*

This was part of her contract. That she not be treated any differently from other drivers. That she wouldn't see her name in the newspapers or magazines next to the word *petite* or *blonde* or *bombshell* or *sweetheart* (she had written them a list, with some input from her father). That she wouldn't be obliged to partake in any interviews she didn't want to. Since she had expressed interest in Hollis, she had received some other offers – but this was her price. This is what Larry had to agree to in order to have her. Once he had, the other offers dwindled, no one else willing to take such a risk for such little reward.

'Thank you, Larry.' He nodded. 'Could we keep this quiet, for now?'

'Yes, that's the idea. No huge announcements. Let's see how the car does on the track, how *you* do on the track, then take it step by step from there. We also have to wait for the all clear from our sales and advertising departments, once people get a sniff of you. What happens to the sales will determine what happens to you, dear.'

'Good.' She nodded, at ease with the practicality of that suggestion. 'I don't want to be embarrassed if it goes south, and we need to do more work anyway.'

By which she meant: she didn't want her *almost* to find out and ruin her *almost-perfect* life.

When she moved towards the door, she saw another wall of memorabilia – but these were the trophies won by Larry's young talents. The ones that he had handpicked and sponsored through to victory as manager. He looked at them, too, with that cherry-sweet smile, his chubby hands clasped on the desk. *This* was his legacy, pinned to the wall like a framed case of rare butterflies.

Even though her first race with Hollis was outside the official calendar of events, after the World Championship, and only seven laps and roughly twelve minutes long, she was feeling a pride so intense that it made her want to scream. Right there in the pit lane, where she waited with the car. She felt so guilty at all her glee that she questioned whether she had killed someone and forgotten about it. Should she return to the kitchen and dig around under the tiles, look for spots of new soil in the back garden? Whom had she buried? There would be some punishment in the afterlife for this extreme smugness, she was sure. But whichever circle of hell she'd be sent to for these thoughts – well, her curiosity got the better of her, and she wanted to see it.

She had already seen heaven: the pit lane at Goodwood Motor Circuit. Noise blended into such a mesh she couldn't distinguish one engine from another. The sweet acrid stench of petrol and tyre-rubber and oil was so pungent that the smell inhabited her. With the mechanical bodies propped and revving in a long trail, the garages opened, she could barely tell the difference between them; and the mechanics and drivers scrabbling around, changing tyres, hammering wheel nuts into place, she couldn't distinguish them either. No one looked for faces in the pit lane. No one looked for anything other than the canister of oil, the stopwatch, the spare tyre.

Unless there was a woman in the pit lane. And then everyone looked for her and at her, and didn't stop looking until they were satisfied. Nothing needed to be said, but their stares exuded threat. Freddy could deal with the looks and the whistles that inevitably came next, but what might come *after* those scared her more than she wanted to admit. What would it be – a hand? And where from? On which part of her? She was suddenly too exposed. It distracted her. And when she was about to drive towards a stack of tyres at 100 miles per hour, she did not want to be distracted.

For that reason, she was already wearing her helmet, having put it on in the Hollis garage. The worst thing was to be a woman in a place where no women are. There was no need to upset this perfect balance of the pit lane. The most equal placc, until it became the least.

Nik threw a wrench at the wall.

'What is it?' Freddy jumped off the pit wall, where she had been inspecting the activity, and approached the car. It was half-covered in tarp, half-guarded by Hollis mechanics who stood in a circle smoking cigarettes.

'This engine is…' he stammered. 'It's…' He turned to her, his hands gesturing.

'Explain it to me.'

'Our engines only have six cylinders, which is less than the others, yes?'

'The Coopers have eight.'

'And the Connaughts have twelve. But this means that all six cylinders in our engine have to work *perfectly*, no blockages, for us to be close to the competitors.'

'And they're not?'

'They are barely showing up, let alone performing well,' he shouted.

'What can we do?'

'This is not something we can *do* anything about. It is too late.' He pawed at his scrappy hair. He secretly adored this stress, its pulsating energy.

She smiled – and he returned it – then walked around to the back of the car, leaned down and looked underneath.

'How essential is the exhaust system?' she asked.

'You want the car to be full of smoke?'

'No, I *want* to go faster. If we remove some of the system, we can make the car even lighter. Cancel out the cylinder issue. It will still be within the weight requirements.' This was the car's advantage – as had been the Puck's. There was less bulk to it. While the engine didn't have quite the same power as some of the others, because Hollis didn't have access to the Italian engineers who were creating multi-hundred-horsepower beasts, its chassis was far nimbler and easier to handle. It may not have the speed to hurl itself down the straights at the same pace as the others, but it could throw itself around the corner without so much braking. She could listen to it as she drove, like an extension of her body, attending to its needs.

'But we have no time…' Nik said, already reaching for the wrench.

'We could skip the practice session. And qualifying.'

He snapped his head towards her.

'*Skip* practice? But then we'll be last on the grid.'

'From the sounds of it, we'll already be last. This will give us a chance not to end the race there. Let's make some changes, we have time. Hand it over.'

Nik placed the wrench in her hand, and she bent down to pry pipes from the floor of the car.

It was difficult to place the reason for her smile: that she was at the race, that she had full authority to be here – or that she was about to miss practice and for once be disadvantaged only because she chose to be.

It didn't mean that she wasn't cursing herself for it when she was sitting on the grid with clean air behind and twenty-two cars in front. Cars that were faster and better built, carrying drivers with more experience and more sense and more chances and no *almost* in their rear-view mirrors.

Not that her *almost* was here – she had checked. Had walked around the track several times, peering into garages, scanning the stands and grassy banks packed with spectators. It was a procedure as necessary as a walk-around of the car to make sure no parts were hanging off that could slip under the wheels and end her race, or someone else's.

From this distance, the five lights above the start line were smaller than the ends of pins and the race banner was illegible. A thick wall of haze rose above the cars in front, cracks emitting from their ready engines. In the coming seconds, she would pass under those lights. Nothing could stop her now. Not from here. She was on the start line, with the others. And no one could tell from the outside that it was a woman in that car, not unless she took off her helmet or elaborated on the F. VAUX painted on its side.

She bounced her foot on the accelerator pedal, her other firmly on the clutch, hand clenched on the brake, and grinned at the hungry yowl that breasted from underneath. The car wanted to eat up the track and spit it out in its own image.

One light. Then two, three. Four red jewels ahead. Five. The lights slammed out, and she swapped her two feet. The wheels spun for a moment, then caught the track and shot her forwards. Straight into the gap between the two cars in front, which were cumbrous, heavy models. She took two places before she even crossed the line. *Twenty cars to go*, she said to herself. And the only voice in her head was hers. Words from Vanessa, from Will, left behind. There was no space for *almost* in a car with no roof and one seat.

Madgwick corner was a wide, rounded bend that could be taken at as high a speed as a driver dared. With her eyes trained on the next two cars in front, battling with each other for the position, she kept her foot hovering above the brake as she manoeuvred the car into the slim gap to their right, finding the inside line. Good drivers never leave a sizeable gap for another to scorch a line through – and these were good drivers. But they hadn't bargained that in her tight Hollis car, Freddy could throw herself into the almost non-existent gap, her right wheel grazing the edge of the grass. While the two were at war with each other, she slipped through and came clean out of the corner well ahead.

The straights: that's where she was vulnerable. Where her car would struggle. But she only had to put up with this problem twice a lap – on the fast Fordwater corner and the long Lavant Straight towards the final bend. In those moments, the cars she had overtaken crept back into her mirror, regaining the advantage she had taken in the previous corners. But at the next one, she would shunt further ahead, she would slip through the impossible gaps, she would find loopholes. Loopholes were her speciality.

With nine cars in front of her, and four laps remaining, she realized that the secret to winning the race, to outdriving death, to outdriving her *almost*, was something other than speed. Not the roar of the engine or how fast a car can accelerate towards a wall. But the driver's handling of the wheel and their ability to find the truest racing line.

The crowds seemed to know it when they hooted at her Hollis and the commentator wailed *Vaux, on the inside, takes another place.* Could it be? That she had discovered the most efficient route around this snake of concrete? That she was one of the best drivers here?

She was a blur to them, and a blur to herself, escaping her body entirely and becoming something other. There ceased to be a divide between the Freddy driving and the Freddy thinking about driving. She was only a mind shooting through the air like a tripped-up comet.

Vaux is in third place now, but it seems… she heard the commentator yell as she swung past the stands for the ninth time, and it seemed she *was* just about to overtake for second. She ignored the ache in her hands from gripping the steering wheel, and braced for the pain at every high-speed corner when her shoulder rammed into the side. The padding had worn through, and the metal casing clocked against her bone. But she could leave pain behind at this speed. She was long past the point of a body.

It wouldn't even be a close finish, she realized, when she took second place on the final lap, because the race leader was thirty seconds ahead, according to the board that her engineers stuck out over the pit wall. Second place was hers, unless the engine packed it in within the next two minutes. She slumped into a gleeful defeat; the steadfast victory of second place, when there was no chance of first. *I suppose I should be happy.* She made all sorts of peaces with herself to cover the snag of disappointment that she wanted to win.

After the chequered flag flew, she manoeuvred the car into the second-place finish spot, leapt out and removed the helmet, walking over to congratulate her fellow podium-sitters. Both drivers hovered their hands near hers when she went to shake them. She heard the lull of silence around her. The crowd, too, had hushed. The commentator, she thought, would be checking his clipboard. *FREDDY VAUX* was the name she had entered under. Hollis hadn't *not* told them about her sex, but they hadn't *told* them either.

Her name was known a little in amateur motoring circles: she had stood on the podium for the Coupe des Dames, won the ladies' prizes in most rallies around Europe, won some of them outright. But this was the professional circuit, and none of that mattered now. These men were legends often known only by their surnames, the fastest in the world. For every newspaper column about some obscure rally, there were dozens of pages about the rivalries in Formula One and Two. Not to mention that Hollis had been keeping the news of her contract quiet until they were certain they had a car – and a driver – who could win.

Several seconds of embarrassment passed. The driver in third turned his back. The winner shocked himself out of it and shook her hand.

'Splendid job, Miss Vaux.' Young and ruddy-cheeked, he had a cocky cockney edge to his speech. He was casual with his limbs but well in control of his body. She nodded.

In that time, the commentator had worked it out and said:

'The young racing dame, Miss Vaux, has taken second place. That marks a record, folks. Not only the first woman to race the Madgwick Cup, but the first to grace the podium.'

She turned to the stands. The audience shouted their support. She waved. They shouted louder. She walked towards them, her hair a mess, the helmet under her arm. Her race suit accentuated her small form, her hips wide enough underneath it to stand out as those of a woman.

The Hollis team celebrated in the nearby garage, but she walked onto the grass beside the track, towards the crowd, as if to say *you see me, and still you shout for me?* And they did. She waved again. When she was close enough to hear their individual voices, someone shouted:

'*What's that all over your face, Miss Vaux?*' She touched her cheek and felt a greasy wet, then inspected her fingers. Black. Oil. Or what happens when you remove your exhaust system, and the soot spits out all over your face and not out the back of the car. Instead of stating the obvious though, she watched the men who were climbing out of their cars, throwing looks her way, then turned to the crowd and shouted the first thing that came to mind:

'It's my face mask!'

The crowd laughed, and her stomach warmed. She saw a reporter write her response down; and she smiled at a photographer as he snapped her. The other drivers were shaking their heads at the remark. It irritated them, and that was just fine by her. They hadn't accepted her when she followed the rules of their game, so why try to play it anymore?

She continued with the bit:

'You've got to work on your skin, ladies!' More laughs. 'You think I wake up like this?'

She turned back to the pit lane, which had cooled into a hostile seethe. The hum of engine revs and wrench-clinks had turned into something spikier. She felt their barbed looks on her. Good riddance, she thought. They had reigned for too long.

'It was *brilliant*.' Larry clapped his hands.

'Yes?'

'*Face mask*? Brilliant.' He was struggling for words. 'Utterly brilliant. Although, I thought the plan was to play it down. *It* being...' he gestured to her person. She sat behind his desk the day after Madgwick, wearing a race suit. He had stolen her from practice, standing in the pit lane and waving his arms around like something was on fire.

'I thought it would be humiliating,' Freddy replied. She fiddled with her naked wedding ring finger. 'Being a woman has always been irrelevant to me, and certainly not useful. I only ever talked about it if they used it as a reason to disqualify me. But I never thought it could come in handy like this... winning support.'

'Winning *my* support,' Larry jumped in. '*And* the sponsors, the gods from up above.'

'Thanks.' She stood, itching to return to the track.

'You might want to stay a moment more, Winifred.'

She lingered in front of the desk.

'The board… and myself,' he continued. She knew he meant only the board. The *myself* was for his ego. 'We've entered two more races in the next two weeks. Same non-championship races, same stakes, and the same script, as long as you agree to—'

'Yes,' she replied, before he finished the sentence. She knew how quickly he could change his mind.

'If you can pull podium finishes for both of them, then the board will be very pleased. We might even be considering a spot in the championship for next year.'

'We… the board…' she stuttered.

'I advised, and it's up to them to decide. You know how it is,' he lowered his voice, although there was no one else in the room. She couldn't help but feel this goofy companionship was forced. Larry fostered the illusion of power – his desk, his business cards. But he was a man who worked for other men.

And why this edge of doubt scraping at her? Why couldn't she simply *enjoy* the moment? There: her *almost*, hitching on her brain. She had everything she wanted – a car, the funding, the races. But at the peak of a mountain, there were only slopes downwards.

'Is that silence from excitement?' Larry asked.

She went to reply, but a knock sounded at the door.

'Yes?' Larry called.

Larry's secretary pushed it open. She had her hair pulled back so tight, Freddy could see her heartbeat pulsing on her forehead. After a look at Larry, she turned towards Freddy.

'Your husband on the phone for you, Miss Vaux.'

'Is he calling to congratulate me?'

'I'm not sure…' The look on the secretary's face said no. 'He mentioned a lawyer. He said it was urgent.'

The secretary pushed open the door and held it wide with outstretched fingers. Larry remained seated at the desk with a nudging smile on his face. Towards the door, towards the desk, Freddy turned her head. Positive and negative charges yanking her this way and that. She followed the secretary out of the room.

'Lawyers, you said?' she asked the neat, scraped-back hair, as she was led to the phone.

She had contacted only one lawyer to see about a divorce, in a casual way, as teenage boys see about a girl. When she returned home from the track and sat around in her father's house, she was faced with long, empty stretches of time. The evenings were never *hers*. The two options were not to think about him at all or to think only about him. Often, she ended up with her hand on the telephone, readying herself to call him. Her father shuffled around behind her, distracting her until she moved it back into her lap. His resistance was quiet, and it began from within.

She had called the lawyer on a whim. In the days before Madgwick, she was steeped in nerves. Reaching for the phone, no one had stopped her. She found the newspaper clipping she had put in her pocket a week before, a secret for herself to find: lawyers specializing in divorce. *Call this number for advice.*

She had been terrified that someone would pick up – which they did, even in the late evening. When a man introduced himself and waited for her response, she froze. After a few seconds, she started to speak, telling him her name and what she wanted, before she froze again and slammed the phone down. What chance would she have, she thought. She would have to convince a court of men that there had been some wrongdoing, that her husband had been cruel or adulterous. It was impossible, she realized. She had sworn she would never tell a soul about the call.

But when her *almost* said hello on the other line, she couldn't help but out with it – before the secretary had even left her alone.

'Yes, I called a lawyer. A divorce lawyer. Just to see.'

'Why would you want to do that?'

And his tone, like that of a clueless child's, told her why she had needed to call the lawyer.

'Why?' he asked again. 'Why would you want to call a divorce lawyer? I heard about it through someone at the club, my wife calling around London offices to ask for a divorce. How do you think that made me feel? I don't know if I can ever show my face there again.'

'I wasn't thinking.'

'No, evidently not.'

She grew angry, then. 'Perhaps I was simply too busy thinking about how we shouldn't have been married.'

'You don't mean that.'

'Because you don't want me to?' A mechanic walked past the phone box and she quietened, smiled at him. He mimed clapping, celebrating her podium at Madgwick. She mouthed back a *thanks*.

'Freddy, you are out of control.'

'Look, Verne…'

'I can't take this anymore, what this is doing to me. I'm going to have to intervene.'

'How?'

'I told you, I know people at Hollis. My father does. We know the board. We can make your contract disappear.'

'No, you can't. That contract is mine. I earned it. You can't take it from me.'

'You don't know the half of it.'

'Why would I believe you, Verne? When you lied about everything. *Everything*.'

'I hate to do it, Freddy, but I will.'

'Then do it. Stop the threats. I'm bored of them. I want to see how you can ruin my life from the other end of a phone. Show me how terrifying you are.'

He muffled huge breaths into the receiver. She shoved the phone down with a *clang.*

Nik appeared near the booth, his stern face lighting up when he saw her.

'Freddy, where have you been? Are you ready?'

'Yes,' she arranged her face into a smile. 'Ready.'

She followed him back to the track. So far, she had managed to keep her husband separate from her blossoming racing career with Hollis, and she would keep it that way. These were two parallel lines, incapable of touching. Neither could influence the other, neither could talk to the other. There was no chance he knew her sponsors, or anyone at Hollis. He was a man who had lied about fourteen Germans. She was certain he was lying about this.

Certain enough to forget about it heading into the next race, which was named after a man who had died on the track the previous year. The trophy was a model of the car in which he breathed his last breath, glued to a wooden block. She couldn't keep her eyes off it when a journalist crept up to her with a microphone and said:

'How does it feel to race for the Jack Donaldson Memorial Trophy?'

'It feels rather odd,' she replied, distracted. 'Like the way we memorialize the man shouldn't be by competing at the same circuit the following year. We should probably change the track so that someone else doesn't die.'

'Is that right?' the journalist asked, scribbling shorthand

into his notebook. She saw the gleam in his eye; she had said something that would make his editor point a finger at him and say *good job.*

Her goal now was disruption. What could she do to twist their tongues into knots in their mouths? What could she do to rattle the rhythm of the races? She was testing how much she could spoil their fun.

'And how are you coping with the Hollis car, Miss? It's much heavier than you're used to, isn't it?'

'Heavy? I don't have to carry it, I just have to drive it.' The journalist laughed, as did the growing crowd of newspapermen around him.

'And Miss Vaux,' another cut in, 'last time you said that you were wearing a face mask. Any cosmetics you'll be using this time around?'

She laughed politely.

'I think this time it's my hair that needs the work,' she whispered to him. 'I spend too much time wearing this helmet and not the one at the hairdressers.'

It was a comment she had heard on her entrance to the paddock that day. The race director, a man named Francesco Cordisaldi, leaned over to another official and mumbled *the only helmet a woman should use is the one at the hairdressers.* She had pretended not to hear. But Cordisaldi would know she had heard when the reporter printed his warped words the following day.

She relished their stunned looks when she held the trophy with both hands an hour later. She inspected the small, shocked face of Jack Donaldson stuck to the wooden block. She wanted to set him free.

The drivers went on to tell all the journalists lining up next to the track after the race that Freddy Vaux hadn't exactly *won* the race. Rather, due to the pelting rain and body-pushing winds, most of the cars that stood a chance of beating her had been wiped out by the slippery track, rogue puddles and gusts of wind that propelled them into the wall. All she had done, really, was hang back and wait for the nine cars that had qualified in front of her to pick themselves off.

When Freddy reached the line of journalists, her race suit soaked in champagne, they asked her what she thought about those comments.

'The only thing I'd like to say is… if the weather was to blame for their DNFs, then why did I finish?'

Because she had kept her distance from the others and carefully positioned her car, looking ahead for puddles. It wasn't that the men weren't smart – they were. But she'd had to be twice as smart even to reach the start line and stand beside them. When they knew ten knots, she had to know twenty.

'Miss Vaux,' another asked, as she cradled the trophy tight against her chest. 'Did you sort that hair out, like you wanted to?'

She rushed her hand to her head.

'Oh goodness, I bet this helmet hair looks just *awful*.' The journalists laughed. Pretending was fun – there was so much she could leave behind when she wasn't herself. At least, until a mechanic came running towards her, an urgent look on his face. A phone call? What was it now? Could she not have one moment of victory?

The mechanic only wanted to let her know that she was needed in the pit lane to deal with the car.

'No one called?' she asked.

'Were you expecting a call, miss?' *Yes*, she wanted to say. She hadn't heard from him in a week, the longest silence yet.

She had won, then. Finally, she had won the race that had begun outside the club on Victory Day. The mechanic handed her the winners' cheque for fifty pounds. In her early days at Hollis, Will had helped her to open a bank account for her modest salary, and she had started to pour her winnings into it.

She had won, and he had admitted defeat.

At the next race, too, there was no word from him. No calls. No assistants or mechanics running towards her shouting *Miss Vaux, your husband on the phone*. Her *almost* was gone. Could it be? That her life *was* perfect now. As perfect as it could be.

She certainly thought so the following week at the Newcastle Journal Trophy, an hour-long, forty-lap race, when she found herself standing on the third step of the podium, the first British driver behind two Italians. This was the best outcome, given that the Italians were considered in their own league. She finished a lap behind them, but two laps in front of fourth place, which made her feel like she was closer to heaven than to earth.

While she stood there with the third-place trophy in her hand, a member of the crowd called out:

'Freddy, what will you do with the prize money?'

She grinned, and caught Larry's eye as he watched the ceremony with the mechanics. She held it for the response.

'I don't know. But I think there's a sale on at Selfridges this week!'

The crowd laughed. The Italians on the podium sighed.

After the podium celebrations, Larry came to the garage and found her on the floor, her back to the wall, cradling the trophy. The mechanics had gone home. The car sat in the centre, half-shrouded in tarp. The room was sterile. Blue squeaky floors, white cinderblock walls, stainless steel tools.

She had been nodding to sleep, until his shoe squeaked on the floor.

'Not sleeping well? Nerves?'

'Something like that.' Nothing like that, but the less Larry knew about her sleepless nights in an empty bed, the better.

'I have to admit, I was sceptical about you at first.' He stood, hands in pockets, looking at the car. 'I heard about the woman in the rallies, the one who killed her co-driver, the one who steered through the Alpine hills like a fiend. The board thought you would be perfect for Hollis, because, while we're established, we were quickly becoming *unfashionable.* Sales were not good. We realized that to sell cars, we'd have to be… imaginative with our promotion. I confess that I never saw you drive in rallies, like I said in Palermo. That was a white lie, but if I wanted to keep my job, then I had to get you on board. In truth, I wasn't keen on the idea at all. But Freddy, I have never been so wrong in my life.'

She stood and put the trophy down on the floor, went over to him.

'You're a remarkable driver. Better than I could ever drive.' He paused. 'I'm going to recommend to the board that you graduate to the championship.'

'The championship? You mean… Formula One.'

'It's run to Formula Two regulations,' he corrected. 'But yes.'

'And the board, the sponsors… they'll agree?'

'I should think so.'

'So, it's official. An official Grand Prix.'

'Near enough.'

'It's official,' she repeated.

'Near enough.' He repeated it twice more. But it was too late. She had delivered this gift to herself. It was hers to have. Hers to hold. No one could take it away from her.

*

For nearly eight months, her life had been almost perfect. Now, it was. The week after the Newcastle Journal Trophy, as autumn had started to dawn, she woke, ate two eggs on two slices of toast, and drove from her father's house to the Hollis manufacturing base while dew melted off the windscreen. She discarded her dress in the changing room someone had hastily slapped a sign outside saying *Ladies*, and put on her racing suit.

She went to greet the mechanics one by one as she walked through the workshops, but none of them could hold her gaze. She went to thank the woman who had her tea waiting for her on the little plastic table near the car, but there was no woman, no tea, no little plastic table – and no car.

The garage was empty, a pale shadow on the floor where it had been.

Her heart thumping, she ran towards Larry's office. The door was closed. She knocked and knocked, rattled the glass until it nearly broke. No one opened it. She ran back through the workshops, asking the mechanics what had happened.

They shrugged their shoulders and looked away. She returned to the empty garage. The bare track. Her hands, tugging at her hair.

Her *almost* had made sure that she had only almost made it.

10. The Gaudy

Larry didn't show up to the factory that day – or the next. And on the third day, neither did she.

Instead, Freddy drove past the turning, stopped outside the nearest pub and went inside. She insinuated herself among a gathering of men near the door, ordered a glass of whisky and gulped it down, the taste of breakfast still in her mouth. She sat there wanting hindsight. She wanted to know that Larry had been under orders from the board, who had been under orders from someone else, and that it was guilt and shame, instead of conspiracy, which kept him away. She'd kill to believe that Verne had committed a thoughtless act of jealousy and that within days he would reverse it. But she had the unfortunate luxury of knowing her husband, his calculations and his schemes, and knew that he would squash a career as he would squash a fly. Without a second thought.

'I don't think I've ever seen someone drink whisky so pathetically.' A voice drawled from the table on her left. She hadn't noticed another woman in the pub. Her brown hair set in a neat bob, she wore an uncreased blouse and a skirt that reached past her stockinged knees towards her shoes, all in the same matching purple. There was a plasticky sheen on her face. And under her eye, the smallest plum-coloured bruise. A black eye blending in neatly, perhaps deliberately, with the rest of her outfit. There was alcohol on her breath, but she wasn't sloppy, as she asked Freddy: 'What are *you* drinking to forget?'

'A career.' Freddy laughed – and the woman laughed with her. But her eyes weren't laughing. There were tears in them.

'Aren't we all…' she whispered. 'I wanted to be a biologist. Now I live in Chiswick and I have three children who treat me like a slave. What did you want to be?'

The way she phrased it, with that edge of past tense, dragged tears into Freddy's eyes as well. She signalled to the barmaid for another drink.

'I still *can* be it. But someone is making it very difficult. He doesn't want me to be it. He's showing me that he can choose and I can't.' Explaining this to the woman, Freddy had the sense she was also explaining it to herself for the first time.

'He,' the woman repeated and played with the ice cubes in her glass. 'It's always a he. I wanted to leave my *he* until he pulled the magic trick of making me not want to do it.'

'What was it? What did he do?' Freddy asked.

'It was the children,' she whispered, as if letting Freddy in on a secret. 'What children could go on without a mother? And he owns them, legally. They're brats most of the time, but then there are the times when I wouldn't want to live my life without them.' She paused. 'What about yours?'

'My what?'

'Your children.'

'I don't have any.'

'How have you managed that?'

Freddy considered the biological explanation, but decided against it.

'My mother gave me some tips once,' Freddy mused.

'Smart woman.' She put down her glass and ordered another. The barmaid nodded, as if she knew what she drank. She had been here many times before.

'We might as well introduce ourselves. I'm Bette.'

Freddy hesitated, before giving her name. 'You seem familiar with this place.'

'Is that a way of asking me why I drink like a fish? I thought you'd know why.'

'What does that mean?'

Bette scoffed, shook her head. Freddy reached for the reasons why she was nothing like this half-drunk battered woman on a barstool at ten o'clock in the morning, but she looked down doubtfully at herself: maybe not battered at this very moment, but still a half-drunk woman on a barstool at ten o'clock in the morning.

'But I loved him, I think,' Freddy said.

'And who's to say I didn't love mine too?'

Freddy pushed her glass away, defeat creeping over her.

'What a fool I've been…' She put her head in her hands. 'Lying to myself about everything he's done, saying it was my fault—'

'That sounds familiar.'

'—and acting as if he was doing it *for* me, as if it was somehow in *my* interest—'

'Also ringing a bell.'

'—even when it was just small things, which, now I see, weren't small. They were *huge*. Telling me not to drive, sabotaging the funds, my life. It was right under my nose, but I might have never noticed until it became something even *I* couldn't ignore.'

'Fists are like that. Hard to ignore.' Freddy didn't even flinch at Bette's statement. A hardened layer had come over her in this pub.

'Perhaps I never even loved him, not *really*. He was just the first person who looked at me like I was a woman and not a little girl.' Bette sipped her drink, letting Freddy get to the end of her thought. 'But I don't know what to do. What *can* I do? He's destroyed my life with a telephone call. What will he do if I'm in the same house with him? It terrifies me, and I hate it.'

Freddy sensed that Bette would understand – that if she poured out her life to this woman, then she would somehow collect it in a glass and hand it back, making sense.

'There's a place you can go to,' Bette said, crunching ice.

'What kind of place?'

'A house, where some women go to… when it's bad.'

She dove into her handbag and retrieved a card with an address scribbled in ballpoint pen. It was smudged with lipstick, crumbs, some splotches of dried liquid. The address was nearby.

'There are several of them across London. Take it.' She held out the card.

'No, I… don't you need it?'

'I have it memorized.' She rushed to correct herself: 'I mean, I don't need it. Another woman in a similar pub gave me this card. She was given it by someone else. I like to think it's been round half of London.'

'And you haven't used it?'

'I told you, I don't need to,' she answered without a pause. 'When I feel like I do, I remind myself of why I stay. Sometimes, when it's particularly bad, like this morning, I've figured out a neat fix to stop me using it.' She pointed to the pub around them.

'This place?'

'I pretend that I've left. I run out of the door in my house shoes, with just my handbag. For a moment, I'm reckless. For a moment, I'm free. And it's enough to keep me going for a while. Until I need to do it again.'

'Is that sustainable?' Freddy asked.

'No, it's not. But it's what I have to do, to keep my world from falling apart.'

Bette was still holding out the card. Her eyes flicked between it and Freddy, pleading with her. Something in Bette's insistent look made Freddy push the card away.

'It would never come to that,' she said finally. 'I'm lucky… I have some money.'

'*Some.* Enough money to live on? A stable income to support yourself with?'

'Well, I could go home to my father. I have friends I could stay with.'

'Friends that aren't his? That he doesn't know about?' Bette pushed.

'You're wrong. You don't know me, you don't know my friends.' She thought comforting thoughts of Will and his estate, imagining him inside the garage, inside the bonnet of the Puck. But she knew that he was currently away at the rallies somewhere on the continent, trying to *find a talent like yours. All I've found so far is a dislike for French seafood*, his last letter read.

She remembered also that afternoon in her rallying days when Verne had arrived at Will's unannounced, after finding out his address. Public school social circles were as small as wedding rings. It was under the pretence of picking her up for a surprise dinner, but she had been forced to sit hip to hip with her husband on the sofa as he questioned a stuttering Will about everything other than his inside leg measurement. As they drove out of the gates, Verne had mused that *he's rather queer, isn't he?* and she had spent the whole drive home examining his face, trying to decipher exactly what he meant. At least he had parted with the idea that Will was his competition.

Freddy was shaking her head. 'I just need to talk to him. I can work this out, I know who he is.'

'It sounds like—'

'You don't know anything about me.'

Bette went silent, then said: 'Suit yourself.' She seemed to relent, before pressing the card into Freddy's hand. 'Take this anyway. And if you need it, then promise me you'll use it.'

'I can't do that.'

'*Promise* me.' Bette's wedding ring dug into her skin as her grip grew stronger. Freddy understood then, that she had to take the card – if not for herself, then for Bette. She nodded, and Bette's grip melted into a squeeze. She whispered softly: 'Be careful, Freddy.'

'I will.'

'And you'll use it, if you need to.'

'I'll use it,' Freddy repeated, she hoped just to please Bette.

'Use it for me.'

She pushed away her half-finished drink and set down some money, hoping – knowing – that she would never see Bette again, and that she would never need the card. It took everything in her not to throw it into the drain out the front of the pub. Women who had failed needed that kind of help, she thought. She wasn't a woman who failed, who had to settle for a life lived in fear. What was she supposed to do – go on living in her childhood bedroom, terrified of familiar creaks?

No one else would salvage her life from this pit, so she had to. And she *could*. Racing and winning throughout these past few months had made her feel invincible. Like her ambition, her hunger was finally being satisfied. Verne had taken her contract from her, but why should he take that confidence too? She would make him listen. They would come to some sort of arrangement, perhaps she could even convince him to go through with a divorce, which seemed the only way forward now. She knew her husband, who he was, his sharp edges and cruelties and his many weaknesses. This time, when she confronted him, Verne would understand. They would sort it out before the week was done.

Freddy knew not only where her husband would be, but whom he was talking to, which suit he was wearing, what he was drinking, whose hand he was shaking and the words streaming out of his mouth: *I won't say I'm going to buy you a drink, because I'm going to buy everyone at least two.*

When the letter arrived in the run-up to Christmas last year inviting him to a reunion at his Oxford college, he hadn't stopped talking about it. *They have to send the invitations so early, you see, because most graduates are busy and booked up, they have to give the notice.* She had dared to ask: *are you busy?* He had responded by marking it on their kitchen calendar and in every diary in the house: 23rd October. She knew the date like her own birthday, because it was important to him. She had been supposed to accompany him to the *gaudy*, as they called it. And what had changed, but the season?

She hadn't told her father about the sudden termination of her contract with Hollis, how it was Verne's fault, how she sat in the car and wept when she found out, how she had taken her race suit and thrown it into the skip of a building site. Her father didn't need to know about this decision either.

When Verne had suggested several months ago that she still accompany him to the reunion *for the matter of appearances*, her father had made her swear that she wouldn't go. *It wouldn't do well to be seen with him in public like that*, he had said. She had agreed, at the time.

Thrill pushed her as she manoeuvred the car towards Oxford, and she remembered that John would be there too, as a member of the same graduating class. She could already see them, stood on the parquet floor under the blackwood beams, the dinkiest glasses of port in their hands, talking with one of the old Fellows in his braided gown, probably reminiscing about that time Verne dared John to throw food at the waiter and he did.

The city was unwelcoming. Its walls rose up like a row of spiney backs as she drove closer, gargoyles with faces skewed in disgust as she passed underneath them. On a precious blue-skied day like today, the spires cut a skyline without remorse. The winding streets kept to themselves, cloaked in their heavy histories.

Packed among the other buildings, the college was difficult to see. She parked outside on the street, waltzed up to the porter and handed him her coat, revealing the dress she had picked up on her way here – the same from Monaco. It was only five in the evening, but the sun had nearly set. The porter let her through without comment. Female academics were argued off the lawns, wives of academics were encouraged to stand on them in their heels.

A static roar came from the Whitstable Room. She paused and looked in on the festivities. It was a small room crammed with people, plush burgundy carpets, cream walls, brass candlesticks and oil paintings. All their voices formed a mash of sound so loud that a scream would drown in the first glass of sherry from the door.

He was on the other side. She crossed the room and hung at his elbow. When he saw her, his eyebrows quivered, then he introduced her to the men and women around him as if the past eight months had never happened.

'And here's my lovely wife, Winifred.'

She shook the Fellow's hand. She shook hands upon hands. Her body had surrendered itself to the room, to Verne. She had never felt less in control, as Verne wheeled her from couple to couple, academic to academic. She introduced herself as Mrs Dawson-Hayes. Miss Vaux from the track was nowhere to be seen.

When she saw his smile, she realized that he thought she was back. That she was here to apologize, to get down on her knees and beg for his forgiveness. It was the smile of a man who was pleased with himself. He thought he had won. He had disciplined his wife.

Only when the procession was moving to the dinner hall did Freddy snap into some confidence.

'Verne, could we talk?' She held his hand and pulled him back.

'After dinner.'

'Now, Verne. Let's talk now.'

'But, the seats will all be taken…' He craned his neck towards the hall, where the couples were sliding into benches. The quad had emptied. She pulled him back towards the Whitstable Room.

'Verne, what did you do?' He closed the door behind him and locked it. She let her hand fall out of his. He removed his jacket and placed it on the varnished wood table near the door.

'I did what I said I'd do. What I *had* to do, for our family.' He approached her, his hands aiming for her hips, and she stepped backwards, the marble fireplace jabbing into her back. 'After you insisted on being so selfish—'

'Selfish? How could I be the selfish one? Need I remind you what happened? *We're broke*, that's what you told me, when we had more money than we ever needed. And now everything I worked for is *gone*.'

'You're talking about Hollis.'

'Of course I'm talking about Hollis.'

She crossed her arms while he stalked the room. Every time she raised her voice, he cringed and looked over his shoulder.

'Who did you speak to?' she demanded. 'Someone on the board? Who helped you ruin my life?'

'Don't overreact, sweetheart. I knew that team wasn't right for you. Racing, it's not right for you.' He shook his head, then reached towards one of the glasses of sherry. He downed it. Then another. He grimaced at its sweetness.

'Why did you do it?'

'You wouldn't listen to me, so I had to. It was the last resort.'

'I came here to tell you that…' She paused, all her gutsiness drying up. What had she come here to tell him? 'That it won't work. I got other offers, from other manufacturers. You can't know every board member. I can get myself onto any team.'

'Since when did you get so cocky?'

'Since your involvement meant I had to.'

'But you understand, don't you? I had to make sure you would focus on our family.' He stroked her arms. 'Did you tell anyone you were coming here?' he asked.

'You mean my father? No.'

'What about Truston?'

'I've not seen Will in a while. He's in Europe at the moment.'

'Then aren't you lonely? Don't you want this? Us?' He stepped forwards, sticky sherry trailing on his breath, and clenched her hands between his. 'We were so great together, Win. Such a beautiful young couple.' Using the words others said about them.

'No,' she pried her hands from his grip. 'I want to leave. Trying to talk to you is pointless.' She tried to side-step him, but he held onto her arm and pulled her towards him. He kissed her, and she kept her lips closed.

When she stepped backwards, he pursued, shoving her into the fireplace. Her head hit the corner, furry pain in the edges of her vision. She gasped and tried to right herself, but he grabbed her arm and pulled her up like a ragdoll; she couldn't even choose how she stood up.

'Then I have to make sure another way,' he murmured. Soon her face was pressing against the cold marble of the fireplace, cracks of oil paint inches away. A belt unbuckled.

'Hold still.' It was what he had said on their wedding night, when she wriggled too much. 'Don't argue with me.' Another thing he had said when she insisted she hadn't let him win the race on Victory Day. Her teeth ached against the mantelpiece, her mouth full of marble, unable to scream. He scrunched up the gown, which seemed flimsy, silly, worthless now that it couldn't protect her from this invasion.

She had never been afraid that her husband would assault her like this, because it seemed reasonable to assume this wasn't something that husbands did. From now, she would have to reassess her fear of everything.

She fought it at first, but there was no stopping him – not here. She had a terrible hunch that if someone were to stumble in on them, they would be more likely to join in than report it, and then discuss it at dinner: *do you remember that time with the waitress in the Whitstable Room?* Her mind floated out of her body and over the buildings.

With her free hand, she grabbed onto the candlestick on the mantle, but he saw what she was doing and pulled it from her, threw it across the room. It landed on the carpet with a dull *clunk*. She could tell he was nearly done, that within seconds it would be too late. It would be over. It would all be over.

Her first instinct had been to return home to her father's. But when Verne shouted *I'll come and find you* as she slinked out of the room, grappling at the torn gown, pulling on her overcoat, past the porter and into the deserted streets, she knew that wasn't an option. Even her childhood home was polluted with him now. As her foot pressed down harder on the pedal of her Baby Austin, she considered staying in her dressing room at the track – but he knew where that was, and there was nothing there for her now anyway. Will's estate was shuttered and empty while he was away, dustsheets on the furniture. What about John and Alice's? Who was she kidding, he knew all these places, even staying with Eric would be dangerous. Her life was his.

The night flung by outside the window as she leaned over to the passenger seat and scrabbled around in her handbag. Had she lost it? No, she knew exactly where it was. She reached for her coat, pulled the card out of her breast pocket, and there it was, smears and all: *7 Sandal Road.*

As she pulled up in front of the house, she felt far away from herself. Like someone had not only scooped out her chest but then thrown the hulled shell away. An echo of an echo.

The street was quiet, residential. Hidden in the winding terraces of an outer London borough, the grey stone terraced house looked like all the others. She couldn't bring herself to take her hand off the car door. She had brought herself here, and that was hard enough.

Then, she heard it: a laugh, from a half-open window, peachy light spilling out onto the road. She let go of the door handle, and said to herself, as she walked up the steps: *it's only for one night.* Or two. Whatever I need. And then I go back home. This is a place for beaten and battered women, she said to herself, and that's not me. It's not. She rolled down her sleeves to hide the bruises that had begun to show since the afternoon.

She knocked. No one answered. She knocked again. No one. After another knock, the letterbox flapped open. Two quick-searching brown eyes looked through. It snapped shut, and the door opened.

A Black woman in a pink dressing gown stood on the other side. She had a cigarette on her lip, with the eraser-tip of a pencil protruding from behind her ear. These weren't details Freddy noticed at the time; her eyes recorded them and passed them onto her brain only days later, when the rest of her body began to work again.

Freddy wanted to say something. Her voice made an effort, but it cracked halfway out of her mouth. Because she felt nothing – nothing except welling shame – she cried. She hoped she would cry herself into an emotion, that the gape of her mouth might explain what was happening near her gut and chest. Once, she had dreamed of a Grand Prix. Now, she dreamed of dreams – having them, her own, again. All she could do was fold into the woman's arms and weep.

11. Sandal Road

Winter 1949/50

Hadley, the woman in the pink dressing gown, introduced her to the others as she entered the house. The front room was so crowded, the residents packed on the floor like sardines, that it was hard to step inside without stepping on them.

'... And that's Lisa, who lost her eye... and Nora, who won't talk much... and Ellie, she's the one with the wobbling chin...' Hadley pointed them out one by one in a stream of insensitive statements that crashed into one another, giving the impression that she was a woman with far too much to say and not enough time to say it. Her hands moved fast, her eyes too, as if it was wasteful to leave one limb to one purpose for too long.

Freddy was in a state she never wanted to return to long enough to describe: quiet, sedate, afraid. She worried that, if she thought about what had happened, she might cry again, and she didn't want to become known as Freddy, *the one that cries all the time.* She leaned back from the thoughts, from her surroundings. Even the carpet underneath her seemed too far away and a shade of red that made no sense to her, the ceiling greasy with scars she hadn't put there and couldn't remove.

From the looks on the faces of the other women they knew this feeling too. But in place of the anticipated empathy, she found apathy. Some, she soon found out, weren't too pleased that she had been welcomed in. Lisa who lost her eye (when her husband beat her so hard he detached her retina) thought that if a woman had two eyes and no bruises on her face then she was probably fine. As did Nora who won't talk much. That was the only thing she said: *what's Princess Margaret doing here?* Freddy glanced down at her torn gown. Battered women were the only ones allowed. But abuse came in all shapes and sizes, Hadley scolded them. Sticks, stones, words. All of it hurt.

The house was like a broken doll's house. With the missing steps in its staircase, its bare floorboards, crumbling plaster, it had clearly been derelict for some time before the women had staked it out. Mattresses scattered on the floor, empty plates, chairs stolen from the street around a table made from chipboard and banister posts. Everything loomed grey, brown, greenish-blue. No one would guess what was behind that smart terrace. Even the windows were scummed from the inside. Any lofty ideas that Freddy had about lady benefactors donating safe houses to troubled women vanished. They were clearly squatting.

'It's a refuge, then,' Freddy managed to say at the end of the brief tour.

'That's a bit formal. I wouldn't say we're there yet,' Hadley replied.

'Collective,' Pat with two sons chipped in.

'Commune,' someone added.

'That's too socialist,' another said. 'We're a haven.'

'Sounds too much like heaven. This is hell.'

'Or purgatory.'

'That reminds me of Catholic school.'

'A safe house.'

'Look, it's just Sandal Road,' Hadley quietened them. 'That's all it is. We have women who work, who look after their children here, who carry on their lives here, who are just… themselves.'

Themselves. It seemed hard to believe that 'Lisa with one eye' or 'Maria from Spain' or 'Pat with two sons' would describe themselves in those terms. Some of these, she knew, were not even their real names. They carried suspicion around like their own skin, and they wore these personalities like the old clothes they had brought – and often that was all they had brought – to Sandal Road.

'Any more questions?' Hadley asked, as Freddy stood blinking at her open face.

'What do they call you?'

Hadley laughed and went on to introduce herself as the one who was not supposed to be here anymore. She was a journalist, she explained.

'*Am* a journalist,' she corrected herself. 'It's not so much my own husband that I'm running from, but other people's husbands. I used to work for the national papers. I took on some cases that others tried to dissuade me from pursuing. Prosecuted husbands, boyfriends killing their girlfriends, things that people don't want to read about at breakfast. After I was fired for going too far, revealing a name, I didn't have the protection of the paper. One of these boyfriends showed up at my flat, although to this day I think the bastard editor *gave* him the address, and the next thing I knew I had a broken arm and nowhere to go.

'But I had access to the record of empty homes in the council. I thought this one might work, for me, and maybe for others too. I used some of my remaining friends in the press to circulate a couple of ads, just a phone number tucked at the bottom of the column under the mattress sales and job adverts. Then when the first few arrived, we circulated the cards.

'There's too many here already,' she crossed her arms. 'I'm sure we'll open more, in time. But it's difficult. It's not designed to be permanent, but it can't feel too temporary either. The point is to leave, not to stay.'

'So why *are* you still here?' Freddy asked, too bluntly. Her manners had gone, and throughout Hadley's explanation she hadn't stopped staring at her neatly trimmed afro – because it was like nothing she had ever seen before, and that seemed excuse enough.

'Look me in the eye if you want an answer to that,' Hadley said, curt but fair. 'And there's three Black women here. I suggest you don't ogle them if you want to get on in Sandal Road. The final thing is, what do we call you?'

'Rich bitch,' someone muttered.

Hadley inched back the curtain and peered out the front window.

'Is that your car out there on the street?' The Baby Austin was glinting in the streetlights.

Freddy nodded.

'Oh, she's *definitely* posh,' another whispered. 'Don't you have some rich *papa* to go and bunk with in his mansion?' Whether it was the mention of her father or the glimpse of her Baby Austin, that comment lit something within her. She lifted her head and said in the loudest voice she could muster:

'I'm Freddy Vaux and I race cars. That's what I do.'

Hadley raised her eyebrows.

'Freddy who races cars, welcome to Sandal Road.'

That immediate connection, that validation from Hadley, had meant Freddy stuck close to her when one day become two, two became ten, and then three weeks had passed and her period was late.

'Are you nauseous at all?' Hadley asked, cooking a tin of beans on the stove. She was halfway through writing several letters and an article, and had bread in the toaster and a plate she was washing in the sink. Whenever Freddy asked Hadley to stop and listen, she only stopped doing one of the tasks she was doing – which, in this case, had been reading a newspaper.

'Yes, but that doesn't mean anything. I've been nauseous since…' She clammed up as Pat with two sons walked into the room, chased by one of them who yelled his tears out of his eyes (*people can tell whose those boys are, because they never leave her side*).

'Pat, please…' Hadley said, but not before comforting the toddler and ruffling his hair. Freddy hadn't told the other women what had happened to her at the reunion, and she thanked Hadley for letting her believe that none of them had figured it out from the bruises on her legs and her cheek, her shiftiness at others' touch. Pat left the room, her son following.

'Do you think you're pregnant?' Hadley said.

Freddy shrugged.

'I suppose the chances are not exactly in your favour.' With her beans cooked, she sat at the table and began to eat them out of the saucepan over the newspaper. *Handle nothing with gloves*, Hadley had said two days into Freddy's stay. *We've all been through too much to beat around the bush.* She had also told her to write a letter to her father and tell him she was staying with a friend in East London for a while:

The last thing we want is the police to come knocking down the door, and you're the kind of person that people will actually go looking for.

'Don't look down like that,' Hadley said, blowing her beans cool. 'There are other options. There are always other options.'

'You're talking about...'

'Abortion, yes. We know a woman.'

'You've had this before?'

'A few times.'

'And?'

Hadley put the beans aside. She reached forwards but knew better than to hold Freddy's hands. 'And we'll wait. We have time. If your period doesn't come, if you start throwing up, if you're sure, then we'll go see this woman. She charges two guineas. We can find the money. But it could be a late period. I have them all the time.

'In the meantime, what's your line again? Cars?' A joke between them: for the first day or two it was the only thing that Freddy could be convinced to talk about. She had bored half of Sandal Road senseless with her descriptions of the Puck.

'There's a race I'd like to enter, but Verne would know about it. I couldn't.'

'Then not yet. But is there something you can be doing? Reading books on this sort of thing?'

'I could study the tracks.'

'Study the tracks, then,' Hadley smiled. 'Just promise me one thing.'

'What?'

'Don't leave like Isabel.'

'But don't you want people to leave? That's what you—'

'Yes, I know. I mean leave… in a different sense. Others will tell you about Isabel. The moment she arrived here she wanted to leave. We convinced her to stay, but she went out to meet with her husband for tea. He brought flowers and cried on her shoulder. He promised to be the man she married. She left, even though I told her, *begged* her, not to believe him. But I let her go. Two weeks later, she's dead. Strangled in her kitchen. We saw it in the paper, a dreadfully written article on page five. *Wife Murdered By 'Peaceful' and 'Generous' Husband.* I'd like to know who would call someone who does that peaceful and generous.' She shook her head, looking out the window.

'It's not your fault, what happened to her,' Freddy said.

'I didn't say it was,' Hadley snapped.

'I know, I'm just saying that if that's what you were thinking, then you'd be wrong. You're not responsible for every woman who walks through that door.'

Hadley looked at Freddy, stunned with this frankness that she'd been the one to teach her. Suddenly frustrated that the conversation had turned on her, she redirected it.

'Look. If you don't want a child, then don't have one,' she continued. 'You are entitled to that. Even if you're pregnant, then it doesn't tie you to him. You're not obliged to be with him, or let him be with it.'

Freddy nodded, realizing this could be her first female friend since Vanessa, and Carrie before that (if what she had with Carrie could be considered friendship). She only wished that she and Hadley had met somewhere different and that their discussions could be about other, trivial things – whether to join the queue for a limited-edition lipstick, which movie-star was more handsome.

'Now, tell me about the Nuremberg ring again.'

'The Nürburgring,' Freddy corrected her.

'Whatever.' Hadley smiled, picking up her pen – spoon in the other hand.

Freddy dozed into half-dreams of racing, but it was never her in the car. A version of her, but not the one lying on a springy mattress in a room with ten other women.

Let's consider this woman behind the wheel, she thought, as she rearranged herself on the mattress for the thousandth time. If it was her from the past, then Freddy wondered if there was some way she could reach out and stop the car from hitting that wall, stop it from leading her to Will, who led her to Hollis, to this room. She was looking back and being asked to consider her faults. *What could we improve on, Winifred?* the nuns had used to ask at the end of every term.

Perhaps the girl in the car wasn't even racing, she was simply driving – fast. She was driving to save someone. Was there someone in the passenger seat? Mothers and children blasted out of their parlours by shellfire. Her own mother, unconscious.

Freddy placed a loose hand over her stomach, thinking of her mother's words. *You should be ashamed of yourself. Driving like that, a hooligan. It's not becoming.* Maybe she was right. *Racing, it's not right for you.* His words, sinking in. What good was driving if she couldn't be great, if she couldn't outdrive death? What good if she couldn't outdrive Verne? What good if it meant she had gone nowhere but to this house with these women?

She flipped between thinking that driving was the silliest thing in the world and the most heroic thing of all. She had moments when she never wanted to think about it again, for all the misery it had brought her, and moments when it was the only thing she deemed worthy of thought. She would lose interest in it – surely. The woman in her dreams had to be a bygone version of her, she concluded.

'How do you know that?' Hadley asked one night, when Freddy recounted this dream. 'Personally, I think dreams are just your cooked brain letting off some steam, but if you have to read into it, then why can't it be the *future* you? A premonition of Freddy who races cars... *after* all this.' She turned over on her mattress, putting her back to Freddy. 'Whether it means anything, we need to get you back in that car so that I can have a break from all your tossing and turning. Finally get a decent night's sleep.'

Freddy thought it over in the dark. She preferred Hadley's theory to her own.

*

The following morning, she sat with Hadley at the kitchen table and drew up a list of twenty names. The names of men she had overtaken, men she had drunk courteous coupes of champagne with, men she had hoped never to speak to again. And now she had to call every one of them and beg for a place in their world.

'You said that you had received *offers* from other teams. Call them back and accept the offers. That's what happened with Hollis, right?' Hadley was munching on peanuts.

'Yes, and no,' Freddy responded, her pen paused above the list.

'No?'

'Those were expressions of interest. I've never seen paperwork from another team. It was never official.'

'Well, that's…'

'Yes, I know.'

The two were beginning to finish each other's sentences. Hadley had the courage – the ability – to say the words Freddy couldn't. And once Hadley had said them, Freddy found that it was as if she herself had, meaning their conversations were never quite conversations, rather a joint grope towards understanding.

More than ever, she was questioning that *other women are a threat* mantra which had followed her around all her life. Where *had* she heard it? Or who had made her believe it? Her mother, perhaps? Her brothers? Long before Victory Day, John and Eric told her that she was slower than them, that she would never run as fast, that she was inferior. In childish ways, but in ways nonetheless, they told her. And she had been an impressionable nine-year-old; she still believed in Father Christmas, so she could believe in her own inferiority. With that belief came competition among her own class. If she couldn't be better than men, she had to be better than all other women – women like Carrie, like John's wife Alice, like the Countess. She had to set herself apart to be worth the skin God had given her.

At Sandal Road, no one was beating anyone else in a race. Rather, the women were off the track, way back beyond the starting blocks. Her commitment to swearing off girlfriends was fading, its sense unravelling. In among all that spite towards them, she had only been left with a deep, pounding loneliness. What use had this belief been to her, other than to isolate her? Where had it got her other than under Verne's thumb, and then here?

As the weeks fell into one another, she threw off the notion that the rape had made her forever the victim, forever *less*. And she had to accept that that's what it was – rape. *Even inside of marriage*, Hadley had said in one of their regular discussions. Night after night, the thirty or so residents of Sandal Road gathered in what a family had once called their living room and took themselves to court among crumbling plaster. Some argued that the fear of violence was worse than the violence itself, some that the violence was worse than the fear; some argued that it was the woman's fault, some that it was the man's; some shared their stories and some never said a word. Freddy mostly listened.

When she heard what had happened to the others, Debbie with a bald patch, Pat with two sons, Ellie whose chin wobbles, she realized that all of them were on the same team. She had always felt a place behind in her solo pursuit of glory. With Hadley and the others, she felt she could go further than ever before.

Immobile and impractical as it was, the telephone directory chained to the phone box at the end of Sandal Road was her most useful stepping stone. Early in the sodden mornings of November 1949, she covered herself in the most robust coat she could find and ran for it through the rain. Her stockings, her shoes, were wet by the time the door slammed behind her. Flicking through the directory, she produced a handful of pennies from her pocket, fished from corners of sofas, the bottom of her handbag, the sides of the street.

She spent two weeks calling Reggie and Peter and Raymond – and Robert, Rob and Bert.

'You mentioned the name Yves before too,' Hadley had said casually at the kitchen table, cracking another peanut.

'Oh, no… I can't.'

'Why not?'

Even though her cheeks went red, even though Hadley knew why, she said: 'No reason. I'll call him.'

'And what about Will?' Hadley asked. 'From what you've said, it sounds like he could probably help you get it all back, like he helped you get it before. Is it because you want to do this all by yourself? There's no shame in accepting help, admitting you need it, that's why most of us are here.'

'He's away on the continent, I've told you this. The last time we exchanged letters, he was in Monaco. Before that he was in the Netherlands. My last letter got redirected. I have no idea where he is.' They had merely resolved to meet for lunch when he returned in the new year. *We'll have plenty to catch up on*, he'd written.

'Surely you could track him down?' Hadley pushed.

Freddy huffed. In the silence, she found her way to an answer.

'Verne knows where he lives, alright? The drive takes an hour. They share mutual acquaintances,' she said bitterly. She was certain that Will would be on her side – of course he would, he had always been on her side – but John's betrayal was still fresh, and it had her thinking the worst of everyone. The week after Verne's impromptu visit to the estate those years ago, Will had said, unthinkingly, *I can see why you fell for him.* He had been charmed.

'So, you don't trust Will?'

'It's Verne I don't trust.'

Hadley nodded resolutely. 'Fine. Let's move on.'

*

The undesirables made her list too.

'You talked about a Roderick something.' This was another kitchen table conversation, and Hadley was plaiting a child's hair. The initial twenty names had quickly been exhausted with little to show for it.

Freddy looked down at her list and all its crossings out, pencil unmoving.

'What?' Hadley asked.

'Roderick Cartwright is… well, he touched me up once at a dinner, and I could never… *never* go begging to him.' Freddy closed her eyes and dredged her memories of the Sicilian celebration dinner. His ridiculous grin. His hand on her leg: *You're the next big thing, 'pparently.* But he had said something else: *I sit on the board of Aspen Motors. If you were interested in being one of our drivers, there are people I could speak with.* She had spun through the tables, caught up in thinking she was a prudish fool. The more she turned over the memory, the more she realized that he was the fool – and a fool with a fetish for the shaved legs of women more talented than him.

She recalled their nightly discussions in Sandal Road and the options that were available to her at this time. There was reporting him, which would get her nowhere. There was calling him to challenge him about his behaviour, which would also leave her with nothing – and possibly less than she currently had, if he took it upon himself to retaliate. And then there was calling him to ask for a place at Aspen, which would perhaps get her something. But then would she be encouraging this behaviour? Colluding with him? Would her passivity make her accountable, if he carried on unchallenged?

She put this to Hadley.

'You're right, about that last part,' Hadley said. 'But we've all had to do things to get ahead that we're not proud of.'

Freddy glanced at the girl with her half-plaited hair who was completely oblivious to their conversation. She felt guilty. But she also needed racing.

Aspen never returned her call. Neither did ten others. Twelve told her she had no chance. Three said they would consider it. And one – a manufacturer named Mackenzie – asked if she could take another call tomorrow to discuss the contract.

She put down the phone and leaned against the wall of the telephone box. Closed her eyes and listened to her breaths. *Her* breaths, all her own. With her body firm around her. It was the first time since she had been made to believe she was nothing that she believed she could be worth anything again, not least a seat in a car.

Rain began to fall. Slow *pats* on the glass at first, and then the drops came crashing in on one another, crescendoing to a busy rush. She pushed out of the box, wanting to feel it on her skin. Her cheeks were already wet from tears before the raindrops even touched them.

Hadley had never remarked on the fact that she

remained stone-faced throughout her first few weeks, which made her think this was the usual state of women who arrived at Sandal Road. Pushed, beaten and bullied with such force that all feeling had been shoved out of their body. Letting it all back in was the terrifying part.

While the rain raged all around her, she turned back to the list and saw one final name, written in Hadley's handwriting: Eric Vaux.

'I don't want to call him,' Freddy had said that morning. As she began putting on her shoes – a scruffy pair of brogues from a previous resident – Hadley had followed her to the hallway. 'I can't trust him.'

'From what I've heard, I think you can. You need someone on your side, someone who can vouch for you.'

'What do I tell him? Do I tell him about…?'

'Now that's a decision I can't make for you,' Hadley held her hands, folding her own over them. She had only recently started to accept the touches of others again. 'But if you want to leave this house, and I don't mean leave like Isabel, then you need someone on the outside you can trust, and it sounds like that could be him.'

It did, Freddy thought. She had heard herself talk about him with Hadley – about how he had helped her with money when she needed it, how he had been the one to break her out of Verne's lies of bankruptcy. But then there was John, and she had never forgotten the severe angle of Eric's neck when he looked up to their brother.

Her suspicion that all Eric's favours were small jabs at John and Verne, because he'd never been welcomed into their inner circle.

Freddy went to close the door behind her, before Hadley yelled *wait* and thrust the list into her hand. She must have scribbled *ERIC VAUX* at the bottom while Freddy had her back turned.

She didn't tell Eric what Verne had done to her for one simple reason: she was almost certain he wouldn't believe her. She was pretty sure that he would wish she'd never shared it with him – and by the end of the phone call, she would wish she had never shared it with him either. Their relationship would be changed forever. In every sentence they spoke to each other and every look, he would see her only as one thing. There would be no going back, and she would be the one to blame.

'It's Freddy,' she said to him in the phone box, too suddenly, hair sopping from the rain.

'Fred? Where are you? Dad said that you were staying with some friend? What happened? What happened with Verne?' She waited for him to finish. He started up again. 'Are you alright? Are you ill? Hurt?'

'I'm fine, Eric.'

'You disappeared for a month. Dad showed me the letter, I've never heard of this friend of yours, Sally-Anne something. Is she from the service? Where are you calling from? Is this a phone box?' She waited until his questions stopped.

'It's alright. I didn't mean to scare anyone. But Verne and I, we had a fight at the reunion.'

'He told me.'

'He did?'

'I don't believe a word of it, Fred.'

Her chest expanded. The rain continued to patter on the telephone box. Tears still wet on her cheeks. His concern felt foreign, but welcome.

'You don't?'

'He said you went there to pick a fight because you'd lost Hollis and you were angry at him.'

'Did he say why I lost Hollis?'

'You disagreed about a car model and walked out.'

'That's not true.'

'What really happened?'

'Verne knows people on the board at Hollis. The next thing I knew, there was no car for me, no contract, no Hollis. I was out on my own. I went to Oxford to confront him. I wanted him to admit it, and I wanted him to apologize, to fix it.'

'I take it that didn't happen.'

'Not exactly.'

'Fred, what are you going to do?'

'I'm going to divorce him.'

A truth she hadn't voiced in weeks – hearing it from her mouth now was a surprise, but it felt good to say it. Eric's words were less of a surprise:

'Dad will hate that.'

'Dad hates most things, so I don't see the problem.'

'How? Fred, how will you divorce him?'

'I haven't thought much about it yet.'

'You need to. You need to contact divorce lawyers, and you need to contact them before he does and charms them.'

'You won't tell Verne?'

'Fred, I haven't spoken to Verne for months. I can't stand him. To tell you the truth, I never could.'

'And you let me marry him?'

'There's no letting you do anything, Fred, that's not fair. You decided to marry him and that was that. No one could change your mind.'

'I was so set in my ways, I was so certain it was the only option, after the war, after the end of the service.' She stopped with the hindsight. 'Will you help me?'

'What can I do?'

There was a sneak of glee in his tone, a mischievous excitement to be in on the conspiracy.

'Tell Dad I'm fine,' Freddy said. 'And not to worry about me. I'm sorting out my racing career.'

'You are?'

'Yes. I'm looking to get a contract. And soon, I might need somewhere to stay, somewhere that Verne doesn't know about.'

'I have a flat that the university pays for. Maureen and I don't use it. Too central for us.' Against all odds, Eric's wife had made an outdoorsman of him.

'I won't be there much,' she promised. 'I hope to be out at races, and it will only be temporary, until I can afford my own place. And divorce lawyers. You know these circles, right?'

'I can make a list for you. Shall I send it to your friend's address?'

'No,' she rushed. 'I'll call in a few days, tell me over the phone.'

'Anything else?'

'If Verne tries to contact you, if he's looking for me… and by that I don't mean seek him out… then tell him that we're done. That I'm done with him, and for good this time. I don't want to see him. He makes me sick. Say that. Those words.'

She could hear the brush of skin against the receiver: Eric nodding.

'Anything else?'

'Not for now… thank you, Eric. Thank you.'

'Of course. But you're alright, Fred?'

'I'm getting there.'

As she ended the call, her heart was swelling with love for him. But there was a nagging feeling that he had never asked, never really pushed to find out what Verne had done to her. He had never asked *did he hurt you? What did he do to you?* He would help, he would always help, but only if he could keep his hands clean. An ally who had nothing to lose in his allegiance.

And just like that, her list was complete.

*

When she returned to Sandal Road, there was another list for her to tackle. She entered the door, shaking off the raindrops, and clicked it closed behind her. Familiar voices from the kitchen wafted down the hallway. She removed her shoes and padded towards the sound.

'Fred, that you?' Hadley's voice, unmistakeable. Delicate and upturned, from years of asking the right questions in the right way.

She stepped into the kitchen. Four women at the table, two at the sink, children tearing around the broken-tiled floor.

'Where am I now on the list?' Freddy asked after a huff.

'Thirty-one,' Hadley looked down at the newspaper she was reading, a cigarette in her hand trailing wisps. The room was dense with cooking fog. Clatters of plates and falling brooms knocking on the tiles.

'Thirty-one? I was thirty-one yesterday.'

'She has to be careful. I've told you this.'

'Don't patronize me.'

'I'm not, Fred, but you have to understand that she could go away for this. She had a scare last week, and she's had to delay appointments and wait for it to blow over.'

'But I can't. If *I* wait for it to blow over, then it will be too late.'

Hadley looked up at her, wide-eyed, as if to say: *what do you expect me to do?*

'I'm not sure I can wait that long.' Freddy fidgeted with her hands.

'What are you saying?'

'Is there anything I can do myself?'

'You want to get rid of it yourself?' Hadley's eyes lingered on her stomach.

A child running circles of the kitchen bumped into Freddy's legs and she swatted it away. She noticed the stares of several women and tried to decipher judgement from envy.

'Look, I've been here before. It will be several weeks before she gets to you, but we still have time. I'll let you know when you need to be worried.'

'You know when that is?'

'Better than anyone.'

'You've…'

'Yes, I paid a visit to her myself before,' she said. She stared into Hadley's brown eyes. Here was a woman who chose her secrets. She knew better, she knew more, she had travelled a road that Freddy was only beginning to set foot on. There was pain, valuable pain, in knowing and having known. There was power, too.

'How are the calls going?' Hadley switched.

'Good. I have another tomorrow to discuss a contract.' She lifted her head.

'That's fantastic.' Eyes lit, both their hearts racing. They were in this together.

*

'You're twenty-five on the list now,' Hadley told her the following morning when she was on her way out the door.

'Really?'

'I went to see her late last night, and there had been some progress. She says two weeks.'

'Two weeks?'

'I know, you'd like it to be…'

'Thank you, Hadley.'

Her conversation with the interested manufacturer – Mackenzie – went exactly as she expected.

The competition manager introduced himself in a curt, clipped voice that made it clear she was an inconvenience. A disruption to his calendar. When he discussed her talent, he used the words *it's there*. Not exactly gushing praise. And the predominant reason (*just so you're aware*, he said) they were considering her as a works driver was because their biggest rival was Hollis and it would please the board (*immensely*) to steal their drivers. At least he was being honest, she thought.

I'd just like to make you aware of some things that are non-negotiable, if we move forwards, he continued. Each sentence couched in hesitance, it seemed at times that he was trying to dissuade her from the team altogether.

There had been *discussions* with the board and *we have come to some conclusions*, he said. *We will have clauses in the contract regarding press and media.*

She wanted to ask *what clauses?* but no need, as he went on to say that the board had noticed that she had relatively little media presence while at Hollis *regarding your gender and its novelty.*

The team wanted to capitalize on it. *Exploit it*, were his words. The man on the phone described it as *valuable*, *lucrative*, and *undeniably something we can use.* He referred to her *face mask* and *helmet hair* lines more than he referred to her skill as a driver. He mentioned four hair product sponsors and only one racing track. Her stomach dropped as he continued.

Her arrangement with Larry had been different. *She* had chosen to act out those stunts after she had already secured her position with the team for her driving skills. And it made Larry like her – and she liked doing it. It had been fun stomping all over their condescending *blonde bombshell* woman driver malarkey, recycling it for her own purposes.

The man on the phone continued. *If* she was interested in furthering the conversation, she should know that there would be more press involvement; journalists would join the training sessions; she would carry out interviews with whomever asked. She would be a tool, he all but said. Nothing but a rake to sweep in money to the company. She would be required to sign with an independent manager who would control her schedule and her publicity. He wanted to make a star out of her – a star that had no say over its twinkle.

It soon became clear that the conversation – if it could be called that – was less to find out what she wanted from the contract and from the team, but more to find out what the team wanted from her, and whether she could go through with it.

When she could get a word in, she thanked him. She spoke about *delight* and *honour* and being *just chuffed*. She swallowed it all back, remembering how Vanessa had rolled up the window in Bob's face.

The only question she asked was about this publicity manager, to which he replied: *he's the best chap we know, there's no need to be concerned*. She hadn't been, before he said that.

When he stopped, the word that slipped out her mouth was *yes*.

He repeated it, and she repeated it back, their mutual surprise loud in the gaps between.

'I should have said no,' she said later, lying on her mattress next to Hadley. Three women and their children had left them that day, and the room was emptier than usual. A hopeful mood had drifted over Sandal Road – someone humming, no knocks on the door. She had been replaying the telephone call in her mind, tossing and turning, until Hadley had said: *just tell me, or neither of us will sleep*.

Hadley turned to her in the dark.

'What's more important to you? Racing, or that people don't point fingers at you and say *a woman who drives!*'

'It's more complicated than that...'

'But it's not.' Hadley, with her talent for binaries. 'You're Freddy, the one who races cars.'

'Exactly, which is why I don't want to be *Freddy, the* woman *who races cars*. Just the racing car driver. They're just using me to get campaigns with hairspray and vacuum cleaner brands. I'm an investment opportunity, like a new product or an engine.'

'But they *are* investing in you, aren't they?'

She had her there. A source of income was her way out of Sandal Road. She was luckier than many of her fellow residents – she had Eric's flat, she had her father's house, she had Will's estate – but still she had nothing of her own. Carpets that were not her own could be pulled out from under her feet, she had learned. Her security relied on finding her own means.

'This is the only team, isn't it?' Hadley checked.

'Yes.'

'And this means that you race again. It means that your life resumes. This means you win.'

'But what about the shame of it? What does it mean for all other women? Like you said, we'll be complicit in the system. How am I going to change anything if I'm going along with—'

'Forget about that for the moment,' Hadley waved her hands. 'All in time. I know I speak about idealism, but there's the practical world to think about as well.' It was like talking with Vanessa again. 'Women will be fine, if you do this. If this is the only way you can race again, then women will manage.'

'You speak for *all* women?'

Freddy saw the outline of Hadley's smile.

'Not exactly, but I'm pretty sure they would be fine with it. Besides, soon you'll be so successful that you'll be writing the contracts.' It wasn't the first time Freddy had noticed her tendency to overpromise. Two weeks had now passed since she was number twenty-five on the list.

On the day she reached seventeen, she went for a drive. The Baby Austin had sat outside Sandal Road since she had arrived. Untouched, forgotten. But beckoning – winks of sun glinting off its bonnet whenever she walked past. It had been too drenched in the past, in her memories of the reunion; she had left her ripped underwear from that night in the footwell of the driver's seat.

The handle of the car door. Frosted shut in the bright December morning. She twisted the key, then yanked, until it cracked and opened. She scrunched up the underwear and threw it in the nearest dustbin. Here the memories and the pain would come, she thought, as she slid into the driver's seat, hands on the wheel. They came, but not as she expected them: overpowering, terrifying. Instead, it was dealt like a verdict: undeniable, conclusive.

As she weaved and tossed through traffic, down empty daytime streets, she considered that perhaps she would never be fixed; that what was growing inside her womb had broken her forever. She would never be the woman she had wanted to be. And her life – the one she had wanted to lead – was over. Suddenly: the thought of a child's head ripping out of her as she gave birth. Sickening.

She veered onto the wrong side of the road.

Oncoming traffic bore down on her. A bus honked and braked but she remained in the lane, hands gripping the wheel, her foot pressed down. Pedestrians noticed. Pointed. This would end the ambition, its persistent need to be fed. It would end the list. It would save her from finding out *what ever happened to Freddy Vaux?*

To her left, driving in the other direction, a man gaped at her. She felt Vanessa in her passenger seat telling her to *remember the little Os where their mouths should be. The shock, the horror, the confusion, that you, Freddy Vaux, are driving past them.* Vanessa, who had died in the most gruesomely stupid way. Her life half-spent, the rest of her rattling around in Freddy like spare change.

In a shock of embarrassment, she pulled back into the correct lane, with ragged and wavering breaths. She continued pulling over, into a layby, where she bent over the steering wheel, her forehead on the leather, hands clamped around it to keep from shaking.

Don't stop for anyone, Vanessa had said. *Don't stop.* She missed her so much – the wit and plunge of her comments, and how they made more sense as time passed.

So this is what it feels like at rock bottom, Freddy thought with a strange sense of relief. There were fewer shadows than she had anticipated.

Questions about the future crowded her mind, swelling the cool foolishness that she had almost never found out any of their answers.

For another hour, she drove the streets, the wheel smooth under her hands, the world slipping away. People: blurred. Shop fronts: blurred. Terraces: blurred. Only the drum of the engine, the pedals, the gears, the slick mechanical complexity working for her, more familiar than her own muscles.

When she returned to Sandal Road and parked down the street, a pain seared her stomach – and then another, before she could recover. Something gushed between her legs. She bundled herself out of the car and saw, on the driver's seat, a dark red splotch.

Despite all the crashes, the slams against the cockpit, the near-deaths of rallying, the closest she had ever come to death – or at least the feeling of it – was miscarriage. Her stomach seemed to fall out, her body weight jostled loose into the toilet. It went on for hours, enough time to knot herself into what she hated to admit was fear. It came with ecstasy and a terrifying, unexpected sadness. All mixed in with the horror that she wouldn't survive it (her mother had described miscarriages in mythological, deathly terms).

She was still on the bathroom floor later that evening, curled into a tight ball as waves of pain rolled through her stomach. As each one grew, she braced herself for it to pass. Someone knocked on the door, but she was in the throes of agony, clenching into herself.

'Fred?' Hadley's voice. She wasn't supposed to be back until late tonight. Recently, she had been paying some of her own visits to the phone box, often waiting for Freddy to return before rushing out the door with her newly drawn-up lists of press contacts and publisher friends; avenues through which she could get her writing out into the world – and herself with it. There was always some dinner these days, some interested party, some old friend.

'Fred, Debbie with the bald patch told me.' *Of course she had* was Freddy's first thought. There was no privacy in Sandal Road. She corrected herself, though, and made a mental note to thank Debbie when this was over. The thought of *this* being over kept her able to withstand it.

She reached up and unlocked the door, pulled on the handle. Hadley melted into the bathroom and curled up next to her in unusual silence. Unprompted, Freddy started to cry. Sobs taking over her. Sobs so thick that she couldn't see out the other side of them.

'I don't understand,' she murmured to Hadley, when she found a break in them. 'I thought… I *wanted* this. I mean, I *didn't* want this.' She paused. 'Did I?'

'I don't know the answer to that, Fred.'

Freddy tried not to think of the baby that might have been, but it was difficult, with blood splattered on her legs. It seemed irrelevant whether she wanted it or not, but the sadness was unavoidable.

'You should go to the hospital,' Hadley whispered.

'No,' Freddy shook her head. 'I'm fine.'

'You're not fine. You don't have to be fine with this, if…'

'I know that, but I don't want this to be remembered. At all. I don't want a record of it, and I never want him to know… or my brothers, or my father. None of them. It dies in this bathroom, and no one ever speaks about it.'

Hadley continued nodding. Freddy wasn't used to being this firm with people.

'At least you don't have to worry about the list anymore. Think of some other girl who gets to climb a place now.'

'I'm glad I could do her the favour. Even though I don't feel particularly generous right now—' Another wave cut her off. Hadley held Freddy's hand, tighter than ever before, and Freddy let her. They stayed like that for a long time, until the pain started to dull, each wave less intense. After a while, it felt less like weathering a storm and more like sailing through it to the other side.

She knew it was time to leave Sandal Road when the competition manager asked for her address and she gave them Eric's flat. Her indecisiveness about whether to accept the strings-attached offer had vanished after that night spent on the bathroom floor with Hadley. Rock-bottom provided an interesting perspective, and she was no longer weary of the publicity manager, the contracts, the caveats. Instead of suffering three lunch courses of negotiation and unpleasant chatter with her new competition manager, she had reached out to shake his hand before the starters had even been served. And now the contract would be waiting for her signature in Eric's flat on the other side of London.

Around three months since she had first arrived, she stood on the pavement looking up at that orderly terrace front. There was a strength, a maturity, in knowing what lived behind it – the pain, the smells, the noises. A naivety had been stolen from her.

Behind those walls, the house was still cruddy, downright awful, nothing short of a total mess. But she had grown to think of life inside as the mess underneath a scab. An intricate network of healing cells and blood vessels and new tissue, shielded from the dirty air. It could be ugly and complicated, but it was vital. She had noticed how women looked after children not their own; how some of them spent their time making cushions and quilts and knot-rugs that punctuated the space with spots of colour; how they cooked and ate and washed and dried in harmony. Helping each other forwards in a hundred different, small ways.

She walked to the telephone box where she had organized her future and made one final call.

'Tomorrow, Eric, I'm moving in,' she told him.

'I'll leave the key with the neighbour.'

'Soon I'll be able to get my own place, this is only for a few weeks, and I can repay—'

'Fred, it's fine. Shall we meet for dinner, once you're settled? Or tea?'

'Alright then.'

'Good. I have something to tell you, that I didn't want to over the phone. And we need to discuss the divorce. I have a list of lawyers, like you said, and I broke the news to Father. He took it remarkably well.'

'Well, he never did like Vernon.' She back-pedalled: 'What is it you need to tell me? I've had enough surprises recently. You can just tell me now.'

'I'm not…'

'Eric, tell me.'

'It's about Verne…'

'Tell me.'

'He's left the country.'

'Where's he gone?'

'The south of France. His uncle has a house there. I believe there's a woman involved.' She appreciated his academic instinct to compress information into short, teachable sentences.

'A woman?' Her heart lifted and dropped at the same time.

'It's the best news for a divorce. Unfaithfulness helps your case.'

'Who is she?'

'An old flame, someone from the social club circles.'

Before she could understand why, tears sprang to her eyes.

'I'm sorry, Fred, I really am, it's a horrid thing for him to do.'

The tears were not for her, but for this other woman. It was concern spreading through Freddy. She had never considered that someone else might have to endure what she had. There was no way to explain this to her brother, who had gone quiet on the other end.

'I'll see you next week. Let's go out. Let's have a good time.'

'I'll make some reservations,' he said.

'All the old haunts. Let's live, Eric.'

'Thank you,' she said to Hadley on the doorstep the following morning. Snow had fallen in the night, spread like thin felt on the pavement. It was thick enough for her to leave footprints. Hadley remained on the covered step.

'All you've done since you arrived is thank me. I'd hate to think that all I've done for you is some favours.'

'No, that's not what I—'

'I know,' Hadley rolled her eyes. 'You're welcome, Fred.'

'After what happened, I didn't even know how to keep breathing.'

'What happened to you should never happen to anyone, and it would be *awful* to suggest that this has made you stronger… *but* it has made you bloody hardy.'

Hadley opened her arms and embraced her. Freddy, after a moment, embraced in return. She knew that she wasn't fully healed, that she might never be fully healed, that fully healed wasn't necessarily possible – but she did know that the wounds were now bright burning fires, and Sandal Road and its residents had helped to light them.

'I'm proud of you,' Hadley continued, tears slipping down her cheeks: the first Freddy had ever seen fall from those eyes that had met her on this doorstep weeks ago. 'The highs are still to come, you know that, right? You are *phenomenal*, Freddy… my *friend* Freddy.'

'It's down to you,' Freddy replied. 'And Pat and Debbie and Nora and Ellie… all of them. I wouldn't be here without you.'

'Now, stop crying,' she smiled, wiping Freddy's tears away while Freddy wiped away Hadley's. 'Go on. If you ever need me, then I'm here.'

'I know.'

'Maybe not in this dump, but I'm here for you.'

'And if there's anything *I* can do for you, just say. I'm not sure what that might be, but you have the number of Eric's flat. Call it.'

'I will.'

Freddy wanted to tell Hadley that it was alright for her to leave Sandal Road. That she no longer needed to drown under her role as founder and carer or punish herself for what happened to Isabel or any of the other women. She was allowed her own life as well, and others would carry on what she had started. But she had a feeling that Hadley knew all this already. Something more inexact than advice had passed between them during their time in this house. The soft hum of sorority, as simple as unringed fingers.

'I'll stay in touch, I promise,' Freddy said.

'And, don't forget, I have press—'

'Press contacts, yes I know,' Freddy completed for her. It was something Hadley had mentioned repeatedly since she told her about the caveats in the contract. She knew the sympathetic reporters *who won't use the words 'bombshell' or 'bimbo'* – television, radio, newspapers, *the works. I'm a friend with friends in high places*, she'd said, meaning the murkiest corners of journalism.

'Drive safe,' Hadley patted her on the shoulder. 'Or don't. I'm not quite sure what to say to Freddy who races cars.'

Freddy thanked her friend one more time before turning to the car. When she started the engine, Hadley had already returned inside and closed the door, restoring the line of terraces to its unruffled anonymity.

12. Monaco Grand Prix

Summer 1951 – 18 months later

For a woman who wanted to spend her life racing, Freddy hadn't spent much of her life doing that at all. In fact, she still wasn't. She was hiding in the bathroom of her hotel lobby, breathing into marble. Deep gushes, in and out, as if the slabs were paper bags.

Knocks started on the door.

'Freddy? You in there?'

Rich knew she was in here, so he was only asking for show. His tone was for show. He was a man all about show. He continued:

'Fred, the BBC want to get a comment and a shot of you before you roll out for qualifying. I need you to get out here, put that helmet on your pretty head and give them a smile. Please.' The please an afterthought.

She kept her forehead pressed to the cool stone, sweat seeping through her race suit.

'Is there something I can do to make you come out of there with a smile on your face?'

She lifted herself off the wall, careful not to topple and pass out.

'There was someone in the lobby who caught me off guard,' she said.

He calculated his response. 'Can I do something about him?' And from that *him*, it was clear he knew whom she was talking about.

'I don't want him anywhere near me.'

'When I walked through, just a minute ago, I didn't see… who I think you're talking about.'

'Are you saying I imagined—'

'No, of course not.'

She walked towards the sink, and the mirror that hung above it. Her blonde hair – a dirtier kind now – was longer than she'd ever worn it before, almost to her shoulders. It was tousled in a way that looked careless. The finest wrinkles had bloomed on her forehead and around the corners of her mouth. Her face was no longer that plain white sheet she had looked at in the club's bathroom on Victory Day. The eyes were the same. They had seen more, known more, but they were the same eyes connected to the same mind and body – which wanted one thing. And he wouldn't stand in her way. Not when she had come this far. *You're on a trajectory to be great*, one of the reporters had said to her that morning, and it was true. She was travelling at a momentum, on a curve, that had taken time and patience to coax into being.

'Please, Fred. We don't have all day. I promise, he's not in the lobby anymore. Please come out.' Her job on the line, but his too.

'We both know that no one's interested in what I have to say.'

'Well…'

'It's true. No one would give a sod about me if I wasn't—'

'We've been over this, Freddy.' He paused; someone passing, perhaps. He was beginning to feel foolish having a conversation with a door. 'Besides, you're about to become the first woman to qualify for the Monaco Grand Prix. The first woman to qualify for *any* Grand Prix.'

'*If* I qualify.'

'You know what I say about the word "if".'

She shook her head, moved away from the mirror.

'And what's that, Rich?'

She opened the door and looked at him.

'That it's a waste of bloody time.'

Since she met Rich, she had been under no pretences that he was a good man. Rooms hated when he walked into them, people turning quiet, flicking their eyes at each other as he barked and spread his cynicism like paisley on carpet; no one would be safe or left unscrutinized – down to the very freckle and stray hair – until he left again. That's not to say that the room wasn't better off after he entered it. No one wanted him – but he was good for them.

For the most part, because of his talent. He knew the public better than he knew his own relatives. Rich had, he explained to Freddy, never wanted to be in publicity – he had begun his career as an actor, only to be booed off the stage for being too rotund a Hamlet to fit on the throne. After which, he began to understand that the reason he wanted to act was the phenomenon of audiences; how they *ooh*ed and *aah*ed and wept and whispered to one another. The fantasy of controlling them. He spoke about that fantasy almost as much as he spoke about the roulette wheel of his childhood – mother, father, uncle, grandmother, who would take him for Christmas this year? It had made him inventive when it came to drawing attention. There had been a need for his inventiveness during the war, and the Ministry of Information hired him to run anti-gossip campaigns that made even those with nothing to hide feel guilty. His was a career built on caring deeply about what people thought. He told the public what they were seeing, and what they were thinking, and he was as sensitive as a nail about it, something Freddy had learned in their first meeting.

A week after she had signed with Mackenzie – her new team – she was given the address of Rich's office. Freddy had never heard of drivers having publicists and managers independent of the team – but her case was unusual. Desperate times, and all that.

In the shabby reception, an assistant showed her to a leather armchair. Magazine covers sprayed the walls: racing drivers with trophies, smiling, some dead, some alive. Old smoke clung to the yellow walls, overflowing ashtrays on little tables.

'He's dead. *Dead?*' Rich's voice on the phone, piercing through the door. 'A racing accident? Just him, no spectators in the line of fire? Yes? Oh, that's *fantastic* news. He's far more use to us dead than alive after his turn this season. I want an obituary in *The Times*. I want a campaign on track safety. I want the funeral to be spectacular. Trust me, the family will thank me when he's remembered as a legend of motorsport.' He hung up.

She had been hoping to hate him. It would make what was to come, the endless *she's a woman who drives!* campaign so much more bearable if she hated the man behind it. He opened the door, saw her, and peered around the room.

She stood and held out a hand.

Dark stubble, rings under his eyes, shirt bulging around the paunch at his stomach – he spent so much time caring what others thought about his clients that he seemed to have forgotten what people thought about him.

'I believe you're looking for me.'

'No, dear, I'm looking for a Freddy Vaux.'

'That's me.'

He looked down at a piece of paper in his hand, surprise lighting up his face.

'Ah, *Miss* Vaux. When they said racing driver, I expected…'

'I know.'

'How delightful. Then that's how the campaign shall begin.'

'Who died?' She nodded to the room, the phone on his desk. Realizing he'd been heard, his face flushed.

'An old client.'

'Was he old, or was it just a client who is no longer your client now that he's dead?'

'The first one. And the second, I suppose.' She had a feeling that it was rare for a person to have the edge on him. But he seemed to be enjoying it. Finally, someone on his level.

Despite her intentions, she liked him, his intense brutality, his intolerance for nonsense. When he called her a bimbo, she called him an idiot. Plus, she was always *Miss Vaux* to him. There were enough 'good' men in the world that she had discovered were not. It was nice to know that there were some who never tried to put on appearances and leave her with a nasty surprise. Both of them, then, were under no false pretences that he was a good man.

Which made his flashes of goodness, rare and fleeting as they were, all the more welcome. He was in the midst of one of them as he led her out of the lobby of Monte Carlo's Hôtel de Paris. She fixed her eyes on her helmet, which he carried, forcing herself to focus on the race. Rich's neck was a spool of rubber, turning his head around the entire lobby to make sure *he* was gone: her husband.

'Either he's left, or he was never here at all,' Rich mumbled.

'He was here,' Freddy snapped back. 'He knew I'd be here, and I suppose he came to gloat.'

She had been due to meet Rich in the lobby nearly half an hour ago, but when the elevator *ding*-ed and delivered her into the bustling space she saw her husband's dark slick of hair in the middle of the crowd. He was waiting for her, hands in his pockets, leaning against the bar, as though he was meeting a friend for their weekly drinks. With dreadful vision, she had almost known he would be here. She could sense him before he arrived, and in the dregs he left behind him. She hadn't been this near to him since Oxford.

Of course, he had never failed to make his presence felt. Even though she had left Sandal Road, moved into her own flat after a couple months at Eric's, and scorched into a successful career, he remained – from his new residence in the south of France – a persistent blight. She called divorce lawyers only to find that he had called them first. When she made cases against him, he professed innocence and love, claiming that the stress of racing had warped her brain; he wasn't having an affair; he had escaped her clutches and fled for fear that she would pummel him. A basket of lies they took to picnic.

With Eric's help, she had eventually found a lawyer uncorrupted by Verne. Either her husband had run out of effort, or he had simply never got to this one yet. But she set the process in motion, took it as far as she could without his cooperation, and had the papers sent to his address with her signature spread all over them. All he had to do was sign, she explained in the accompanying letter. By signing, he also admitted to the cruelty that she had meticulously detailed in documents presented to the court – law changes in her lifetime had extended the grounds for divorce beyond adultery, if it could be proven.

But she never received a response, nor any signed papers. A court date came and went, and he never appeared. She had to conclude that, while he had no interest in winning her back (his sudden flight to the continent with his new lover was more than a temporary arrangement), he couldn't divorce her, because then he'd not only be a man that lied about shooting down fourteen Germans but a man who had failed at marriage. He was determined – as Eric had told her – not to let that man come into being. He would do everything in his power to make sure that the divorce would never go through. And all he had to do was disappear.

At least until he felt like confronting her about it, far from the courts and the lawyers' offices. On her turf, where it would hurt most.

'Don't think about that now,' Rich said, reading her mind. 'You've got a qualifying to get to. Interviews to give. We can manage that later.'

She nodded, and as the two spilled out onto the bone-white hotel steps a crowd waited for her. Her crowd. She wouldn't have believed it if not for their chanting: *Freddy, Freddy, Freddy*. One held a cardboard sign that read *Woman on Wheels*, and another: *The she-devil speed-devil.* They never failed to tread the line between flattering and insulting – a line Rich loved to toe.

But she had to thank him for it. As much as she chafed at that *only woman on the track* label, as much as she felt the growing pressure to advocate for women in motorsport, and as much as she had barked in Rich's face that *equality is not having to act differently*, she owed him. He had made her the *rising star* of motor racing when she was neither a *star* (had never won a major championship race) nor *rising* (hers was more a jagged series of rises and falls). He had made her career – made it not exactly what she imagined, but made it into something. Something that might even be a beginning for other women, she thought, when things were going particularly well. He had saved her, and her dreams – which had changed since her stint in Sandal Road. If she had to suffer the chanting and the signs and interviews, then she would. If it was what she had to do to keep herself on the track, for herself, for others, then she could grin and bear it.

This furore around her addition to the starting grid also alienated her competitors. When she first walked into the pit lane, she had been surprised by their initial acceptance of her. She had expected a legion of Bobs making jokes and vulgar remarks, and there were a few who felt it necessary to get these comments out of their system. But she soon realized that it was only the smaller men at those lower levels of racing who cared about the gender of the person beating them. The men racing in the championship had other concerns, their confidence was harder to dent, and most treated her with respect – congratulating her for her toughness, for making it in the sport, for her courage in the car. Not in any condescending way, and not because she was a woman. But since this *Woman on Wheels* circus had struck up, they kept their weary distance. She couldn't blame them.

As she pushed through the crowd, she saw his handsome face bob above the lagoon of heads, wearing the same sunglasses that he had worn on their honeymoon. Between the chanters, Verne. He was always stewing somewhere in her success. It was almost as though he could sense when she had forgotten him.

Rich saw him too this time. He guided her by the elbow around the corner and into the drivers-only area. Engines puttering in the minutes before qualifying, mechanics shouting at each other in Italian, French, Dutch. Smoke hissing on her left, two drivers in an argument on her right. Rich pierced through it like a needle, while she lagged, glancing behind them.

'He didn't make it into the area. It's fine,' Rich said.

They paused, and Freddy couldn't look up from the cobblestones.

'Why are *all* their floors white?' she asked, pointing to it. She could see Rich stare at her trembling hands. 'Do they not know we're here to *stand* on them? What happens if someone bleeds on these, huh? You'd never get it out.'

'Fred,' Rich held her shoulders. 'I need you to stay calm. He's here, but he's not getting through. I'm here. There are lots of others around. Besides, he's just a man.'

She looked up at him.

'That's precisely the thing to be afraid of.'

In their periphery, two reporters with microphones, notepads and a video camera approached.

'Bugger, the BBC. Like hounds in the night,' Rich muttered. 'Can you keep your wits about you for a few more minutes, before qualifying? Please?' They had come far enough in their relationship to demand favours like this. She nodded.

'Just pretend he's not here. For the next few minutes, he's not.'

'Who's not here?' the journalist asked, his pen poised over the pad.

'Oh, a colleague of mine, should be on his way,' Rich responded quickly.

The journalist seemed satisfied with this answer; he didn't write it down. The two of them were in tweeds too heavy for the hot and blue-skied Monte Carlo weather.

'Miss Vaux, how does it feel to be on the brink of qualifying for your first Grand Prix?'

She cleared her throat and adopted the voice that she and Rich had chosen for her interviews: high-pitched, sweet, breathy.

'It's exciting to be here. Monaco is a very special country. It's one of the greatest tracks to race. I've never raced a Grand Prix at this track, only the rallies for the Coupe des Dames.'

'Do you feel left out among all these chaps? Does anyone ever ask you what you're doing here?' A laugh on his lips, but she responded sincerely.

'Of course, all the time.'

He nodded, swallowing. 'Yes, and is that hard for you?'

'Very much so. I wish there were some other girls here to keep me company. Perhaps one day there will be.' Instead of the fake smiles and lines about helmet hair and face masks, this honesty felt more purposeful. She had ceased pretending.

'And why do you do it, Miss Vaux? What do you enjoy most about racing?'

'When I get in that car, almost everything else disappears.' *Your Grace Kelly smile*, Rich had said.

She caught sight of the dark slick of hair above the tents. The reporter took a new line:

'Miss Vaux, do you have any comment on the allegations about Will Truston, your former manager?'

'Do I *what*?' The mention of Will's name shocked her. She had seen him a handful of times since emerging from Sandal Road, since his return from Europe, but his presence in her life had dwindled. Stuck on the future, Freddy was hesitant to tell him about what had happened in Oxford and a slight coldness had elbowed into their friendship with this new secret.

'Miss Vaux?' Behind the camera, Rich shook his head *no.* The reporter looked up at her, eyes ready to drink in her words, the camera lens gaping. Looking between both heads, all she could focus on was Verne. Watching his every move.

'The allegations about Will Truston… that he was arrested for *indecency*.'

'*Indecency*,' she repeated.

'Yes, Miss Vaux. Do you have a comment on the allegations?'

The dark slick was moving towards her, she was sure. Her mouth moved of its own will.

'Well, if you call *that* indecent, then…'

'Call what indecent? Miss, do you not deny the allegations against Will Truston?'

'No, I…'

'There has been speculation about his—'

'Right.' Rich grabbed onto her arm and looped her towards the Mackenzie tent. 'Video only from now on, boys. Just a shot of Freddy getting into her car, her final chats and preparations with the mechanics, and then she pulls out and heads off.'

'But she won't deny his… she *admits…*'

'Those comments are not to see the light of day,' Rich growled. Which, of course, meant that they would see the brightest daylight the reporter could find. Freddy walked towards the car, leaned against it. She wanted to be out of here, when all she had wanted was to be here. With her mind all wrapped around itself, she realized – far too late – what she had done to her friend. A few thoughtless words and she had ruined him.

The cruellest thing about racing, Freddy thought, was that even once she had secured sponsorship, secured a car, trained and tested it for over a year, boosted herself into some press-digestible personality, transported the car to Monaco, memorized the circuit and practised it countless times, she still had to qualify if she wanted to race. Which meant driving the car around the specific circuit in a specific time with a specific gap to the leader to secure her spot on the starting grid for the following day.

She already knew that spot wouldn't be in the top five. The race officials penalized those who failed to get their cars ready for the practice sessions by restricting the top five positions to drivers who had been in attendance for all of them – and with her media commitments, her close encounter with Verne, and the fact that her car was one of the worst, she had only attended two out of four.

Of the thirty cars in Monaco, it was common knowledge that half of them wouldn't qualify. Not all 2.5-litres were fast enough to hit that one-minute-forty-second time for the lap. In a less-than-perfect car, she had to complete the lap perfectly for even a chance at a spot; the others, in their beastly Ferraris and Maseratis, could walk to a front-row start with half the effort she put in. Facts like that spoiled the myth of fairness she liked to believe. Racing was both surprising and devastatingly predictable.

These were the facts that she tried not to think about as she gave a thumbs-up to her mechanics, started her engine and rolled into the pit lane. She tried not to think of Verne, what she had said about Will, what allegations the reporter had been referring to, and what, most importantly, would happen to Will now. She could do nothing about these things while strapped into the driver's seat. Usually, her efforts not to think were successful, so it worried her that her foot slipped on the brake pedal and her helmet seemed to crush her head; and it worried her that she was worried. She had got over all that, hadn't she? *When I get in that car, almost everything else disappears*, she had said to the reporter moments ago.

The noise of a backfiring engine drew her attention, and she snapped her head towards it.

Yves Le Brocq wheeled past her, in what was possibly the worst open-wheeled car she had ever seen. Its side panels were bulged and bulky, the nose too long, the wheels too large; it was the overstuffed armchair of racing cars.

'I've missed you on the track,' he shouted. 'Where have you been? Did they lock you in a cupboard somewhere?'

'Something like that. Mackenzie are committed to my *image*,' she replied over the noise of rousing engines.

'Of course, the *lady* driver,' he said it mockingly, but not as though she was the one being mocked. He had one arm over the edge of the driver's cockpit, one on the wheel, and he leaned back as though he was taking his convertible for a drive through the countryside. Yves was a man, she understood, who had nothing to lose; he'd already *had* it all, and he had thrown it away: Ferrari, championships, women. He had worn them like outfits and then, bored, moved on. He had poured endless money into a car manufacturer under his name – Le Brocq Motors – which created hideous cars, and then drove those hideous cars at tracks that cost a fortune to enter. A flippancy she could only dream of. A contradiction that, strangely, attracted her.

'My image, you know, is something I'm keen to cultivate also,' Yves said, gesturing to the right side of his face, which was pocked with scars. Half his right ear was missing – *attached to an olive tree somewhere in the outskirts of Catania*, she had overheard him saying. He was battered, bruised – but not ugly.

And certainly not what she should have on her mind, Freddy told herself, as she notched her car forwards to keep up with his. They moved through the narrow lane, soon funnelling onto the starting grid where they would queue and wait to begin the hour-long session to determine their places for tomorrow's race. Her heart had rocketed up to its usual pre-race pace. She busied her mind with images of the racing line.

*

But as she accelerated down the straight towards the harsh Sainte Dévote corner, as she tried to focus on the plan for the lap, Verne kept butting into her thoughts. Mid-turn, she was seized with an electric disgust at herself. This was her first Grand Prix, and he had stamped his footprint all over it.

Accelerating once again, she started scaling the uphill straight of Beau Rivage. The air was stuffed with a thick, clammy marine fog that was waiting to burn off. There was so much moisture in the air. Her hands were wet with it. All the blood seemed to be crowding to her heart.

She scooped around the Massenet bend up to the Casino, picked her way around the Station Hairpin, before a clean squeeze through the Tunnel – all to prove him wrong. When she had finished the first lap, her crew marked down the time and held out the placard over the barriers. It was thirteen seconds off the pace. She took a deep breath. It was an opener. A first attempt. She had an hour to get it right. But she now needed an out lap; three minutes of slow crawl around the outside. Then, she had to do it again, and she had to do it perfectly. Mackenzie's car was lumpy, nothing like her Puck. She had asked for it to be modified for her, but they refused: *This is how others drive it, you'll drive it that way.* If only they treated her like everyone else in all the other aspects of her contract.

On her second attempt to hit the qualifying time, she tried to think of everything but Verne. It worked better, and she took the first corner with confidence, her lungs more open than before. She fixed her eyes on the next bend and visualized how early she would nudge the car over to the inside line, her hand already on the gearstick ready to ratchet down the gears, and then up them again. Already, she huffed with effort, her body training every muscle to grapple the machine around the twisted track. It was a delicious tired, and she swelled into it. Her head filled with the smell of burned rubber and oil.

There were corners without crowds where the only sound was her engine, and she breathed in time with her gear switches. In the busier corners outside the casino and the marble-columned hotel where the crowd sat on terraces with spritzes, in white cotton shorts and sockless feet in boat shoes, everything simply faded.

The corners had begun to open themselves up to her, show their weak spots and where to place the car. Her hands were sweating, the goggles clammed onto her face. As she approached Tabac corner, spectators packed up against the balustrade, dark heads of gelled hair, the sun glinted off a slick of oil on the track – and before her hands could even counter the skid, she knew she would crash.

What she didn't account for was that Yves Le Brocq would be so close behind her, almost on her tail – and when she headbutted the wall, the nose of her car scrunching up like a paper ball, he drove over her. His wheel kissing her ear. Another car behind him added to the growing pile-up – and then another, and another.

Freddy felt the thuds of them as she hung limp in her seatbelt, white-backed bugs scrabbling across her vision. Above her eyebrow and along the top of her head, the pain was intense. When she tried to lift her hand up to feel her cracked helmet, it remained numb at her side, the wrist dangling in her lap.

She had to get out of that car. Her senses both dulled and heightened, she heard huge dollopy drips of fuel smacking onto the road underneath; distant seagull cries and engine shrieks; a near hissing; tyre squeals. More fuel on her face – or was that just sweat? Her heart – was it beating too fast for her to hear it or had it stopped? There was pain, but it was a distant call; she chose not to answer it. Instead, she pulled her legs free from the crushed nose and up to the seat. With her good arm, she helped herself out of the cockpit and slumped onto the track.

The first piece of safety advice she had ever received was: if you crash, never take off your helmet. But it was compressing her head; she could almost hear her skull splintering under the pressure, and with two hands she pulled it off and threw it to the side. She slid down further until she lay on her back, flat on the track. A brief blue pinhole in the clouds appeared above her. Until a body blocked it, and a hand from that body reached out towards her.

'You shouldn't take off your helmet,' Yves murmured. She was filled by an intense and misplaced envy that he had walked from his car unscathed and now stood above her, offering help.

She swatted his hand away with her tender wrist. The spike of pain forced her to roll to the side, folding the arm into her chest. Yves lowered his face near to hers. It was the closest she had ever been to him, the dark luggage under his eyes, the nicks on his face.

'It looks broken,' he said, gently lifting her wrist, weighing it in his hands.

She snatched it back and lugged herself to her feet. Blinking through what she suspected was blood, she lifted her eyes. The audience stared down at her, hands on their mouths, elbows on the white balustrades. French, Italian, English, all talking about her. *The woman who crashes.* Leaning over the balcony and looking onto the harbour road where her car smoked in a twisted heap of metal.

There it was, unmistakeable: the face of her husband, creased in concern. The past eighteen months, all her efforts at distance, collapsed.

She forced her eyes to skim over him. The last thing she needed was for him to know she was aware of his presence. Instead, she looked around her at the drivers unspooling themselves from wrecked vehicles that spilled smoke and oil onto the track. The sight was almost apocalyptic, broken souls falling out of broken bodies. She counted seven of them.

'You nearly killed me,' she shouted at Yves, who was helping another driver out of his car. Tears had begun and she scrubbed at them. *Not here, not now.* If they needed more excuses to ban her from the sport, then she was giving them plenty. 'I nearly got your tyre tracks tattooed onto my cheek.'

'How was I supposed to stop?' When he knew the other driver was alright, Yves left him leaning against his car. Soon, other help would crowd in. Ambulances and race stewards would rush towards them, even spectators would pour onto the track. But for now, it was them alone.

'Last time I checked, cars have brakes.'

'I have them, and I pressed them, but I can't change the laws of physics.'

'I thought you could do everything, Yves Le bloody Brocq.'

'Don't make a scene.' His cheeks had begun to redden. She had drawn him into it now. 'Don't be hysterical. Why can't you just *drive*, without all the theatrics, huh?'

Why *couldn't* she just drive? If only it was that simple. It was the question she had been asking herself since she had first sat behind a wheel.

'That was *unavoidable* and you know it!' She pointed to the splat of oil on the ground. 'You would have hit it and spun, like I did.'

She turned her back to Yves, looking for breaths her body didn't want to give her. Her eyes drifted up to the audience. Vernon was talking to a man on his right, probably a fellow spectator. But then her husband turned towards the track again, his face scrunched tight – no longer in concern, but something else.

Jealousy.

Could it really be? That of all the things he could choose to be in this terrifying moment, her husband had chosen to be *jealous* of Yves. Both for being the one to touch her and be there when she needed him – and the one to rile her up. What was he thinking? That only *he* had the right to make his wife that angry? She hated herself for the petty thoughts barging into her head. Her husband problem spilling onto the track like a rogue patch of oil. Vernon had miscalculated one thing, however. Out of the two of them, *she* had the power at this track, and he was going to have to watch her take it.

She swivelled, walked towards Yves and shoved him. Yelling at him again, asking him why – *how* – he could be so careless with their lives. In the middle of her assault on him, Yves' eyes flicked behind her towards the audience. Did he know who was up there? Who was watching this?

Whether he knew or not, Yves played into her hands. Rage was his natural state – where he felt most comfortable, most himself. The smallest hint of a smile played at the corner of his lips.

'You go too fast,' he shouted back, his accent becoming stronger.

'Someone told me that before.'

'Maybe they were right. Maybe you should have listened to them. You won't survive in Formula One with that attitude.'

'You won't survive in Formula One with that car.'

He walked past her, colliding with her shoulder as he did; stocky, well built, he almost knocked her off her feet. When she stumbled, he turned back to catch her and remained holding onto her shoulder, his concerned face close. Their lips level.

Eventually, the stewards trickled in, the Monégasque men who urged her to lie on a stretcher and dabbed at her face with stinging alcohols and asked her how many fingers they were holding up. Three. She had never been more certain of anything in her life.

Six hours and one-and-a-half bottles of wine later, she had decided which write-up of the crash was the worst: the one in which she was the mother of Verne's non-existent children.

'*Mrs Winifred Dawson-Hayes*,' she read aloud to Rich, '*who is separated from her husband, must have put the fear of God into him, when he realized that the mother of his children was not only out on the track but sprawled on it*. I suppose the chap writing this rubbish would be relieved to know that neither Verne nor I have any children.' She sat cross-legged on the bed in her hotel room, the evening papers spread around her, and her arm bandaged and propped on a cushion. It was, to her relief, merely sprained. Rich lounged in an armchair next to the open balcony doors. The sky had cleared, and the remnants of a warm Mediterranean evening seeped in. She could see stars from the bed. The room, populated by hundreds of honeymooners over the years, was stale of love.

'I wonder if I have sons or daughters,' she said, tossing aside the newspaper to the stack on her left.

Rich mused: 'I can't tell whether it's bad reporting, bad manners or bad men.'

'How about all three?'

She had expected worse, considering the questions served to her in the lobby by rogue reporters. Some had asked whether it was the ongoing divorce case with her husband that had distracted her or Vernon's presence at the race messing with her racing line (how they knew he was there, she would never know). And what *was* her line anyway? Why had she been aiming so close to the apex of Tabac? One of the opinion pieces had suggested that she had been *in a state of hormonal flux*. 'I didn't crash because I was on my bloody period,' she'd said to Rich as she threw the newspaper at him.

Then there were those that brought Yves into the picture, suggesting – assuming – that his swaggering sexual energy had blown apart her braking pattern, that the whole crash had been an elaborate wooing ritual. 'If I want to get in Yves Le Brocq's underwear, there are easier ways,' she'd said. When Rich had drunk enough wine, he let slip what the commentators had said: this is what happens when a woman gets behind the wheel. Perhaps it had taught her a lesson. Not to stick her nose where it doesn't belong, stop meddling with a world that clearly wasn't hers. The

Monégasque track had shown her who should drive on it – and it wasn't her kind. Track, oil, tarmac and cement were not subtle teachers. They had given her a smack, like any good husband disciplining his wife.

Not one newspaper had thought to suggest there might be an oil patch on the track, or that it had been the one thing shared by all: a mistake. Women weren't allowed to make mistakes. There had to be a reason for her to fail.

Rich sloshed another gulp of wine into his mouth, wiping his lips with the back of his hand. He was the most unmarried man in the universe. And she had a feeling he'd like to keep it that way. When she was in the medical centre, he had spent the afternoon carrying out damage control: interviews with the press about her condition, manoeuvring reporters away from the car, telling Vernon in no uncertain terms to *fuck off.* He was tired from cleaning up her mess.

'Did you get through to Will?' she asked. With the last of the newspapers, she had run out of ways to distract herself from her other mistake of the day.

Rich shook his head, mid-swallow of wine. He gulped, opened his mouth to say something, then closed it again. He was not the sort of man to tell her that it would be fine.

'I'll try and get through to him tomorrow morning,' she said, not looking him in the eye. 'First thing.'

He nodded. 'There's nothing you can do about that right now. Focus on things that you *can* do something about.'

'Alright. What's going to happen with Mackenzie? When they find out I didn't qualify, I'll…' She trailed off, remembering Hollis, the empty garage, the pub, and where it had led her. And how long it had taken to climb back.

'There's four more races in the calendar. Belgium, France, Portugal, Italy.' He counted them on his fingers. 'That's four more chances. All you've got to do is qualify and complete a Grand Prix and that sets you in good stead for a position on the team next year.'

'I know, but do you believe me, when I say that it was a mistake?' she asked.

With his eyes closed, head leaned back against the wallpaper, he nodded.

'I didn't see it until it was too late, and then when I tried to avoid it, I couldn't. Maybe that means… I'm *not* good enough.'

'Fred, you wouldn't be here if you weren't good enough.'

'That's not what I mean.' These thoughts had been repeating themselves in her head as she had lain in the medical centre, and it felt good finally to confront them. 'I don't think I'll ever be *great*, Rich. I've not earned it, I've not worked for it. I've always been ambitious, but ambition only gets you so far. There's the hours, the encouragement, the… But if I had driven more, raced more, practised more, then I would have seen that oil patch *before* it was too late, and I would have qualified. I'd *be* there on the starting grid tomorrow, among the best in the world.' She expected Rich to dive in, but he was loopy on the wine, rolling his head on the wallpaper.

'I *did* want it. I wanted to be great, I wanted to win. But it's just not possible.' Into her mind came her father's face as he explained *the blunting* that afflicted her mother and her bitterness that came afterwards. Her mother's ambition had its wings clipped. The same was happening to hers.

'Even though I've made it here, and I'm proud of that, I think maybe this is all I can ask for, which seems unfair, doesn't it? I'm jealous of the men who can aspire to win, when really all I can aspire to do is race. And it would never be *just* racing. That would be all I've wanted to do, so it's not fair that it doesn't feel like enough. Because it has to be. Do you understand, Rich?'

He wasn't listening. She didn't mind. These revelations were mostly for her.

Wrapped up in them, she almost missed the shadow that scraped past the door of her hotel room. Feet shuffled down the carpet and paused. Her breath hitched in her throat and she remained still. The feet stayed put. Moved off and returned again. Then moved off, then returned. Most of her knew it wasn't Verne, it couldn't be, he didn't know the number of her hotel room – but after Oxford, when she had thought he would never do what he did to her, she questioned everything. She knew now that he was a man who would not only crush a spider but crush a career and think nothing of it. He would come to her hotel room. He would knock. He would play nice. He would ask her to drink with him.

She pushed herself off the bed and padded in bare feet to the door. There was breathing on the other side of the wood, when she pressed her ear to it. Were these his breaths? Rich let out a snore behind her.

She grabbed onto the handle, and pulled the door open.

Yves Le Brocq stood in the hallway, hand lifted to knock. In loose trousers, a cotton shirt, sandals. Untucked, ruffled, unlike Yves.

'Oh,' she let out.

'Oh?'

She spent a second torn between whether she hadn't wanted him to show up at her door or whether she hadn't *expected* him to.

'I came to see how you were,' he gestured to her arm.

'Not to apologize?'

'Forget it.' He shook his head and walked down the hall.

'Wait. Yves.'

He paused with his back to her, then turned.

'It's not broken,' she said.

'That's good.'

A pause opened up.

'Is that really all you came for?'

'I needed to ask you a question.'

'Yes?'

He hesitated, a slight smile on his face. 'It's something I can only ask you over a martini in the hotel bar.'

'Yves, I can't.'

'Why?'

Verne. She had opened the door expecting it to be him. He could be in the building. He could be in the bar. All the more reason, she thought, to go with Yves. But what would it look like if she was at the hotel bar with Yves? People would think of her as she had thought of Vanessa – on an extended tour of the drivers.

'Rich will kill me,' she whispered, looking back to the room.

'Who is Rich?'

'He's in charge of… what I look like to others, the press.'

'It's late. There's no press in the hotel.'

'There's always press somewhere.'

'I know how to hide from them. I have been in this business a long time.' He looked behind him at the noise of an opening door somewhere in the hotel – his attention was waning, her chance disappearing.

Prude, pregnant, married, modern. Where did Yves fit? His gleaming smile wouldn't even fit on a piece of paper, let alone in a tickbox – and in this hallway with its many doors, the categories overlapped and bled into one another, useless now that Yves was here outside her room at midnight. She'd always thought that one day these categories would explode into one another and die with their own fusion, but now it was here. If she wasn't married, or pregnant, a prude, or even modern, then she would have to be herself.

'Let's go,' she said – and fetched her purse from the room.

Yves, it turned out, knew nothing. He had no idea about the discrimination she had faced, no idea of what had happened between Verne and herself (his nose was clean from the gossip pages), no idea why her only option was to drive for the worst team on the grid (except his), or why she had paused so long before she agreed to a drink with him. She toyed with the idea of keeping him in his dark.

'Did you know that I'm the first woman to compete in a Formula One World Championship race?' she asked him over the second martini. 'That there's been more atomic bombs dropped than women to enter the championship.'

He squinted, sceptical.

'There's been none before?'

'Why would I lie?'

'Not lie, but perhaps you have it *wrong*.'

'Zero is an easy number to remember.'

'What I don't understand,' he continued, 'is why that matters so much to you.'

'But it is shocking, no?'

'Yes, but perhaps if you focused less on that and more on the racing then it wouldn't be the case.'

'Trust me, Yves, that's not why there are no women in cars.'

'Well, no, that's because…'

'Why?' She held an olive halfway to her mouth. He grinned and looked down at the bar. She had no money for these drinks and she had to assume that Yves was planning to pay for them. 'Tell me, why is that? I want to hear.'

'Women don't like cars.'

'How do you know that? Have you spoken to every woman in the world?'

'No, but it's…' He looked around the bar. She saw the thin patches of silver-grey on the side of his head, above where the cheeks were littered with scars and scrapes. It was past midnight and the pianist was surviving on fumes, his hands recycling the same tune at different octaves. The waiters polished the glasses with mindless stares. Only a few couples remained, dotted around. The romance of the evening had passed, leaving dined-at tables in its wake. Yves and Freddy were too late, behind it all. He pointed towards a woman on the other side of the bar. 'Take her.'

The woman had diamond earrings so large that Freddy could see the stretch in her lobe. She had on thick makeup, black-lidded eyes.

'That is a woman who is not a driver.'

The laugh that came out of Freddy's mouth caught her off guard; she hadn't given Yves permission to draw it out of her.

'One woman proves your point?'

'No, but—'

'I agree,' she cut in. 'But,' Freddy lifted her finger, 'she *could* have been. You're saying women are less interested in cars or motor racing, and you're right. But men are very rarely interested in dresses.'

He swallowed a gulp of martini with a pained look.

'What do you mean by that? I'm not…'

'And it makes sense, because boys are not told to wear dresses. Men are not encouraged to sew or knit or embroider, and so there are very few who do that. It is the same.'

'The same as…?'

She was surprised by his slowness, when it came to matters like these.

'You're supposed to be a *fast* driver. Keep up.'

'This is not a race.'

'I'm saying that if we aren't encouraged to drive and buy motorcycles and fix engines, then it makes sense that we don't. You make the rules and call them facts.'

'It can't be as easy as that.'

She let out a spiky laugh.

'No, of course not.'

'I don't appreciate your laughter.'

'I can tell.' She smiled. Ridiculing a man who was not dangerous to her – it was fun. 'No, it's so much more complicated. But exposure is necessary. *That* is when there will be the same number of women in this sport as men. When the same number are given the opportunity to choose.'

'But women are still less likely to be inclined than men. Besides...'

'Our physical characteristics?' Freddy challenged him.

'Yes.'

'What about them?' He had no defences against her arguments, because he had never heard them. 'I understand when it comes to women in a running race, but in the same car... what else could be more equal? We are as cunning and... scrap that, we shouldn't be *comparing* ourselves.'

She hadn't been this passionate since her discussions with Verne. Discussions that had ended with a kitchen full of smashed crockery and his fist knocking her to the ground. Yves' hand stayed by his side. Instead of anger, there was desire. Red, radiating desire.

'And this is what you were encouraged to do?' he asked. 'Drive and buy motorcycles and fix engines.'

She let him switch the conversation, which he knew he was losing; she had practice with back-and-forth conversations like this from her many evenings in Sandal Road.

'Not intentionally, but yes.'

'Not intentionally?'

'My father owned a car manufacturer, not a household name and only of passenger vehicles. If he had his way, then I would have never seen a car. But I demanded to drive. He taught me.' She found herself explaining her father's half-support for her, his inward rebelliousness but outward conformity. Like a chocolate truffle with acid inside. The words flowed out of her as her brain turned numb with vodka. 'When I knew the basics, I taught myself. I was inclined to it. Just as I was not so inclined to dresses. And diamond earrings.'

'If a man bought you diamond earrings, you would throw them in his face.' No one had ever looked at her more directly.

'A man has never bought me diamond earrings. I don't know what I'd do with them.'

As the night progressed, he wanted to know more. Ignorance was clearly not something he was often acquainted with, and she noticed the irritation in quirks of his face. She noticed them like tells in a tennis player's serve, and soon began to anticipate and predict his questions and how to answer them. He laughed in the pauses she left for him, and she laughed in the pauses he left too.

When she turned to her drink, and a curl of hair fell over her face, he brushed it back. She reached out and touched the chunky cross swinging at the open neck of his shirt. He became candid. She let him.

'Le Brocq Motors is not a viable company unless the car makes it out of qualifying. If not, our fuel sponsors will leave us.'

'But you have more than enough money to keep it going, no?'

'No, that's gone. Racing is not a lucrative sport, not if you're me.'

'What does that mean?'

'My temper drives people off. Ferrari has its influence everywhere, and while I used to win, while I won the championship for them, no one will sponsor me now.'

'Why not control it, then? The temper.'

'I…' He trailed off. The question had disturbed him. He travelled in circles of racing drivers – and racing drivers were men, and men didn't ask questions like that.

'You have no family money?' she saved him.

'Do I look like I have family money?'

'I always assumed, with a name like Le Brocq…'

'Then you assumed wrong. All my money is my own. My career is my own, and this temper is my own. At least, with this company, I can set my own rules. I can choose what car I race.'

'Even if it is the worst car on the grid.' It slipped out before she had a chance to catch it. She froze. To her surprise, though, he laughed.

'Not as bad as yours,' he gasped between laughs, and she did too. She looked to see if the other couples in the bar were watching them, but everyone had left. The piano was unattended, run dry. When she asked for another drink, the sole waiter informed her that the bar was closed. Hours had passed.

Yves insisted on a walk to the harbour. She played at hesitance for the appropriate amount of time before agreeing. She let him hold her hand. And drape his jacket around her shoulders, even though she could see his blue lips in the cold pre-dawn. She let him put his arm around her and tell her things about Monte Carlo she already knew. She let him tell her she was beautiful and then she let him believe no one had told her that before. All the while she let herself remember how she had walked similar paths on her honeymoon and how that had ended – and would end here, with Yves.

As the early morning dew passed over her, wet needles of mist on her cheeks, she told herself this couldn't be real. Surely, it was some ruse, some game between them – even if it did feel delightful. But what if it *was* real? That would make her… what would that make her? Falling for him? Caught up in these thoughts, she started to draw away from him until:

'Why do you race?' He tried to make it sound unrehearsed, as he looked out onto the flat bay. But he had asked it without prompting and left her ample gap to reply. He cared a great deal about her response – almost as if it would validate, or make way, for his own. He asked the question because he needed to talk about his own answer.

'Well, for me, it's never been only about the thrill, or the feeling. I adore those things, I do. Who wouldn't? But it's giving yourself up to the car and the track, escaping it all. I want to drive away from fear and pain and all of it, and it gives the illusion that I can do that, that I can outdrive it all. For a moment, I'm untouchable. I can be faster than whatever is following me.'

'You talk about driving as though you have a complicated relationship with it.'

'What driver doesn't?'

'You'd be surprised,' Yves scoffed. They had seated themselves on the harbour wall, the streets dead. The Tabac corner only up the harbour road from them, too close for comfort.

'There's the irony,' Freddy continued. 'Driving is caught up with all the things I'm trying to outdrive. I suppose the illusion remains, and perhaps for one split second it came true today, somewhere between my second and third qualifying lap, but it's a losing battle.'

She had never spoken these words aloud before, but now that she had, she felt the weight of them exit her chest. It was like swapping out two hearts for one.

'Why do *you* race?' Now was the chance for him to let her in.

'I race because if I don't then I might die, and I race because it might kill me.' He ploughed into the statements. 'This is not something I tell people. But you are not just people.'

'Yes?'

'At fifteen, my father died.' He looked out into the bay – not at her. 'He was a fisherman and another boat tore a hole in his. One day, he left early and never returned. It's an island near France, where I'm from. A British island, but my mother was French, so I was raised French. We were outsiders there.

'I felt very low, after he died. My mother was fragile, and I blamed her, because I felt fragile too, and I thought she must have infected me with it. I always thought that when someone died, it made you want to live more. But it only made me want to die with him. I couldn't leave my mother, not on that island by herself. So I found a compromise.'

Freddy went to look down, but decided against it. She didn't want him to feel ashamed.

'I realized that I could drive so fast that it felt like the edge of death,' he continued. 'It's unfortunate that the way I threw myself into it also meant I was incredibly good, and I was encouraged to continue. If only all these people around me knew why I was doing it. It is a bit like you, Freddy, the complications all tied up in racing. I know I should stop. I am beyond my best. But I always have to find a way to keep on racing, and if that's using every penny I have to build the worst car on the track, then I will do it. I have to. I am always angry at the world when it chooses to keep me alive for another race. I don't race to win. I race to die.'

'It's what keeps us going, but also what holds us back,' she said after a long time. They had come to this revelation together. 'The thing that lets us escape is the thing that traps us. It is tied up in a mess of our lives, but it *is* our lives.'

'You understand. I knew you would understand.'

When she let him kiss her, she let herself kiss him.

13. Belgian Grand Prix

She tried to avoid the topic of Verne as much as possible; Yves tried to discuss it as much as possible. Where was he? Who was he? What was happening with the divorce? She had been led to believe that love affairs existed in a realm far removed from the legal fictions and paperwork of marriage and divorce. She assumed that lovers typically didn't ask about husbands and children (*are there any?*). But her knowledge of affairs consisted of her mother's and little else.

A rather narrow pool on which to base her perceptions, she realized, when her affair with Yves developed in the weeks after Monaco. They spent two more days in the hotel – during which they watched the Grand Prix from the balcony, attended the dinner and shook hands with their competitors – as well as two nights, where they shared Yves' hotel room and she crept out early in the morning before Rich appeared at her door with a list of interviews for the day.

From observing her mother's efforts and the dramatized affairs in films, she had always thought that such a secret would consist of complex misdirections, staged scenarios and absurd lies, but she found this secret remarkably easy to keep. There was barely any keeping to it – no one asked, no one noticed. If she had been wanting to have some glamorous, illicit affair, then she would have been disappointed; there was no elaborate cover-up, no scandal. It was two adults sleeping in the same bed now and then.

And talking – about now, and about then.

'What about this Vernon?'

'You mean my husband?'

'I understand you're still married.'

'You *know* I am,' she said, mixed up in his sheets on their final night in Monaco.

'Why?'

She turned her head to look at him. 'I want to end it. I want to divorce. I have sent him *signed papers.* But it's not so easy. It's caught in limbo. And I don't have the money or the contacts to fight him.'

If she had been in a film, they wouldn't be talking about this in bed. But they had already done all they could as many times as they could do it in one night. This was all that was left.

'Could I help?' he asked.

She kissed him hard on the lips.

'No, but I appreciate the offer.'

'Could I not talk to him and… persuade him?'

She leaned up on her elbow. The thought of Yves confronting Verne sent quakes into her stomach.

'No. Please, no. He will be *encouraged*.'

'You're sure?'

'I'm sure.'

He patted her arm in resignation.

'Verne was here, during the qualifying. I haven't seen him since.'

She rarely let Yves win when it came to revealing information about her husband. Since Sandal Road, she had avoided sharing with anyone what Verne had done to her, how she had ended up in Sandal Road – or that she had ended up there at all. Out of shame, out of personal pride, or out of something else, she planned to keep it that way. But this night she was tired of holding things back from Yves.

'Here to talk?' Yves asked.

'I don't think so. Here to intimidate. Terrify. Make me change my mind. He's still convinced that I'll realize the error of my ways. Stop with the divorce and save him the embarrassment, protect the Dawson-Hayes name from the tabloids.'

'And does he?'

'Does he what?'

'Terrify you?'

She paused, considering the question. 'He didn't used to.'

'And now?'

'Yves, please. Stop. Let's not talk about this.' She leaned her head back on the pillow. 'Very little terrifies me… And that, I think, is the problem. A little fear could have made my life easier. I could have leaned into the blunting far easier.'

'What is this word, *blunting*?'

She smiled at Yves' crinkled forehead.

'It's nothing.'

'Because I don't understand?'

'You'll never understand.'

'I'll never…' He pretended to be angry, and tickled her – she let out a loud laugh, covered her mouth when she realized how late the hour was, but that pushed Yves onwards to make her laugh – and then moan – louder.

When the Mackenzie team packed up the following morning to drive the train of equipment and vehicles up to the Ardennes Forest for the race at Spa, she asked Yves when he planned to get there. He said he would arrive the day after her, but he had to attend to some business in Paris first. They would have three weeks to practise on the track and prepare for qualifying. Neither of them could afford to lose out on another race.

The Ardennes Forest may have led her further into the fairy tale of her affair with Yves. Trees thickened on the side of the road, and toadstools clustered in little red crowds near tree stumps; hills rolled one into another, cluttering the horizon with wild beauty. Rain showers dumped water on them, the water evaporated in sudden sunshine, more fell, and the push-pull left the air wet and humming. Black-barked hollows, time-loosening valleys, pots of gold and unmapped lands awaited her in northern Belgium.

She barely noticed the purple ring around Yves' eye when he arrived the following morning. *A friend, who is a terrible influence, and I were mixed up in a bar fight*, he explained as she kissed the bruises. Merely the most recent ones that he had collected in situations like this, she presumed.

Through a quilt of rain, she practised with Yves, taking turns timing the other's laps, advising each other on the racing line, when to brake for the corners, which gears to use, which tyre compounds. Mackenzie were not too impressed that she was training so closely with Le Brocq Motors – but she argued that taking advice from a two-time Monte Carlo Rally winner could do them no harm.

Rich, meanwhile, had returned to London to sort *an issue with another client*, and the outside world slipped away with his absence. In the evenings, she went with Yves to the local inns and sipped Belgian beer; the pubs where ivy hid brick, and they were the only ones who spoke their language.

When the morning of qualifying came, there was still no sightings of Verne. She had scoured the paddock and pit lane and stands and tents and bars, and couldn't find a trace of him. She was almost angrier than if he'd actually shown up – she had pierced her dreamy state to look for him, and it had been for no reason. He was not here.

It was only the worst, most paranoid and painfully narcissistic part of her that assumed Yves and his shiny black eye had something to do with this absence.

She went looking for Yves and found him with his car, tapping on the tyres and checking for pressure.

'What have you done?'

'Sorry?' he asked.

'My husband isn't here.'

'That's a good thing, no?' He straightened, and she loved that they were the same height; his scarred face level with hers.

'Yes, of course. But he's not here. It's suspicious.'

'Can't you be happy?' He threw the wrench to the floor.

The past three weeks had proved she could.

'Where did you really get that black eye?'

'I told you where I got this from. I told you the truth.'

'Was it the truth? Is it from him? Did you have something to do with the fact he's not here?'

'Don't be ridiculous. Why would you ask me that?'

'Don't answer a question with a question. Yves, look at me. Did you have something to do with it?'

'No,' he said, firmly. 'I listened to you. Don't talk to the bastard, you said, even though I'd like to do more than just talk with him. He's not here because he's a coward, he can't confront you. Not while I'm here. And I'm not going anywhere.'

He moved towards her, put his arms on her shoulders. She looked around, but no one took the faintest interest in them.

'Please, don't let it ruin our time here,' he said. Their gaze connected.

He was right. Why should she let it destroy her Arden? She had earned this, hadn't she? This was what the world was supposed to feel like, right? This sense of looseness and glee – perhaps this was what it was like to be a man.

'I'm sorry, I won't think about it.'

Eventually, she overcame the suspicion that Yves had a hand in her husband's absence. He wasn't the sort of man that lied, nor had the imagination to invent hypothetical Parisian bar fights with enough details for a painting (champagne bottles had been used as weapons). Verne wasn't here to spoil this weekend, so she shouldn't spoil it herself. She was where she wanted to be, with a man she wanted to be here with – these sentences, she chanted to herself. There was no reason to let Verne in.

'Come,' Yves patted her on the shoulder. 'I hear they are making an announcement soon, something about a last-minute change in regulations.'

'To do with qualifying?'

'Perhaps,' he nodded, and looped his fingers through hers. They wandered over to the stewards' desk, where others were crowding, but she could already hear the news spreading through the drivers and mechanics. Whispers that turned louder, rolled into one another and turned true:

Due to weather, it had been decided that all drivers would be allowed to compete. There was no qualifying session. She would race in a Grand Prix.

Hand in hand with this revelation came another, when she saw a bright white suit among a crowd of mechanics. She knew immediately that it was Will.

There's someone I should say hello to, she mumbled to Yves, touching his arm, and threaded off through the crowd before he could ask who it was. Apology was already on her lips. It had been waiting there for days, and she was desperate to get the words to him finally, to tell him that she could never be sorrier for anything in her life.

Since her mishap at the Monaco Grand Prix in front of the camera, eyebrows had raised and remained there. Talk of the *allegations* and the *arrest* had swirled only more violently. *What has happened with Will Truston and why has he all but disappeared from the grid?* wrote *Motoring Weekly*, in an attempt to turn rumour into comment. *He's not been on the grid for a while now. Instead, he opts for the sidelines as a consultant engineer for British Racing Motors while overseeing Truston Motors from a distance, after he retired from driving nearly a decade ago. That was after the death of his* dearest *friend Peter Bracknell. But his encounter with the police earlier this year has certainly ruffled some feathers at BRM and now he's even less inclined to be seen at the track, at least during daylight hours.* She had the article memorized – and the memory of gut-dropping shame when she read it for the first time.

The tabloids couldn't resist getting their pound of flesh either. *Is it true that racing man Will Truston was caught in an indecent act in Mayfair this March? That he was arrested with another man at one o'clock in the morning outside a disreputable establishment popular with queers? His longtime Truston Motors partner Freddy Vaux certainly didn't deny it when asked several weeks ago in Monaco.* Statements phrased into questions so that they could actually print this stuff.

The talk among drivers was even worse, because of its silences. Gapped sentences and wordless phrases drilling holes in conversations with men she used to trust. *Did you hear about Truston, that he's… inclined to sample… you know what?* The look between them when his name came up. Just enough silence to say what needed to be said. People had circulated rumours about *queer old Truston* for years – but now she had given them the edge that it could be true.

Will had been so careful to cultivate his appearance; it had taken years, an entire career, for him to craft. She'd had no right to point out the oil marks on his suit. Only he could do that. Only he could decide when he wished to expose who he was. He was not ashamed of it, she knew, but he was also a man of care, who cared for his reputation and realized how his world would react if they knew everything. He was true enough to himself while remaining safe within the confines of that world, and he was proud of the balance he had struck for so many years.

A balance she had ruined.

She had continued reaching out to him, of course, in the days after she made those comments so unthinkingly to the press in Monaco. Endless calls to Will's estate to warn him of what was to come, offering her help and support and whatever he needed from her, even if that was to never speak to her again. But news travels fast, faster than her, and, when she was left listening to dial tones and the phone line kept disconnecting, it was clear that Will did not want to talk. She had debated travelling back to England to see him while Yves was in Paris, but something kept her from following through. What would she say to him that could possibly be enough?

Will stood with his back to her. She could tell from the tension in his neck that he was trying to figure out an issue with the engine. He always clenched and unclenched his fists when there were problems with the wheels. For anything else, he rubbed his foot into the dirt.

She tapped him on the shoulder. He turned, revealing a split in his lip and a bruise on his jaw. He looked her up and down, then turned back to the mechanics as if she had been a stray gust of wind.

'Will,' she pleaded.

He ignored her.

'Will, please.'

He turned, snapped.

'Can I *help* you, Miss Vaux? Or is it Mrs Dawson-Hayes? I can never remember which you prefer.' Cruelty was something he didn't do well, and he had to work at it. His face wore the effort.

'Will, can we talk? I'd like to apologize.'

'For what?' He kept turning to and from her. 'Do you want to apologize for my lip or my jaw.'

'For all of it. There's no excuse, but please let me explain. I want to make it up to you.'

'Make it up to me?' He raised his voice, then lowered it. He calmed his nerves, smiled, all those years of acting like someone else quickly kicking in. His eyes settled on the fringe of forest nearby.

He stormed off behind the pavilion, heading into the woods. She was expected to follow, and he led them to a clearing. It was puddled and grubby with rain, harsh bolts of sun poking through the canopy of trees.

'I was hoping not to see you here,' Will said. He faced away from her. 'Because if I did, I wouldn't be able to stop myself from talking to you and saying everything on my mind… saying something that would mean you'd never talk to me again.' He paused. 'I want to ask you how you've been, but I can't because you caused me such *trouble*, Fred. And I don't even think you realize. You have no idea what you did with your comments. My life as I knew it was over.'

She let him speak. It was the least she could do.

'*One time*, I stayed out too late. For just *one* moment, I forgot the world I lived in. And I was hoping to get away with it, I nearly *did*, if not for your attempt to… I don't know what it was. To *defend* me? *If you call that indecent*, you said. People had mostly shut up about the arrest when Monaco rolled around, but you just… the can of worms was open again.'

'I didn't mean—'

'I know you didn't, which is even worse. You were just careless. You might as well have told them everything. At least that would have stopped the speculation. And the speculation, Fred… the speculation is *eternal*. No one gets bored of it.'

He stamped around, kicking at stumps and weeds. His face was the same choirboy pale, with new fine seams in his forehead and around his mouth. 'I can't enter a room without people turning silent. I was walking along the pavement when this happened,' he pointed to his lip. 'I was out to get dinner when some policeman recognized me from his motoring magazine and said I was too near a particular end of town. They made up some reason to take me to the station where they shoved my head against the wall and made me stay the night and vomit into a steel toilet.'

He turned away, but she had already seen the tear fall before he wiped it away. 'I'm afraid, Fred. All the time now.'

'Will, what can I do?'

'There's nothing you can do. Our hole has been well and truly dug and, if you say anything else to the press or goodness knows who else, then we'll only be digging it deeper. You'll just confirm it even more, and it will look like I asked you to save me.'

He stepped closer, and she saw the tautness in his chin. Releasing his secret had only caused him to seize up more.

'I'm getting *married* again, Fred.' He winced at the word. 'After this race. How ridiculous is that? I'm going home and saying "I do" for the *second* time, can you believe? That's what you've made me do. It's the only way I could put a stop to it. The only way to at least salvage my reputation out of all this.' He threw his arms around. 'And before you ask, she's got nothing on Vanessa.'

'Will, I'm so sorry.'

'No,' he said. 'I'm not accepting it, at least not until you stop this…'

'Stop what?'

'What are you *doing*, Fred?' She didn't think he wanted an answer from her. 'What are you doing messing around with Yves Le Brocq? Are you still married to Vernon? Don't look at me like that, everyone knows about Yves. You're playing into their hands with this silly love affair.'

'No, it's not like that—'

'You're becoming exactly what the drivers all expected of a woman on the grid. They're probably just ignoring it because they're waiting until you're done with Yves and move on to one of them.'

'Will, stop it. I know I hurt you, and I'm sorry. I wish I could take it back, but—'

'You think you've *found* yourself driving, but I think you've lost it. Somewhere between the first corner and a pit lane that never wanted you in it. You think you're so mature, because of what you've been through and all that you've suffered, but—'

'You have *no* idea what I've been through!' she exploded. 'What I've had to sacrifice to get here. Who I've had to become.'

'It's not the same and you know it,' he raised his voice to match hers.

'Why are we *competing*?' she pleaded. 'We're supposed to be on the same side.'

She had no clue what she was doing, what she was saying, but she'd also never had a friend she cared so deeply about.

'I was distracted, when I said what I said.' She looked to the ground. 'Vernon was there, in Monaco.'

'I don't care that Vernon was there.' Will threw up his hands. 'He's *gone*, he's not here. Why are you still married to him? If you really wanted to divorce, then… go on, admit it.'

'Admit what?'

'Admit that you could have solved it by now, you could have asked your father to sort it out, and he would have. But there's a part of you that still wants him. Because you need whatever it is that he does, the way he puts you down, to justify your racing and your outspokenness, all of it.'

'No,' she cried out. 'You don't know what he did to me. He… forced himself… on me…' She broke off, looking away. The trees shook in a breeze. Another rain shower was on its way. Her Arden, completely shot.

His stance changed, softening.

'Fred, I'm sorry, I didn't know…'

'You're sorry, I'm sorry, we're all sorry!' She chucked her arms out, walking away from him.

'Freddy,' he pursued her, grasping at her wrist. She shook it off. He held back, understanding.

'I told myself that if something like that ever happened to me, then I'd blow my brains out. I had to learn how to *want* to live again. I healed just enough, in the end, but Monaco was so soon afterwards. I wasn't prepared for him. I lost my head. I'm sorry. Please, Will.'

He nodded, sadly. It wasn't forgiveness, not yet, but the promise of it. Freddy hadn't been expecting forgiveness.

'I need to get back, Fred. I have an engine to fix.' He said it calmly, his temper cooled.

'Will you be at the next race, in France? We could talk properly then.'

'No. The only reason they asked me to come to Belgium is because I happen to be rather good at fixing problems that others can't. And I've been asked – *told*, more like – to step into a role on a board where I'm not visible.' He paused, sighing. 'I'll be busy with the wedding as well.'

Her cheeks burned with embarrassment; she bit her nail.

A rift had opened between them, with her secret and her breaking of *his*. The problem was trust – they had put too much of it in one another, both of them unfamiliar with how to lay their lives on other people, and it had led them here. Freddy had no idea how to repair it, at least not now. She had the sense that it would take years. Perhaps that's why his final comment stung so much: 'It's only fitting. I began your career, and you ended mine.'

He walked out of the forest and back onto the track, leaving her in the clearing alone.

Early on the morning of the race, she left Yves in bed and showered in the wood-panelled hotel bathroom.

Halfway through washing her hair, it struck her: *I'm the first woman to wake up in this position, on a Grand Prix morning. I will be the first woman to line up on that start grid.* It was a moment, she only let herself admit now, that she had been dreaming of. Her head was clear and silent after this small revelation. She hoped that it would mean something to anyone but herself, but for now she was unsure.

So, she carried on: dressing item by item, building the layers between her body and the outside world with thermals and race suit and boots. It was hot and humid, but she wanted protection between her small, bulky body and that of the car.

When she reached the race paddock, it was deserted, cars lined up, tents dripping in morning dew, wrenches strewn on tarmac. As she walked the track one final time, numbers flashed through her mind: 13 drivers; 36 laps; 508 kilometres; three hours of racing time. From her calculations last night in bed, she would place seventh, at best – and that would be behind Yves in sixth. It would take roughly four miracles for her to come anywhere close to winning.

She put her back to the start line, surveying the grid, and counted the number of years since she had nearly missed the beginning of the Daily Express Rally with Vanessa. *It's a race to get to the start line*, she'd learned, and now she was here, feet firm on the white line. She allowed herself a moment to wonder if Vanessa would be proud.

The paddock, when she returned, was strangely bereft of media. She imagined that the woods had batted the reporters off, left them somewhere tangled in ivy and microphone wires.

Verne was nowhere to be seen. Will was nowhere to be seen. Yves was nowhere to be seen. She scolded herself for considering these absences.

Engines began to cough and burst into life. The crowd poured into the grandstands. And from here, no one could tell who she was or what made her different, and she couldn't tell either. She was a new species embedded in the old. She was here because she was a racing driver and she had earned this spot.

She was starting in twelfth, due to her practice session time. As she climbed into the car, she saw the exhausts in front leaking thick black smoke onto the ground. Her mind was both thrown and never more focused. Mechanics scattered from the grid like ants. The lights grew one after another until there were five red beacons ahead.

Then they went out.

She released the clutch, dissected the shunt with the accelerator and shot off the line. Before the first corner, she had overtaken two cars – two cars who had poor starts (one of them no start at all), but she was ahead of them and that's all that mattered. Tenth.

Three laps later, fire spiked from the engine of the car in front – an Australian driver whom she couldn't remember the name of. The flames grew higher, and she swerved to the other side of the track to give him a wide berth. She wouldn't dare get out of her car and help. None of the others would have done it for her. Vanessa wouldn't have done it. She moved up into ninth.

Mackenzie's car might not be fast, but it was reliable. She could bash it against the barriers and it would bounce back. It threw itself around the corners. It couldn't be fazed. Unlike the car in front of her, which gave her eighth place when it transformed into a lobbed ball of flames freewheeling down the track. She thought she heard a scream, but she pressed on the accelerator and the car groaned forwards.

Somewhere in that surge, she felt that familiar thrill deep in her bones as cars around her overheated and stalled, and she burst through to take their place. She had notched into the rare and familiar sense of power. From then, the race flew.

In the penultimate lap, by which point she was running in fifth, she saw the opportunity to overtake. It was a high-speed corner, so the bravest won. The driver who didn't slow their pace, who took the boldest inside line and let their fear lie, took dominance of the track. She ploughed into it, the rear of the car in front growing larger, larger, until she was alongside it. When he realized, he tried to press into the empty track, but she was already there, she had already taken the space. She squeezed the accelerator even further, the nerves in her body tingling and looping around each other in strange shambolic hugs, her hands gripping the wheel. She came around the corner, and the other driver dropped back as the track straightened. She lodged into the straight, shifted the gear, and pushed the car as fast as it could go. He was trying to crawl back the advantage she had gained, but at the next corner she was ahead of him, snatching the apex before he could sniff it and shooting into clear air on the other side. She watched him drop backwards in her mirror, not even turning around to look.

She had found it: the perfect line. She had entered that place beyond her body, stepped out of her skin and left it somewhere on the track behind her. The want to be nothing. To disappear into the stretch, turn into motion, slough off her gender and become a soul moving through air, without attachments. So relentlessly herself.

She had been searching for that her entire life. In these moments, the flickers at high-speed corners, she found it. Remembering all the time that it was only a split-second flash, a minute arrangement of wheelspins and engine howls. It was nothing but everything, and never often enough.

She had always assumed that the driver can never know for sure what's waiting for them around the corner, and satisfaction with a lack of control was what made winners. It was what Will had told her years ago, that drivers had no choice but to ease into this powerlessness, give themselves over to the racing line – that undeniable black stripe scorched onto the tarmac. She had believed ever since that being in control was a fable. It was the track and its bends that controlled the driver. But when she swept the sickle of that curve, she decided that this was rubbish. Weak drivers surrendered to the curve and whatever surprises it would present. The stronger drivers ploughed into them, eager to collect their prize on the other side. Freddy focused on what was waiting for her around this corner. Fourth place. Her career. Yves.

The chequered flag flew above her, and she lifted her foot from the accelerator; her tyres burned as her heart squeezed its fast elastic pulses. The car slowed; she rolled around the lap, before pulling to a stop with the other cars.

For a moment, the huffs still spilling out her mouth, she sat there in the driver's seat. Stunned at what she had done. Fourth position in a Grand Prix. Three points in the championship. Three points to her name.

When Yves parked beside her in the seventh place slot, and she climbed out of the car to embrace him, there were tears in her eyes. With the sweat thick on her forehead, she removed her helmet. The sun made her squint. Yves fell away to speak with his team members. The pit lane closed in; crashes and wheel guns and brake cranks all at once.

She became cynical too quickly, starting to wonder why fourth place felt like she had won. Dread crept in, telling her this was the best she could do. This was all she could hope for – and fourth was not a place on the podium, fourth was not something that people remembered. She would return home without a medal or a trophy or a laurel of green leaves. As empty-handed as she was when she arrived in Belgium.

Perhaps that's why her fourth place felt tarnished.

Or, more likely, it was because someone was dead.

'Russo…' the surname was all she heard, rippling through the crowd of drivers and mechanics and strategists. His number was thirty-two, and she had seen it veer off the track. Whether she had been the one to nudge him off, she couldn't be sure.

Yves came towards her and held her shoulders in his hands.

'Russo…'

'Yes?'

'Did you see?'

'No, I was so focused on… he went off early though?'

'They say,' Yves said, looking elsewhere, 'that his Maserati crashed into a ditch beside the track, one that should have been filled in. He told them to keep the race going when they rescued him, but it's… I have just seen a priest making his way to that corner of the track.'

'What happened? Did he get a puncture?'

Yves sucked up the tears he wouldn't let fall, shaking his head. Platitudes of varying sincerity filtered around the pit lane: *No driver, no matter how good he is, can avoid death…*

'Yves, I can't believe… I came *fourth*,' she whispered.

'You heard about Russo?' He looked confused.

'Yes, I heard. It's awful…'

'This is a time of *mourning*,' he hissed. 'You wouldn't understand. When a driver is hurt or killed in championship races, we do not *boast* about our position. It's disrespectful.' She saw jealousy in the curl of his lips. It was tough to tell where it was aimed: at Russo, for achieving the goal of death; or at her, for finishing in fourth when he had to settle for seventh.

The drivers began to pour onto the track, where an improvised vigil had sprung up. Someone with a megaphone had already begun to sing the Italian national anthem for Russo. A bouquet was on its way to the fateful corner. Arms interlinked with hers. The sky broke open to rain.

Through it all, she could only think that no one had poured out with flowers and anthems for Vanessa, when a crash had broken her skull in two.

In the hours afterwards, she told herself it was fine. More than fine. She had finished fourth. She had finished. Her competition manager at Mackenzie had called and said she was on course to keep her place on the team for the next championship. She was elated – hesitant but elated. Planting her feet on the ground as she listened to him talk. No longer expecting rugs to be pulled out from underneath her.

On a spare few days before practice began for the next race of the season, the French Grand Prix in Rheims, she took the train, then the ferry, back to London to rest in her flat. A stack of letters waited for her on the table next to the door, which her landlady had placed there.

Several letters down, she found one with a first-class stamp. The return address was the offices of the Fédération Internationale de l'Automobile in Paris. No one wastes a first-class stamp on bad news, she considered, and ripped into it, reminding herself what was perfect in her life: Yves, fourth place, that she would race the French Grand Prix next week.

But, according to the letter from the Federation, she would do no such thing.

14. Home

'Because of Monaco? I thought that what happened in Monaco *stayed* in Monaco. Or what happened on a racetrack *stayed* on that racetrack.' She was shouting down the phone to Yves, her coat still on, the bags abandoned by the door.

'Yes, but Monaco is like the crown jewel of racing, it's… you can't mess with Monaco. The Federation doesn't like it.'

'Are you defending them?' She scrunched the letter in her hand.

'No, of course not. It's a level of discrimination I have never seen before.'

'Because there's never been a woman try to race the French Grand Prix before. It's so much easier to discriminate when there's no precedent. And until there is one, which would have been me, there never *will* be one.'

'Yes…' His voice trailed off and she heard laughs in the background.

'Where are you? I called your hotel.'

'I'm with some friends in the hotel bar. Why don't you come out here?' He was in Rheims already.

'There's no point now, is there?'

'Yes, of course. But you could watch?'

'I will *not* spectate. If I'm in Rheims, then I want to race.'

'Yes, but they won't let you.'

'Which is wrong.'

'Which is wrong,' he repeated, but the words sounded rehearsed and tinny.

'It makes no sense. In Belgium, there was a pile-up not so different from mine. And what about Russo's crash? The wheel from his car struck a driver unconscious. What makes mine different?'

Her crash in Monaco had given the authorities reason to suspend her on the grounds of her *dangerous driving* rather than her chromosomal make-up; she had given them the permission to discriminate, and to do it so that it looked like responsibility instead.

'Except...' Yves paused, waiting for her to swoop in and save him from saying it. But she waited, stubborn, clicking her shoe on the wooden floor. 'Except that you are a woman. It is antiquated and it is rude...'

'It is *sexist*, Yves.'

'Yes, it's sexist, but it's the Federation. I don't see how you expect to change their minds. You cannot unmake what is already made.'

'I never intended to *unmake* anything, but for the love of…' She covered the receiver and swore out the window, which she had wrenched open. The apartment was thick with days of embedded heat. She composed herself and continued, 'I knew that I would never win a championship, not in that hunk of metal Mackenzie gave me, and not without the years of practice and experience that I'll never have on those men. Trust me, I never thought that by scoring points in the Belgian Grand Prix I had changed the world in any grand way, but I thought it would mean *something*. I thought that… I'd done it. Not that I'd *solved* it, but that I had proven we were worthy of being there.'

'That is what terrifies them.' Yves' voice was softer now. 'What you have done is open the door. They're terrified that you *have* changed everything, and these men in these offices do not like change. I know this.'

'How, Yves?'

The background bar noise poured through the phone.

'The President of the Federation, I know him well. In my career, he has been good to me.'

'*Good* to you?'

'Yes.'

'Could you speak with him, get him to change his mind?'

Another pause.

'That I cannot do.'

'Why?'

'He won't change his mind.'

'How do you know?

'He spoke to me in Belgium, and he said to me, before the race, as I walked towards my car, that...'

'What?'

'He said that the only helmet a woman should use is the one at the hairdressers.'

She picked up the letter and saw the name at the bottom: Francesco Cordisaldi. She recognized that line; he had used it on her before, in her rallying days – and now he was President of the Federation. He had not changed. Nothing she had done made a bit of difference. The same lines, the same looks, the same old ways.

'Freddy?'

'I can believe he said that.' In the past, these nudges backwards had propelled her forwards. She remembered how she swam across the river to race, how she drove twice as hard to beat those who refused to stand on the podium with her – there had always been novelty to that, a childish game of barriers that she could supersede. But here was the biggest backward push yet. She feared that this one would take the spring out of her and push her back to the beginning, where she would remain.

The hardest bit is getting to the start line. Vanessa's voice in her head, always. Vanessa wouldn't let her give up – because that's what she had begun to consider on the phone with Yves, Freddy realized, the crumpled letter in her hand. It's what she had been considering since she opened it and read those words: *RACE BAN.*

Vanessa. She still had Vanessa to make proud. Championship points? She'd scored them. She could score more of them. This was nothing. *Nothing*, she forced into her mind.

She asked Yves once more to speak to the Federation President on her behalf. He refused.

'Because it puts myself at risk,' he said. 'He has the power to disqualify me.'

'You won't because you're scared what will happen to you?'

'Don't say it like that.'

'Like the truth?'

'Don't be angry.'

'I'm not. I'm just confused, and a little disappointed. You won't stand up for me, even though you know it's the right thing to do.'

'*Is* it the right thing to do? Is it not best to take this disappointment and wait until the next race. He could have banned you from the entire competition, but it is only one race.'

'He will do it again, for Portugal, for Italy. Once I let it happen, it happens again.'

'If I vouch for you, there's a long list of crashes that he could use to ban me from races too. I can't live with that. You know I race to live.'

'And so do I? Why am I not allowed that claim too?'

'You don't understand, Fred. My career is so fragile. If he finds fault with Le Brocq Motors, I don't have the money to rebuild it again. I can't throw it on the line for you. I love you, but I can't do that.'

'Then perhaps you don't love me.'

'Love shouldn't need to be *proven*,' he pleaded.

'No, it doesn't. It should be there, ready, waiting to help.'

'Not everything revolves around you, Freddy.'

'That's not—' she broke off in a half-yell, half-scream. Then the line cut.

She held the phone for several more minutes, wondering if this conversation meant it was over between them. He had pirated their exchange, turned a conversation about racing so quickly into an argument about their relationship – or had she been the one to do that? The seamless transition between the two topics made her uneasy.

While she wanted to be at a bar in Rheims, she ended up somewhere wildly different: her father's house.

As she left the car on the gravel drive, she tried not to think about the fact that she was returning to where she began. The garage, to her left, where she first climbed into the Baby Austin, the spot on the drive where her mother had fallen. If the past was here, then surely she had some sway over it, she thought. Surely, she could yank the small Freddy out of the driver's seat and tell her what she's getting herself into; surely, she could tell herself not to drive her mother to the hospital because death would catch up anyway. She might have avoided this very moment where she looked at the drive and realized she had gone nowhere, and done nothing, at all.

After Yves, she called Eric to blow off her anger about the French Grand Prix. His response had been more satisfying, his tone reliably sympathetic. But even he couldn't offer her the answers she was looking for, and after several minutes of *sorries*, he simply said:

'Please, come for tea. Tomorrow.'

'I don't want to be drinking tea. I want to be racing. I could go to France, I could pressure them in person. I can't let them win, Eric.'

'Is there someone else who could vouch for you?'

She had already debated whether to contact Will – he knew a co-president or two – but decided against it.

'No.'

'Then this letter seems like a firm *no*. You said there's no appealing it. So, in the absence of racing, tea. At home.'

'Home?'

'Father wants to see you.'

'I don't want to go home.'

Since she had begun the process to divorce Verne, her father's steady stream of supportive letters (written out of the sight and mind of his friends) had slowed. From their contents, she assumed that it wasn't disappointment, but rather shock. *This wasn't done in my day* appeared twice in one letter. *We moved on in pain* was another with the faintest shadow of envy behind it. Her parents had never even considered divorce, for the sake of appearances – even if that's all their marriage was.

Since disappearing to Sandal Road, signing with Mackenzie, and beginning her racing campaign in Formula One, she had become a curious creature to her father. His hands, through the letters, had reached out to her, but she had avoided him, and this house, because she worried that he might not quite know what to do with her.

'I haven't seen him in...'

'A couple years, I know,' Eric finished for her. 'All the more reason to come tomorrow. Please, Fred. I have something for you.'

'What?'

He paused.

'Eric, tell me. I hate surprises.'

'The divorce came through yesterday. Verne signed. Lawyers signed. It's done.'

She sat down. The phone almost slipped out of her hand.

'Why didn't you tell me that at the start of the call?'

'Because you wanted to talk about racing.'

Only a divorce could get Freddy in her father's drive again, she thought, as her feet crunched the gravel. She knocked, twice. When the door opened, it was John.

Her father still couldn't make tea. At this point, it had to be a deliberate effort to keep a slice of the war alive, Freddy realized, because she figured it out as she sat staring into the cup: he reused the tea leaves too many times. There was no need for it anymore and yet he still reused them. Consider it muscle memory, practice or just plain stubbornness – he was living in the past.

John sat on another sofa in the parlour. A sofa she had play-wrestled with him on when she was five and he was twelve. There was a tear in the edge where she had gripped on for dear life, and a crook in the armrest where he had kicked at her and missed. Their father had never known what happened to it and she'd sworn she would never tell.

Eric sat next to him, talking his tongue out of his mouth. About the weather, about his wife, about his teaching schedule, about their memories. Whenever the hot air had stilled the room into a silence, and the talk had stopped, he began again.

Her father nodded, without adding anything. Until there came a stop and Eric's eyes slid left to right between herself and John.

'I don't like the idea of my children not getting along,' her father murmured into the silence.

'I'd say that it's more than simply not getting along,' Freddy said. She looked at John, waiting for him to speak, but his eyes remained fixed on the low table with the tea things. She couldn't remember the last time she had seen him. Silverstone? That dreadful New Year's Eve? His broad shoulders from the war years had narrowed into a slouch. Creases from all the laughs had settled into fine wrinkles and his hair was combed back sharply, more scalp exposed than before. The shine of his locks had become a gelled sheen. He was thinner than in his rugby-playing days. Where he had been so full of movement, now he was still, with his eyes fixed on something else on the low table: a large envelope.

She grabbed for it, brushing aside the porcelain with a tinkle (her father catching the nearly tipped cup), and ripped the envelope open. There it was, what she had been waiting so very long for: Verne's signature scrawled next to hers, which had been on the creased piece of paper for over a year. Beneath the initial typewritten form, a small stack of paper with Verne's confessions of adultery. His affair with a woman he had known since childhood whose name was not mentioned other than as a nickname. Pages of letters sent between him and this woman, dated from that awful autumn in which Freddy had walked the woods thinking they were broke. She had assumed he was off salvaging their lives, never even suspecting that he was the centre of someone else's. The sheer depth of her naivety shocked her.

She was unsure whether to be disappointed by this outcome or not: the divorce had come through, and that's all that should matter. But the fact that he had agreed to it on the grounds of an adultery – when she had filed it on the newly permitted grounds of cruelty and desertion – was an odd, disorientating blow.

It felt dismissive to slide the documents back into the envelope and forget about the whole thing, and yet it felt counterproductive to keep her hands occupied with the stack of paper. She had never known anyone to successfully divorce, and the law that allowed her to do it was so new that she was unsure whether a cocktail party or a prolonged period of mourning was in order. There was only one question she needed answered:

'Why now? What made Verne change his mind?' She tried to stop that part of herself that suspected Yves had something to do with it.

'Actually,' Eric broke the silence. 'It was John.'

'Not exactly,' John spoke for the first time.

'Why?' Freddy asked her oldest brother. 'You hated that I wanted to divorce him. I thought you'd made up your mind that Verne was God and I was the devil. Old boarding school code and all that.'

'Winifred,' her father scolded.

'I did think that, for a while.' John looked out of the window. 'I was angry at you, Win. I had been led to believe that marriage, children, was proper, what's done. It was a belief that kept me going, through the war, and after it, too.' When he paused, she nodded at him to go on. 'The problem is that when I launched into this great adventure of marriage and adulthood myself, with Alice, I realized that… well, it's not quite so wonderful as all that. I thought you were being stubborn and making life difficult for Verne, but then with Alice, we argued, she made decisions that I disagreed with, we've raised fists at each other…'

'Are you divorcing Alice?'

'No, no, of course not,' he waved her away. She remembered with shame when Alice had written to her, and Freddy had ignored the letters one after another until they stopped. She resolved to reach out and discuss things with her – even if those things were her own brother's marriage. She resolved to be a friend.

'Then…'

'Please, let me finish. I realized that marriage is very difficult. It breaks a back. Wives have minds of their own, and I love Alice's mind, even if it took some getting used to. What I'm saying is…' He knew it wasn't coming out right. 'As time wore on, and I saw what Verne had done, that he was clinging to that myth we had been told as boys, about being masters of houses and women, I felt ashamed that he was my friend, and that I had remained his friend through all of it. I knew then he had failed, in so many ways, and he was not right for you.

'I went to him in France, several weeks ago, and told him that he had to end it in law. He had ruined our friendship, and he had hurt you, he had hurt the family, and he was lying to himself to think you could stay married and live separate lives.'

'You made me doubt myself, John, for a long time,' Freddy said. 'For someone I loved to tell me that I was wrong and that I had to listen to Verne. You know how cruel that was, right?'

'I do now. I'm sorry, Freddy, for all that I did. I was blind in so many ways. I hope you can forgive me and put all this behind us. I want you to move on and race, race, Fred, like you're supposed to.'

She had always thought, as the younger sister, that she would be the one who needed to be forgiven for her naivety. And while she might not be ready to forgive him now, she had a feeling that she would soon.

Eric had remained quiet throughout this exchange. Their gazes met, understanding between them. Her time in Sandal Road (or, as he knew it, *at a friend's*) and all the conversations from those months still remained their secret. In this moment, she felt she owed him an apology, for doubting his kind acts and seeing them as petty revenge for an unpleasant boyhood. These were not only the actions of a good brother, but the actions of a good man. His loyalty was lifesaving and nothing more. His kindness was simply kindness, no agenda. It seemed so obvious now, and insulting to voice that she had ever thought that at all, so she held his hand and smiled for two. John had some making up to do, but perhaps she did as well.

It was unclear as to why her divorce was a family event, and why her brothers wanted an even share in this step, but now they were here and gathered she was not unhappy about it.

John continued, 'Also, he admitted that he never shot down fourteen Germans.'

'He's never shot down a German in his life,' her father grumbled.

Under her heart, the conclusion to it all: she didn't know how much time to spend on rejoicing the divorce, because she didn't want to be here with the divorce papers at all. She wanted to be in Rheims, halfway down the final straight.

Now she could burst forth, *now* she was unleashed, *now* she was free.

Four laps into the Portuguese Grand Prix, however, her engine was not on the same page. With the heat like a monster in the cockpit, sweat fuming from her every pore, it blew. Big gulches of black smoke poured out the back of the car as she braked and rolled to the side of the track. Then, fire. She could feel the hungry warmth on the back of her neck, the smell of molten metal as the car melted away behind her. Stewards helped her from the car and doused it in water while she looked on at the wreck.

Yves assured her, when he found her in the empty garage after accepting his third-place trophy, that she *wouldn't have been in with a chance to get near the points anyway.* He was right – she had qualified last, a minute off the pace, and her car was stale from disuse and unprepared for the hot street track. *Mackenzie makes their motors in Scotland, so it's no wonder they can't handle this weather,* he said. She was relieved when he kissed her after offering these stilted condolences, their argument about Rheims forgotten.

Her engine went again in Monza the following week. The temperatures reached over thirty degrees for the final race of the season, and she knew it would never be able to withstand it. She had driven expecting to hear that *ka-plush* and the smoke. The only consolation was that it came in the fifty-sixth lap out of seventy, and she was the last to retire, so finished eighth. Yves too retired, his engine with similar faults, but it gave her no satisfaction.

What had she been through it for – Verne, the divorce, Sandal Road – if she could only settle for the best loser? For a best-season finish of fourth place? Winning the championship was off the cards, but surely she was doing it for something grander than herself. As she stood next to the wreck of her Mackenzie, half-black and the engine on the floor, a sooty stumped heart, she had the dreadful sense that it would only ever be for her. Mechanics were clearing away cars, loading them into lorries, folding up toolboxes and equipment. The championship season – her first season – was at an end.

Rich approached, picking tobacco off his tongue. His brow was scrunched tight as he bumped into another driver who swore at him. Rich was shifty – but not clumsy.

'Hello there,' he whistled through his gapped and yellow-stained teeth. Much too polite for him, she thought. He had never said *hello* in his life, but always dove straight into the conversation.

'Hello,' Freddy replied.

He was also never short of words – short or long ones. He sat on the crate next to her and tried out some silence.

'What is it, then?'

'I need to talk to you—'

'Mackenzie are dropping me,' she said, overlapping with his final *you*. The words still surprised her when she said them aloud, even if she had known it was true since Portugal.

Rich began a slow nod, then fell into a head shake.

'Not exactly, not yet.'

'The car is the problem.'

'A bad workman always blames his tools.'

'Not in this case. I know that Mackenzie cuts corners. I've done what I could with that car. Monaco was an oil spill that I saw too late. Then, in the other races, the engine was to blame. A good workman shouldn't blame his tools, but if the head of the hammer keeps falling off whenever he tries to hit the nail, then I think he has a good case against them.'

He nodded, slowly.

'I believe you. Mackenzie has a reputation for their substandard engines. But that doesn't mean they can't blame it on you anyway and not sign you again.'

On instinct, she kicked the car wreck.

'All I'm saying,' Rich continued, unfazed, 'is that it wouldn't be unwise to consider other options.'

'Should you be telling me this? You work for Mackenzie.'

'I work for myself,' he said firmly. 'Mackenzie may be

paying me for now, but *you're* the one I care about, Fred. It will always be that way, understand?' She nodded. 'I've seen this before. Mackenzie are ruthless, and they'll drop you too late so that there won't be any team spots available before next season starts. You'll be left out in the cold. But...'

'But what?'

'Well, if you decide to *leave* Mackenzie instead of being shown the door, that will give you credibility. Mackenzie won't like it, but you can make a statement saying the car wasn't up to scratch, you think you're a better driver than they give you credit for. It would make you look ruthless too.'

'Ruthless?'

'Yes, ruthless is good.'

'I'm not sure I want to do that. Mackenzie gave me a chance to get back in the game.'

'But they'll leave you high and dry without a second thought,' Rich said. His bluntness shocked her into understanding.

'Who else would have me on their team?'

'In truth, I'm not sure that anyone will, and most of the teams are already full.' It was nearing *too blunt*. 'But you've got me on your side this time.' She remembered her office in the telephone box on Sandal Road; she had called and called until her voice was hoarse.

She sat next to him again. Leftover fumes swilled in the air, and she breathed them in with a heavy smile.

'You just want to race, right?' he asked.

She looked at him. Had he heard all that she'd said in the Monaco hotel room, when she thought he was asleep? He had been snoring, hadn't he?

'If that's what you want, then I want it for you.'

'Because I'm your client?'

He shook his head.

'No. Because I'm your friend.'

She squeezed his shoulder, and they looked at the blackened car, as if waiting for it to come alive.

Yves made a proposal that night during pillow talk, after she told him about her conversation with Rich.

'I have a team,' he said to the dark hotel room. She remained silent. 'And you have talent.' Another pause. 'If I wanted someone else on the team, then I would want the woman who shares my bed.'

'Because she shares your bed, or because she has talent?'

'That's what you heard?' Yves shook his head. He moved upright, and she moved with him. Empty Prosecco bottles clinked at the foot of the bed from where they had toasted the end of the season, although neither had much to celebrate. Freddy had wanted this to be a serious conversation, but the bed was the only place he quieted long enough for her to bring up anything she wanted to discuss. It was where she had some power.

'Yves, I'm grateful for the offer. It's so kind.'

'This is not kindness. It's a real offer, because you need to be on a team. A talent like yours is not to be wasted.' He seemed almost offended to be called kind. That was her Yves. 'You know this situation like yours happens to all drivers, it has nothing to do with your womanness.' It was a word Yves used too often – despite her telling him that it was not a word.

'But won't *you* want to drive?'

'We can be teammates, no? Or I have been thinking of having a year as the reserve driver. Put all my energy into improving the car instead. Either way, you don't need to worry about taking the position from me.'

'But…'

'But what? Why all these reasons to say no? Say *yes*. We can train together and race together. Isn't it a dream?'

Isn't it? He was looking at her expectantly, waiting for her to explain this hesitance. She was waiting for the hesitance to explain itself to her too.

Her mind returned to their argument about the French Grand Prix, when he had refused to speak to the President about her race ban. She had concluded then, with some confidence and closure, that her problems would not be solved with Yves. Neither his kisses nor his embraces would mean anything outside the bed, as lovely as they were.

This new step complicated that conclusion. It unnerved her, and it was a step she had promised herself she wouldn't take, where her relationship blended with her racing career. If she accepted this offer, then she would be tied to Yves, personally, professionally, irrevocably. His decisions would affect hers. If the two of them argued, or disagreed, or broke up, he could fire her. He could stop her from racing. It felt like a loss of the independence she'd won with Mackenzie.

'I'm concerned that our relationship could…'

'It will only make it better.'

'Better than this?'

'Yes. I promise.'

Still, she hesitated. As her affair with Yves had whipped itself up like a tornado, she had questioned it. Whether it was the *silly love affair* Will had called it in Belgium, or whether it was more – and how it was possible that each moment could be more wonderful than the next. What she had with him was too good, and she had been waiting for a turn like this when it would all go wrong.

But she knew that no other teams on the grid would accept her, and that Le Brocq Motors was her only shot at a place next season. It was what she had to do to continue to race.

She found herself nodding.

'Yes, Yves.'

'Yes?'

'Yes, alright.'

He laughed, embracing her.

'I feel as though there should have been a ring.'

'Yves, don't say that.'

So he kissed her instead, until she could barely breathe.

How far she had come: her husband not allowing her to drive, and now her lover saving her career.

15. Monaco Grand Prix (Again)

Summer 1952

S*wimmingly* was the word she used to describe her time with Le Brocq Motors so far, but she failed to tell the interviewer that she was not a good swimmer. Nevertheless, he licked his pen and smiled at her, and she thought he was so delighted with her answer he was going to eat his ballpoint.

'I can only imagine how wonderful it must be to work so closely with a great friend like Yves.'

She nodded, and he nodded, and he would get nothing else out of her apart from:

'Yes, so wonderful.'

Lies were easy to tell herself; she had been doing it for months now.

The interviewer flicked to another page in his notepad, the hotel reception bustling around them, and she rubbed at her neck, sore from a collision with a wall of tyres the day before. Impulsively, she had ordered a Shirley Temple when the interviewer suggested they get drinks from the hotel bar, but now she regretted it. The drink felt childish, and she couldn't stop staring at the sickly, glistening cherries sitting on top of the ice.

A car engine started outside the window, and she turned her head to the noise; she was jumpy, short on sleep. She wished this interview had been in her hotel room, somewhere quieter, but she was sharing a small double with Yves on the basement floor, which looked out onto a cement wall – nothing like the last time she was in Monaco. Le Brocq Motors or LBM, as Yves called it, was not flush with cash; her car was held together with tape and scrap metal. Her third race in Monaco, she had a sense, would not be the charm.

The interviewer crackled his papers. She had been in enough of these to know that meant her absent-mindedness was not appreciated. After all, this meeting had been a favour set up by Rich, who had split from Mackenzie when she had. Yves had suggested it as well. *Perhaps on the day before qualifying, so that we can boost the name.* She knew him well enough to know that *perhaps* did not mean perhaps.

'Why don't you tell me about how these past months have been, testing and training on the track with Yves?' he offered. 'Spare no detail.'

The past months unfolded in her mind.

*

When Freddy signed with LBM, Yves had forgotten to mention Taff – whom, she hated to admit, she hated. Of course, she hadn't expected to be the only driver on the team, but she also hadn't expected to be teammates with a German who called her *Fraulein* and asked whether she had missed the turning to nursing college (*with these women that want to be near danger and death, they should have been nurses,* he explained); who grabbed her fingertips for a *lady handshake*, and made most of the discussions revolve around his car and what he wanted for it, because, as he always reminded her, he was *the number one driver* and she was *the number two.*

She approached Yves about it after their first session on the track, and he wafted it to the sky.

'Taff's an old friend. He's a little bit… *direct*, but I promise you he's alright once you get used to him.'

'If you'd said that I'd be racing with Wolfgang von Taffnen on my team then I would have maybe thought twice about signing with you.'

Yves paused with a pad of paper in his hand.

'Would you?'

Her voice went small. 'Maybe.'

'Come on,' he murmured and had hooked his fingers into the belt loops of her trousers and pulled her towards him. She swatted at his hands.

'We talked about this, Yves.' *When we're on the track,*

you're the team principal and I'm the driver, she had said. And she had said it once more, and twice more, every time he forgot and kissed her on the cheek or tapped her bottom – loving, instinctive movements that he couldn't help himself making. She let him sometimes, because that overspill of affection into his hands and lips was endearing. But it muddied their heads, the partnership, everything, when Taff saw them and told her *there are easier ways to secure a spot on a works team*.

Taff was just one of many things she and Yves bickered about in the months over winter when the season was in recess. Another was the car. She asked him how he won a race in *this piece of rubbish* and he said *with skill* and neither of them spoke for a week, not even in the bedroom. He had built the car for himself, based on his stocky body and his thick limbs with their muscles packed vacuum-tight beneath the skin. When she sat in the same car, she dinked against the sides like a pinball. It was a car that would never win. It was worse than Mackenzie's – *and that's saying something*, she spat.

'Then don't say it,' he spat back one day when the rain lashed down onto the track and the two had retreated to the garage. Raindrops flicked off his hair as he shook it.

'But it doesn't drive well,' she continued. Their voices echoed in the metal-and-cement box; the track was deserted, the drains overflowing.

He countered: 'I have poured so much time and money into this endeavour, and I have taken a *risk* on you. *For* you.'

'No, don't do that. That's not fair. You've done this for yourself, because you wanted to remain on the grid, you *had* to remain on the grid. It is your survival method but it is *killing* you.'

'You are… ungrateful.'

'Ungrateful? You're a has-been. You're the one who should be grateful to me. You think you're a legacy, that you've won the championship once and you're untouchable. But the car is not good enough, not for me.'

More than she hated Taff, she hated the words that came out of her mouth. She was tearing down the man who wanted to love her, whom she wanted to love, and it terrified her all over again. She had a sudden, aching desire to have done it all differently. She hated the circumstances that had led her to this argument. She had wanted to be here, but never with a man, not tied to him, dependent on him.

There was passion in their arguments, an intense twisted passion. Half of their disputes collapsed into kisses, for lack of knowing how else to end them, both fumbling to remove their clothes in the empty cockpits of disused cars. Poor track wardens walking in on their attempts, which made her laugh so much it hurt her stomach.

There were moments when she caught sight of herself in the bathroom mirror, choked on her toothbrush, fumbled with the hairbrush, when she asked herself: *what are you doing?* Why was she ruining something good? Her love for him, and her love for racing – only one of them would survive this new stage of their relationship, she feared.

She was confused too often now. She had never resolved the hesitance that haunted this affair, and now it was too late, and she was left wondering at high-speed corners whether the man clicking the stopwatch on the side of the track was her lover or her boss, and what she wanted him to be. He gave her instructions about racing lines while they were horizontal on bad mattresses, his missing-fingered hands drawing arcs in the air above their heaving chests. The taste of his kisses still in her mouth as she asked whether he had finalized the chassis design. He referenced these discussions in front of others – *it's like I told you last night* – and she shouted at him to not bring up their midnight conversations with Taff and the engineers, and so he stopped giving her instructions altogether. Misunderstandings were the norm. She skipped testing sessions because of arguments in bed; he skipped the bed because of arguments in testing sessions. There was no distinction between their midnight hours and daylight ones.

All the worst thoughts about herself resurfaced. Her passion mistaken for anger – and sometimes the other way around – she batted her way through arguments that made neither of them feel good. Most were about Ferrari, and how she would kill to drive for a team like that. He might not be a man who lied about shooting down fourteen

Germans, but he was a man who had walked away from the best racing team in the world. Foolish was the word, she thought. He never raised his fist at her, he never threw anything at her, but he threw spanners at walls and punched them until his knuckles were stinging and blue.

She could break it off. It was 1952, she had divorced one man – and she could leave another. Yves was not possessive, not like Verne. He would mourn her, but he would move on, and so would she.

If only she had not put herself in this position. Where she had to make the decision between her love, or her career. These months had proven she could not have both.

When she finished her fabricated recap of *the wonderful year of training and collaboration*, she capped it with another *swimmingly* for the interviewer. He didn't write it down and she could tell the word was tired. She was tired, old news. The novelty of the *woman on the track* had worn off. The reporters and their lack of interest made her miss something she had always wanted to cast off.

After the interview, she left the hotel and elbowed through the heaving streets towards the pit lane. Far above her were those tightly packed beige and white apartments that she had seen on her first descent into Monte Carlo, breathing wonder all over her rally car. She remembered how the harbour and the sky were competing to be the brightest blue. The city had seemed so perfect, racing so pure. It had seemed impossible to drag the complications of love and life into those sacred lanes, but she had been wrong on both accounts.

Tyre rubber dirtied the everyday streets, and the make-shift racing signage and barriers were falling apart. Even the stucco of her hotel was dripping its gold all over the pavement, people picking it up on the bottom of their shoes.

She saw two children sat on the sea wall, their legs dangling over the edge, pretending to drive. One pushed his foot down on an imaginary pedal, another pulled an imaginary wheel to the left and both of them lurched – then laughed.

The saving grace: in among all these overlapping strains of her life, these entrails and bad seeds sowed in the wrong patches, this dirtied racing, this cracked love, *she* had grown. Somewhat older, questionably wiser, and slightly less desirable – but herself nonetheless.

And *she* was here, in Monaco, to drive. That was all she wanted to do. It wasn't perfect, it never would be. But it was her.

She stopped at the edge of the pit lane, her eyes resting on Yves as he tapped the car and gave a thumbs-up to an engineer.

By finding herself, she had found she did not – could not – want him. Not like this.

But before she could break it off with him, she needed to qualify. She had surely cultivated here for herself the worst-balanced life.

As she walked through the pit lane, loud shouts and voices stirred her, and she cowered when shoulders bumped into her own. Men pushed her aside as they moved past. Without her, it would all continue to flow, like a river she had never disturbed.

Yves didn't notice her approach. He spoke in quick French – occasional Italian – to one of their engineers. There was no point trying to understand what he said; even the little French she spoke couldn't catch up to his fast rolls of language.

'Yves,' she shouted. And on her tongue was: *I need to speak with you about us.* What she said was rather different. 'How's she looking?'

'She is…' He looked to the engineer with a frown and shared a shaky hand gesture.

'What does that mean?' Freddy asked.

'She'll get you round the track.'

'Is it the gearbox again?'

'It could be.' The engineer chuckled behind them.

She wanted to say *have you tried to switch the pedals out?* but her mouth tripped into the other words this time. 'I need to speak with you.'

He paused and kept his eyes fixed on the gloves – as confused as she was about her statement. He was not in racing gear, but in starched white pleated chinos and a navy-blue polo, the gold cross swinging above his chest. The outfit a man might wear to take his girlfriend out for ice cream.

'What?'

'Have you tried switching out the pedals? It worked last time.'

'No, not yet. We don't have time. What do you need to speak about?'

'Why don't you switch the pedals?'

He slipped back into the conversation about the car. But when she meant to ask about *the strategy for the session*, she said: 'Yves, can we do this any longer? It's good for neither of us.'

'You're talking about…'

'The car. I'm talking about the car.' She waved her hands and leaned over the cockpit, fiddling with the steering wheel. He leaned over it next to her, half their bodies outside the car, half in the cockpit.

'I want to try and work through this, Fred. I need this, I need us.'

'*That's* the problem,' she replied – and neither she nor he knew whether she was talking about the gearbox or about them.

'You need me. I need you.'

'That kind of need and desperation, it's not good.'

He opened his mouth, unsure how to reply. She ploughed on.

'The gearbox, we need to replace it.'

'Replace it?' His face stuttered, unsure which conversation to give his attention, which answers to offer. 'But we don't have time.' Racing – racing was always easier to discuss.

'The old gearbox, even though it's sturdy and it wants to work… it perhaps isn't the right one for the car. It was at some point, it certainly was, and they fed off one another, and *used* one another—'

'I never used you.' Yves' face dropped in embarrassment.

'—and the car will be forever grateful to that gearbox for what it offered, but the two should part ways so that the car can move on faster, and the gearbox can be fixed in the workshop.'

'Will the gearbox,' he replied, 'fit with another car?'

'I'm not sure. Perhaps you will.'

'You?'

'It,' she said, firmly.

'I don't want to do this. Gearboxes are hard to find. And hard to replace.'

'But it's for the better.'

His face scrunched.

'No. We don't have time.'

Over a tannoy, she heard: *The qualifying session will begin in thirty minutes.* Yves turned over his shoulder and spat some French at the engineer. He took Freddy's helmet off the table and put it in her hands.

'Not now. This is not the place for it. The gearbox stays. You drive.'

She tried to argue with him, but he held a finger to her lips.

'This is too important. LBM relies on our performance

here today. We have to be in the top sixteen of twenty-four.'

'But…'

'No,' he edged her out of that conversation.

Yves kissed her on the cheek, the force of his lips surprising her into silence.

'We have practised. The car can do this. You can do this.' He smiled and retreated into the garage, where he put on earphones and spoke into a radio.

She walked the car further down the pit lane with the mechanics, trying to lock her head into the laps ahead of her. She had no idea whether she had or hadn't told him it was over.

Two laps in, the car lurched, the pedal shuddering under her foot. Her neck took the brunt of it, but she had to ditch the lap and divert into the pit lane.

'Change it!'

'We don't have time,' one of the mechanics shouted. She looked over their shoulders at Yves who remained in the garage, hands on his hips, watching from afar.

'What am I supposed to do?' She threw her hands up at him.

'Go again, there's still half the session left!' he yelled over the scream of engines and wheel-slips.

She smacked the side of the cockpit and swore, but shoved down her foot and drove off in the shuddering, failing car. A quick look at the leaderboard as she passed the start line told her what she already knew: she was off the pace. Currently nineteenth out of twenty-four, she was three places away from a qualifying slot. She needed that slot.

As she began the lap again around Monaco's familiar streets – *she* began it, she reminded herself, *she* had the control – her heart twanged. Each corner was a challenge; she had to choose the best line, she had to lose as little time as possible, brake as late as possible. Qualifying was about maxing out her limits. If that meant she didn't breathe, or that she folded her car into the side, then so be it. That was racing.

But she drove not for the love of driving – although she loved it still. She drove to outdrive Yves, as she had driven to outdrive death, her mother in the backseat. She drove to drive herself out of Yves' life, to prove herself good enough for a spot on another team and a career that was separate from him. Manically, frantically, she tried to show she could be a race driver; she could risk her life; she could do what the others on the track did. She was never only thinking about the track, and whether that was her fault or someone else's, it was a fault nonetheless. She couldn't be one of them. She never simply drove – that was never allowed.

When the lap came to an end, she had dropped to twenty-first. She lifted her foot from the pedal for the out lap, an odd metallic taste in her mouth. Blood, she realized. She had bitten her lip open.

Her final chance came around. Two minutes remaining. For the final time, she threw herself into a qualifying lap. It would all be worth it, and worth continuing, if she made it to sixteenth. There was nothing else to it, she told herself – but, too busy telling herself, she missed the braking pattern on the first corner and went into it too fast, so she had to take some gravel with her as she circled into the next straight. *Another second lost*, she thought. The qualifying time became harder to meet, and, while she pushed every ounce of her body into it, she felt further than ever. She felt tired.

There comes a time, she considered, when failure was that and that alone. Wood sometimes bows. Rafters snap. Apples rot. Perhaps she was simply not good enough, her or the car, and she would never even be within touching distance of the best. She was simply a woman with ambition and not the tools to realize it.

Even though she didn't want to, she held Yves' hand for the announcement of the qualifying results. There had been a discrepancy with timings, and the fastest driver, then the fifteen slower than him, had to be calculated anew, which would take several minutes. She couldn't remember whether he had grabbed her hand, or she had grabbed his; the moment had begun to take on the hue of memories, already tinged with regret. Yves' hand became a ghostly, disembodied squeeze from the past.

'This is it,' she whispered.

If we don't qualify at Monaco, then the season is over, Yves had mumbled over eggs and bacon in the hotel restaurant. She hadn't eaten a bite.

'You were looking promising for your final lap.'

'I didn't feel it.'

'Don't blame the car if we don't qualify.' Yves had built and designed it himself, and what he meant was: *it will be personal.* That he had said *we* too made her stomach keel in, as though someone had punched it. If she had success, it was half his. If she failed, it was all hers.

'Gentlemen…' No ladies. *'The qualifying results are in.'* The voice boomed over the tannoy. *'The drivers with a place on the start line tomorrow are…'*

He read out sixteen names, one of which was Taff's, and none of which was hers.

Yves dropped her hand and she breathed.

It was a task not to lose him in the crowd. Bumping shoulders, elbowing men out the way, she pushed towards the glass doors of the hotel, following him. Thick walls of people on either side, closing in.

'Yves,' she called, as she entered the lobby, but he was gone. The porter pointed to the hotel bar, and she nodded a *thank you* and followed his finger.

He was stood at the bar, his hand already accepting a glass quarter-filled with whisky. He threw it back and turned towards her, shook his head. Le Bar Américain, with its potted plants and white marble walls, was grey and empty, ashen shadows on the floor. Waiters polished glasses in the lull of late morning. Where it had been lit and warm before, now it was cold and silent.

A chandelier drooped above her like a tear that no one had wiped away, and she remembered Victory Day and the club; how boys swung from chandeliers and threw down their shirts to the girls waiting below. In another bar, with another man, she had thought: *What would the nuns say?* Prude or pregnant. Married or modern. All of it an old madness.

'Why, Freddy?' Yves asked. 'Why did you have to do it today?' He strode towards the terrace. She followed him.

'Do what?'

'Raise *us*. You needed to focus. And you didn't. Now, it's lost. It's all lost.'

'I *was* focused.'

'No,' he shook his head. 'No, you weren't.'

The terrace door was locked. He rattled the handle, but it didn't move. The waiters kept their eyes on mops and glasses. He tried the next door – also locked.

'When else could I bring it up, Yves? You never want to talk about what's happened to us since we started working together.'

'That's not true.' He turned to her.

'You must realize that we can't do this any longer. We bicker and we fight and we can't separate what happens on the track from off it.'

'*You* are the one that can't separate it. I can. Because…' There was more on his tongue.

'Because what?'

'It's your *constitution*.'

'My *what?*'

'Your womanness.'

'How many times have I told you that's not a word? You never *listen* to me.'

'Since when did racing become so complicated, huh? Since women were involved.'

She scoffed and walked off towards the bar. The waiters had made themselves scarce. *Probably wise*, she thought.

His footsteps were light on the carpet, but she felt the loom of his shadow.

'I've been asking myself that too: when did it become so complicated?' She kept her eyes trained on the polished wood. 'I never intended it to be like this, but I didn't have a choice. The men were security, were money and sponsors. I had to let others and all of it in, to be successful. I don't think I'll ever have racing without the complications. It's not in the cards for me.'

'It's Monte Carlo, sweetheart, this is the city of gambling.' He tried to touch her hands, bitten and chapped, and she moved them away.

'This won't go back to how it was before. You need help, Yves, and I can't give it to you.'

He scrunched up his brow, crossing his arms.

'I don't need *help*. Sick people need help. I'm not sick.'

'You drive a tin can around a racetrack at a hundred miles an hour to feel close to *death*. If that's not sickness, then I don't know what is.'

'Don't—'

'Look, I'm washed up at twenty-seven—'

'Twenty-seven is young, Freddy.'

'—divorced, a failure in the sport. I know you can help, but I need to find my own way, another team, another chance...' She stood back as his arms came towards her for an embrace. 'I don't want to be tied to you. It's been a dilemma since I started. I can't race and only race—'

'Then don't race,' Yves said. 'If you can't do this without dragging everything into it, then don't race. I have to race. I was born to do it, and I'll die if I don't, but you seem to hate it and everything it does and everyone it involves. Leave it. Move on. Perhaps this is not what you were meant to do.'

'I never used to hate it.'

He was right, she realized. Her hate for the sport had grown in equal parts with her love for it, like the roots of a flower. It was a relief to admit that it was hate, that gloopy dread in her stomach when she approached a racetrack now, when she entered into conversations about the car. She hated it.

She dreaded her next sentence.

'I think I need to leave. I need to leave you, and I need to leave the team. And I need to leave now.' Relief poured in after she said it, her chest no longer weighted with the disappointment from not qualifying.

Muscles in his jaw twitched, he cracked his knuckle – and she flinched.

'What will I do if you leave?'

'You have Taff,' she whispered. The two of them were so close now. 'You have yourself. You know the car better than anyone.' In his sour face, she could see he'd been hoping for a less rational answer.

'You're contracted until the end of the year.'

'I never signed anything, Yves. It was a contract of words and promises.' His eyes searched her face as he tried to remember the contract – but there *was* none. 'It's your car, Yves. You drive it.'

'At Zandvoort, next week?' he asked.

'I'm not going.'

'Not even to watch?'

'I don't know.' How quickly she had turned from competitor to spectator. 'But I can't do this any longer, Yves. None of this feels right.'

Behind them, the waiters unlocked the terrace doors. Freddy moved towards them, eager for fresh air. Instead, she smelled petrol fumes. Black smoke, burnt rubber. She looked onto the pit lane with its bustle of activity, the boom of exhausts and blackened faces. The distant clash of tools faded into a tapestry she was no longer part of – that she had quite possibly never been part of.

Yves stood beside her, his mouth clamped shut. Perhaps he was afraid of what would spill out.

'Are you angry?' she asked.

'About the qualifying, or about us?'

'Both,' she said.

'I'm angry that they're *both*.'

'I am too.'

He looked down at the marble banister.

'You'll change your mind,' he said.

'About which one?'

'Both.' He choked on a small laugh. 'You're wrong about us. You've got yourself into a lie about racing and love. When you realize that, and when you know what I'm saying is true… then you know where I'll be. On a track somewhere, driving in circles.'

He gave the wall a light smack and walked off.

16. Dutch Grand Prix

Sand dunes filled the train window. White mounds with green tufts, sifting and silting out their layers under the blue skies; the straw-like grass beaten by decades – centuries – of wind.

Then, above the scoops of dune, a grey line of track. A banked corner, at a sharp forty-degree angle that made her hold her breath. In the second that the track remained within the window, a white car shot round, pushed up to the top of the corner for the clearest line, and then fell down again and headed for the straight somewhere beyond the edge of dune.

Despite resolving not to do this, she was on the train to Zandvoort. She was a spectator now – someone who read about the Monaco Grand Prix results in the newspaper; someone who was not *in* the pile-up that happened at the exit of Sainte Dévote when Taff's car slid off the line on its own oil, but only saw the photographs the following day. She told herself she was only trying on this life outside the driver's seat, to see if she could bear it; she could already feel herself itching for the wheel.

Yves had asked her to come in a short note:

> *Ferrari will be there, and they asked me to be a reserve driver next season. There's some forgiveness, and this could begin my career again. Please come.*

He had written it on hotel stationery, and left it in reception for her when she checked out. She hadn't seen him after he left her on the terrace – she was glad of it. Not because of anger, but because she couldn't trust herself not to fall into *yes*es like lovers into hay. *You're wrong about us*, he had said – and continued to say over and over in her head in the hours afterwards.

Stood in the reception of the Monte Carlo hotel, drivers and engineers milling about, she had set her lips and scribbled: *LBM is your team. It's your car. You drive it.* With no word of whether she would be in Zandvoort in two weeks' time. She had walked out of the hotel, determined never to return.

But she had found herself unable to return home either. It had seemed too final, too decisive. Instead, she had taken a bus to the first French town outside the Monaco border and walked into the first hotel. Standing at the check-in, she had realized her funds were dangerously low. Financial management had never been a skill of hers, and she had shivered when the clerk informed her of the nightly rate. Since she had moved from Mackenzie to LBM, her fee had halved, and Yves had insisted there was no money for drivers' expenses or travel, so she had been paying out of her own pocket for it – never really keeping an account of that pocket. Ashamed, she had trudged to a boarding house where she rented a room for a third of the price and spent two weeks stuck in a kind of limbo. Without Yves, without racing, without her career, she had a grant total of nothing.

Now, a country away, she alighted from the train. As she walked through the little Dutch seaside town and then along Zandvoort's wide, flat beach, she was glad to be out of the boarding house. Its patchy red carpets, dim rooms and flaking plaster had reminded her too much of Sandal Road. The air at the coast was clean and fresh. Birds strained to fly against strong gusts. Families pitched windbreakers and tents on the beach, with children of indeterminate sex scattered on the sand, their tanned bodies only slightly darker than the surface. Mothers shouted after them, fathers sat in the chairs. It was beautiful, but like a painting in a museum – distant, and something she would never think to take home with her.

She wore unwashed trousers and a stained polo shirt that she realized belonged to Yves long after she had taken it with her. Her unpinned hair spun around her head in the coastal winds.

Approaching the track, the crowds began to thicken. Fathers with sons marched down the dunes to catch a glimpse of the racing. It would start in less than an hour and the final practice session was under way. She knew the schedule, knew the track, but she would not be driving it.

There was some relief when she looked up and saw that a thick cloud had moved in. Moments later, rain began falling – light, then heavier, until families were running. The fathers picked up their sons and sprinted to the nearest shelter. She too was running, heading towards the tunnel that filtered people out onto the banks near the track. The roar of drops was like applause. The drains gurgled, and small rivers ran down the road. She waited in the tunnel for the rain to end, and when it did she walked up onto the track.

Practice had been cut short, unsurprisingly, and people walked across the track to hike up the surrounding banks and dunes. She joined them, finding a vantage point near the pit lane from where she could see the drivers. No one recognized her. Some part of her put that down to the fact that her head had always been in a helmet and her face half-covered with oil and smoke. But another part imagined the conversation with Rich. All their efforts had been wasted. Their efforts to *make* something of her had failed. She felt like a gambler disillusioned with the game. She had never entered the sport to be known – but by being known, she could have helped others enter. Like Vanessa had done. Her trials didn't need to have a reason for them, but there could have been a conclusion, a result. The next thing someone would write about her, she thought, would be her obituary.

Scanning the pit lane below, she looked for Yves. For LBM. For Will. From this heavenly height, she looked down on them, at the same distance from which she had watched her brothers and Verne play rugby at school. At every match, no matter how fast she ran onto the pitch or from which angle, someone would catch her and lug her back to the sidelines, where she would receive a smack on the ear while the boys fell into hysterics.

Near the LBM garage, she saw a driver pull up and jump out the car. Before he took off the helmet, she knew it was Yves. The anger in his hard body, coiled and spiralled for years. Like twine taut around his bones. He threw the helmet at one of the mechanics and began to shout at anyone nearby, pointing at the track, pointing at his wet race suit. Yves hated the rain. It stopped him from driving, and the only time he would be happy not driving – the only time he would ever be happy – was when he was dead.

In between his shouts, he looked up at the bank where she sat. She tucked herself behind another spectator, and Yves' eyes skipped over her. She hadn't realized until then, but if he saw her, if he had run to her, she would have fallen into his arms. She would have driven for him. There were no rules against switching drivers for the race, if a car had qualified. And she had arrived in time. She could have raced, if he had asked. She had checked in the rulebook the previous night.

Minutes passed, and she could see heads bent and hands gesturing to standing water, discussions taking place on whether to delay the start due to the wet track. None of the drivers would want to. *Rain doesn't stop us*, they would say. *Men are not paper, they can withstand some water.* She could hear this chorus from where she crouched on the dunes.

The drivers soon put their helmets on and got in the cars, the mechanics gave thumbs-ups, slapped the sides. The cars drove to the grid, waited. In the second before the lights went, seagulls blurted, and she tilted her head to the sky and closed her eyes.

It should have been her in that car.

It still should have been her when, on the second lap, it went wide and crunched over gravel. On the tannoy, the commentator spoke disapprovingly of Yves: *A clumsy turn there from the experienced driver in his own car. He'll have to do better than that if he wants to get out of eleventh place.* Yves would take that to heart. He was probably swearing inside his helmet.

It still should have been her after another two laps, when the car took the banked curve – that same corner she had seen from the train window – and sailed up towards the top. It was exquisite to watch. Her breath caught in her throat. But on the wet track, the wheels lost their grip and the car continued to slide upwards – and further upwards and over the top of the bank and into the air. The car dropped out of sight, a telegraph pole fell, and then a body flew through the sky.

17. Le Mans

May 1968 – Three months until Le Mans

Like a seabird without feathers, she had always thought. It was so much easier to think of it like that in the following years, rather than as what it was: Yves' limp body thrown from the car, his skull crushed.

Freddy sat in her old Porsche, the engine idling. She had been planning to take out the key and walk across the car park and through the doors onto the track for her first day of practice, but then her memories had come knocking. Even after fifteen years, the memory of Zandvoort and the crash was like an uninvited guest that she was never able to shoo away. Its arrival was so familiar, she would know when it was coming, brace herself for it. And once it began, it had to play itself out until the end.

Died on impact, they told her after the *incident*, when she sat with two medics and told them again that she was not his wife. One of them was wrapping her forearm in bandages, and another shining a torch in her eye. A steward was on her left, chastising her for her *intervention*.

When the body tore through the air and disappeared, she had shot up and run down the dune. She pushed aside the stewards and mechanics in the pit lane and ran onto the track. None of the drivers had stopped, but she had seen a gap in the cars and sprinted to the other side. No one had stopped for Yves.

This was the part where the images rolled into one another. She must have scaled the steep bank and climbed over the top to see a smoking, sparking hash of metal and man nestled in a sand bunker. For reasons unknown to her, she went to the car, which had started to burn. She knew he wasn't in there, but she had told herself that men didn't fly; it must have been a bird she had seen. *He must be in the car*, she had muttered.

The burning accelerated and she reached out her hands to the empty cockpit. The flames licked her, and she recoiled, stepping backwards. Far off on her left, she saw a hump in the grass, which could have been a mole-hill. Because it couldn't have been Yves. It couldn't have been Vanessa; she would never sit still.

She often wished she could have seen his face, but arms dragged her backwards. Stewards, medics, dragged the *incensed mistress*, as the newspapers called her, back from the car and the body and onto the sidelines.

She blamed the blurriness of what happened next on the rain, which had started again. It only made sense that the memory was waterlogged from here on. All she knew was that somehow, she walked off the track, and out of Zandvoort. Perhaps she had walked to the train station, perhaps she had walked all the way to Amsterdam, sodden, before she walked home and into another life – and even though she had spent that long walk telling herself that she would never race again, in the end she had walked back here, to the place she left behind.

She swiped the key from the ignition, and stepped out of the car.

The doors to the track were locked and chained up with an almost medieval rigour. From outside, she could hear the distant gearbox shifts and engine starts – but she could have been a world away. Someone had really gone to town on these. She tugged at the chain, wiggled the locks, rattled the doors, ignoring the ever-present discomfort from the lump in her breast. Something in her stomach dropped and she was mumbling *no*, *no*, *no* to herself. She had come this far. She walked up and down the side of the track, searching for another door, but found none. Not even one that said *staff* or *personnel*.

Instead of another door, instead of a key, she found a fire extinguisher attached to the wall and ripped it out of the holster. She hammered down on the chain until it let free. The door swung open. She placed the fire extinguisher back in its position, regaining her breath, while in her head Vanessa said something about doing exactly the same thing.

That spool of liquorice-black track greeted her on the other side, already hot in the spring sun. A haze rose from the tarmac, the past written onto it in skids and petrol spills. A track was never clean, she remembered. Idioms and sayings came back to her, the grooves in her brain that she had filled with sod and soil slowly returning to life. She had not been back in so long that the smell was strong enough to fog her brain. Tar and petrol and brake fluid so thick she could almost feel it coating her tongue – once she steadied herself, acclimatized to it, she realized: it was delicious. She had no idea how she had been away for so long.

As she began striding towards garage number twelve, voices drifted towards her from the stands. Three low male mumbles. With a faint European lean to them too.

'I've never *heard* of her before,' one voice said.

'She scored a point or two in Formula One. And made podium at the Coupe des Dames.'

'A race for women.'

She put a silent step forwards and saw the three heads down at the front, surveying the track. They were supposed to be hidden, but hadn't made much effort. Glasses and suits on each one. Briefcases propped up next to the plastic chairs, their hands clasped in their laps.

'You know, what does she *do* now that she's not a racing driver. A housewife? This is why he's invited us here, to watch and decide whether she's good enough.'

The heads all nodded.

She set her face and clocked her heels on the floor as she walked in the upper rungs of the stands. They turned, one at a time.

When their faces stared up at her, she looked down and said:

'You want to know what I am? I'm a racing driver. That's what my line is.' It was unwise, and a little silly, and she regretted it the second the words left her mouth. But the hurt from *What's My Line?* was still raw and the outburst gave her a temporary relief. She left before they could form a response.

She found the garage and walked right in.

Inside, there were two young drivers in race suits. A man and a woman, both petite as buttons. And beside them, bending over the bonnet of the car, with his finger on the engine, grease staining the sleeve of his linen suit, was Will Truston.

'You made it.'

'Only just. I had to break open the doors to the track. They were locked.'

'You didn't use the driver entry?'

'I couldn't find it.'

'It moved.'

'That would have been helpful to know.'

She had driven straight to Will's from the BBC studios. Buried deep in Berkshire, and buried deep within his estate, buried deep underneath a car – she had known just where to find him when he told her there was an opening on his Le Mans team and to *come see me as soon as you can*. He added that it was *time that you catch up with your old friend*.

By which he meant the Puck. She had crunched down the gravel drive and stood outside the workshop, arms crossed, examining it. Their car had been modified, matured over the years as the latest updates came into force, but it was still that same compact whip that she had helped to craft. The car followed none of the precedents, none of the other models, with her tight aluminium frame that Freddy knew almost better than her own. Legs protruded from under the chassis and she called out:

'What have you done to our car? You've painted it orange.'

A head and shoulders emerged – and a wide grin to go with them.

'Well, we wouldn't want anybody to overlook her, would we?'

'But she'll do that on her own. No need for the bells and whistles.'

'Sometimes it doesn't hurt to stand out a bit,' he grinned back. They quipped these riddles and half-answers across the gravel drive as they had once thrown wrenches and spanners over the engine that now lay nestled in the car.

The years without Will – roughly seven of them – had been unbearable. He had been like a phantom limb in those months after their encounter in Belgium, too present but never there; she would wait for him to laugh at a joke with her, only to realize he wasn't in the room. It was after she read about the new sports car division he'd founded that she reached out, tentatively. A brief letter signed with an *F* to tell him that the company's sports car was the *ugliest little thing I've ever seen. Probably why it's so fast.* He replied with a *shut up, Fred* so comfortingly familiar she knew it meant *send another letter.* She sent more. There were polite meet-ups in nice bars every year or so; at the last one, she made fun of him for his knighthood or lordship or whatever it was. It was forgiveness, at last – or the closest the two of them would ever get to it.

When they became too casual, when the memories became too close, she quickly found ways out; she kept him at arm's length – it seemed safest for all. His anger had waned, but he never missed a moment to assert that he had made (remade) himself a good life. His new wife had a son from a previous marriage, Paul, who became his and whom he loved. He was resigned – and content in that resignation – to unhappiness. Laid back in a lucid dream that he was planning never to wake from.

He exited the workshop, wiping his hands on the overalls and grimacing at the grease on his pale skin. In his early sixties, Will still had that choirboy complexion.

'How is she?' Freddy gestured behind him.

He turned to look at the car, some of the guts splayed throughout the workshop.

'She's not ready. We still have lots of work to do before Le Mans.'

'We?'

'My son has been helping to prepare.'

'How old is Paul now?'

'Eighteen, if you can believe it. He's started racing in rallies. I tried to convince him to choose another line of work, but he seems quite set on it, poor boy.'

She shook her head, looking at the ground. 'When did we get so old?'

She closed the gap between them, not afraid that he could read the answer in her eyes. They embraced. When she pulled back, she said:

'What's for dinner?'

'You know already,' he clasped her hand and led her towards the house.

Cheese soufflé, of course. The hardest soft dish to make. And the only thing that he could make, he said in that boast which was not really a boast. Just as he had on the day they first met. When that was finished, washed down with several glasses of wine, the sun made a move to set. The afternoon had a nostalgic feeling about it, as though the minutes were freezing in amber.

'I thought you were out, Fred,' he said at last.

'I was, but…' she trailed off.

'Why now?'

She blinked away what he could see in her eyes.

'Is it your husband?' Because she had found another, eventually. A good one this time.

'No, that's fine,' she responded. 'David has nothing to do with this.'

'Are you sure? I know what…' This was another bone between them – that when she needed him, she had left him in the dark and chosen Sandal Road instead.

'Will, stop. I'm sure. I want a car, not a saviour. I want someone to sponsor me to drive around in a circle three hundred times, to prove that I'm not dead yet.'

He nodded, silenced. Then began to clear away the dishes. Absent-mindedly, he said: 'They're saying Le Mans will be over three hundred and fifty laps this year, with the speed of some of those damned Ferraris.'

'You helped me once,' Freddy continued, ignoring his comment. 'Help me again. One more time, I'll make that car move as fast as anyone ever could. You know I can. I helped to build her. For goodness' sake, my body is the model for those seats. That car is built for me.'

'The car has changed, Fred,' he turned to her, his back to the kitchen counter, and lit a cigarette between his long, thin fingers. 'It's been a long time.'

'I can do this, I can—'

'If I agree,' Will cut her off. 'Then I need insurance.'

'Insurance?'

'You're older. That's just a fact. You've been out of driving for some time. That means I choose the rest of the team, and I need some back-up drivers, understudies, that could step in if you felt… unable to proceed.'

'Who would these drivers be?'

'I have some kids in mind.' To her look: 'You were a kid once, remember? The young upstart that people wanted to throttle for their talent. Now I have some of my own. You'll have to teach them about the car. Show them how our Puck bites.'

'Are you saying I can't do it?'

'Not at all. I'm saying you can.'

'Am I your driver or your coach?'

He turned towards her, a smile spreading on his face.

'What do you want me to say, you heathen? I betroth to you my car, my love, my kingdom.'

'That works.'

The two shook hands – and the sun had still not even set.

Rich had come all the way to her house so that he could express, in person, his lack of enthusiasm for the idea.

'I was worried that it wouldn't come across over the phone,' he had explained when she'd asked what he was doing on her doorstep early on a Saturday morning. She had left a message with his secretary on the Friday night that she was planning to race Le Mans with Truston, expecting that he wouldn't see it until Monday. She should have known better.

'Alright,' she replied, unconvinced. Letting him in. If he had changed over the years, then she had missed it. He was a plump man of thirty when she first met him, and now he was a plump man of fifty. Still his voice had that laboursome, heavy growl and his distaste – for all things, including himself – was clear.

Several minutes later, over cups of tea, he said:

'Isn't it too late? Aren't you too…'

'I'm forty-two, not dead,' she snapped.

'I know but this is *Le Mans*. It's twenty-four hours, it's three hundred laps—'

'They say it's going to be three-fifty this year—'

'Well, I'll tell you what it is, Fred, it's ridiculous. You don't race for fifteen years and then you think you can stroll into Le Mans.'

'You were the one who forgot to tell the BBC that I'd given it all up. *You* wanted me to get back into it.'

'Yes, but not like this. This is a bit *extreme*, isn't it? It's sudden. And with Truston?'

'What's wrong with Truston?'

'Has the funding behind Truston agreed?'

'Will *is* Truston.'

'Not anymore, the rumour goes. I heard he's selling up to foreign investment.'

'He didn't mention it.'

'No, I bet he didn't. This needs consideration, Fred. You don't launch into decisions like this.'

'What makes you think I haven't considered it?'

Aspen, Porsche and BRM – she had arranged meetings with all of them about their Le Mans teams, she told

Rich. But after her meeting with Will, she had attended none of them. The deal was finalized before she left his estate, and she spent the next two evenings on the phone with Will as he went through training schedules and car models and sponsors and why she was needed at the track on the coming Monday. There was no time to waste.

'Does that sound alright?'

'You should have asked me that before you signed the contracts.'

'I didn't sign any contracts.'

'None?'

'Not that I remember.'

'That you—'

'It's all lined up.'

He swallowed some budding anxiety along with two large gulps of tea.

'What is it really, Rich?' Freddy asked. 'Why did you come here?'

He put down the mug, saying: 'I know that *What's My Line?* must have hurt.'

She shrugged. 'I've been through much worse.'

She felt bad for saying it when she saw Rich's face draw down in sadness. It was a great honour to be someone's only friend – because she had a suspicion that that's what she was to Rich. 'The show and then… *this*. It feels erratic. I just don't want to see you get hurt again.'

She clutched his hands over the table.

'I have to do this,' Freddy said. 'For myself. For others. You never met her, but there was a woman named Vanessa who was the first one to tell me I could race. That I *should* race. She always said that it was her duty to encourage other women to drive, show them it was possible, and, well… I don't think I've done my duty. Not yet, at least. And I don't want to run out of time to carry on the project that Vanessa spent her life working on.' It had taken her short-lived career, and the hiatus after it, to come to this conclusion.

It was clear he wanted to tell her that she *had* done her duty – but they both knew that Freddy wouldn't believe him. He drew his hands out of hers.

'I suppose it's pointless asking you to be careful,' he sighed. 'You're never careful, which is why you're so bloody fast.' She smiled. 'There's one thing I want to ask of you, though.'

'What?'

'Let me handle the press on this one, alright?'

'Alright.' She went to carry on. 'But—'

'I know, I know, motoring magazines, only the best for Freddy. There's always the *Ladies' Home Journal*, though. You made quite the impression on *What's My Line?* in that pink number and the phone's been off the hook with calls from their editor. What do you think? Want to be their cover star?' He was laughing before she delivered the punchline:

'I'd rather drown in shrimp cocktail, thank you very much.'

*

Freddy knew Rich wouldn't take it personally when she did the exact opposite of what he'd asked. Minutes after he left, she picked up the mint-green phone on her desk and called the only broadsheet newspaper she read.

'Hello, yes. I would like to speak with Hadley Turner. Of course, you're right, Hadley Southern. Yes, put me through to Hadley Southern.'

She opened the window in the study and pushed her head out while waiting for the secretary to figure out the connection. At high spring, the grasses were dewy and sun-soaked and the fields were full of yellow life.

'Hello?' It was unmistakeably her voice on the other end, unchanged in all this time.

'Hadley?'

'Fred? Is that really you?'

'I have a scoop for you.'

'No one uses the word scoop.'

'I'm just a humble racer, what would I know about the high-flying world of journalism?'

A tinkle of a laugh. It was deceptive, and not to be mistaken for gentle. That voice had wounded politicians, ended careers, saved lives.

'What do you need?' she asked, straight to business, even though the last time they spoke was more than a decade ago. It could have been construed as rude, but Freddy knew it was just Hadley. 'We're in the middle of trying to get tomorrow's paper sorted, and I need to get home to the kids soon…'

'Hadley, I need an old friend. That favour you once promised. I'm racing again.'

'You're—'

'Le Mans. I'm racing it. How about this for the headline? Racing pioneer returns to drive Le Mans in tremendous final act—'

'Final act? What's that about?'

Freddy shook her head.

'Why do you have to be such a good journalist?'

'Okay.' She heard the other woman smile on the other end of the phone line. Hesitant, but not unsupportive. 'What can I do?'

'A write-up. Feature. The works. Will would appreciate it, and it would be good for sponsorship. Besides, it would be nice to have something in print about me before an obituary.'

'Fred, what's wrong? You sound ominous.'

'I'm a racer. I'm always ominous. The closer to death, the better.'

'You're insufferable.'

'Don't put that in the profile.'

'You can't tell me what news to write.'

'The story is yours. I'm telling no one else. It's an exclusive.'

'This isn't because of something else, is it?' Her concern was comforting. It was clear that even if

Hadley wasn't *there* in Sandal Road, she was always *there*.

'You said outside Sandal Road, remember…'

'I prefer not to,' in a clipped whip. Then: 'I need to check with the editor.'

Freddy knew that Hadley was senior enough at the newspaper to take on whatever jobs she wanted. What Hadley needed to do was think about whether she wanted to see Freddy again. After what they had been through together, Hadley was considering whether she could dive back into that tunnel. What risks of memory it might incur. She would have to hold her daughters and think about how she had made it to where she was. Over the years, apart from the occasional letter and call, they had seen each other only once. This meeting over scones and tea in an East End café had wordlessly been considered a mistake. They had merely spent the half hour looking over their shoulders, reverting to painful memories and versions of themselves that they would rather had remained in the past.

'Please. This would mean the world,' Freddy said.

'You know I hate trite comments like that. I'll see what I can do.'

Later that day, Hadley called again. Freddy's husband caught it while she was out on a walk, and he scribbled down the message on a scrap of paper he left on her desk:

Lunch. You're paying.

*

At first it was the pain that kept her from going near a race car – and from getting inside one. Vanessa, Yves, even Will, she had lost them all. Those who had helped her, had pushed her forwards and held her on their shoulders. A pain so intense in those weeks after Zandvoort that she could see it in the corners of her eyes. After several months, it mutated into another reason not to race, something worse, something selfish: the belief that *she* had killed him. Because of everything she had dragged into the racing, polluting it with her problems and her loves and her needs, she had dirtied it and caused Yves to die. This twisted life, where she needed men so that she could drive, and then shunned men for the shame of it, this twist of driving and love and life, had turned deadly. She couldn't be near a car again or she'd kill someone with it. *Women drivers.*

Even now, it made no sense that she had returned to the track, that she was standing in front of Will and his two young drivers, a brand-new race suit embroidered with her name folded neatly on the table.

'Please, Fred.' He gestured her further into the garage. 'I want you to meet some people. Delia and Mark.'

'My hip replacements,' she murmured, looking them up and down.

'We're not *replacements*. We're a team.' Mark put a hand forward and she slapped hers into it.

'Fred has never been the best at teamwork,' Will mumbled.

'What was it that you did again?' Mark asked. 'Scored

some points in Formula One, and won some rallies in your day.'

'Something like that.'

It felt like she was back on *What's My Line?*

Delia looked up at her. Big brown eyes and a scrub of brown hair wild on top of her head. There was almost nothing remarkable about her, and Freddy figured that Delia liked it that way. She tried her best not to, but she saw herself in Delia. Which made it all the more heartwarming when—

'I listened to it on the radio, when you won those points,' Delia said. 'Belgian Grand Prix 1951. I was seven.'

Freddy couldn't find the right response, so she looked at Will for help. He was grinning.

'Right, that's enough talk. Shall we?' Will flicked his eyes to the car. The other two had begun to take positions and wheel it out when Freddy stepped in.

'Stop, stop,' she began, then reeled back.

Will straightened and leaned back from the car. He gestured to the open air with a slight quirk to his mouth. 'Go on, Fred. Tell them.'

She bit her lip.

'It's just… you don't want to push on the sides there. Push at the back. You won't bend the side pods then.' She showed where to put their hands, noticing the look Mark exchanged with Delia.

After a sticky moment in which Freddy expected them to ignore her, the two younger drivers moved to the back of the car and placed their hands where she had directed. She helped. It was light to the touch, the frame almost stretchy under their hands, like the thin fabric of an airplane wing.

She glanced at Will but he looked away. He was wearing glasses, she noticed. He had never worn glasses before. And the way his shoulders fell, slumped forwards – that was also something she had never seen before.

In the corner of her eye, though, Delia was putting on a helmet.

'What are you doing?' Freddy asked.

She paused, the helmet sitting on top of her head.

'I'm going to do a lap.'

'You're going to *do a lap*?'

Mark narrowed his eyes. Will, behind them, was smirking. She didn't need to turn and see it. She could hear it.

'Have you memorized the racing line? Figured out the gear shifts, the braking zones, the speeds?'

'No, I thought I would just…'

'Can I?' Freddy gestured to the helmet. 'I memorized the circuit last night. I want to show you something.'

Delia handed it over.

'Can I?' Freddy checked with Will.

'Teach them, Fred.' Will nodded, his eyes sparkling. 'It will make them better drivers.'

Several days later, she held a stopwatch at the side of the track as Delia did her seventy-sixth lap of the day. She was shouting at her that it was not good enough in the most encouraging way possible.

'They're here.' She stiffened in surprise at Will's hand on her shoulder. She turned – and behind him stood Hadley with a photographer, both talking to Rich, who threw his arms around and made them laugh. Hadley wore an expensive-looking bottle-green skirt suit with a matching hat sitting atop a neat afro of curls, her lips buttered to a shine. In Sandal Road, beauty had been something they had all been too bitter and distracted to commit themselves to, and Freddy had never noticed how striking she was.

Will approached them, touched Hadley's shoulder. She turned to him, smiled at something he said, Rich shook his head and then made a comment that sent all three into hysterics. The sun shone down on them all. They turned and looked to Freddy.

With sudden clarity, she knew why she was here – all she had learned, that twisted mess she'd been through with these people, she wanted to share it. Before it was too late. Her end: another's beginning.

18. The Interview

Hadley had already warned her at their lunch that she wanted to *use* her story.

'What do you mean *use*?' Freddy had asked over the appetizers.

'You know my kind of work, what I'm interested in?'

She did. Since Sandal Road, she had read all of Hadley's articles: the investigations into harassment of female workers at the canning factory; the opinion columns on women's rights and racial justice; her slim book about their refuge in London, which spawned other refuges throughout the country; even the features on female intellectuals and politicians, which were stuffed with quips against racist and patriarchal hierarchies. From the other side of the print, Freddy had been in awe of her friend.

She was aware that she wanted to *use* Hadley too, but that conversation over lunch still left her uneasy. It was a conversation laced with words like *change*, *movement*, *bigger picture*, *feminism*, which seemed to fall like anchors around her story. She understood these words, and she was glad to be in a world where newspapers were printing them in headlines, but she worried whether her little career could possibly match up to what Hadley was planning for it. It had been a long time since Freddy had looked into the lens of news cameras and said that she wanted to see change, and she was unsure whether she had the voice for it anymore.

It was that unease which made her agree to Rich's *Motoring Weekly* interview as well. The day before her interview with Hadley, she had met with a journalist named Scott. His thick brown hair was chiselled into neat gel lines, and he carried a briefcase with a Filofax in which he had written *female driver (name?)* in the midday slot.

Like his face, the questions were open and safe: *What was it like being the only lady on the track? What made you want to drive? Why have you decided to race Le Mans now?* Sat in the stands, her helmet on her lap, her legs crossed, she answered in smiley platitudes about her *fantastic time on track with the boys*. It had been *too much* for her to continue racing after seeing so many dear friends die behind the wheel, she told him. She had wanted to get married and settle down. She gave him a whitewashed account of her career that was simply a record of all she had achieved. She offered statements devoid of details that didn't invite follow-up questions: *I was fearless in that car. I was told I drove too fast and took too many risks, but how else is one supposed to be a racer?*

By the end, she had stuffed him silly with what everyone wanted to hear – the kind of bland woman-bucks-the-trend narrative that even men could stomach with their bourbon, a tale of encouragement, spirited passion, warm anecdotes. He nodded his head in total satisfaction.

She had saved the truth for Hadley.

Trackside, Hadley sensed her lingering uncertainty. She had taken off her suit jacket and shooed away Will and Rich, much to Rich's displeasure. They sat in the front row of empty, rickety stands looking onto the track, which was bordered by adverts in bold black letters. Logos left and right. It was late spring, but the sun was hot. Freddy wondered whether the two should find shade. It was supposed to rain in April. She fidgeted. Nothing about this was right.

'Let's begin with family.' She poised her pen over an empty line.

'Why did you agree to this?' Freddy said suddenly, pulling at the collar of her race suit. Hadley lowered the notebook, a small smile on her face.

'I'm supposed to be asking the questions.'

'I know, sorry, but why?'

'It's a favour for an old friend.'

'Yes, but apart from that. Would you have done it otherwise? Is this *worth* anything?'

Hadley looked as shocked as when Freddy appeared in an evening gown on the doorstep of Sandal Road.

'Of course it's worth something.'

'To who?'

'To anyone who cares about equality and progress and—'

'And what about the people who don't? People who think I'm doing this just to spite the men who were *mean* to me, to air dirty laundry and all that.'

'Stop overthinking this. If it's the truth, then…'

'Right, right,' Freddy repeated. She rearranged herself in the seat.

'Are you ready?'

'Yes.'

'So, let's begin with why you started racing.'

'That's difficult to… it's about Verne and…' She mumbled. Hadley's face dropped and her pen remained still. Eventually she set it aside on the seat next to her.

'You know, you don't have to do this. It's not particularly ethical if journalists are extracting comments from a source when they really don't want to talk. If you don't want to, then no one will blame you.'

'I do, I do.' She reached across Hadley and picked up her pen and notepad, put them back in her hands. 'Ask again.'

Hadley eyed her and reached into her handbag.

'Let's try something different.' She pulled out a small tape recorder and pressed a button. 'It's better than me writing down all those notes. Let's start with an easier question. How did you learn to drive?'

That was something she could answer.

'It was my father.'

'Did you ask him?'

'No.' Freddy shook her head. 'Of course not. I'd never ask to drive. And I would have never asked, if I'd known how hard it would be to fall out of love with driving.'

'Why did you fall out of love with it?'

'I had to.'

'Why?'

'Because driving with my father was probably the only time I've ever been able to drive freely.'

'What do you mean, drive freely?'

'Without…'

'Fear?' Hadley offered. Freddy frowned.

'Without constant obstacles, whether that's discrimination in the sport, money, my first husband…'

'Tell me about him.'

With this lead in, Freddy found she could. Victory Day was the beginning of the end for her, and for so many other women, she explained. War had unleashed their skills and their desires to be drivers and mechanics and soldiers, and when it was over they were expected to return to their husbands. Still a child, she needed a rock to steady her through that uncertain time, and Verne was there. He challenged her, with his disdain, his lack of encouragement. And she had loved the idea of him – perhaps she had even loved him once, which made it all the worse when he lied to her. She hated how much of her story belonged to him and always would – but this narration into the tape recorder, with Hadley's nudges forwards, seemed like a way to reclaim it, to put it on the record from her side. Sweating under the sun, Freddy pushed herself to explain it all, how she had ended where she had – and why.

She described what happened when she tried to divorce her husband, and how her racing career took a step back after the reunion. And how that word – rape – was one she had never wanted to use, even after it had happened to her, because it would be something she had to confront. Her telephone box office. Her return to the track. Yves.

It was going so well until she reached Zandvoort. Her words crumpled under her.

'I can't. I don't think I can.'

Hadley paused the recorder with one hand and wiped away Freddy's tears with the other. 'If you don't want to…'

'I don't.'

'Then don't.' She waited with Freddy for the tears to slow, then passed over a handkerchief. 'Fred, you don't have the responsibility to change racing forever, or end discrimination, you know that, right? It's like that time a wise woman once told me that I wasn't solely responsible for every woman who walked through the door of Sandal Road.' She shared a knowing smile with Freddy.

Hadley looked off at a distant car scooting around the track; it was driving away from them, but soon it would turn and race in their direction. She was deciding whether to go back there: Sandal Road, the pink dressing gown, that crumbling kitchen.

'I'll forever owe you for telling me that. You know I left not long after you?' Hadley paused, wondering. 'I wouldn't say I left *because* of you, you don't get *all* the credit, but…'

'You introduced yourself to me as the one who wasn't supposed to be there anymore.'

'And I wasn't.'

'So what did it come down to, in the end?'

'Well, it was *partially* you. I don't think I've ever met another woman so self-absorbed, so completely selfish about what she wanted and needed.' Freddy knew this was not intended as an insult. 'I was so concerned about looking after everyone else that I forgot about what I wanted in life. Something about you and your trips to that bloody phone box made me realize that it had gone on too long. So I went back into the world, back to the newsroom. Now I have my girls.' She smiled. Freddy remembered how Hadley had looked longingly at Pat with her two sons, sometimes ruffling their morning hair at the kitchen table.

'I'm glad that you found your way out.' Hadley nodded, and a comfortable silence lulled between them. Freddy's eyes floated to the tape recorder. Hadley followed her gaze, then looked back up with a sigh. 'So, what about the interview?'

'You want to know what I really think?' Hadley said. 'I think you're a woman who has done some remarkable things in a car, and suffered some terrible things outside of one. You've learned how to get close to the top, and you've got closer than any woman before you. Share that. The *achievements*. Share what you know, what you've learned, how you beat it and got that far, because you made it bloody far, Fred. You belonged there. You were the first woman to make it all the way around a championship race. The first of many women, hopefully. You scored points in a *Grand Prix*.'

'How do you know that? That was years ago.'

'I'm a good journalist, I did my research. Besides, I followed every race.'

'You did?'

She nodded.

'Of course I did.' She looked again at the tape recorder. 'Sharing your story, *all* of it, forget it.'

'But you said you wanted to use—'

'I know what I said, but legacies are fickle things, Fred.'

Freddy nodded. If there was anyone she wanted to be patronized – or chastised – by, it was Hadley. Hadley was the one who knew things.

'I thought I wanted to bare it all. I thought it was my duty, it's what I *had* to do.'

'It's not. Not at all.' She pulled Freddy in for an embrace. 'You being there, in those cars, on those podiums, that's enough. You training that kid Delia, that's enough.'

With her friend's words, Freddy remembered how she had been devastated when she was barred from the French

Grand Prix – she thought that she had failed everyone, that she had achieved nothing, made no difference. She remembered when she woke up on the morning of her first Grand Prix in Belgium and wondered if her place on that start line meant anything. Her pursuit of individual glory – she had been happy to leave that by the wayside. But she had never been able to let go of her failure to achieve anything larger than herself. She had never outdriven her own death, had never left anything behind. But perhaps she had. She pictured a seven-year-old Delia cheering her on through the radio. Telling her friends about it at school the next day. The first woman to score points. It was a huge relief to know that she had already done something good.

'The recording. Will you keep it?' Freddy asked, in a way that made it clear she was decided.

'Not if you don't want me to. I can tear out the tape right here.'

'No, don't do that, I might change my mind one day. Or the world will change instead. Will you keep it safe?'

'I'll guard it with my life.'

'I'm sure a filing cabinet will be fine.'

They shared a grin. Freddy felt better knowing that it existed, told, on record. For now, she was afraid that the full story of her career would dissuade women from getting behind a steering wheel. But she knew enough about feminism (thanks to Hadley's opinion columns) to know that they were cresting a new wave, and there were bound to be more to come. Perhaps she would last long enough to ride the next one – and if not her, then her story. Carried over the waters like a message in a bottle, waiting for new shores.

It was nightfall by the time Hadley left the track. After her tears had dried – on Hadley's handkerchief – the two had talked for hours about their lives since Sandal Road, and the years that followed: years in which Hadley had married her dream man and had given birth to children who had their own wishes and dreams. Cut back the flowers and so much can blossom in its place.

Freddy spent the final portion of their interview explaining the chronicle of how she met her second husband, David. After Yves, after her decision to stop racing, she committed herself to adulthood. She went to the dentist, to the chiropractor, to the doctor. She wanted to fix every inch of her body, and hoped her mind would follow in its own time. Riding a breeze of productivity, she wrote and applied for secretarial, teaching and engineering roles, and heard back from most with the explanation that she had *no relevant experience*. She had experience, experience in a forgotten wing of the armed forces, experience manoeuvring a bend at over a hundred miles per hour, but she couldn't type one hundred words per minute so they weren't interested.

When she was rushing down the corridor to one of her appointments, she fell into a doctor's arms – then proceeded to fall for him. David explained on the second date that he was unlikely to want children, and she explained on the third that she would never have them; on the fourth he agreed; on the fifth he proposed. And the sixth was their honeymoon to the Lake District. She sat in the passenger seat as they drove away from the church, listening to the cans smack the pavement as she leaned her cheek against the cool window.

One week before leaving for Le Mans, she drove through a green and yellow Sunday afternoon to her father's house, where cackling flowed out the windows onto the drive. These were the laughs of old men in the midst of something *frightfully* important. Her father's weekly game of cards, with his friends from the club. In all these years, she had never known which 'club' they belonged to – whether it was a golf club, a social club, a motor-racing club. She had never been allowed into their sanctuary to ask.

She walked down the hallway like a ghost in a manor. There were small messes everywhere, on chests and the stairs. She drifted towards the drawing room and put her head around the door.

Seven men sat around the table, clutches of cards in their hands, fanned decks, smoke swilling around their heads. The blinds were drawn on the bright afternoon and low lamps spilled drops of light onto the table.

As she opened the door wider, the smoke gravitated towards the new gap in the room and her father looked up. A wide smile came over his face.

'Darling!' He stood and walked over, laughing as he bumped into someone else's chairback. He folded her into his arms. 'Darling, darling. What are you doing here?'

'Is this…?' one of the others began.

'It's the racing driver! The last time I saw you,' another man chipped in, standing and hovering his hand near her waist, 'you were this tall.' She remembered that day, when she had pattered down the corridor to the card room, peeped in the door, was spotted by the men, and accordingly shooed away.

But no one told her to go away now.

'My wonderful daughter, the racing driver,' her father said.

'Hello everyone.' She shook their hands when offered.

'Are you alright? Is it too much? Do you want me to…' he whispered, gently touching her shoulder, his eyes softening. He knew about the lump, of course. The last time she came home it had been to tell him. They had cried about it, reminisced for a moment, then cried again and harder the second time. His stiff upper lip had returned before long, which had been more comforting than anything else.

'No, finish your game. Please.' She laughed – and it was a real one. 'Please. I just thought I'd drop in as I'll be off soon.'

'Well, you *must* join us now.' Her father pulled on her arm like she was another chap.

'Yes, yes,' the rest of the room chorused, finding a chair, pouring her a glass of whisky, dealing her a hand of cards. She relented and sat down. Her father rubbed her shoulder, and she held his hand. Its creases were deeper than she remembered.

When the other players asked questions about her, she couldn't edge a word in. Her father did all the talking. He knew her career like a biographer, listing off her races, her wins. *But Monte in '48 was a tough one, wasn't it, Fred?* And he rushed off to find newspaper clippings he had saved, and passed them around the table like bread.

When the card players had left, Freddy sat with her father outside on the bench, soaking in the final dregs of sunshine.

'You might not want to tell *them*,' she nodded her head towards his departing friends, 'but I'm not sure that Le Mans will be my finest hour. I'm already tired, getting clumsy, and we've not even got to the endurance practice sessions yet. My lap times are not what they used to be.'

'Yes, but we know why that is, don't we, Winifred?' Like Rich, he too had not been keen on Le Mans. But this chastisement had clearly come out harsher than intended, and he added a little *sorry, dear.*

He sipped his tea; she had taken one sip of her own and fed the rest to the flowerbed when he wasn't looking. Silence, and a murmuration of birds, passed.

'Do you remember what you said to me when I told you that I wasn't going to race anymore? After Zandvoort.'

'That there's more to life than racing.' She sneaked a look at his wrinkled face, his quickly turned white hair. All that stoicism had kept him young, she thought – at least on the inside.

'I was angry that you never tried to convince me to return. I thought that maybe you were *relieved* I'd finally decided to throw in the towel. That quitting was what you wanted me to do all along, for me to stop pursuing this stupid hobby that was never meant for women.'

'That's unfair, Winifred.' With his stare, she sank back. 'Of course not. You know how I felt about your mother and her wasted talent.' They looked at his slippered feet.

'I know.'

'The reason I didn't encourage you when I should have was… because I saw what had happened to your mother. I saw how bitter it made her.'

'The blunting, you mean.'

'Exactly. It was selfish, but I didn't want to have to blame myself if you never made it. If I had pushed you, coaxed you into a hole that then swallowed you up, I don't know if I could have lived with myself.'

'Because you knew that racing would never… that I'd never make it.'

'Not because of your talent. Because of how it is.'

'How it is,' she sighed.

'I wanted the best for you, like every father does for their daughter, and I worried that driving wouldn't *be* the best. I knew it wouldn't.'

'But what about the Daily Express Rally, after Vanessa died? I could have killed you for making me drive home.'

'You would have become a timid, terrified little thing had I not done that. Besides, you were a child then. When you quit racing after Zandvoort, you were most definitely not. You were old enough to make your own decisions.' He raised only one of his eyebrows as he looked sideways at her. 'I trusted you to know when it was time to stop.'

'And Hollis? You wrote to them, told them to take me on.'

'Hollis was different. I had to get you away from that *imbecile*.' He paused, disgust washing over his face. The distaste for Verne had never left his mouth – nor hers. Not even these many years after her first husband had died.

Verne had been driving down the Amalfi Coast with his new wife when the car went over the cliffside. The news had come to her via John and she had been confused about how to feel. It was the fate she had wished for him in her darkest hours, but it felt too neat and she got no satisfaction from it. Gods died on Mediterranean rocks. He died without regret, without repentance, without change. He left a world that still loved him, and which he still loved.

She had attended Verne's funeral, sitting in the back row of a village church. Members of his family whom she hadn't seen since their wedding clotted the pews. No one had recognized her. She escaped before the procession to the cemetery. The last thing she left in Verne's life – her last word – was the echo of her shoes as she pattered out of the church.

She could tell her father regretted bringing him up.

'I'm so sorry, for how it is. I knew how hard it would be, and I thought that I could protect you from that. But I should have known better.' He clinked his wedding ring, which he still wore, against the mug.

She wanted to tell him not to apologize, but it didn't feel right, considering how insistent he was to do it.

'I was terrified of what would happen when I left,' she said, 'that I would become bitter and twisted like Mother. That I had nothing else but the racing. And I loved it, for a time. Until the love became complicated.'

'Are you talking about Yves Le Brocq?' He put his arm around her. 'I'm sorry about him.'

She looked down. 'I fell into a bit of a hole, after he died.'

She remembered it still, those months afterwards. The empty wine bottles piled in the corners of her trashed flat, the way she isolated herself from her brothers, her father. She had always promised herself that she would never fall to pieces over a man, and that's exactly what she had done.

But she had been mourning more than Yves. At that point, she had already resolved to quit, and she was mourning the tracks and their comforting inevitability. She had loved that she could follow the corners and the straights and end where she started in a familiar rhythm.

Suddenly in front of her was a road with so many junctions and turns and roundabouts and endless, endless miles – and she'd had no idea what to do with them. Eventually, she had navigated her way. With help from her family, David's patient words, and that strength forged inside her long ago.

'There's more to life than racing,' she repeated her father's words. 'But in there, you were so proud of the racing.' She pointed back to the dining room, where cards sprinkled the table.

He shook his head.

'No, I was proud of *you*. Not the racing, but the woman that you are. You are so strong, stronger than I have ever been. Maybe your will was something that you didn't want to be tried and tested, and maybe it shouldn't have been, but by God, are you splendid.'

She smiled at him, and he returned it.

It took hours for the sun to set.

19. Rochefort

Three weeks before Le Mans, everything hurt. It had hurt four weeks before, and five weeks before too, although she had ignored it. But now that she was at the practice track in rural north France, the hurt pulsated into her fingertips when she pulled on the gearstick, twinged in her elbow when she turned the wheel. It was a chore to drag her body around the track, her lungs were raw and tired, and she had started to think that she would rather sell a limb than continue in the car.

Mark and Delia had noticed too, fetching her extra cups of water and offering to take over her slots. She had seen Will more often in the stands with the European investors, pointing in her direction, making pleading gestures with his hands. There was no article from either *Motoring Weekly* or Hadley yet, and, when she chased both of them with a polite query, their responses of *we are waiting until closer to the race* sounded suspiciously like *we are waiting in case you don't race.* Since Hadley's reassurances during their interview, Freddy had felt her reasons for putting herself through this gradually leaving her.

The doctor had warned her this would happen. She would be operating at half her capacity. *You will feel scattered and short of breath, with sharp and painful headaches and stomach aches.* He had told her not to take on any strenuous activities and she had told him she would do nothing of the sort.

She tried to channel the nights during the war, when her heart would ride its beats and breathlessness was a gift. When she had driven to save lives – and now she couldn't even drive to save her own. Death sat in the passenger seat. Death, she considered, had outdriven her, and there was nothing she could do about it.

When she exited the car at the end of the session, Mark and Delia had already left the track, their helmets side by side on the bench. Freddy had never been more certain that two people were sleeping together. She had walked into the garage countless times to see them fling apart with such force that Mark would hit the wall, and they arrived at the track at such precise intervals apart from one another that it had to be planned. But she tamped down her smirks; if they wanted to keep it a secret, then let them. She had once wanted romance, there was no reason to rob them of it.

On one occasion when she entered the garage and caught Delia alone, she left the silence as long as she could before:

'Are you getting on well with Mark?'

She froze, her hands halfway to a peg. Then resumed.

'Yes.'

'He's a lovely chap.'

'Yes.'

'He's not made any moves, anything… *untoward…*'

'No, goodness,' she looked at Freddy, shocked. 'Besides, if he did, then I would probably kick him where it hurts. I'd have no trouble doing that.'

'Oh, right.' Freddy forced out a polite laugh and returned to sorting her own race suit. As Delia left the room, Freddy realized that she had never noticed how loud her heel clicks were until now and how confidently she pumped her feet down. Part of her knew that this was just Delia – a confident girl, with a brash voice and an impressive command over her body. But part of her also knew that Delia belonged to a new generation of confident girls with brash voices and command over their bodies, a generation that hadn't been told they could never drive. Delia hadn't needed her advice. She had already decided whether and how much to lean on a man. A slice of jealousy passed through Freddy like a contraction.

As she looked around the empty garage, she thought about Mark and Delia in bed. Their young, lithe bodies on the mattress. It was difficult not to think about it, once the image had pressed its way in.

'They're probably in missionary right now,' a voice murmured behind her. She whipped around to see Will, leaning against the frame of the garage.

'How long do you think it's been going on for?' Will asked. 'Delia and Mark, I mean.'

'A few months.'

'Ah, to be young…'

'Or not to be. Youth wasn't exactly…'

'Yes, but old age isn't much better.'

'Speak for yourself, old man.' Their laughs passed. Silence – or as close to silence as possible at a racetrack – settled.

Will broke it. 'Do you miss him?' He knew what she had been thinking, the smell of new sex in the room. It was only a matter of time before he asked about Yves. Still, the question caught her off guard.

'That's a harder question than you think.'

'Trust me, I know how hard that question is.'

'Because the answer is yes, of course.'

'Of course.'

'But it's more complicated.'

He nodded, knowing that she would elaborate at her own pace.

'What about Peter Bracknell, do you miss him?'

'Yes, every day,' he said without hesitation, turning away as his eyes became wet and red-rimmed. She wondered why he tried to hide his despair, before putting it down to habit. 'But you're right that it's complicated. Missing someone will always feel a little unhelpful, perhaps self-indulgent. Even if it is the measure of true love. How much we miss someone after they're gone.'

She nodded, sighing. 'What I miss most are the moments before his death, when everything seemed possible. When it wasn't my fault.'

'It was never your fault.'

'It was. It still *is*,' she insisted through Will's shaking head. 'But there were moments *before*, when I hadn't killed him.'

'You didn't kill him.'

'I did. And it's not just that you could *argue* I killed him, I actually did. No question about it. I killed him, and I miss him in those moments. I've forgotten what it feels like not to have that *guilt*. I should have been in that car. He never should have raced that day, all because I was stupid enough to tempt fate, to think I could be a racing driver and a woman with a heart—'

'For goodness' sake, Winifred.' He sliced off her rambles. The sound of her name in his mouth made her embarrassed. 'I am genuinely quite astounded at how long you have believed that ridiculous story. *Enough* with this *tempting fate* act, don't think so highly of yourself. A woman in a car is fetching to some but, trust me, fate does not care whether you sew dresses or race cars. Physics, metal and a racetrack killed him. If only you'd seen it then for what it was, a horrible accident, not something that you caused… God, I just wish for five seconds you'd stop acting like Eve, like you need to be punished. You didn't eat an apple, you didn't get us kicked out of Eden, you just drove a bloody car. If only you had seen it then, if you had stuck with it, you could have been great. You *were* great.'

Not knowing how to respond, she stood there awkwardly until:

'I know I should have carried on. I should have locked everything about him away in a safe at the back of my head. But I didn't want to forget him so quickly. And I was terrified of what would happen if I put my foot on another pedal. All I could think was who else would die because I wanted too much for myself.'

'A career is not wanting too much.' He took her hands, this raging, rattling affection still working its way through his body, then embraced her. She was touched at how fiercely he cared for her, even after everything she had done.

She hadn't told him about the lump – and she had no plans to. But there was a knowingness in their embrace; he could tell that she was fragile, unwell.

'Come,' he pulled away from her and nodded his head towards the door.

'Where?'

'Let's get a drink.'

'I probably shouldn't…'

'Freddy, if you think I'm talking anymore about the past, or the future for that matter, in this miserable garage then you're sorely mistaken.'

'But…'

'I won't hear it. You can have one whisky.' Her doctor told her she couldn't. He also told her not to do Le Mans.

'I'm going to Rochefort for a few days,' she said, in the cool dim light of the French bar. Pop music fanned out from a stereo across the room, along with the clicks of pool balls and whoops from teenagers. A good thicket of smoke, which Will added to with his cigarette.

'Down the coast? With the retired folk and all that?'

'Quaint, I believe it's called.'

'You once called it the place you'd like to see out your final days.'

'Peaceful, yes.'

'Well, is it the best time?' he asked, taking another drag. Now that he didn't drive, Will was careless with his health. He smoked, he drank, he couldn't scale stairs without losing his breath. He drove, but only for recreation, and only convertibles, and only when the sun was out.

'I need a rest. My body needs a rest.'

He nodded, tapped his cigarette into the ashtray. Their conversations had always had a pattern, and that pattern set out that he was the one to keep the conversation moving. But he was silent.

'Will, I'm sorry.'

Distracted, he turned.

'Oh, I don't want to hash that out again.' He put his head in his hands, playing at exasperation. He was talking about Monaco. He was talking about what she said. Wounds heal – but scars take their place.

'Not for that, although I *am* sorry, I'll always be sorry.' She continued: 'I'm sorry this time for being an old woman who can't drive like she used to, and can't drive like the car deserves.'

The pattern also dictated that he batted away her modesty – but she wasn't being modest, and he couldn't bat away truth.

'But you are planning on driving Le Mans still, aren't you? I'm all for a minibreak, Fred, but this trip to Rochefort, it's not…'

'I'll be at the start line, one way or another. You know me.' She clasped and unclasped his hand. They shared a sad look. 'The investors would certainly be happy if I never made it there. *I'd* certainly no longer have me there if I was paying for it.'

'Investors…' he mused, twiddling his lighter with his fingers. 'Don't you mean the owners?'

A cheer from nearby teenagers almost drowned it out.

'You sold?'

'Months ago.'

'Because…' she began for him.

'Because it was time. Time to get out of it. I'm getting too old, Fred. I'm well into my sixties, and my career is beyond over.' He glanced at her. She looked down at the table. 'That's not aimed at you, dear.'

'You don't seem sad about it.' He was tired, shoulders bent forwards, but his bright blue eyes still sparkled.

'Not for the price I sold it to them.' He grinned and she did too. 'At first, I hated the bastards when they came calling, but then I realized that I couldn't hold on to it forever. I could leave and move on. This racing business has never been kind to me, and that's not to say it was kind to anyone, but I've lost enough years of my life to it.'

'Why didn't you say anything?'

'I was embarrassed that I wanted out. I thought people would have told me to hold on longer, to stand my ground. I didn't want to be convinced out of it.' He signalled for another drink. 'Did I tell you that it was Vanessa's decision to set up the company? After we married, she was in charge of it all at first. I thought that if I ever sold it, then I'd somehow be letting her down, and giving away what she started. But then it made more sense to pass it on. She'll continue to live in that car as long as it moves. In this car, she'll live forever.' Tears came to his eyes.

'I think about Vanessa too,' Freddy saved him. 'All her advice that she gave me. That's what's important, to pass that on. Not to hold onto it for myself. But to share it with others.'

He reached a hand forwards. 'You know that you don't have to race Le Mans. You've got nothing to prove, not even to yourself.'

She took his hand.

'Thank you, Will.'

'For what? There's so many things that come to mind.' He laughed lightly through the tears.

'Just, thank you. For saying that.'

Freddy found she had nothing else to say. She simply wanted to hold his hand, for as long as he wanted to hold hers. He suggested another round. They made two toasts: to the past, and to the future.

Rochefort, where she set off for the following morning, was a place that existed in both. The past: because its shuttered streets hadn't changed since they were laid; the pastels had faded somewhat but the same cafes remained on the same streets run by the same families. Driving to Rochefort – where she and her husband rented an apartment for several weeks in the summer – was akin to driving back to a place before complications and politics stepped into the world; locals sold melon plants for coins and children skipped down streets. It was a living antique.

The future: because it would always be there for her. That's what she had decided one night on the balcony of their apartment, as the town square rolled around in the orange light of sunset. When she needed it, it was there waiting.

After her drinks with Will, she had made arrangements to rent the apartment. Her husband had been due to join her in Le Mans after the bulk of the practice sessions were over, but she told him to find her in Rochefort instead. When Will asked her what he was supposed to tell Delia and Mark, she said: *Tell them that getting to the start line is the hard part. It will reassure them.*

Half of Rochefort's beauty was the drive there. Endless snakes of road, with spring green fields on either side, and pale blue skies above, the odd puffy cloud sprinkled here and there. If heaven had nine circles, as hell did, then this was its ninth. She shot like a bullet through the French countryside, her hands guiding the wheel with expert patience.

Thank goodness the roads were quiet, because she was in a rally again. Driving down from Glasgow, or across the Alps; hours that she had spent in the Puck, in the cabs of Imps and Sunbeams, shouting at her navigator who crouched over a map. Staving off tiredness. The wind nudging the side of the car. Icy conditions on the road that made her slip and slide. As she drove onwards, she drove through them all again in her head; this body had driven them all.

She drove onwards round the generous curves. She was driving into timelessness. Those familiar movements of the wheel, the bandy from foot to foot of clutch and accelerator, took her to a plane where she had driven all the rallies and all the races. It was reassuring to know that in that line that she took around the bend of the curve, in the way she dipped the hill, there was a place where she would always exist as a driver, recorded on the plane for others to see.

The future folded out before her, as the past bunched itself up, and she saw herself not racing Le Mans. Instead of historians – the kind she imagined on Victory Day – it was journalists that she saw. She saw the journalist from *Motoring Weekly* salvage and sew together an obituary about her life with a black and white smile; there would be no trace of Le Mans in there, because it was depressing to read about someone who had almost done something. Perhaps she had died before the race even took place. Maybe she had given him enough to patch together a version of her life, with enough dates and recollections that it almost made sense. That it would almost be a record of who she was. And she saw Hadley keep those tapes hidden away in an envelope marked *FREDDY*. Perhaps she would throw them away after the dust built up, perhaps she would forget about them. Her fate, her legacy, her history, were in another's hands – but she could trust Hadley's. She had put her life in them before.

It had begun at the end; but another beginning was now here, at her end. In the way that Delia took the high-speed corners, Freddy would live on. In the way that Mark shifted down gears, Freddy would live on. Vanessa would live on. Yves would live on. In that plane where she drove for the sheer thrill and beauty of it, all of them would live on, and none of their lives would matter. If this was defeat, it didn't feel like it.

The sign – *ROCHEFORT* – appeared. As the car took the corner, she leaned towards the window. With a smile, she remembered all the previous leans, and her shoulder remembered them too. The road curved hard up ahead. She clutched, then began to descend through gear shifts. Her foot found its way to the brake. Quick clutch and swap. Her mind ahead of herself, outside of the car. She kept to the outside of the road for as long as possible, until she reached the corner, braked, and found her racing line, straightening for a long, uneven stretch. A hill and dip approached. She drove over it and onwards, onto the other side.

Author's Note

Winifred 'Freddy' Vaux is a tapestry of three women primarily: Maria Teresa de Filippis, Rosemary Smith and Lella Lombardi. Moments and shades from the lives of other female pioneers in motorsports have blended into Freddy's story, but it was Maria Teresa's bet with her brothers that became Freddy's bet on Victory Day; it was Rosemary's appearance on *What's My Line?* in 1966 that became Freddy's on the same show; and it was Lella's achievement as the only female driver to score points in Formula One that became Freddy's too.

Very early in the research process, I found there was no way I could restrict myself to the life of just one of these individuals when their voices in interviews and articles were all so strong. Whether that was Maria Teresa's abrupt response to a question about her nerve to take on the men in a man's world – "It never worried me, all of that. I just wanted to race" – or Lella's claim that she only complained about the inequality of Formula One because no one listened to her when she suggested changes to the car. "I am not a feminist, only a free and independent woman," she said. Lella was also the one to quip that the weight of her car was no bother: "I don't have to carry it, I just have to drive it." If this novel only succeeds in encouraging you to seek out their incredible stories and voices, then I will consider it a great success.

In all aspects of motor racing in the 1940s, 50s and 60s, I have done my best to research, recreate and describe things how they were. That said, I have chosen at points to diverge from the historical record for the purposes of our story. Most of the rallies and races are real, some are not. The dates and locations of races have occasionally been shifted a few months or years and car models have been amended or modernized at times. For example, there was no Monaco Grand Prix in 1951 due to budgetary concerns, and the Monte Carlo Rally did not start again after the war until 1949 (not 1948, as in our story). As for car models, the Puck is an amalgamation of several different models from that era; the engine behind the driver concept was true, but stolen from the Cooper open-wheeled cars.

In this vein, I also decided not to dive too deeply into the details about how the war and post-war period affected motorsport, partly because I'm not sure I could do this topic justice, and mostly because I feared that such a level of detail would alienate readers who were newcomers to this world and whom I wanted to be able to access and enjoy Freddy's story.

Well-known figures in the sport are also absent because *The Racing Line* is ultimately a work of fiction and, in the words of Walter Tevis, author of *The Queen's Gambit*, "... it seemed prudent to omit them from the cast of characters, if only to prevent contradiction of the record". To that end, the car manufacturers Truston, Hollis, Mackenzie, LBM and Aspen bear resemblances to real teams (Hollis is loosely based on Rootes, for example) but are my own inventions. British Racing Motors, Porsche and Ferrari are the only real teams and car manufacturers mentioned in the novel, and Ferrari the only one at any length. Because who could write a book about motor racing without including Ferrari?

Acknowledgments

No racing driver can get their car to the chequered flag without the hard work of a huge team of mechanics, engineers, strategists, coaches and many more experts back at the factory. So it is with novels. A massive thank you to the diligent team at Atlantic who worked to get this book to the shelves. Designers, sales, marketing, publicity. In particular, thank you to my wise and fair editor Rachel Imrie for being so patient with me throughout this entire process. Thank you also to my agent Ciara McEllin for her continued support and encouragement.

Thank you to those who facilitated my research and provided valuable knowledge. Namely, the Jersey International Motoring Festival and Alex Salmon, who drove me around in his rally car at 100mph. You had no idea I was researching this novel at the time, but the experience (including the part where our brakes started leaking black smoke and we were red-flagged) was invaluable in informing how Freddy experiences these speeds.

Also, Kate Wright and Lisa Leventhal, whom I encountered while working as a journalist and who educated me about the complexities of coercive control and the many forms of domestic abuse. I admire your ongoing work with FREEDA.

I wrote this novel while working at the *Jersey Evening Post* and edited it while working at Ogier, so thank you to my colleagues and managers in those workplaces for their support, understanding and enthusiasm.

I'm thankful to wonderful friends: Katie, for your ongoing wisdom (you do a much better job than any thesaurus); Charlotte, for fuelling (pun definitely intended) my McLaren and F1 obsession; Charley, for the band names; Sarah, for letting me sleep on your sofa and for everything else; Jodie and Christie, for being ace revision partners and my unofficial therapists.

Thank you to my actual therapist. I might not be here without you.

Thank you to all those *trailblazing* female drivers (the number of times I had to read that word during research…) who inspired me to stick to my racing line: not only Maria, Rosemary, and Lella, but Susie Wolff, Jamie Chadwick, Abbi Pulling, and Doriane Pin. What you do is remarkable and I hope to see one of you lining up on the start grid of a Grand Prix very soon.

Speaking of Grand Prix, thank you to my favourite driver Lando Norris for winning the Monaco Grand Prix on the same weekend that I was editing Monaco Grand

Prix scenes. That was pretty cool. If you or McLaren ever want to host me for a race or anything like that, then I'm free whenever.

Last but not least, family. Because of my dad, I grew up knowing the names Lewis Hamilton and Jenson Button like they were our relatives and hearing the commentating of Martin Brundle coming from the living room on Sunday afternoons. I might have been more interested in princess dolls at the time, but, when I started to watch the Grand Prix with you and Sean, thank you for welcoming me into your world and answering all my questions about tyre compounds and pit strategies. Sorry Mum. Thank you to all three of you for dealing with me. I love you very much.